Lo
Summer

*Two determined women, two strong men,
trying to protect their hearts...but could
it be love that will keep them safe?*

Grace Under Fire by Beverly Barton

'Ms Barton deftly mixes romance and suspense into a
heady adventure that will stir your senses.'
—*Romantic Times*

An Honourable Woman by Lindsay
McKenna

'When it comes to action and romance, nobody does
it better than Ms McKenna.'
—*Romantic Times*

Long Hot
Summer

Beverly
Barton

Lindsay
McKenna

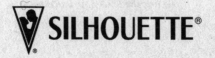

SILHOUETTE®

*Silhouette and Colophon are registered trademarks of
Harlequin Books S.A., used under licence.*

*First published in Great Britain 2004
Silhouette Books, Eton House, 18-24 Paradise Road,
Richmond, Surrey TW9 1SR*

LONG HOT SUMMER © Harlequin Books S.A. 2004

The publisher acknowledges the copyright holders of the
individual works as follows:

Grace Under Fire © Beverly Beaver 2003
An Honourable Woman © Eileen Nauman 2003

ISBN 0 373 60186 7

81-0704

*Printed and bound in Spain
by Litografía Rosés S.A., Barcelona*

GRACE UNDER FIRE

by

Beverly Barton

To Linda, LJ and Lori, who helped me plot this book.
Ladies, here's to frantic, last-minute trips to
Wal-Mart, camouflage condoms, fat-free
pudding and Ouija boards.

Prologue

Grace watched Dean bouncing their baby daughter on his knee. Emma Lynn's soft blond curls peeked out from beneath her pale pink bonnet and her big blue eyes sparkled with laughter. Emma Lynn loved her daddy. Grace's heart swelled with pride. She had given this precious gift to the man she loved, and in the years to come, perhaps a brother and a sister would join their perfect family. Life was so incredibly wonderful, so rich and full and delicious. Grace thanked the good Lord every day for her many blessings.

When Dean set his daughter on her feet, she toddled precariously across the green lawn, moving directly toward the tall, elegant, silver-haired man who held his arms open for her.

"Pa…aa," Emma Lynn said as her grandfather swept her up into his big, strong arms, the same masterful arms that had held and protected Grace all her life.

"How's my big girl, my little moonbeam?" Byram Sheffield planted a kiss on his granddaughter's forehead.

Emma Lynn began jabbering, some of her words quite distinct while others only mimicked the English language.

Grace lifted a glass of lemonade from the wicker table beside her ornate white wicker rocker. She loved this time of day, early evening on the back veranda. The day's hot, humid swelter had faded into a warm, moist twilight. She'd been born and raised in this old Louisiana mansion that had once ruled a thousand acres of the Belle Foret plantation. Six generations of her family had lived and died in La Durantaye parish and she and both her parents had been born right here in St. Camille. Her roots ran deep in this rich, fertile earth. Dean and she would raise Emma Lynn to cherish her heritage, yet teach her to become her own woman, with a vision for the future.

Grace closed her eyes and savored the moment, storing it for future reference.

Suddenly the warmth disappeared. Cold air surrounded her. Had a summer storm cropped up, bringing rain with it? she wondered. She opened her eyes, intending to suggest to Dean they go inside before the storm hit, but Dean wasn't there. Where had he gone?

"Daddy?" she called, but received no answer.

She couldn't see her father. Couldn't see Emma Lynn. And where was Belle Foret? Where had her family and her home gone? What was happening? She cried Dean's name repeatedly, but he didn't respond.

Had she fallen asleep and was now dreaming? Surely that was it. Wake up, Grace, she told herself. End this nightmare. End it right this minute, do you hear me?

"Mrs. Beaumont?" a pleasant voice spoke to her and a gentle hand touched her face.

Grace's eyelids fluttered open. She looked up at a middle-aged woman with a kind face. When Grace opened her mouth to speak, she realized she couldn't. Something prevented her from fully opening her mouth. She tried to lift her hand to touch her face, but her arm felt as if it weighed a ton.

''It's all right, Mrs. Beaumont. You can't speak because your mouth is wired shut, but you'll be able to speak again soon. For now, just blink your eyes once for the word yes and twice for the word no. Do you understand?''

She blinked twice. No, she did not understand at all. Only a few minutes ago she had been at home with Dean and Emma Lynn and her father. Where was she now? How had she gotten here? And where was her family?

''You understood to blink,'' the woman said. ''What is it that you don't understand? Are you confused about where you are?''

Grace blinked once.

''You're in St. Camille Hospital. You were in an automobile accident. Don't you remember?''

Grace blinked twice.

The woman sighed. ''I'm Andrea Woods, your special duty nurse. Your cousin Joy Loring hired me. You've been in the hospital for two weeks now and just this morning they moved you from intensive care and I came on duty. You've been coming in and out of consciousness for several days now. Don't you remember Dr. Drummond explaining to you what happened?''

Grace started to blink twice for no, but stopped herself. Dr. Drummond? The image of a stocky, bald man wearing a white shirt, blue tie and cream-yellow suspenders flashed through her mind. And she could hear his baritone voice speaking to her slowly and softly. As she recalled what he'd said, she tried to block the words, not wanting to hear the truth. With every ounce of her fragile strength she fought against remembering.

''Oh, you poor thing,'' Nurse Andrea said, then tenderly wiped away the tears cascading down Grace's cheeks. ''Your body will heal in time and someday you'll be able to rebuild your life. For now, you must rest and let me take good care of you.''

Grace lay there on the cold, sterile bed in her private room at St. Camille Hospital and prayed to die. She had absolutely nothing to live for now. Dean was dead. Daddy was dead. With a strength born of determination, she lifted her hand and laid it on her flat stomach. And the child she and Dean had longed for—the little girl Grace had envisioned many times since the moment she found out she was pregnant—would never be born. She had even chosen her unborn baby's name, Emma Lynn, in honor of her two grandmothers.

She could hear Dr. Drummond saying, "I'm sorry, Grace, but you miscarried the baby."

Grace pleaded with the Almighty. *Please, God, please, take me, too. I want to be with Dean and Daddy...and with my little Emma Lynn, who never had the chance to live.*

Chapter 1

Elsa Leone placed the morning mail on the ornate Jacobean desk, then hurried into the adjoining kitchenette to prepare her employer's morning beverage, a rich cinnamon-flavored cappuccino. She loved her job as the personal assistant to the owner and CEO of Sheffield Media, Inc. The pay was above average for such a position, the personal benefits were excellent and her working relationship with Grace Beaumont couldn't be better. Elsa had worked for the company the past ten years, as a receptionist for seven of those years; but during that time she had been attending night classes at St. Camille Junior College, hoping to improve her chances for a promotion. Then miraculously three years ago when Grace had taken charge of her father's media empire, she had looked within the company for a replacement for her father's middle-aged assistant who had retired shortly after Byram Sheffield's death four years ago.

Elsa worked busily, wanting everything to be perfect when Grace arrived. Although professionally and socially they were worlds apart, Grace insisted Elsa call her by her given name. Being allowed that privilege, along with receiving fair and courteous treatment, Elsa had grown to not only admire her boss, but to care for her. She would even go so far as to say they were good friends.

"She's not here?" Hudson Prentice, the senior vice-president of Sheffield Media, Inc. stood in the open doorway.

"No, sir." Elsa glanced at the carved mahogany antique wall clock. "It's five till."

"So it is. And our Grace is seldom early and never late."

"Yes, sir."

"Buzz me when she arrives. I've made reservations for Dumon's for lunch and I don't want her making other plans." Hudson stared quizzically at Elsa. "She doesn't have a prior lunch date, does she?"

Elsa liked Hudson Prentice well enough, but thought him a bit of a stuffed shirt. Somewhere in his late thirties, with brown eyes, brown hair and of medium build, he was a rather nondescript-looking man, despite his expensive suits, weekly manicures and salon-styled hair.

"Not that I know of, Mr. Prentice, but she doesn't always inform me when she has a personal lunch date."

Lifting his brows, he stared at her, contradiction in his eyes. "Grace doesn't have lunch dates unless you count her outings with that silly cousin of hers." When Elsa didn't respond, he asked, "There isn't someone that I don't know about, is there?" He shook his head. "No, of course not. She would have told me."

"I'm sure she would have, sir."

Hudson Prentice wanted Grace. Everyone who worked for Sheffield Media, Inc. knew it. Elsa smiled. Probably two-thirds of La Durantaye Parish knew it. The poor man had done everything but get down on one knee and beg Grace to marry him, but she gave the impression of being oblivious to his unrequited love. Elsa figured it was easier for Grace that way. She was less likely to hurt Mr. Prentice's feelings if she feigned ignorance.

Of course, she wasn't sure which the man loved more—Grace or her money. The curse of every wealthy woman.

Mr. Prentice backed out of the doorway. "Yes... well...buzz me when she—"

"Good morning." Grace Beaumont arrived at precisely one minute till nine, and looking like a breath of springtime in her white linen suit and pale yellow blouse. Grace was a classically beautiful woman, with natural blond hair and vivid blue eyes. Tall and slender, with an aura of elegance and fine breeding, she exuded cool sophistication.

Hudson turned and smiled. "Don't you look lovely this morning."

"Good morning, Grace." Elsa brought the cappuccino over to Grace's desk and placed the mug on a mono-grammed earthenware coaster.

Grace entered her office, put her dark-green leather brief-case on the right side of her desk, then pulled out her large, hunter-green, tufted-leather swivel chair and picked up her coffee cup.

Hudson Prentice hovered in the doorway. Grace glanced at him.

"Is there something you need?" Grace asked pleasantly.

He cleared his throat. "I've made reservations for us at Dumon's for lunch."

"Is there a special occasion I don't know about?"

"Have you actually forgotten?"

"Forgotten what?"

"This is your anniversary," he said.

She looked at him, a puzzled expression on her face.

He sighed dramatically. "Three years ago today you took over the reins of Sheffield Media, Inc."

"Oh." Grace offered him a wavering smile. "How sweet of you to remember. Then, yes, of course, a celebratory lunch would be nice. We'll include Elsa, of course."

Hudson Prentice looked as if he'd been slapped. Elsa couldn't help feeling sorry for him. He'd wanted an intimate lunch for two, and any third party would alter his well-made plans.

"No, really, I don't want to intrude," Elsa said.

"Nonsense," Grace insisted. "She won't be intruding, will she, Hudson? After all, I couldn't manage without the two of you. You're both indispensable to me and to Sheffield Media."

"Yes. Certainly, Elsa, you must join us." Hudson backed out of the office again, like a commoner respectfully easing away from a queen. "I'll call Dumon's and make that lunch for three."

"Make it for four," Grace told him.

He stopped abruptly and looked directly at her. "For four?"

"Yes, Joy mentioned stopping by to pick me up for lunch today. She phoned last night. She's been to New Orleans on a shopping spree and is dying to tell me all about it."

He swallowed, then nodded, a rather pitiful disappointment evident in his fading smile and sagging shoulders. "Lunch for four then."

Grace didn't even seem to notice when he left. She put the crystal glass mug to her lips and sipped the frothy cinnamon coffee.

"There seems to be quite a bit of mail this morning," Elsa said. "I've set aside an extra thirty minutes for you to take care of it before your appointment with Mr. Carruth."

The phone rang. On the second ring, Elsa lifted the receiver. "Ms. Beaumont's office. Elsa Leone speaking."

"This is Orson Sidney down in Bayou Cuvier. We've got us a big problem here at WBCL. Our biggest advertiser is threatening to walk. They got all upset over a political ad that we started running a couple of days ago. All the sweet-talking and ass kissing I've done hasn't calmed them down. I think it's something Ms. Beaumont is going to have to handle."

Grace flipped through the assortment of envelopes stacked on the blotter in the center of her desk.

"Oh, dear," Elsa said. "Hold one moment, Mr. Sidney."

Grace glanced at Elsa. "Orson Sidney?"

"Yes, ma'am. It seems he has a problem with an advertiser. I'm afraid the mail will have to wait until later." Elsa handed her the telephone. "This will probably take awhile."

Grace shoved the morning mail aside, took the phone from Elsa and said, "Good morning, Orson, I hear we have a problem."

Elsa excused herself quietly, closing the door behind her as she left Grace's office and went into her own. Grace would probably be tied up on the phone for the next couple of hours—maybe longer. But in the end, she would find a compromise that would suit everyone. The woman had a knack for diplomacy. One might say a true gift. Of course it didn't hurt that she was beautiful, charming, intelligent and had become quite business-savvy in the past three years.

Elsa had watched the transformation and was sometimes awestruck by Grace's abilities. Her being an astute businesswoman had been a trait she'd come by honestly. After all, her father had created an empire for himself that spread out all over Louisiana, and parts of Mississippi, Arkansas and Texas. Elsa hadn't really known Grace before Mr. Sheffield's death, but she'd seen her a few times in person and numerous times in the society pages of the *St. Camille Herald*. Everybody in La Durantaye Parish knew who Grace Sheffield Beaumont was. The daughter of one of the richest men in the South and the wife of the state's attorney general, Dean Beaumont. Both from prestigious old-money families, they'd been called the golden couple. Dean and Grace Beaumont had had it all. And in the tragic events of one summer night almost four years ago, they had lost it all.

Not once in the three years Elsa had worked at Grace's side, day in and day out, had Grace ever mentioned the accident or the fact rumors abounded afterward that Grace had suffered a nervous breakdown. Whether the rumors were true or not, Grace showed no signs of whatever torment she'd suffered. She was, at least outwardly, highly competent, unemotional and always in control. But Elsa suspected that beneath that dispassionately calm, serene exterior, she was still in mourning.

Jed Tyree had never seen Dundee's office manager Daisy Holbrook as anything less than calm, skillful and confident. But today, as the old saying goes, she was running around like a chicken with her head chopped off. Of course, even Dundee's CEO, Sawyer McNamara, seemed a little nervous. No, on second thought, nervous was the wrong word to ever describe the super-cool former federal agent. Sawyer was anxious. Anxious that he, the office staff and the agents he'd been able to round up on short notice would make a favorable impression on the owner of the agency, Sam Dundee. Having been hired by former Dundee's CEO, Ellen Denby, Jed had never met Sam, but he'd heard all about him. Hell, the guy was legendary around here.

"Mr. Tyree, didn't you get the memo about dressing appropriately today?" Daisy gave him a disapproving glance as he walked by. "Mr. McNamara requested suits and ties."

"I don't own a suit," Jed told her.

"Then at least go put on a tie."

Always Ms. Efficiency, Jed thought. And never shy about stating her opinion, but usually in a more diplomatic manner. Her sharp tone expressed her nervousness.

Jed reached out, put his hands on Daisy's plump shoulders to bring her to a standstill. "Slow down, take several deep breaths and—"

"Is my craziness showing?" Daisy laughed. "It's just that I know how important it is to Mr. McNamara that Mr. Dundee's visit comes off without a hitch. After all, it is the first time Mr. Dundee has come to Atlanta since Mr. McNamara became CEO."

Jed patted Daisy's shoulders. "I don't own a tie, but I'll see if I can borrow one from Frank or Vic."

"Thank you." Daisy released a sigh.

Jed meandered down the hallway until he came to Frank

Latimer's office. Frank was a big guy, tall and muscular, but trim. He was wearing a suit today, as usual; and as usual he looked like he'd slept in it. Frank had the unkempt appearance of TV's Detective Columbo and was every bit as shrewd.

Jed knocked on the open door. Frank glanced up from where he sat behind his desk.

"Come on in."

"You look like you have a fresh haircut," Jed said. "And you even shaved."

"We're supposed to look our best," Frank replied in his thick South Carolina accent. "The big man's on his way in from the airport."

"Yeah, so I hear." Jed glanced at Frank's cheap blue-and-red striped tie, and wondered where the guy bought his clothes. "You wouldn't happen to have an extra tie, would you?"

"I've got two more at home."

"Ms. Efficiency just told me to find myself a tie."

"From the way she's been acting this morning, I'd say Daisy missed her calling. She should have been an army drill sergeant."

Jed chuckled. "So, who around here might have a tie?"

"Other than Mr. Beau Brummell himself?"

"Yeah, Sawyer probably keeps a dozen in his office."

"If Dom were here, he might have one." Frank nodded toward the office next to his. "Try asking Vic."

"I thought Vic was still in Miami."

"Got in late last night and Sawyer requested his presence in the office today."

"Bet he's not too happy about that."

"About as happy as I would have been."

Jed grinned, then headed next door. He found Vic Noble standing by the windows overlooking the street below.

"Got a tie I can borrow?" Jed asked.

"Sorry, I didn't bring a spare." The tall, lanky former

CIA operative turned to face Jed. "Have you ever met Dundee?"

"Nope."

"Ellen hired you, didn't she?"

Jed nodded. "And you came on board right before she retired."

"Yeah. I believe Rafe Devlin was the first agent Sawyer hired."

"Never thought I'd say this, but I sure as hell wish I had Devlin's assignment. Overseeing the security for a cotillion ball in Savannah seems preferable to putting on a tie and showing off to the big boss to make Sawyer look good."

"Ah-hem." Standing in the doorway, Sawyer McNamara cleared his throat. The new CEO of Dundee's looked like a damn model straight off the cover of *GQ*. Tall, physically fit and almost a pretty boy. Almost, but not quite. There was always an expression in McNamara's eyes that issued a warning: *Dangerous. Tread lightly.* "Heard you were looking for a tie." He held out a beige silk tie that would coordinate perfectly with the long-sleeved brown shirt and brown slacks Jed wore.

"Should I apologize now or should I just wait for my punishment to come later?" Jed asked.

Sawyer's lips twitched, but he didn't smile.

Lucie Evans came up beside Sawyer, who glanced at her briefly, frowned and then replied, "No need to apologize, Tyree. I do want the entire staff, including all agents present today, to look and act like professionals…because I want Sam Dundee to know when he chose me to replace Ellen Denby, he made the right choice."

Lucie expressed herself with a mocking frown and an odd, rumbling groan. Jed couldn't suppress a chuckle. Everybody at Dundee's knew about the ongoing feud between Sawyer and Lucie, both former FBI agents, who mixed like oil and water. What surprised everyone was the fact that Sawyer didn't ask for Lucie's resignation once he became the head honcho. Then of course, maybe he had.

And maybe Lucie—being the stubborn, tenacious Lucie they all knew and loved—had told Sawyer to go…well, to go take a flying leap.

"What is that you're wearing?" Sawyer asked Lucie as he surveyed her from head to toe. Disapprovingly.

"It's a dress."

"Yes, so it is. Don't you think a suit would have been more appropriate?"

"Look, your royal high-muckety-muck, I came in to-day—on my off day—because you asked me to. I'm attending an afternoon wedding in Smyrna and I won't have time to go home and change."

The six-foot redhead was built like an Amazon. No model-thin, fragile creature was their Lucie. She filled out to perfection the hot-pink and purple floral dress that hugged her every luscious curve. "I think you look lovely," Jed said.

"So do I. You look like a flower garden," Frank added.

"Why, thank you, gentlemen." She smiled at Jed and Frank, then gave Sawyer an eat-dirt-and-die glare.

Daisy came flying down the hall. "They just rang from downstairs. Mr. Dundee has arrived. He's in the elevator."

Jed draped Sawyer's expensive beige silk tie around his neck, tied it quickly and followed the others down the hallway toward the elevators. His mind flashed back to when he'd been a boy and had watched while his uncle Booth inspected his household staff and personal bodyguards. This little show here today to impress Sam Dundee was a minor skirmish compared to the battle Booth Fortier's underlings had fought on a daily basis to keep their boss content. Sawyer McNamara wanted to impress his employer because he admired and respected the man, because to Sawyer doing a good job was a matter of honor. Booth's employees had sought to please him out of fear. No one Jed had ever known could put the fear of God into a person faster than the notorious godfather of the Louisiana Mafia, a man to whom killing came as naturally as breathing.

Frank Latimer jabbed Jed in the ribs, bringing him instantly back to the present moment. A huge, blond man with the build of a football linebacker stood in front of him, his big hand held out in greeting.

"Sam, I want you to meet Jed Tyree," Sawyer said. "He became a Dundee's agent last year. We're lucky to have him. He's former Delta Force."

"Did you know Hunter Whitelaw?" Dundee asked as he took Jed's hand in a firm, friendly exchange. "He was former Delta Force."

"Yes, sir. I served under him for about a year before he retired. He's the one who recommended me for my job with Dundee's."

"Fine man. Hated to lose him, but he made the same choice I did. He found a less dangerous type of work when he got married."

One by one Sawyer introduced the office staff and the agents who were present, then the big boss man invited everyone to lunch. He had reserved a private room at Peaches, a local downtown bar and grill that always hosted the crème-de-la-crème of private security agents whenever Sam Dundee was in town.

Grace returned from a festive lunch at Dumon's with a slight buzz. She'd indulged in three margaritas, while she'd done her best to put on a happy face for the others. For Hudson in particular. The dear, sweet man had thought it only appropriate to celebrate the three-year anniversary of her assuming the CEO role at Sheffield Media, Inc. What had never entered his mind was the fact that the only reason she had taken over was that her father had died. And her cousin Joy, who seldom had a serious thought in her head, had rattled on and on about May Beth Chapin's darling twins…little four-year-old boys. Not once had Joy considered the fact that discussing children, especially children who were the same age Emma Lynn would have been if Grace hadn't lost her child before she'd had a chance to live, might not be all that pleasant for Grace. But she suspected that Elsa understood how difficult it had been for her to smile and chitchat. And smile. And smile. And smile. Her young assistant seemed wise beyond her twenty-eight years, which made Grace wonder if some tragedy in her life had gifted her with such sage perception.

Grace slammed the office door behind her, then marched to her desk. Staring down at the stack of mail she'd never gotten a chance to look over this morning, her vision blurred momentarily. Oh, God, why had she drunk that third margarita? And why had she agreed to the celebratory lunch in the first place? She should have known that the memories would return like a tidal wave, washing over her, bringing with them the melancholy she continuously battled.

"You did it because you didn't want to disappoint Hudson," she said aloud as she plopped down in her swivel chair. Everyone, including Hudson himself, had expected the board to name him as CEO of Sheffield Media, Inc. After her father's untimely death, Hudson had run the company for ten months, handling everything with his customary competence. And no one, least of all Hudson, had dreamed that Byram Sheffield's socialite daughter would use her power as the major stockholder to claim the position her father had held during his lifetime.

No one had understood why she wanted the demanding job; and she had not felt compelled to explain her reasons. What could she have said? *I desperately need something to do, something that will require most of my time and attention, something that will keep me from going stark, raving mad.* For nine months after she had buried her husband, her father and her stillborn child who had existed inside her body for over five months, she had lived in limbo, little more than a zombie who went through the motions of living. She had cried until there were no more tears. She had ranted and raved and vented her anger. And she had gone through months of grief therapy with the best psychologist in the state. After all, money was no object. She was one of the

wealthiest women in the South. She was Grace Sheffield
Beaumont, who had once been the luckiest woman in the
world.

Emotion lodged in Grace's throat. Damn those margaritas! She usually had complete control over her feelings, a
hard lesson learned from necessity. For self-protection. To
keep from going insane. But liquor had always affected her
strangely, making her weepy and silly and—

Damn the margaritas. Damn Hudson for celebrating her
three-year anniversary as CEO. And damn Joy for talking
so cheerfully about another woman's beautiful, healthy and
very much alive four-year-olds.

Before she realized what she was doing, Grace swiped
her hand across the top of her desk and sent the stack of
unread mail sailing off the edge. Damn Sheffield Media, Inc.
Her job was supposed to keep her so busy and wear her out
so completely that she never had time to think about the
past, to remember what had been and what would never be.
It had been almost four years since her world had been
turned topsy-turvy. Four long, lonely years where each day
was much like the day before, a routine of mundane habits—eating, sleeping, bathing, working. Trying to make it
through another night in a house filled with memories. Some
had thought she should leave Belle Foret, buy a condo in
town or even move the headquarters for her father's company to Baton Rouge or New Orleans. But she couldn't
leave her family's ancestral home. It was the only thing she
had left that she truly loved. Everything else had been lost
that night nearly four years ago when a hit-and-run driver
had crashed into their car and sent it careening over a steep
embankment.

*Don't do this to yourself. Self-pity serves no purpose. Get
on with what you have to do.*

Grace scooted back her chair, stood and then bent down
to pick up the scattered mail. Not bothering to neatly arrange
the array of envelopes, she dumped them on her desk and
began methodically going through them, sorting them into

let-Elsa-handle, consult with Hudson, and take-care-of-yourself stacks.

Halfway through the chore that should have been done first thing this morning, she glanced at the return address on the envelope she held. New Iberia. Who did she know there? They had no business connections to that city. She studied the plain white envelope. No name above the return address. Elsa must have assumed the letter was personal.

Grace removed the single page of eight-by-eleven paper and unfolded it. Not handwritten. Typed. No signature. An odd sensation shuddered through her. What was that old saying? Ah, yes—she felt as if someone had just walked over her grave.

She read the letter all the way through once, but couldn't comprehend what she'd read. Then she read it again.

Mrs. Beaumont,
I believe you should know that the accident that killed your husband and father was no accident at all, but a coldblooded, premeditated plot to destroy your entire family. Your husband had uncovered damaging information about our governor, Lew Miller, and was investigating the connection between Governor Miller and organized crime in Louisiana. Your husband believed our esteemed governor was in bed with Southern Mafia kingpin Booth Fortier. He was very close to finding the evidence he needed, and your father was set to go public with this evidence, using Sheffield Media's vast television, radio and newspaper resources in the state. The reason the hit-and-run driver who caused your husband to wreck his car that night was never found is because Fortier had the man executed so he could never tell anyone what happened. But I know. And my conscience will not allow me to keep silent any longer.

Grace held the letter in her trembling hand. Who could have sent her such a horrible letter? Who would be cruel enough to torment her with some fantastic story about the governor, a Mafia boss and her husband? Why would anyone tell her such wicked lies?

She balled her hand into a fist, crumpling the letter in the process. Lies. All lies. The car wreck had been a horrible accident. The highway patrol had believed some out-of-control drunk had smashed into them on River Road and just kept on going.

But wasn't it odd that they never found the drunk? They never even found the car the man had been driving. It was as if he had vanished off the face of the earth.

Fortier had the man executed so he could never tell anyone what happened.

It was a lie. Every word in the letter was a lie! It couldn't be true. It couldn't be. Lies. Lies. All lies.

But what if it wasn't a lie? What if it was the truth?

Chapter 2

Jaron Vaden wiped his damp hands along the outer edge
of his thighs, the threadbare denim cool beneath his sweaty
palms. This May wasn't any hotter in South Louisiana than
any other had been in the past, but then it wasn't the heat
that had Jaron perspiring. Although his red T-shirt clung to
his shoulders and chest with perspiration, a cold chill rippled
along his spine as he passed Booth Fortier's home office.
The door was shut, which meant Keep Out. No one dared
to disturb Booth; no one entered his private domain without
an invitation. Not even Charmaine, whom many outside the
immediate household thought had her husband wrapped
around her little finger. Jaron knew better. His sister might
be the wife of the most powerful crime boss in the South,
but her influence over Booth was insignificant. He'd seen
his brother-in-law give in to Charmaine on several occasions, when it suited him to please her. But he'd also seen
Booth slap Charmaine halfway across the room when she'd
dared to interfere in one of his business decisions.

Jaron heard two voices talking behind the closed door,

but he couldn't understand what was being said. He paused just past the doorway and listened. The louder, deeper voice belonged to Booth. He couldn't make out the other voice because it was much quieter and softer. Everyone spoke with reverence in front of Booth. Out of respect. Out of fear.

Jaron hated his life and hated himself for ever being stupid enough to get sucked into this sewage of corruption and mayhem. He wanted out. He'd been part of the syndicate operation since he'd been eighteen and had been looking for an easy way to earn a fast buck. He had brought Charmaine into this cesspool, this underbelly of society. He blamed himself that she was now tied to Booth Fortier for life. His wife. His whore. His slave.

There was only one way to escape—money. Lots of money. Enough to fake his death and Charmaine's and set them up for life in South America or Europe. He'd been making plans for over a year and yesterday he'd driven into New Iberia and mailed a letter to St. Camille. Step #1— make contact with the wealthiest woman in Louisiana.

He had written just enough to whet her appetite, to make her curious. By now, Grace Beaumont had probably read the letter and was trying to decide if what he'd told her was true or not. But after she thought things over, she'd come to the only logical conclusion. Once she had accepted the accusations against the governor and Booth Fortier as the truth, she'd be ready to bargain with him for the proof that would prove her husband's and father's deaths hadn't been an accident. He didn't have the original documents, of course. Booth kept everything locked away safe and sound at the bank. But he had photocopies in his home safe. Almost as good as the real thing. Enough for Grace Beaumont to take to the police; enough for a judge to issue a search warrant.

Once he had the five million, he'd tell Charmaine about his plan. She'd be scared. Hell, who wouldn't be frightened out of their mind at the thought of double-crossing Booth.

But they really didn't have much choice. It was either risk everything, including their lives, or continue living in hell.

Jaron hurried along the hallway that led to the den. On the far side of the room, a set of French doors stood slightly ajar. When he drew nearer, he heard his sister's muted laughter, as if she'd covered her mouth with her hand. She couldn't even laugh out loud for fear it would displease Booth.

Someone else laughed. Louder. Robust. A man's deep-throated chuckles. Someone not afraid for Booth to hear him.

Jaron eased open the French doors and glanced outside. Stretched out on a padded wooden chaise, Charmaine lounged by the pool. Her round, voluptuous body was tanned to a golden hue from endless, mindless hours spent in her bikini outside in the hot Louisiana sun. Of course, it didn't hurt that both she and Jaron were biologically prone to café-au-lait complexions. His mother had said they had Creole blood, but his Aunt Hattie had whispered that their great-grandmother had been the quadroon mistress of a rich Creole doctor.

A big, masculine hand shoved Charmaine's waist-length auburn hair to one side, then lathered her back and shoulders with colorless suntan lotion. She turned her head slightly, just enough so she could glance up and over her shoulder in order to look at the man who was touching her so tenderly.

Damn, they were fools! What if Booth saw them? Would Charmaine be able to explain why Ronnie Martine had his hands all over her?

Jaron stepped outside onto the deck that ran the length of the sprawling old house. A hundred and fifty years ago, the place had begun as a large raised cottage, and had been expanded over the years into a six-thousand-square-foot house. Booth's father had purchased the house and twenty acres for back taxes when the widow whose family had owned the house for generations fell on hard times. Booth's daddy had been a shrewd businessman—and every bit the heartless bastard Booth was. At least that's what folks around these parts said.

"Booth's home, isn't he?" Jaron said, his question more a warning than anything else. "I heard him talking to someone—"

Charmaine gasped when she saw her brother standing only a few feet away. Despite the surprise in her eyes, she managed to smile. "He's holed up in his office with Ollie."

"Ollie? You mean Oliver Neville, his lawyer?"

"Yes, silly, what other Ollie do we know?" Charmaine flopped over on her back. Ronnie Martine capped the lotion bottle and placed it beside the chaise on the concrete patio that surrounded the pool. When Charmaine glanced at Ronnie, her whole face brightened and her cheeks flushed. "Thanks."

"You're welcome, Mrs. Fortier."

Ronnie wore a pair of tan cotton slacks, a white short-sleeved cotton-knit shirt and a pair of brown leather sandals. He was a big guy, about six-one, with massive shoulders, ham-hock arms and tree-trunk legs. He'd been working for Booth nearly eighteen months now, a trusted employee; but there was something about the guy that bothered Jaron. Something other than the fact he obviously had a thing for Charmaine—and she for him.

Was Booth out of his mind giving Ronnie the job as Charmaine's personal bodyguard? That was like asking a fox to guard the henhouse. He didn't know how far things had progressed between his sister and her protector, but if they weren't already screwing around, it was only a matter of time.

Another reason he'd had to put his plan into action a bit earlier than he'd figured on. He had originally thought he'd send the letter to Grace Beaumont a couple of months from now so she would receive it on the fourth anniversary of the car wreck that had killed her husband and father. But with things heating up between Charmaine and Ronnie, he realized he had to get his little sister safely away from Louisiana before Booth found out she was betraying him with another man. If he even suspected what was going on, Booth would kill Ronnie and Charmaine.

Ronnie walked across the patio toward the round wooden table, reached down under the open umbrella-shade and lifted the pitcher of lemonade the housekeeper had prepared at lunchtime. Jaron came up beside him. Ronnie offered him the glass of lemonade he'd just poured.

Jaron shook his head, declining the offer. "You need to be more careful," Jaron said, his voice only a whisper.

"Huh?" Ronnie squinted his inquiring eyes.

"I can see what's going on with you and Charmaine," Jaron said. "If Booth ever picks up on any vibes—"

"There's nothing going on between Mrs. Fortier and me. You're way off base with that kind of accusation."

"I'm her brother. I love her. I don't want anything bad happening to her," Jaron explained, not buying Ronnie's denial. "Anything else bad, that is. Being married to Booth is bad enough."

"You've said too much," Ronnie told him. "I like Mrs. Fortier. She's good to me. And I'd never do anything to cause her harm. But I work for Mr. Fortier and my allegiance is to—"

"Yeah, yeah, sure. Theoretically your allegiance is to Booth, but—" Jaron glanced decidedly at Ronnie's crotch. "We both know you'd feed your best friend to the gators for a chance to screw my sister."

Charmaine sat up quickly and glared at Jaron. "What are you two talking about? You both look so serious."

"Business," Jaron replied.

"Business, business, business." Charmaine's full, pink lips formed a sassy pout, then when she was certain both men had seen her sultry expression, she sighed. "That's the only thing y'all ever talk about. Booth's always sending me out of the room so he can talk business."

"Did I hear my name mentioned?" Booth Fortier stood just inside the open French doors.

Jaron swallowed hard, then turned to face his brother-in-law. Booth Rivalin Fortier wore only the finest clothes. He had his own tailor in New Orleans. He kept a barber and a manicurist on retainer. The man prided himself on his personal appearance. With a strenuous exercise routine, he kept his five-eleven, fifty-nine-year-old body in prime condition. Vanity, pure and simple. Booth was a proud, vain man. When he'd started going bald in his mid-thirties, he'd tried a toupee and even considered plugs, but at forty, he'd shaved his head, giving his appearance a Yul Bryner exoticness.

Charmaine lifted her sheer see-through robe off the foot of the chaise, slipped into it and sauntered across the deck toward her husband. "I was just complaining to Jaron and Ronnie that all you men ever talk about is business."

When she drew near, Booth reached out, grabbed Charmaine around the waist and pulled her up against him. He nuzzled her neck. She giggled. Jaron knew a fake giggle when he heard one.

"Business pays the bills, *mon petit chou.*"

Charmaine sighed dramatically, then turned just enough so that when she rubbed against her husband, her right breast brushed his side. Booth gazed at her, lust in his eyes. And Jaron noted something far more dangerous than lust. Obsession. Booth's slender, manicured fingers slid down Charmaine's back and grabbed her butt. He glanced at Jaron and then at Ronnie, as if saying, *This is mine. Ain't it fine.*

Jaron could only guess what went on between his sister and her husband behind closed doors. But he suspected it was often brutal. More than once Charmaine had tried to explain away the bruises on her beautiful body.

God, he had to get her away from Booth. And soon. Before Booth found out about Ronnie. If that happened… they'd all die.

* * *

With no one other than herself residing at Belle Foret, Grace had cut the household staff down to only a housekeeper and a butler/chauffeur, both having been in her father's employ since before Grace's birth thirty years ago. Laverna and Nolan Rowley were in their late sixties, a devoted couple, who had always seemed like family. Laverna received assistance from daily maids who worked for a local agency, so now her job mainly consisted of preparing meals. Since the tragedy four years ago, Laverna and Nolan had spoiled Grace shamelessly, more so than ever.

While Laverna placed the silver service on the tea cart in the front parlor, Nolan headed out into the foyer on his way to answer the doorbell's insistent ring.

"Will there be anything else, Miss Grace?" Laverna used her apron to swipe nonexistent dust from the edge of the tea table.

"No, that's all. Thank you." When Laverna reached the door, Grace called to her. "Please, if anyone telephones while my guests are here, take a message. I don't want to be disturbed."

"Yes, ma'am."

The minute Nolan opened the front door, Grace heard the squabble and walked quickly toward the foyer. Dear Lord, what horrendous timing. Joy and Hudson had arrived on her doorstep simultaneously. The two had taken an instant dislike to each other the moment they met in Grace's hospital room nearly four years ago. Joy called Hudson an insufferable dork and he referred to her as the brainless twit. Of all nights, why tonight? Grace asked herself. She didn't need this. Not when she had to make an important decision and wanted the advice of her closest confidantes. Maybe Joy wasn't the most intellectual person Grace knew, but her bubbly little cousin had a good heart. She was someone Grace had been able to count on, since their childhoods, through the good times and bad.

"All I asked was why, if you had to take a cab over here instead of driving yourself, didn't you remember to bring some cash with you?'' Not giving Nolan a glance, Hudson stormed into the foyer, Joy walking quickly to keep up with him, her cheeks splotched with color and her eyes shooting fiery darts. ''And why on God's green earth did you tip the driver twenty dollars? With my money! That's obscene. It's ridiculous!'' Hudson threw up his hands in disgust. ''What am I saying? Not only are your actions ridiculous, but you're ridiculous. Just look at yourself. No self-respecting woman wears those outdated clothes like you've got on. You look like my great-aunt Mozette did when she gave one of her garden parties.''

Joy grabbed Hudson's arm, then paused in the foyer. She blessed Nolan with her sweetest Southern belle smile. ''Evening, Nolan. How are you this evening?''

''Just fine, Miss Joy. And you?'' The butler didn't return her smile, but his watery blue eyes twinkled.

Joy had always had a way of making people like her. Everyone except Hudson. Grace couldn't figure it out. What possible reason could Hudson have to dislike Joy? Grace supposed it was because Joy disapproved of him so vehemently.

Hudson tried to disengage himself from Joy's tenacious hold, but the harder he tried to escape, the tighter she held onto his arm.

''Damn it, woman, will you let go of me?'' Hudson demanded in a harsh yet quiet tone.

''I didn't drive myself over here tonight because my car's in the shop. My precious Jag is sick. And I don't have a chauffeur the way Grace does.'' Joy gave Hudson a pathetic wide-eyed look, like a soulful puppy dog, her long, thick lashes fluttering ever so slightly. ''And my goodness, Huddie, you act as if I won't reimburse you for the money I borrowed to pay the driver.''

''Good evening.'' Grace moved into the foyer to meet her cousin and business associate. ''What seems to be the problem?''

"No problem." Hudson slapped at Joy's arm, trying to free himself from her clinging grip.

When he finally gave up and forced a smile as his gaze connected with Grace's, Joy whipped her arm away from his and rushed toward Grace.

"Give Huddie some money, will you?" Joy requested. "A fifty will be enough. I had to borrow a little from him to take care of the cabdriver, and he's making a scene about it."

"Will you please stop calling me Huddie." Hudson's cheeks flamed bright pink.

"But isn't that the pet name your brothers and sisters gave you when you were a child?" Joy asked guilelessly. "I thought that's what Grace told me."

"I haven't been a child in years." Hudson grimaced, his expression just a fraction short of malevolent.

"Sometimes I find it difficult to believe you were ever a child." Joy breezed past Grace and floated into the front parlor. Joy seldom simply walked. She breezed into, floated along, sauntered, meandered and strolled; but never just walked. Then without glancing his way, Joy said, "And for your information, *Hudson*—" she emphasized his name "—you're the only man of my acquaintance who disapproves of the ladylike way I dress."

"I'd appreciate it if you two would set aside whatever personal differences make both of you act like competitive children whenever you're around each other," Grace said. "At least for this evening."

"I apologize." Hudson squared his shoulders and stood ramrod straight, as if Grace was his commanding general preparing to inspect the troops.

"Oh, Gracie, sweetie. It's all my fault." Joy hugged Grace, then planted an affectionate kiss on her cheek. "I'm afraid Huddie—er...Hudson brings out the worst in me. I promise I'll behave myself...for tonight."

"I must admit that I'm curious as to why you called this meeting," Hudson said.

Before Grace could respond, Nolan opened the door for Elsa Leone, Grace's trusted and valued assistant. During the past three years, she had come to think of Elsa as a good friend. The young woman was, as Grace's daddy would have said, smart as a whip. Efficient to the nth degree, Elsa had proven herself time and again. Although the two had shared personal moments, neither had taken the opportunity to pour out their hearts to each other. Grace knew the basic facts about Elsa's life, but had respected the woman's privacy as Elsa respected Grace's. Grace did know some of Elsa's history. She was the eldest child of four. Her father had died years ago, leaving Elsa with a mother who drank too much and worked too little. The sister just younger than Elsa was married and lived in Lake Charles. The youngest sibling was mentally handicapped and attended a private school that cost Elsa a fortune, despite the scholarship the little girl received. The only brother was a freshman at St. Camille Junior College. Troy had gotten into some trouble in high school—drinking and drugs—but Elsa believed he'd finally gotten his act together.

"I hope I'm not late," Elsa said.

Brown-eyed, sable-haired, with a slender build and of medium height, Elsa wasn't the type who stood out in a crowd. But she was quite pretty, if one bothered to take a second look.

"Right on time," Grace replied. "Please, come join us in the parlor. Once Uncle Willis arrives—"

As if on cue the doorbell rang. When Nolan opened the door, a stocky, ruddy-faced man entered, a jolly expression on his round face, his pudgy cheeks flushed from the warmth of the humid Louisiana evening. Uncle Willis was Willis Sullivan, her father's old friend and attorney. Grace had known him all her life. He wasn't really family, unless you counted the fact that his sister had married one of her daddy's first cousins once removed.

"Evening all." Willis's thick Southern accent rolled off his tongue like molasses over hot biscuits. He was a rotund man of average height, with thick white hair and a full beard and mustache, both neatly trimmed. In his tan summer suit, he looked like Santa on vacation.

Once the round of greetings ended, Grace ushered everyone into the parlor and closed the massive pocket doors. With her guests all seated, she turned to face them.

"I didn't mean to sound so mysterious when I telephoned each of you, but this…this wasn't something I could talk about over the phone."

"Heavenly days," Joy said. "You certainly know how to make a body curious."

Grace took a deep breath. "I received a letter today. It was sent to the office. The envelope was postmarked New Iberia."

All eyes focused on Grace. Quivers of uncertainty rippled along her nerve endings. Although she had somehow managed to make it through the afternoon at work, her mind had never wandered far from the mysterious letter.

"The letter was typed and not signed." Grace paused. Dear Lord, how could she say the words aloud? How could she repeat such damning information? "Whoever wrote the letter wanted me to know that he—or she—is certain that the hit-and-run driver who crashed into Dean's car and sent it over the ravine wasn't just a drunk driver. Dean's death and Daddy's death weren't accidents. They were targeted to be killed that night."

Murmurs of disbelief rose throughout the room, but it was Uncle Willis who spoke. "Are you saying that this person, who didn't even sign his name to the letter, claims Dean and Byram were murdered?"

Grace nodded.

"Why?" Hudson asked. "Why would anyone want to harm your family?"

"Good question," Joy said. "I can't imagine either Dean or Uncle Byram having an enemy capable of such a terrible thing."

Just come right out and say it, Grace thought. *Tell them.*

Name the enemy who is more than capable of murder.
"What if that enemy was Booth Fortier?" Grace's heartbeat
hammered deafeningly inside her head.

A stunned silence enveloped the parlor.

"*The* Booth Fortier?" Hudson's eyes widened; his mouth
gaped.

"The letter accuses Governor Miller of being 'in bed'
with Fortier," Grace said. "Supposedly Dean was working
on unearthing the evidence to prove it and he'd told Daddy
and Daddy was set to use Sheffield Media, Inc. to—"

"Byram never mentioned a word of this to me." Willis
shook his head in disbelief. "My God, if this is true...it
would mean Dean and Byram really were murdered."

"Wasn't it possible that Daddy didn't tell you because
he was waiting until Dean had the evidence in hand?"
Grace asked.

"Of course, it's possible." Willis frowned. "And the
fewer people who knew what Dean was doing, the better.
It makes sense. And they wouldn't have told you because
they wanted to protect you. You know how old-fashioned
Byram was. And Dean, too."

"I think the whole thing is ridiculous," Hudson said.
"It's a hoax. Someone's trying to upset you."

Grace glanced around the room, first to Elsa, then to Joy.
"What's your opinion?"

"I don't think you can dismiss the letter as a hoax," Elsa
said. "If you believe there's a possibility that what it states
is true, then you will have to prove it."

"But that could be dangerous." Joy's usual vivaciousness
waned and Grace could sense the fear she felt. "I think you
should call the police."

"And tell them what? All I could do is show them the
letter. I have no proof whatsoever." Grace walked over to
the antique secretary, opened a middle drawer and retrieved
the notorious missive.

"The police could dust for fingerprints," Joy said.

"Probably wouldn't do any good." Willis tsked-tsked. "This sure enough is puzzling."

"I called y'all here because I want your advice." Grace waved the letter about as if it were a fan, then slapped it down on the open drop-leaf secretary's desk. "I have to make a decision. The right decision."

"Call the police," Joy said.

"Throw the damn thing in the garbage and forget it," Hudson told her.

"Hire a private investigator to look into the allegations," Elsa recommended. "Find out if it's really possible that the governor is in Booth Fortier's hip pocket."

"I agree with Elsa," Willis said. "Hire a private investigator for now and if he uncovers anything that links Fortier to Lew Miller, then go to the police."

"If we're voting on this, then I cast my vote with Elsa and Uncle Willis." Joy's lips curved precariously, as if she had intended to smile, then thought better of the idea.

"Oh, all right," Hudson added. "What harm can it do to have someone check into the allegations and prove them unfounded?"

Grace sighed with relief. The four people she trusted most in this world had given her the advice she'd wanted to hear. "I'm glad y'all agree with me. I came to this same conclusion earlier and made some inquiries. I needed each of you to support my decision. Thank you."

"There are any number of decent private firms in Louisiana," Willis said as he moved toward the tea cart. "Anyone else care for something to drink?"

"I'd love some coffee," Joy said. "Cream and sugar, please."

"I've chosen a firm that's based in Atlanta," Grace told them. "The Dundee Private Security and Investigation Agency. I checked them out and found that they're considered one of the top agencies in the country, definitely the premiere agency in the South."

"I take it that you haven't contacted them, yet." Elsa joined Willis at the tea cart.

"Now that we're all in agreement, I'll call first thing in the morning. I want an agent here in St. Camille as soon as possible."

"Why not call them tonight?" Elsa suggested. "I'm sure someone will take your call, an answering service probably." Elsa instantly took over the job of hostess, serving first Willis and then Joy before preparing a cup for herself.

"Would y'all stay awhile? I asked Laverna to prepare enough supper for guests." Grace didn't want to be alone when she made the call. And she didn't want to spend the evening alone, thinking about the letter, about the implications. Simply dealing with her family's deaths on a daily basis was difficult enough. How would she cope if she could prove what the letter stated was true?

You'll make sure the ones who are guilty pay…and pay dearly.

With Haviland cup and saucer in hand, Joy advanced on Grace, pausing at her side, a sympathetic expression on her china doll pretty face. "Are you sure you really want to dig up that particular can of worms? You'll have to relive that night…and remember all your losses. And if there's a speck of truth that Booth Fortier was somehow involved, then your own life could be at risk if you start snooping."

Grace grasped Joy's chin, forcing her cousin to look her squarely in the eyes. "If you were me, would you leave it alone? Would you be so afraid for your own life that you'd allow—"

"I'm not as brave as you are." Joy clutched Grace's wrist and pulled Grace's hand away from her face. "But, yes, I suppose I'd do exactly what you intend to do. I'd need to know the truth. I'd have to know." Joy set her cup and saucer on the secretary, only inches from the letter, then reached up and placed her arm around Grace's shoulders. "If Uncle Byram and Dean were murdered, then you could wind up a victim yourself. I'd just die myself if anything happened to you.''

"I'll be careful," Grace promised, then added, ''but you know as well as I do that since the night I lost my family, my life hasn't meant much to me. I'm not afraid to die because I really don't have anything to live for, do I?''

"Oh, honey, don't talk like that. I just can't bear it.''

Grace kissed Joy's cheek, then slipped away from her and picked up the telephone on the secretary. She flipped open the address book lying beside the phone where she'd written down the number for the Dundee Agency; then with everyone watching her, she made the call.

Chapter 3

Jed Tyree took the private elevator directly up to the suite of offices on the sixth floor and arrived at the Dundee Agency at nine-fifteen. Sawyer McNamara had phoned him at home and asked that they meet tonight about an assignment Sawyer had handpicked Jed to oversee. On a gut level Jed felt something was off about this job. He'd heard an odd tone in his boss's voice. For some reason, Sawyer had been reluctant to discuss even the most minor details about the assignment over the phone.

As Jed neared Sawyer's office, he noticed the door stood wide open so he saw plainly that Sawyer wasn't alone. With his hip resting against the side of his desk, Sawyer was deep in conversation with Sam Dundee, who presided over the room in the chair behind the massive desk. Across from the desk, in a large wing chair, another man, in a black suit, sat with his legs crossed. The stranger possessed a swarthy complexion, sleekly styled dark hair and an air of comfortable authority.

When Jed approached the open door, Sawyer glanced at

him, then eased off the desk and came forward to meet him. "Come on in," Sawyer said. "We've been waiting for you."

A hard knot of apprehension tightened in his belly. What the hell was going here? Jed wondered. Why was Sam Dundee sitting in on this meeting? And who was their visitor?

Sawyer escorted Jed into the room. The man in the wing chair stood and offered his hand. Jed eyed the neatly manicured fingers on the guy's right hand and noted an onyx and diamond ring; then he looked right into the stranger's face. The guy's yellow-brown eyes narrowed as he studied Jed, who shared a quick handshake with him while Sawyer made the introductions.

"Dante Moran, this is Jed Tyree."

Moran stared at Jed so intensely that he wondered if perhaps they'd met before and Moran was trying to figure out where.

"Jed, this is Special Agent Dante Moran," Sawyer said.

Now Jed knew something fishy was going on. "You're a Fed."

As if to say: *that's that,* Sawyer slapped and then rubbed his hands together, the quick, loud sound breaking the tension radiating around the room. "Why don't you have a seat, Jed, and we'll get right to it."

Jed nodded, then took the matching wing chair across from the one into which Moran eased his long lean body.

"I received a call tonight from Grace Beaumont," Sawyer said as he backed up against the edge of his desk, making sure he didn't block Sam Dundee's view. "Mrs. Beaumont is the widow of Dean Beaumont, who was the attorney general of Louisiana four years ago."

At the mention of Louisiana, Jed's mind sent up a red warning flag. He'd left the state behind him—everything and everyone—seventeen years ago. He'd never returned, not even for a brief visit. Hell, he hadn't even made a phone call home.

Jed didn't respond in any way; he simply waited for Sawyer to continue, which he did.

"Dean Beaumont and his father-in-law, Byram Sheffield, died in what was believed to have been a hit-and-run accident almost four years ago. Mrs. Beaumont survived the crash. And the driver of the other car disappeared without a trace. The crime is still unsolved."

The more Jed heard, the less he liked where this scenario was leading. Before his uncle's name was even mentioned, Jed knew that somehow, some way, Booth Fortier was involved.

"Today Mrs. Beaumont received an anonymous letter telling her that the deaths of her husband and father were actually murders, not the result of an accident," Sam Dundee said. "She wants to hire Dundee's to investigate this allegation. We've chosen you to head up the operation."

"And if I don't want to accept the assignment?" Jed asked, then looked pointedly at Dante Moran.

"You know where this is leading," Moran told him. "You know why you're the perfect candidate for this job."

"Let me guess—Booth Fortier is involved." Jed's jaw clenched. He had spent a lifetime trying to put more than distance between himself and his mother's brother. Only in the darkest, loneliest moments of introspection did he allow himself to remember the past.

"This anonymous author claims that Dean Beaumont was on the verge of providing proof that Fortier has his hooks into Governor Lew Miller." Moran's expression didn't change one iota. "The Bureau has reason to believe these claims are true."

"And if that's the case, then Booth Fortier was behind the murders of Beaumont and his father-in-law," Sawyer said.

"So you want to send me to Louisiana to do what?" Jed's lips curved into a mocking smile. "You think because there's a biological connection between Fortier and me that I'll be able to unearth the truth...quicker...easier...than another Dundee's Agent?'' Jed scanned the room, his gaze taking aim at Sawyer and Sam for a split second, before he returned his sharp glare to Moran. ''If the Bureau has an interest in this situation, why not send one of your own down there?''

''We're taking a risk here, trusting you,'' Moran said. ''But as you well know, before you were hired by Dundee's, they did a thorough investigation into your past. You're clean as a whistle. Not one black mark against you. And you've had no contact with your uncle since you left home when you were eighteen.''

''Get to the point.'' Jed didn't like the way the conversation was going. No matter what the Bureau wanted or why, it had to be bad news for him.

''Seventeen years ago, you contacted the Bureau about your uncle.'' Moran continued. ''You claimed Fortier had murdered your father and you wanted him brought to justice.''

''Yeah, and I was patted on the head and sent on my way.'' Jed recalled the arrogant son-of-a-bitch who had pointed out that Jed had no proof, that the accusation was worthless, that it would be Jed's word against his uncle's.

''The agent in charge at the time made a mistake,'' Moran said. ''He made a decision without consulting his superiors.'' Moran cleared his throat. ''Special Agent Clark overstepped his authority by automatically refusing to use you to infiltrate Fortier's close-knit family. It seems Clark had his own reasons for not taking advantage of your ties to Fortier.''

''Mind telling me what those reasons were?''

''The guy didn't trust you. He was skeptical when it came to mob informants. Actually, he had a major chip on his shoulder when it came to anyone associated with the mob,'' Moran explained. ''He figured you'd either get scared off or you'd wind up dead before the case would ever go to trial. He made a bad judgment call, one we didn't know about for years. Not until after his death eighteen months ago.''

"So what's the deal?'' Jed asked. "Lay it on the line for me, will you? You can't possibly want me to infiltrate my uncle's organization at this late date. He'd never buy my coming home and doing the prodigal son bit.''

"We want you to go to St. Camille, work for Mrs. Beaumont as an investigator and while there, pay your uncle a visit. We're not expecting a reconciliation, but it's a known fact that Fortier still has a soft spot where you're concerned. He'll see you. You know he will.'' Moran waited for a response; he didn't get one. "Be up-front. Tell him you're working for Grace Beaumont. Act skeptical, tell him you don't trust him, ask him if the allegations against him are true. But give the guy a hint that you might not hate him, that you've had second thoughts about blaming him for your father's death. Make him think you want to believe he didn't have Ms. Beaumont's father and husband murdered.''

"And putting on this little act will get us what?''

"Seventeen years ago you desperately wanted to help us bring Booth Fortier down. Here's your chance to help us do that and also protect Grace Beaumont's life in the process. Once Dundee's starts digging, it's only a matter of time before her life is threatened. We both know that.''

"Why not send one of your agents?''

Moran clicked his tongue, but said nothing.

"You've already got someone in place, someone working undercover in my uncle's organization.''

Moran remained silent.

"Damn you, Moran! Something's gone wrong with your inside man.''

Moran's expression didn't confirm or deny Jed's statement.

"You need a contact person between your guy and the Bureau, someone with a personal connection to Fortier,'' Jed said. "Booth might question my motives, but deep down he'd want to believe that he has a chance of making things right with me. My uncle has a warped sense of family, so he'd like nothing better than to bring me back into the fold."

"Then you'll do it, won't you?"

"Yeah, I'll do it. You knew I would." He glanced around the room, his gaze pausing on each man in turn.

"We were fairly confident that we could count on you," Sawyer said.

"Retribution's been a long time coming, Tyree," Moran told him. "But with your help, we stand a good chance of splitting Fortier's crime syndicate wide open."

Grace emerged from the white Mercedes, locked the vehicle, smoothed the wrinkles from her coral linen shirt and headed into the airport terminal. More than once during the past ten years, St. Camille's little airport had been put on the extermination list, coming close to being shut down. But every time, the influence of local politicians and Sheffield Media, Inc. managed to keep the planes flying in and out of the small Louisiana town.

Having arrived early, Grace waited inside the terminal. She sat in an uncomfortable, hard plastic seat and checked her watch continuously. Her entire support contingent had offered to come to the airport with her this morning—Joy, Hudson, Elsa and Uncle Willis—but she had declined their offer. Nolan had wanted to drive her here in her father's Rolls, but she'd nixed that idea immediately. She wanted her first encounter with the Dundee agent to be just the two of them. In the next few weeks—or perhaps even months— she and a man named Jed Tyree were going to be working together to prove the validity of the accusations against Governor Miller and Booth Fortier. It was imperative to the mission that he and she form a bond of trust and cooperation.

The minutes ticked by, each moment seeming like a dozen, as she waited impatiently. Finally twenty minutes later, the arrival of Jed Tyree's flight was announced. She joined the dozen or so others who were meeting that flight as they congregated together to greet the incoming passengers. Grace watched as, one by one, men and women disembarked. Four, eight, twelve. There he is, she thought. She wasn't sure exactly how she knew that the man she was looking at was Jed Tyree, but she knew. He was tall—probably six-three—with shoulders that would fill a doorway. His dark, curly hair appeared to have been combed with his fingers. A day's growth of beard stubble covered his cheeks and chin. And his attire was casual. Very casual. A light-blue cotton knit shirt clung to his broad chest and muscular arms. And a pair of well-worn jeans hugged his hips. With every move he made, Jed Tyree's body screamed, ''I'm a man!''

Grace swallowed. The very idea that she would be even remotely affected by this man's blatant masculinity unnerved her. Not once since Dean's death had she felt the least bit attracted to another man. *You're not attracted to this man,* she told herself. *You've simply noticed how virile he is.*

The man glanced around, obviously looking for her. He scanned the few remaining people waiting, then zeroed in on her. His eyes widened. He grinned. But suddenly the grin vanished, replaced by a worried frown.

She took a tentative step toward him. ''Mr. Tyree?''

He nodded.

''I'm Grace Beaumont.'' She held out her hand.

He hesitated. She heard a low rumble coming from his throat and thought he'd murmured something that sounded like ''son-of-a-bitch.''

When she continued holding out her hand, he finally grasped it and gave her the quickest handshake she'd ever exchanged.

''We can pick up your luggage and then—''

''This is all the luggage I brought.'' He hoisted the black canvas bag over his shoulder.

''Oh. All right.'' She motioned for him to follow her.

"I'm parked in the adjacent lot. I'm afraid we don't have valet parking here."

"Lead the way."

Grace glanced over her shoulder—once—and caught him staring at her behind. Feeling self-conscious, she tried to not sway her hips as she walked.

When they approached the Mercedes, she punched the button on her keyless entry pad and the trunk flipped open. Without being told what to do, Jed dropped his bag inside, closed the trunk lid, then hurried around to the driver's side and waited for her to unlock the door. The moment she pushed the pad again, he opened her door for her. He didn't look like a gentleman, Grace thought, but by this gesture alone he showed he could act like one.

"Thank you." She smiled at him. He returned the smile. The bottom dropped out of her stomach. This wasn't happening! No way. What was wrong with her? Why did he make her feel like a young girl encountering her first real man?

Grace slid behind the wheel, strapped her seat belt, started the engine and turned on the air conditioning. Although it wasn't quite June yet, it was already warm and humid. The minute Jed fastened his safety belt, she backed out of the parking slot and drove onto the city street.

"Have you ever been to Louisiana, Mr. Tyree?" Grace hoped some idle chitchat might relieve the tension tightening inside her.

He didn't respond immediately, as if he had to think about his answer. "Please, call me Jed. And as a matter of fact I was born and raised in Louisiana."

"Really?" Grace forced herself to keep her eyes on the street, to not sneak a peek at her passenger. "Where are you from?"

"Beaulac. It's a little place between Baton Rouge and Lafayette."

"Beaulac's not far from here. We have a radio station there."

"Sheffield Media, Inc. is a pretty far-reaching empire. I understand it spreads over into Mississippi, Oklahoma and Texas."

"Have you done your homework on me?" Grace hazarded a glance at him. "I'm afraid I don't know much about you other than your name and that your boss, Mr. McNamara, assured me you were the right man to head up this job."

"Not much to know, ma'am. I joined the army at eighteen and stayed in for fifteen years. I've worked for Dundee a little over a year. No wife. No kids. Never been married."

"I suppose you know my personal history."

"Yes, ma'am. Dundee's always compiles a file on all clients. Just basic stuff. Nothing too personal. Not unless it affects the case."

"Murder is very personal, isn't it, Mr. Ty—Jed? So I suppose you know the facts about the car wreck that killed my husband and my father."

"I'm sorry about what happened. I understand you almost died, too."

"A part of me did die," Grace admitted, then wondered why she was so forthcoming with a stranger.

"I think I understand."

No, you don't understand, Grace wanted to shout. *You can't possibly understand. No one can.* Not unless they have survived an accident that killed the other members of their family. Not unless they, too, have lain in a hospital bed, and silently prayed to die.

Grace whipped the Mercedes through early morning traffic, which wasn't terribly heavy in a small town like St. Camille, but dense enough to slow their progress from the city limits out into the country where Belle Foret was located.

Jed observed Grace Beaumont as she maneuvered her car through traffic and onto the highway leading out of town. At the airport, the moment he'd realized the gorgeous, long-legged blonde approaching him had to be Grace Beaumont, he'd cursed under his breath. He supposed he could right-fully be accused of being a ladies' man; he'd certainly en-joyed his fair share. But during his time at Dundee's, he'd made it a personal policy to not become involved with a client, which usually wasn't a problem. But he could see trouble with a capital T written all over Grace Beaumont. What red-blooded man could look at her and not get aroused? She was absolute perfection.

Yeah, Tyree, she's perfect—but not perfect for you. Not even for a brief fling. How do you think she'd feel if she knew you were Booth Fortier's nephew? Especially if it turns out that Uncle Booth was behind Dean Beaumont's and Byram Sheffield's deaths… Hell, what was he thinking? Of course his uncle had ordered their deaths. And if Jed knew his uncle, Booth Fortier had wanted all the occupants of the car to die that night. Grace had barely escaped; and once his uncle became aware that she had now instigated an investigation into their deaths, she would be in grave danger.

Jed couldn't allow himself to become personally involved with this woman. It wouldn't be fair to either of them. And from what he'd learned about Grace through the files Dun-dee had put together on her, she'd been hurt more than enough for one lifetime. He had to keep things strictly busi-ness between them.

While in Louisiana, he'd be walking a fine line, trying to balance the truth with the lies. He'd be working with Dun-dee's and the FBI to find evidence that substantiated the accusations in Grace's anonymous letter. He'd be guarding Grace as closely as possible, even before the first threat was made on her life. And it was only a matter of time until that first threat happened. Also, once the time was right, he would make contact with his uncle. That meeting was some-thing he dreaded. But for their plans to work, he had to visit Booth. Several times. He had to convince his uncle that, after all these years, he was willing to give him the benefit of the doubt. And he had to find a way to make contact with the federal agent who had infiltrated his uncle's organization. Undoubtedly something had happened recently to make it impossible for the agent to contact anyone in the bureau without jeopardizing his position.

"We're here."

Grace's soft, sultry voice instantly snapped Jed from his thoughts. He surveyed the area as she drove the Mercedes through the white wrought-iron gates that opened at a touch of her finger on the automatic control inside her car. A long paved drive, lined with massive oak trees dripping with Spanish moss, led to the old antebellum mansion. Consisting of three stories, the first was graced with whitewashed brick pillars across a wide veranda and a second story balcony was decorated with white columns and fancy white wrought-iron banisters.

Grace Sheffield Beaumont had been born into a life of wealth and privilege, with a pedigree that could be traced back to Europe. Until her father's emergence into the media industry forty years ago, the men in Grace's family had been gentlemen farmers since before the Civil War. And the women had all been ladies of breeding. Quality. Not a peasant in the bunch.

And what had Jed's family been? Several generations back, when Grace's ancestors had been pillars of Louisiana society, Jed's had been pirates. In the past century they had been bootleggers, racketeers. Criminals, the whole lot of them. And one noteworthy relative—his mother's father, Vernon Fortier—had become the head of a crime syndicate, the job taken over and his territory enlarged by his only son, Booth. Without any children of his own, Booth had been grooming Jed to follow in his footsteps, but had been careful to keep his nephew out of the mainstream. Jed had been given the best of everything—everything that dirty, illegally earned money could buy. Most of his life he'd heard the rumors about his family, his uncle in particular, but he hadn't wanted to believe them. Growing up he'd been sent to private schools, taken to Europe for vacations, expected to attend a top-notch university. But then the summer after he'd graduated from high school, he'd learned something that changed his life forever.

Jed's mother, who had spent most of his life secluded in a private sanitarium for mental patients, had told him that her brother, his beloved uncle Booth, had murdered the man she loved—Jed's father—when he found out that Lance Tyree had gotten her pregnant before their elopement. At first he'd thought his mother's accusations were simply the ramblings of a disturbed mind. But when he'd confronted his uncle, he'd seen the truth in the devil's black eyes.

Grace parked the car in front of the old mansion, then got out and started for the steps leading to the front veranda. The minute her foot hit the first step, the massive double wooden doors opened. A small, gray-haired man in black slacks and white shirt stood in the open doorway. The butler, Jed figured, Nolan Rowley, who'd worked for the family over thirty-five years.

"Come inside." Grace invited him in with a sweep of her hand.

"May I take your bag, sir?" Nolan asked.

"No, thanks. I can manage it myself."

"Very well, sir." Nolan turned to his employer. "Will you need me to drive y'all into town this morning, Miss Grace?"

She shook her head. "Not today, thank you, Nolan."

The old butler-cum-chauffeur nodded and quickly disappeared down the back hallway. A divided spiral staircase possessed a good part of the massive black-and-white marble-floored entrance foyer. Glancing up, Jed could see all the way to the third floor, which he figured had once been the servants' quarters and might still be.

"Laverna has aired out and prepared a guest room for you. I thought you might like to unpack—" Grace eyed his lone canvas bag "—and freshen up—" she glanced at his beard stubble "—before I take you into town to Sheffield Media's headquarters and introduce you to the staff."

"I'm about as fresh as I get," Jed told her, putting a humorous glint in his eyes when he smiled at her.

"Oh, I see." She avoided looking directly at him. "Well, you can deposit your bag and unpack if you'd like. And if you'd care for breakfast, Dora can prepare you something—"

"I'm not much of a breakfast eater. I grabbed coffee and a couple of doughnuts at the Atlanta airport before takeoff this morning."

Grace huffed ever so softly, then said, "Let me show you to your room."

Jed got the distinct impression that Miss Grace didn't approve of him. Good. Let's keep it that way, he decided. If she found him a bit rough around the edges, if she didn't like him, it would be easier for them to maintain the distance necessary for their professional relationship.

Grace Beaumont was about as luscious a lady as he'd come across in many a year. She was like a ripe peach hanging precariously on a limb, ready to be picked. And if there weren't a hundred and one good reasons for him to keep his distance, he'd take a sweet, juicy bite out of her.

Rein in your libido, Jed cautioned himself. The last thing he needed while on this assignment was a love affair. Hell, everything was already complicated enough as it was.

Chapter 4

Elsa met her brother at the back door, catching him as he tried to sneak into the house. She'd been up all night, worried sick, half out of her mind, because he hadn't come home or called. Her greatest fear was that he was back on drugs. He'd been doing great lately, ever since going through rehab his senior year in high school and enrolling this past fall at St. Camille Community College. Troy wasn't a bad kid, just easily manipulated by others.

"Where the hell have you been?" Elsa studied her nineteen-year-old brother, looking for any signs that he might be high. Although he looked a bit scruffy and needed a shave, he seemed to be sober.

"Who are you, the police?" Troy asked defensively.

"I'm the woman who has been a mother to you since you were a kid, that's who I am. I'm the sister who put her own life on hold to make sure you and Sherrie and Milly had food in your bellies and clothes on your back. I'm the person who worries about you."

Troy shrugged his slender shoulders. Built like their dad,

her brother was tall and lanky, almost skinny. He wore his dark hair shoulder-length and had his ears, his nose and his tongue pierced.

When he tried to sidestep her, Elsa grabbed his arm and swung him around to face her. "Where were you all night long?"

He jerked free and glared at her. "I'm nineteen frigging years old. I don't have to report in to you. Haven't you figured that out yet?"

Elsa inhaled deeply, then released her breath as she counted to ten. "I thought we had a deal, one you've lived up to for nearly a year now. I pay the bills and you go to school and keep your nose clean. Has something happened to change that?"

With his back to her, he shook his head. "Nah, not really. Not yet. It's just…well…I got a part-time job and I got a girl."

"Are you saying you were working last night or are you telling me you stayed over at some girl's place all night?"

Troy glanced over his shoulder sheepishly. "Both actually. The job's in a warehouse down at the waterfront. My new girlfriend picked me up afterward and I spent the night with her."

"I see. You could have called, you know." Why didn't his explanation relieve her worries? she wondered. Maybe because it was too little information, too late. "When did you get the job? How long have you been working? How'd you meet this girl? Who is she?"

"Damn, what is this, the Spanish inquisition?"

"Look, Troy, I was up all night. I called every friend of yours I could think of. I checked with the hospital and even with the police to see if you'd been in an accident. I had to call in at work this morning to let them know I'd be late because I didn't know what had happened to you."

"Hey, I'm sorry, okay." Troy sucked his cheeks in as if trying to curb his explosive temper. "I'm not back on the hard stuff. I swear. I drink a few beers now and then and that's it.''

Crossing her arms over her chest, Elsa waited, expecting a reply to her questions.

"I met Josie at school this quarter. She's taking a secretarial course. She shares a place with a friend and works at the diner over on Fifth Street." Troy glanced down at the floor. "And before you ask, yes, I'm being careful. We…uh…I always use a condom."

Elsa let out a loud, exasperated breath, closed her eyes and prayed for patience. And while she was at it, she prayed that Troy was telling her the truth. All she needed at this point in her life was her brother knocking up some girl and her winding up having to raise the baby.

"What's the name of the place where you're working?"

"It's just a warehouse. I'm not sure about the name. I help load and unload crates off trucks and boats. The guy pays me in cash. It's good money for a few hours work."

Elsa didn't like the sound of it. "What's in the crates you're helping load and unload?"

"How should I know?"

"Drugs?"

"Hell, Elsa, get off my back. I said I don't know what's in the crates…and I don't care. Josie told me that a guy she knew had a good paying part-time job, so I applied for the position and got it. I thought you'd be pleased. Aren't you the one who's always griping about money?"

"What's the guy's name?"

"What guy?"

"Your boss?"

"Curt Poarch."

"What if I want to talk to this Mr. Poarch, how do I get in touch with him?"

"No way." Troy's face flushed; his body language became hostile. "Stay out of my business."

Before she could say another word, Troy stormed out of the kitchen. Elsa followed him down the hall and into his bedroom. She stood in the doorway and watched while he stuffed a knapsack full with his underwear and clothes.

"What are you doing?" she asked.

"I'm moving out, that's what I'm doing. I'll take what I can this morning and I'll come back for my other stuff later—after you've left for work."

"Where will you live?"

"Josie will put me up for a few days until I find a place of my own." He grinned mockingly. "Who knows, maybe we'll get a place together. Split expenses."

"This man—Curt Poarch—must be paying you pretty good if you think you can rent your own place, keep up your truck payments, pay for your schooling—"

"I'm outta here." Troy hoisted his canvas knapsack over his shoulder and all but shoved Elsa out of the way as he moved past her.

"Troy." She raced down the hall after him. By the time she caught up with him, he was outside, dumping his knapsack in the cab of his older model Ford pickup.

"Think about what you're doing," Elsa said, as he slid behind the wheel and slammed the door. "What if the guy you're working for is doing something illegal? Is it worth that kind of risk just to make some fast, easy money?"

He cranked the engine, shifted the gears into Reverse, and said, "It's a hell of a lot better than working for pittance the way you do at a job where you have to lick Ms. Rich Bitch Beaumont's fancy high heels every day." With that said, he backed out of the driveway and sped onto the road.

Elsa heaved her shoulders as she sighed heavily. God in heaven, where had she gone wrong? Hadn't she done everything in her power to help Troy, just as she had Sherrie and Milly?

For the time being there wasn't much she could do, short of praying. If Troy needed her, he knew where to find her. In the meantime, she had herself and Milly to support.

Elsa checked her watch. If she left now, she would be only two hours late. That was two hours of pay she couldn't afford to miss and she didn't want to use a sick day because she saved those days in order to volunteer once a month at St. Camille Haven, the private boarding school where Milly lived during the week. It was a school for children with severe learning disabilities. For volunteering one day a month, they reduced Milly's tuition by a small amount.

She knew that if she'd taken Grace Beaumont up on her kind offer of assistance in paying the tuition for St. Camille Haven, she wouldn't constantly be struggling to make ends meet. But she would not accept charity from anyone. Not even from Grace. Besides, she was well aware of the fact that Grace had arranged for the scholarship that paid over fifty percent of Milly's bills at the school.

Elsa made a mad dash to the bathroom, ran a comb through her hair, swiped on some lipstick and checked her appearance in the full-length mirror attached to the back of the door. She looked presentable. That was good enough. She detoured through her bedroom, grabbed her keys and handbag, and rushed out to her car, all the while praying Troy would come to his senses before he got in over his head with the wrong people.

A two-story structure that blended in nicely with the century-old buildings in downtown St. Camille, the headquarters for Sheffield Media, Inc. presided over two acres of land within the city limits. Consisting of several small buildings resembling raised cottages, so prevalent in Louisiana, and connected by white lattice-covered breezeways, the administrative center looked more like a mini-community than a business site. Grace gave Jed a tour of the entire compound, introducing him as "Mr. Tyree, who will be working for me a few weeks in an advisory capacity." She hadn't elaborated on his job description and no one had asked for more information.

Jed opened doors for Grace as they made their way into the heart of the complex, which was alive with activity. All the employees were friendly. They smiled, greeted them and paid the proper respect to the CEO and her guest. Did any of these people know who he was and what he was doing here? Probably not.

"Exactly who knows about the letter you received?" Jed asked.

"Four people other than myself…and the person who wrote the letter." She paused by the desk in an outer office, then glanced around as if searching for someone. "My senior vice-president, Hudson Prentice, who is also a good friend, my cousin Joy Loring, my lawyer and family friend, Willis Sullivan, and my personal assistant, Elsa Leone, who doesn't seem to be here this morning."

A wide-eyed young woman with a mop of curly carrot-red hair emerged from Grace's private office—Grace's name on the door declared the space as hers.

"Oh, good morning, Ms. Beaumont." The plump redhead left the door wide open, moved aside and stood at attention. "Elsa phoned. She'll be late coming in. A problem with her brother. But she gave me exact instructions. Your mail has been opened and placed on your desk and I just put a mug of cappuccino on the coaster. I used the crystal mug, per Elsa's instructions."

"Thank you, Avery." Grace entered her large, elegant office, then glanced back at the young woman. "Did Elsa say what the problem was with Troy?"

"No, ma'am, she didn't."

"Mmm-hmm. All right, thanks. When Elsa arrives, please tell her I wish to speak to her. And for now, will you inform Mr. Prentice that I'd like for him to come to my office."

"Right away."

Jed wasn't surprised by Grace's air of command. He figured she'd been used to giving orders all her life, so it would have become second nature to her. Call him a male chauvinist, but what amazed him was how someone so young and beautiful could be savvy enough to run a multimillion-dollar media empire. After all, from what he'd read in the Dundee's report on her, she hadn't worked a day in her life until three years ago when she'd stepped in to fill her father's shoes as not only owner of Sheffield Media, Inc., but as the CEO. She'd been born and bred to be a society wife, as her mother and grandmothers before her had been.

"You asked to see me?" A rather ordinary-looking man, of medium height and build, stood in the open doorway.

Jed studied him briefly. The guy was a bit of a dandy with his expensive clothes, Rolex wristwatch and perfectly styled brown hair.

"Hudson, please come in and close the door," Grace said, and her senior vice-president scurried to do her bidding.

Jed wondered if all the men in Grace's life were such willing slaves. Probably. He pegged Grace for the type who, when she snapped her fingers, expected a man to come running.

Hudson Prentice eyed Jed with the kind of speculation he translated as the guy trying to figure out whether Jed was competition. Competition for what? What else—Grace Beaumont's affections.

"Jed Tyree, this is Hudson Prentice."

"Thirty-six, unmarried, lives alone, no pets, no children. Graduated magna cum laude, with an MBA from Tulane. Hired as an assistant by and for Byram Sheffield. A loyal employee for almost fifteen years. Now senior vice-president, good friend and confidante of Grace Beaumont." Jed recited the info, and noted the way Hudson's brows rose and a tenuous smile hiked the corners of his mouth.

"You seem to have me at a disadvantage, Mr. Tyree." Hudson offered his hand. "You know a great deal about me and I know nothing about you."

"All you need to know is that I'm a Dundee agent hired by Ms. Beaumont to investigate some serious allegations." Jed shook hands with Prentice, whose smile quickly disappeared.

"Hudson, I want you to arrange for an office for Mr. Tyree. Move some people around, if necessary," Grace in-

structed as she lifted the crystal mug from her desk and
sipped the cappuccino. "I want him in this building, fairly
close to me."

"Yes, of course. It will take some time to—"

"I want it done this morning."

"Certainly."

Grace eyed Jed over the rim of her mug. "Tell Hudson
what you'll need. Computer? Fax? Copier? Extra phone
lines? A secretary of your own?"

"Yes to everything except the secretary," Jed replied.
"Dundee's will send someone to act in that capacity, if I
find I need it. By not using one of your people, we lessen
the chance of more people knowing about your private business."

"Good idea." Grace sat down behind her desk, then
glanced at Prentice. "That's all, Hudson. Thank you."

Prentice looked like a kid who'd been told to go to bed
without any supper. Staring down at his feet, he cleared his
throat, then glared at Grace. "Couldn't Elsa handle all of
this? After all, how will it look to the employees to have
me at Mr. Tyree's beck and call? I am the senior vice-
president."

Grace set her coffee mug on the coaster, placed one hand
on the desk and the other on her thigh. "I apologize. I had
no idea you'd feel demeaned by helping Mr. Tyree settle
in. But Elsa has been delayed this morning by a personal
matter, so if you would, I'd appreciate your at least arrang-
ing for an office for Mr. Tyree."

"Grace, I—I didn't mean to imply that—"

She held up her hand in a Stop gesture. "No, no. It was
my mistake entirely."

With that said, she dismissed Prentice, who gazed at her
pathetically and slunk out of the room like a whipped dog.

Jed wondered how a guy who could so easily be cowed
by a woman had ever been considered CEO material?
Hadn't he read in the file on Grace that Prentice had temporarily replaced Byram Sheffield for ten months after his

death? The only explanation that made sense to Jed was that Prentice was in love with Grace, which made him act like a tongue-tied fool only around her. Otherwise, the man was just an idiot. And he didn't think a man with Byram Sheffield's reputation was the type to have suffered fools gladly.

"You should put him out of his misery," Jed said.

Grace's head snapped up; she glared at him. "Pardon?"

"Nothing." Jed shrugged.

"My relationships with my employees are none of your concern."

"Yes, ma'am." Jed clicked his heels and saluted her.

She glowered at him. "Was that supposed to be funny?"

"Sorry, I couldn't resist. It's just no one would ever suspect that under that cover-girl beauty beats the heart of a commanding army general."

"Look, it's none of your business—"

"You've already made your point."

"Hudson thinks he's in love with me. I pretend not to know how he feels. But he also resents the fact that I took over for my father when he expected to be named permanent CEO. I want him as a friend. I need him as an executive. So I walk a fine line as far as our working relationship goes."

Jed nodded. "Are you trying to tell me that your Hitler routine was strictly for Prentice's benefit?"

"I'm a woman whose claim to fame prior to my father's death was being a prominent socialite. How do you think my employees would have reacted to me if I hadn't come in here on the first day with a hard-ass, I'm-the-boss-attitude?"

"I see your point."

"What is it with you, Mr. Tyree—do you have a problem with strong, aggressive females? If so, I suggest you get over it for the duration of this assignment, while you're working for me."

"I'll do my job, Ms. Beaumont, but there's one thing you should know—I don't jump through hoops for anybody, so don't expect it.'' Without giving her a chance for a rebuttal, he nodded toward the outer office. ''I need to make some phone calls, get the ball rolling. My boss is supposed to have contacted the local authorities to see about getting me copies of the accident report and the file on the subsequent investigation into the wreck that killed your husband and father. We'll start there, see if there's anything that might indicate the hit-and-run wasn't accidental.''

''Use Elsa's desk until Hudson can arrange for you to have your own office.''

When Jed walked into the outer office, Grace followed him, then paused at his side when he sat down at the desk.

He glanced up at her. ''Yeah?''

''For your information, I do not expect anyone to jump through hoops for me.''

''If you say so.''

Grace huffed. ''Why begin with looking into information about the accident? Why not investigate the allegation that Governor Miller is involved with Booth Fortier?''

Should he be totally honest with her? Jed wondered. Should he tell her that Sawyer, Special Agent Moran and Sam Dundee had all agreed that Jed shouldn't start digging into the governor's supposed involvement with the syndicate until they had several Dundee agents on the job and a couple of Feds in place? Once they started the investigation, it was only a matter of time—hours or days—before both the governor and Fortier would learn about it. And when they discovered who was behind the probe into their affairs, Grace Beaumont's life would be in imminent danger.

''We've already started putting out feelers from Dundee's headquarters in Atlanta,'' he told her. ''Once our other agents, Domingo Shea and Kate Malone, arrive tomorrow, they'll be involved exclusively in that investigation.''

With a somber expression on her face, Grace said, ''It's going to get really ugly, isn't it?''

''Yeah. Real ugly, real fast.''

''Do you earn double pay for double duty?''

"Double duty?"

"Don't play dumb with me, Mr. Tyree. It doesn't suit you. You and I both know that very soon you'll be acting as my bodyguard."

Jaron checked to make sure the door to his room was securely locked. He couldn't risk having one of Booth's people walk in on him while he was composing his second letter to Grace Beaumont. He didn't like living under the same roof with Booth, but agreeing to live here was the only way he could keep an eye on Charmaine and try to help her however he could. Booth treated him well, for an underling. The big man trusted him. And why shouldn't he? Jaron had bowed and scraped to Booth most of his adult life. If Booth said jump, Jaron asked how high?

Sitting down at his desk, he turned on his laptop computer and stared at the blank screen. He had already worked out the details of where, when and how she would have to deliver the money, but that information could wait for the next letter. This time, he would simply explain that he was in possession of evidence that would link Governor Miller to Booth Fortier and for five million dollars, he would put that evidence in Grace's hands. And as a bonus, he would add all the details he knew about the "hit" put out on Dean Beaumont and his father-in-law four years ago.

Jaron typed as fast as his hunt-and-peck technique allowed, being careful just how he worded the letter. As soon as he finished, he hit Print. The minute the sheet rose from the printer, he snatched it out and read it hurriedly, then immediately deleted the letter from his computer.

A noise outside his room alerted him to possible danger. He folded the letter and slipped it into the inside pocket of his sport coat. Sweat popped out on his upper lip. He listened. Heard nothing. He inserted a four-by-nine envelope into the slot in the printer, typed out Grace Beaumont's name and work address at Sheffield Media headquarters, then put the letter inside the envelope, added a stamp and returned the message to his inside coat pocket.

There was that noise again. Footsteps? Then his doorknob jiggled. Jaron swallowed. Perspiration dampened his palms.

Get a hold of yourself. There's no way Booth can suspect you of anything. You're letting your fear get the better of you. You've got to act like a man with nothing to hide.

Taking a deep breath, he stood, straightened his shoulders and crossed the room. He unlocked and opened his bedroom door, then glanced up and down the hall. Braced casually against the wall several feet away, one of Booth's devoted employees, Curt Poarch, grinned at Jaron.

"You want something?" Jaron asked.

"Hey, man, sorry if I disturbed you. With your door locked, I figured you were taking a nap or humping somebody or jacking off or—"

"What do you want?"

"As you know, Mr. Fortier just left for a couple of days in New Orleans," Curt said. "Before he left, he told me to take any questions or problems to you."

Inwardly Jaron sighed with relief, but outwardly his body language didn't change. "Yeah, so?"

"We got a big shipment coming in tonight and I'm gonna need some extra cash to pay the part-time guys. Mr. Fortier said you'd handle it since you got the combination to that safe."

"Yeah, sure. Just tell me how much you need and I'll see that you get it."

"Thanks, Mr. Vaden. And sorry I made a crack about why you had your door locked."

"No apology needed," Jaron told him. "When you get to know me better, you'll learn I like my privacy. That's all there is to it."

"Yes, sir."

Jaron put his hand on Curt's shoulder. "Let's go get ourselves a nice cool drink and you can tell me if any of the temporary boys you've got working at the warehouse are candidates for permanent jobs.''

Curt grinned. ''A cool drink on a hot day sounds good to me. And as far as promising workers, there's this one kid—reminds me of myself a bit when I was his age. Eager to please. Smart. Follows orders without question. Got himself an expensive playmate, if you know what I mean.''

''Sounds like our kind of guy. What's his name?''

''Leone. Troy Leone.''

Chapter 5

"Are you sure there's nothing I can do to help?" Grace asked, wanting desperately to alleviate Elsa's pain.

"Thanks for the offer, but I'm afraid there's nothing anyone can do at this point. I've talked to Troy until I'm blue in the face." Elsa's effort to smile failed miserably. "I would do absolutely anything to help him. You know that. But I can't help him if he fights me every inch of the way. He's damned and determined to do what he wants to do."

"Perhaps we could offer him a part-time job here at Sheffield Media," Grace suggested.

Elsa shook her head. "I have a feeling that the part-time job he has is paying him ten times what a job here would pay. And that's what has me really worried, more than him moving in with some girl who is probably…" She stopped short of calling Troy's new girlfriend a tramp, but Grace got the idea. "Anyhow, I'm afraid whatever is going on at that warehouse is illegal."

"I could call and talk to Chief Winters—"

"No!" When Grace gave her a puzzled look, Elsa explained. "We have no evidence that there's anything illegal going on. If the chief of police has one of his officers poke around down there... Oh, God, Grace, what if the police catch Troy committing a crime? He would go to jail. And even though his juvenile record is sealed, he did have a few run-ins with the law right after he turned eighteen."

Neither Grace nor Elsa had heard the office door ease open, so when Jed Tyree said, "Want me to run a check on the place?" both women gasped simultaneously.

"Sorry, didn't mean to startle you," Jed said. "I thought y'all heard me open the door."

"How much did you hear?" Grace asked.

"Enough to know that your assistant—" he nodded to Elsa "—that Ms. Leone's brother might get into trouble with the law on his new job."

Ever mindful of her manners, Grace said, "Elsa this is the Dundee agent I hired, Jed Tyree. Jed, my assistant and friend, Elsa Leone." After a moment of awkward silence, Grace asked, "How discreet could you be in checking out the warehouse where Troy is working part-time?"

"No, please, I can't afford—" Elsa protested.

"Consider it a freebie," Jed said, then responded to Grace, "I could be so discreet that no one connected with the warehouse would know I'd even run a check."

"That's discreet enough." Grace turned to Elsa. "Is it all right with you?"

Elsa nodded. Any other woman would have been in tears by now, but not Elsa. Years of being strong and tough and responsible had hardened Elsa. Grace understood that particular self-protection technique all too well. A person could endure only so much suffering and disappointment before erecting a giant shield around her heart.

"All right," Elsa said. "As long as the police aren't involved. I figure if Troy continues on his chosen path, he'll eventually wind up in prison. But I don't want to be the cause of it by sending the police to check on him."

"We understand, don't we, Mr. Tyree?"

Jed hesitated and during that momentary pause Grace noticed an odd expression cross his face. It was as if he truly did understand Elsa's concern. Had he ever been in a similar situation? she wondered.

"Yeah, we understand," Jed said.

Elsa offered them a fragile smile. "Thank you, Mr. Tyree."

"Call me Jed. And as soon as I find out anything, I'll let you know."

Elsa nodded, then said to Grace, "I'll get to work now. I'm so sorry I was late this morning."

"You had good reason," Grace replied.

The minute Elsa exited the room and closed the door behind her, Jed faced Grace. "You know the odds aren't in her favor."

Grace's gaze connected with his. "Meaning?"

"Meaning her brother is headed for big-time trouble and we all know it. He's got a high-paying part-time job at night in a riverfront warehouse. There's a ninety-percent chance he's working for Booth Fortier."

Grace's heart lurched at the mention of the monster's name. "Isn't that quite a leap? You're assuming—"

"I'm assuming nothing. Booth Fortier controls organized crime in Louisiana. Everyone knows it, including law enforcement, but the guy's been too smart all these years to ever get caught. He prides himself on being able to flaunt his wealth and power and thumb his nose at the police, the state boys, the Feds... He thinks he's invincible, which makes him twice as deadly. But it also makes him vulnerable. It's his major weakness."

"You seem to have learned a great deal about Fortier in a very brief period of time." Grace sensed that Jed's assessment of the mob boss came from something more than recent research on her case. "Did you know about Fortier before you took this assignment?"

"Yeah, I knew about him. Don't forget I'm from Louisiana."

"I see." But she didn't; not really. Not unless Jed Tyree had been in law enforcement, which he hadn't been—or unless for some other reason he'd kept tabs on Fortier's career. Was it possible that Jed had suffered a personal loss, as she had, at Fortier's command?

"I'll have the warehouse where the kid works checked out. It shouldn't be too difficult to find out which warehouse it is," Jed said. "Now, back to the case at hand—I've gone over the accident report from four years ago and taken a look at the photos of the scene. I agree with the police. From the evidence, it appears to be nothing more than a drunk driver who lost control of his vehicle and hit the car your husband was driving. But..."

"But?"

"If the other driver was so intoxicated that he couldn't control his vehicle, then why didn't his car go over the embankment the way your husband's car did? It is possible that his erratic driving, swerving back and forth, saved his life, which is what the police think."

"That's not what you think, is it?"

"My guess is the other driver wasn't drunk, he knew exactly what he was doing and once he'd made certain your husband's car crashed over the embankment, he turned just in the nick of time and went on his merry way. He'd been hired to do a job, told to make sure it appeared to be an accident. The guy was a professional."

"If he was a professional, why did Fortier kill him?"

"We don't know he was killed, do we?"

"But the letter I received said—"

"The letter you received said a lot of things, made a lot of accusations, none of which we've proven. Not yet. Whoever wrote that letter, wrote it to get your attention. He wants something. He'll contact you again."

"What?" Grace spun around and glared at Jed. "He said in the letter that his conscience was bothering him. Are you saying he—"

"To have that type of inside information means he's either one of Fortier's boys or he's close to Governor Miller. My guess is that he belongs to Fortier. He's double-crossing the head of the crime syndicate, which in Fortier's world is punishable by death, so this is no soul-cleansing confession. Believe me, you'll hear from him again. That's why I want your personal phone line here at the office tapped and your home phone as well.''

"You think he'll call me?"

Jed nodded. "Either that or he'll send another letter."

"When?"

"Soon. He can't afford to waste time. Once Fortier realizes that you're having him investigated, he'll know why...or least he'll be able to make an educated guess. Then he'll start looking around at those closest to him and figure out who has stabbed him in the back. Out of fear for his life, our guy is working on a strict timetable.''

"I'm impressed," Grace admitted. "You seem to know an awful lot about the way these people think. But I suppose you have to possess that type of knowledge in your line of work.''

Jed didn't respond.

"What's next?" she asked. "Where do we go from here?"

"A great deal of investigative work is done by computer these days, so Dundee is already taking that route. And when Domingo and Kate arrive tomorrow, they should have a report for me. They'll be doing the hands-on investigation, but I'll be coordinating their efforts along with my own and with what's being done at Dundee headquarters.''

"If you need an office at my house, you can use mine. My father had a state-of-the-art home office and I've taken full advantage of it.''

"Sounds good. Thanks for the offer.''

"Okay." Grace's whole body relaxed as she willed the tension to drain away. She'd learned how to release negative energy and wipe her mind clear. The technique helped, but it worked on a temporary basis only. But even temporary relief was better than none. "Are you about ready for lunch? I can have Elsa order in for us or we can go out. Your choice."

"I need to tie up a few loose ends," he told her. "Then I'll be ready to leave. I'd like to take a look around St. Camille, familiarize myself with the town. Besides, I'm in the mood for Crawfish Etoufe."

"I know just the place. Beula's Crab Shack, over on Avenall. It looks like a seedy dive, but they serve the best Crawfish Etoufe in La Durantaye Parish."

"Give me ten minutes."

"All right."

Jed grinned at her, then winked just as he turned and headed out the door. A peculiar quiver radiated through her tummy. She couldn't remember the last time a man had winked at her. Or the last time she'd responded to an innocent flirtation.

Be very careful, Grace, a warning voice inside her head cautioned. *An innocent flirtation could easily turn into something serious, something you aren't prepared to handle.*

Why was she entertaining man-woman thoughts about Jed? She wasn't sure she even liked the guy. Okay, so she might not like him, but she was attracted to him. No use in denying the truth. There was something unique about Jed Tyree, something undeniably appealing.

Jed dialed the digital phone number for one of the two undercover Dundee agents already in place—the two Grace Beaumont didn't and wouldn't know anything about. Not yet. Rafe Devlin answered on the second ring.

"I need for you to check out some warehouses down by the river," Jed said. "This isn't directly connected to the case, but it just might have ties to Fortier. Check the warehouses owned by Garland, Inc. first. Garland, Inc. is controlled by Fortier. See if you can find out what comes in and out during the nighttime hours. And see if a kid named Troy Leone is working part-time there."

"Leone? Isn't Grace Beaumont's personal assistant named—"

"He's Elsa Leone's little brother. Probably getting in over his head, thinking about nothing but making some big money the easy way."

"Been there, done that, got the scars to prove it," Devlin said, a hint of humor in his voice.

"Call me on my cell phone when you find out something."

"Will do." A slight pause. "Hey, did you know that when Dean Beaumont passed the bar and went into private practice, back when he was a green kid, he briefly worked for Oliver Neville?"

"And Neville is?"

"He's been Fortier's lawyer for the past fifteen years. An odd coincidence, don't you think?"

"Yeah, but it could be just that—a coincidence."

"Maybe. But then again it's possible the evidence Beaumont was so close to getting on Fortier and Governor Miller was going to come from Neville."

"And if Neville was the source, then Neville could be our letter writer."

"Bingo."

"It's worth checking into," Jed said.

"I'm already on it."

"Rafe?"

"Yeah?"

"Make sure—"

"Yeah, yeah, yeah. I will. I'm not stupid. I know what I'm dealing with here. I won't take any chances and I won't make any mistakes. You're the one who's in the most danger. You'll soon be walking into the lion's den."

"I'm familiar with the territory."

"Familiarity doesn't make it any less dangerous."

"Right." Jed paused for a split second as long-ago memories flashed through his mind. Memories he'd spent a lifetime trying to erase. "Just let me know about the warehouse ASAP. Okay?"

"Sure."

Charmaine Fortier had made a decision, one that might put her life in danger. But she didn't care. Not anymore. For months now she had pretended she wasn't falling in love with Ronnie Martine; she'd tried with all her might to resist her feelings. And even though Ronnie hadn't made an overt move or said anything that indicated he felt the same way, she knew he cared about her, too. Of course he was loyal to Booth, as were all Booth's employees. But unlike most of Booth's other boys, Ronnie didn't seem to be afraid of him. Not the way Jaron was. Her brother practically quaked in his boots every time Booth entered a room. And with good reason. Booth had a reputation of eliminating anyone who displeased him. She didn't know it for a fact, of course, but she didn't doubt for a minute that her husband had ordered the deaths of countless people. And whenever he took his vile temper out on her, she wondered how many people he had murdered personally. There was an evil in Booth that fed off other people's suffering. Off humiliation. And death.

If he ever finds out about you and Ronnie, he'll kill you both, she reminded herself.

"Turn off at the next right," Charmaine said. "I want to take a ride by the river before we go home."

"Yes, ma'am."

Ronnie acted as her chauffeur and bodyguard, a position Booth had assigned him six months ago. Booth always chose a bodyguard for her within the ranks of his personal staff, the boys he kept around him, the ones who lived in the house with them. During the fifteen years they'd been married, he had rotated her bodyguards on a yearly basis, which meant Ronnie had only six more months to be at her side.

They'd taken Charmaine's silver BMW convertible, a car

Booth had given her on her birthday two months ago—her thirty-fifth—when she'd decided to run into town. She was thirty-five goddamn years old. One day she'd been Booth's twenty-year-old bride and the next thing she knew she was his middle-aged prisoner. Yeah, that's exactly what she was—a prisoner. He had never allowed her to go anywhere without an escort, not in fifteen years. She was watched over day and night. Guarded, but from what she didn't know. Or maybe she did know. Wasn't Booth afraid she would betray him, that given the chance she'd turn to another man for the love he was incapable of giving her?

Jealousy was one of Booth's personality disorders—only one of many. When he'd married her, he'd known she still had feelings for someone else, but he had been so sure he could make her forget her first love. Whenever her performance in the bedroom had been less than he expected, he'd throw up the fact that she had been soiled goods, that she hadn't come to him a virgin. And she would never forget what he'd said to her the first time he hit her.

"So help me, I'll get Jed Tyree out of your system even if I have to beat him out of you."

As the late springtime wind whipped through her hair while Ronnie drove her along the bumpy gravel road, Charmaine let her mind drift back to her teenage years, to when she'd first met Jed. They'd been sixteen, both of them a little wild and looking for fun. Jaron had just gone to work for Booth a few months earlier and was in awe of his boss and encouraged Charmaine to cosy up to Booth's nephew. Jed had been her first love, in every sense of the word. And she'd thought he loved her, too, during their teenage affair. But after Jed had left so suddenly at eighteen and hadn't asked her to go with him, she'd hated him. Hated him enough to marry his uncle two years later. What a fool she'd been. Not a fool for having loved Jed, but to have believed marrying his uncle would be a sweet revenge.

"Do you want to stop anywhere, Mrs. Fortier?" Ronnie asked. "Or do you just want me to keep driving?"

"There's a little house not far from here, about a half mile down the road." She and Jaron had grown up in that shack by the river, just the two of them fending for themselves after their mother died when Charmaine was twelve. They'd never known their father. Hell, they didn't even know if they had the same father.

"You planning to visit somebody?" Ronnie glanced at her quickly then returned his gaze to the road.

"I'm going to pay a visit on some old memories."

"Pardon?"

"I used to live in the house," she told him. "Back before I married Booth."

"Yes, ma'am."

She tossed back her head, closed her eyes and let the afternoon sun warm her skin while the humid breeze caressed it. Right this minute, she was free. Gloriously free. Booth was in New Orleans. And she was alone with Ronnie. Away from the house. No prying eyes to spy on them.

"Have you ever been in love?" she asked.

"What?"

"I said have you ever been in love?"

"Yeah, sure I have."

"Was it wonderful and passionate and—"

"We were young. Got married. Had problems. Got a divorce."

"Are you still in love with her?" *Please, say no,* Charmaine prayed. *Say that you don't love anybody but me.*

"It was a long time ago," Ronnie said. "So long ago I barely remember."

"Then it wasn't real love. I remember Jed, you know. Even though Booth thinks he's erased his nephew from my memory. He hasn't."

"Mrs. Fortier, I don't think you should be—"

"There it is!" She squealed with delight, then sighed when she noticed the dilapidated state of the old house. "Lord, what a pitiful sight."

Ronnie pulled up in the weed-infested driveway, the dirt

path almost totally obscured by vegetation of various varieties. "Do you want to get out? Looks a bit shaky to me. Might not be safe."

Charmaine flung open the door and stepped out. "I was a lot safer in this house than I am in the one where I live now."

Ronnie got out and joined her as she walked toward the ramshackle front porch with rotting floorboards and a sagging roof. He came up beside her, his gaze scoping out the area, his open palm hovering over the small of her back. Hovering but not touching.

She paused before she reached the rickety front steps, turned slowly and smiled at him. "I came here for another reason. Other than to visit some old and very pleasant memories." He waited for her to continue, his gaze downcast as if he didn't want to make direct eye contact with her. "I brought you here for a reason."

"Yes, ma'am."

"Don't you want to know what that reason is?"

"If you want to tell me."

"The first time I made love, it was in this house. One cold winter night when I was seventeen. Jed Tyree was the sweetest, most tender lover."

Ronnie cleared his throat, then shifted uncomfortably.

"I don't still love Jed, if that's what's bothering you. I just love the memory of him."

"Mrs. Fortier—"

"It's just the two of us. Call me Charmaine." When she reached out and laid her hand on his chest, she felt the hard, steady beat of his heart.

He stood there, stiff as a board, unmoving, except for his eyes. His eyes devoured her.

"I brought you here because I want to make some new memories," she told him. "New sweet memories to add to the old ones."

"Ma'am, I don't...you shouldn't—"

Charmaine slunk closer, lifted her arms up and around his

neck, then pressed herself against him. "I want you to make love to me, Ronnie. Here in this house. No one will ever know. Only the two of us."

He hesitated for a split second before he reached up, grabbed her arms and flung her away from him. "I'm taking you home right now, Mrs. Fortier. And we're both going to forget this ever happened."

For just a moment, she felt the sting of rejection, then she looked at Ronnie and saw how desperately he was struggling to remain in control. It was so obvious that he wanted her as much as she wanted him, but he was fighting his desire.

"All right. We'll go home," she said. "But we won't forget. We can't forget. And tomorrow you'll drive me into town and we'll make this same detour on our way back. Think about it tonight. Think about the two of us... naked...making love...over and over again."

Ronnie swallowed hard. His hands knotted into tight fists. Charmaine tilted her chin high and walked toward the convertible. She could have forced the issue today. Right now. And Ronnie would have made love to her. But she didn't want to seduce him. She wanted him to be unable to resist her. She could wait another day. After all, she'd been waiting seventeen years to fall in love again. One more day couldn't possibly matter.

Chapter 6

"That was the best Crawfish Etoufe I've eaten in years,"
Jed said as he held open the door at Beula's Crab Shack
and waited for Grace to exit.

"Didn't I tell you? The place really is a shack, but the
food is to die for."

Grace smiled. Sweet and genuine. Instinct told him that
she had no idea how sexy her warm smile was, how alluring,
especially since she possessed such a cool, aloof sophistication. His gut tightened. He wanted to touch her; run the
back of his hand over her cheek, down her neck, and dip
his fingers into the vee of her silk blouse.

"Walk or ride?" she asked. "It's really sticky outside
today because of the high humidity, so you might prefer the
air-conditioned car."

It took him a second to dislodge his lustful thoughts and
realize she was talking about the tour of St. Camille he'd
requested before lunch.

Since there was little chance, this early on, that Booth
Fortier knew anything about Grace having been contacted

by a traitor in Fortier's ranks, any danger to Grace was probably nonexistent at this point. However, all that would change once the investigation into the allegations went into full swing. An investigation of this type, especially with the FBI involved, wasn't something that could be rushed. By tomorrow at this time, the wheels would be fully set in motion and after that everything would switch from slow gear into high. But before that happened, Jed wanted a chance to get to know the woman whose life was in his hands. Not only would a casual, relaxed tour of St. Camille give him the opportunity to acquaint himself with Grace Beaumont, it would also allow him to get the lay of the land. Whenever he began a new assignment, he always tried to make time to check out his surroundings, and that included the town or city. The more he knew about his employer and his or her environment, the better he could do his job. At least that was the way Jed worked.

"Which do you suggest?"

"Despite the heat and humidity, I recommend the walk. It's really the best way to see the town. And unless we dawdle along the way, the tour won't take long. Downtown St. Camille isn't all that big, only a few blocks."

"Then why don't we shed our coats, dump them in the car and tour the town on foot?"

"Let's go."

She headed for the parking lot shared by three restaurants side-by-side along the street and a voodoo/magic shop on the corner of Avenall. After opening the back door of her Mercedes, she removed her lavender jacket to reveal a sleeveless, V-neck silk blouse that clung to her high, round breasts. After folding her jacket and placing it on the back seat, she turned to Jed. He'd already removed his jacket— one of only two sport coats he owned—and was in the process of folding it when he heard her gasp. He glanced at her face, then followed her line of vision to the hip holster he wore.

"Where did…when did…?"

He patted the weapon. "I'm licensed to carry the gun. Dundee's handles all the legalities that affect us whenever we cross state lines or work in foreign countries."

"I don't like the idea of your..." She frowned. "At present you're working as an investigator, not a bodyguard, so why is the gun necessary?"

"It's not." Jed removed the holster and placed it beneath his jacket on the seat. "Is that better?" There was no reason to tell Grace he carried another gun strapped to his ankle. A seasoned professional usually had a backup weapon.

"Yes, thank you. If someone had seen you wearing a gun, they might have reported it to the police."

"I thought you and Chief Winters were personal friends. All you'd have to do is explain to him that I'm working for you, as a bodyguard. Your being who you are, he'd buy that."

"How did you know Charles Winters and I are friends?" Her eyes widened with realization. "That Dundee report on me really was very thorough, wasn't it?"

Jed grinned. "Thorough enough, as far as preliminary reports go."

"Then the second report you're expecting will no doubt list my shoe size, my bra size, how many fillings I have in my teeth and whether I sleep in pajamas or a gown."

He tossed his unfolded coat into the back seat of the Mercedes, atop her neatly folded jacket, then surveyed her from head to toe. "I don't need a report to give me that type of info. My guess is you wear a size seven and a half shoe, a thirty-four C-cup bra..." His gaze lingered over her breasts, then moved up to her face. "I'd say no more than three or four fillings in your teeth and as far as what you sleep in..." He paused, imagining her in silk pajamas, then in a sheer see-through gown. "A woman with a body like yours should sleep in the raw...and you probably did when your husband was alive. But now, I peg you for the silk pajamas type."

Grace stared at him with a mixture of wonder and disbelief in her eyes. "Shoe size correct. Bra size correct. I have six fillings in my teeth. As a kid I loved sweets." She took a deep breath. "And I sleep in silk pajamas."

Jed noticed a tinge of color in her cheeks. Anger? Embarrassment? A bit of both, he figured.

"Should I apologize?" he asked.

"For what? For being too forward, for getting a bit too personal?"

She studied him, the intensity of her gaze informing him that his brash comments hadn't rattled her in the least. But he knew better. Deep down inside, Grace Beaumont was just a little unsure of him…and of the effect he had on her.

When he remained silent, she said, "I assume it's your nature to act the way you do. Just keep in mind that whatever effect your boldness has on other women, it's wasted on me."

"I think you just accused me of something…not having good manners probably." She wouldn't be the first to tell him that he was often tactless. "And just what effect do you think I usually have on women?"

Grace slammed the car door, looked up at him and offered him a cold smile. "I think you're used to women falling all over you. Now, shall we take our walk? I can give you a tour of the town in an hour."

She had adeptly ended the personal aspects of their conversation and changed the subject. *Guess she put you in your place,* he told himself.

"Lead the way," he said.

Jed fell into step alongside Grace as they left the parking lot and began their trek by following Avenall over to the next block. She pointed out several buildings, explaining that this particular section of town was, for the most part, close to two hundred years old. They passed two blocks of renovated structures dating back to the early nineteenth century.

"My father did a great deal to help restore many of the old buildings downtown," she said as they crossed the street onto Raleigh, which ran north to south. "Of course St. Camille isn't the tourist spot that New Orleans is since we're a small town, but we get our share of the Louisiana tourist trade. And we have a 'Tour of Homes' every spring, in late April, and again in the fall, in early October."

As they continued their walk around town, numerous people spoke to Grace and gave Jed curious stares, but she didn't introduce him to anyone, nor did she linger in conversation. By the friendly yet deferential way the citizens of St. Camille treated Grace, he concluded that they liked her, but didn't really know her on a personal basis; that everyone respected her, but many understood they weren't her social equals.

Jed had been to St. Camille in the past, but he remembered very little about the small, centuries-old town. As a teenager, he'd had no interest in history or culture, but seeing the town through Grace's appreciative eyes gave him a different perspective today. She pointed out four banks, two other restaurants, and several lawyers' offices, including the house where the man she referred to as Uncle Willis had his practice.

"That house is on the historical register," Grace said. "Uncle Willis had it restored as closely to the original as possible."

Jed nodded. "Mmm-hmm."

"Not your thing?" When he eyed her quizzically, she elaborated. "You're not interested in your heritage or the historical significance of Louisiana architecture or history of any kind or—"

"Hey, why don't we just agree that I'm an uncouth barbarian and leave it at that." He paused in front of the two-story structure that housed the *St. Camille Register,* a local weekly newspaper. "We can even go in and take out an ad in the paper stating the fact." He had overreacted and he knew it, but there was something about Grace's lady-of-the-manor attitude that grated on his nerves. She was so...so untouchable, which made him want to touch her all the more. Made him want to drag her down to his level, and get real-life dirty with her.

"Did I hit a raw nerve?" she asked.

A loud rumble of thunder echoed nearby. When a streak of wide, bright lightning zigzagged unexpectedly through the sky, Grace gasped. Her gaze collided with Jed's. They stood there in the middle of the sidewalk staring at each other for several seconds. Another boom of thunder preceded a closer lighting strike, a sound so powerful that it rattled the windowpanes in the old buildings along Main Street.

Suddenly raindrops plopped onto the sidewalk, splattered on their heads and bare arms, warning them to take cover. But before they were able to respond, a torrent of rain descended. Jed grabbed Grace and pulled her into a narrow alleyway that ran between the St. Camille Register and the renovated Little Theater Playhouse. A small covered alcove at the back entrance to the theater provided a modest barrier of protection from the isolated springtime rainstorm.

Jed's arm tightened around Grace, pressing her body against his. She clung to him, shivering, her hair and face damp from the rain, as she hazarded a glance up and into his eyes. While he stared at her, his body hardened. He'd never seen anything more beautiful in his life than this flawlessly lovely woman wrapped in his arms. Striking blue eyes looked at him, her gaze riveted to his. When her full pink lips parted ever so slightly, all he could think about was how much he wanted to kiss her.

Another thunderbolt roared, followed by vicious lightning. When Grace trembled, he splayed his hand across the small of her back, then lowered his head to hers. She eased herself up on tiptoe as she prepared for the inevitable. Jed covered her mouth with his, instinct urging him to ravage her; but the moment their lips met, the very hunger of her response gentled his possession. When his tongue came into play, sliding inside her mouth, exploring, she accepted his invasion without protest. The kiss deepened and intensified.

Whether it was his doing or hers, he wasn't sure. More than likely a mutual action. Within seconds all reasonable thoughts left his mind; desire ruled him completely.

She smelled of fresh rain, a natural feminine sweetness and an enticing floral perfume, ever so subtle. Her scent assailed his senses as did her taste. A hint of the sugary breath mint she'd eaten after their meal lingered on her tongue. Her mouth was soft, pliable and eager. Her tall, slender body melted into his, the feel of her arousing him unbearably.

God, he could devour her. Every luscious inch.

She whimpered, but at first he thought nothing of it, then when she ended the kiss and tried to break free, he realized she had come to her senses. She had, but he hadn't. He wanted more. So much more. Reluctantly, he accepted her withdrawal. He buried his face against her neck and ran his hands down to cup her buttocks. She made a sound something between a gasp and a sigh.

"Please, release me," she whispered, her voice throaty, wispy.

He dropped his arms to his sides and lifted his head, but his gaze met hers and held.

"If you don't stop looking at me like that, I'm going to kiss you again," he told her.

She glanced away, then crossed her arms and ran her hands up and down, from elbows to shoulders and back. From within the dry security of the alcove, she studied the downpour. He sensed she wanted to run from him.

"Should I apologize?" he asked.

As she continued watching the rain, she replied, "What happened just then was mutual, as much my fault as yours. So, no, there's no need to apologize. We just need to make sure it doesn't happen again."

"Despite my admission of being a barbarian, you should know that I don't customarily drag women into alleyways and ravage them."

A tentative smile played at the corners of her mouth. "I

haven't been kissed like that—there hasn't been anyone since my husband died. I haven't shared even a kiss with another man."

Jed sucked in his breath, then blew it out in a huff that expressed his surprise. She hadn't been with another man since her husband's death. She hadn't been kissed in nearly four years. No wonder she had responded to him with such passion.

"And here I thought I turned you on." Jed grinned.

Her smile blossomed when she looked at him again. "You did…you do. I guess you affect me the way you do other women after all. But that doesn't surprise you, does it? You have to know you're a very attractive man."

"Why thank you, ma'am."

"But regardless of that fact, I'm not interested in whatever you're offering, be it a one-night stand or a brief affair. Our relationship will remain a professional one. Do I make myself clear?"

"Quite clear, Ms. Beaumont."

Grace looked up at the sky. "I think the rain is tapering off a bit. Now would probably be a good time to see if we can make it back to the parking lot before another downpour sets in."

"Why don't you stay here, give me your keys and let me run back to get the car?"

"All right." She snapped open her small shoulder bag, dragged out the key chain and handed it to Jed. "It appears that even a barbarian can sometimes behave like a gentleman."

Acting purely on instinct, Jed kissed the tip of her small, pert nose; then before she could respond, he closed his hand over the keys in his palm and dashed off into the light springtime rain.

Jaron stood in the shadows and watched Charmaine, who wore a scanty bikini as she paraded around in front of Ronnie. She was trying to seduce the poor fool. He understood his sister as no one else did. She was hot for Ronnie Martine; and that meant she would stop at nothing until she trapped him. She must think herself in love or she wouldn't take such a huge risk. He wondered if they were already lovers, if they were taking advantage of Booth being away in New Orleans. If so, they'd better be careful and not let anyone else catch them mooning over each other. Not only was Booth's small squad of personal "bodyguards" devoted to him, so was the household staff. Some out of awe, others out of fear alone.

It would only be a matter of time, perhaps weeks, perhaps even days, before the love affair between his sister and Ronnie would become obvious to the most casual observer.

Jaron patted the envelope hidden away in his coat pocket. He had intended to drive over to New Iberia and mail the letter to Grace Beaumont this afternoon. But Booth had called and sent him out on a job with Curt Poarch—overseeing a daytime shipment at the riverfront warehouse. Now he was glad he hadn't gotten the chance to mail the letter. He didn't dare waste the time—the one or two days it would take for the letter to reach St. Camille. With Charmaine and Ronnie's relationship heating up, Jaron knew he had to accelerate his plan. He'd drive into New Iberia tonight, find a pay phone and call Grace Beaumont. With Booth in New Orleans until the end of the week, now was the perfect time to get the documents out of the safe and exchange them for the five million he was certain Grace would pay him.

Charmaine's sultry laughter echoed through the open French doors. Nola, the housekeeper, came to an abrupt halt on the patio, the stack of fresh towels for the pool house teetering in her arms. Charmaine stood on tiptoe and ran her long, coral nails across Ronnie's lips, over his chin and down his throat.

God in heaven, why wasn't Charmaine being more discreet? What if Nola telephoned Booth and told him that his wife was carrying on shamelessly with her bodyguard?

Jaron shook his head. No, don't worry, he told himself.

Nola is fond of Charmaine. She would never betray her, never jeopardize her life.

This time it had been Nola who'd seen Charmaine up to no good. But what about next time? Jaron removed his cigarette lighter from his pants pocket, pulled the letter from his coat and set the edge of the letter on fire, then let the damp evening breeze scatter the ashes.

On his way out of the house, he spotted Curt in the den and called to him. ''I'm heading out for a while. Got a hot little number waiting for me.''

Grinning broadly, Curt nodded. ''Nothing like a hot piece of tail. I need to take a night off from the warehouse sometime soon and get me some. If this gal you're with tonight is any good, let me know.''

''Sure thing.'' Jaron closed the door behind him, then halted on the front veranda. He took a deep breath. Sweat moistened his palms and dampened his shirt. He would call Grace Beaumont tonight to set things up and call her tomorrow with the particulars of the exchange, after she'd had time to get the money. Then day after tomorrow he'd have the five mil. Once he deposited the money in a bank account in the islands, he'd arrange for an ''accident,'' so he could fake his and Charmaine's deaths. With a little luck, everything would come off without a hitch and by the weekend, he and Charmaine would be out of the country and free of Booth Fortier forever.

Grace didn't have much appetite for supper. She'd eaten a huge lunch at Beula's Crab Shack; and afterward she'd taken refuge with Jed in an alley alcove where they'd shared a kiss that had her lips still burning—and had set a fire that still raged inside her. As much as she'd tried to forget that kiss, as much as she'd tried to rationalize the way Jed had made her feel, she'd thought of little else all afternoon.

Shortly after Jed and she had shared the evening meal, she had excused herself and rushed off to the sanctuary of her room. Now was not the time to suddenly discover her sexuality had at long last come back to life. Jed was an employee, a trained investigator and bodyguard. He had been in her life for one day. One day! Never, in her thirty years, had she ever kissed a man she'd known for only one day; nor entertained thoughts of making love with him.

In high school and college she'd had a reputation for being a good girl. Grace Sheffield didn't put out. She'd been engaged—briefly—her senior year in college and had believed herself to be madly in love with Marty Austin. But Marty had resented Grace's loyalty to her father.

Marty hadn't understood the strong bond between her father and her, a bond that had strengthened greatly after Grace's mother's untimely death when Grace was sixteen. Elizabeth Ann Sheffield's death had devastated her husband and daughter. From that day forward, Grace tried to make her father happy, even if that meant bending over backward to please him. She had felt that it was the least she could do for her mother, a woman Grace had so adored. Marty had wanted her to marry him and for the two of them to forge a new life together as Peace Corp workers. Her father had said Marty was a worthless bum who'd never amount to anything. When the time came to choose between the life of privilege she knew as Byram Sheffield's daughter and the unknown and uncertain future as a poor man's wife, Grace had chosen the easy route. In retrospect, she realized she'd been more in love with love than with Marty.

Marty had been her first lover, her only lover, until she'd married Dean Beaumont, a brilliant lawyer, ten years her senior. She had admired and respected Dean. They had instantly formed a genuine rapport based on similarities in backgrounds, likes, beliefs and future plans. Her daddy had thought the world of Dean and had encouraged their relationship. She had loved Dean. He'd made her very happy. Their life together had been everything she'd hoped it would be. And then it had ended. Suddenly. Tragically.

She had never even considered the possibility that she might love again, that someday she would want another man. But rough-around-the-edges Jed Tyree had opened the door of possibility, had given her a glimpse of what it could be like to live again. Really live instead of simply exist.

The telephone rang. Grace ignored it. Laverna or Nolan would pick up on the fourth ring. Whoever it was, she didn't want to talk to them. What she needed was a long soak in the garden tub in her bathroom. A bubble bath. With some soft music, a few scented candles. Quiet time. Stress-reducing time. Tomorrow would be soon enough to deal with all her problems.

Just as Grace chose a pair of beige silk pajamas from her closet and headed toward the bathroom, a soft rapping on the door interrupted her plans.

"Miss Grace, there's a phone call for you," Nolan said from outside the closed door.

"Please, take a message," Grace replied. "I'll return their call tomorrow."

"Miss Grace, you might want to take this call. The man said if you didn't talk to him, you'd be sorry."

Grace's heart caught in her throat. It was him. The man who'd sent her the letter. Jed had told her that he might call, but she hadn't seriously believed he would.

"All right, Laverna, I'll take the call. And would you please tell Mr. Tyree about the call and ask him to come to my room immediately."

"Yes, ma'am."

Grace glanced at her hands. They were trembling. Her stomach fluttered and a tingling nausea churned inside her. She tossed the pair of pajamas on the foot of her massive four-poster bed, then hurried toward the nightstand where the antique-inspired French phone rested. Her hand hovered over the receiver for a split second, then she lifted it and mentally prepared herself for whatever was to come.

"Hello, this is Grace Beaumont."

"Listen very carefully," the voice said. "I won't repeat myself. I have documents that will prove Booth Fortier controls Governor Lew Miller. I want five million dollars in exchange for that proof.''

''Five million is a lot of money.''

''Not for a woman as rich as you.''

The bedroom door opened quietly. Grace glanced at Jed as he entered the room, a portable extension phone in his hand. Oh, Lord, Jed was listening to her conversation with the caller.

''How do I know you're telling me the truth?'' Grace asked the caller as Jed came toward her.

''You don't ask any questions. Just get the money together. I'll call you tomorrow and let you know when and where to bring the money for the exchange.''

''But I need some sort of—'' The dial tone hummed in her ears.

Jed set the portable phone on the nightstand, then reached out and took the receiver from Grace's death grip and returned it to the cradle. He wrapped his big hand around her small wrist.

''We'll get those taps put on the phones here and at Sheffield Media ASAP,'' he told her. ''Our guy isn't wasting any time. Looks like he needs that money fast. He's desperate to get his hands on it and leave the country before Booth Fortier finds out what he's done.''

''So, do I believe him? Should I get him the money?''

Jed nodded. ''Call your banker. Tonight. Start the ball rolling. Whether we give this guy any money or not, we need to make it look as if we intend to.''

''Do you think he has proof of—''

Jed caressed her wrist, causing her tight fist to relax. ''Yeah. Maybe. Probably.'' He paused, then looked directly into her eyes. ''Be sure you want to go through with this, with all of it—the money exchange, the investigation. Booth Fortier is a formidable opponent. He plays dirty. And he plays for keeps.''

''Four years ago my life ended,'' Grace said. ''If Booth Fortier was responsible for my husband's and father's deaths, then he killed me, too, that very night. Don't you see, Jed, I have nothing to lose. I've been dead inside all these years. If Fortier was behind the hit-and-run driver's actions, if it was murder and not an accident, then I want him to pay for what he did. I want him to suffer. I want him..." Grace hadn't realized she was crying until her tears hit Jed's hand that held hers.

Jed pulled her into his arms. She went willingly. The feel of his strength surrounding her comforted in a way nothing else ever had, not since she'd been a child and her father had consoled her after all her little girl crises. Although her reaction to him confounded her, she couldn't help but give in to his protective embrace.

"Nothing will ever bring back your father and your husband, but you're alive, Grace, very much alive. And you'll love again. You'll marry again."

She clung to him as the silent tears trickled down her cheek lying against his hard chest. "I lost more than my husband and father that night. I lost my baby. I lost Emma Lynn. God didn't spare her life. He didn't give me even that much."

"You lost a child?" Jed asked, gazing down at her.

"My little Emma Lynn died before she had a chance to live. I was almost six months pregnant."

"Damn! Grace, I'm sorry. I'm so sorry." He pulled her closer to him.

"I don't believe in happiness anymore. I don't trust God. I will never—ever—care for anyone that much. I'd rather be dead inside than know that kind of pain again."

Grace doubted that Jed understood her reasoning, doubted that anyone who had not experienced the kind of losses she had could possibly comprehend the extent of her torment. Numbness was preferable to agony. Existing was better than risking being hurt if she took a chance by truly living again.

Chapter 7

The telephone rang at eleven o'clock, waking Oliver Neville with its insistent clamor. He roused from sleep, blinked his eyes and yawned. Who the hell would be phoning him at this time of night? he wondered, and could think of no one other than his most notorious client—Booth Fortier. By the fourth ring, Oliver managed to rise from the overstuffed lounge chair in his den, where he'd fallen asleep tonight as he did almost every night. Between the fifth and sixth ring, he lifted the receiver.

"Hello."

"Did I wake you?"

It took Oliver half a second to realize his caller wasn't Fortier. "You shouldn't be calling me. There mustn't be any record of contact between the two of us."

"I'm at a pay phone near a gas station off Interstate 10. Believe me, I don't want anyone to know that there's a connection between the two of us. Now or in the past."

"Is there a problem?"

"Well, Ollie, now that you ask..." Self-satisfied chuckles

hummed through the phone line. "Yeah, there's a problem. A big problem."

"Concerning?"

"What the hell do you think it's concerning—it's about Grace Beaumont."

"Any problems you're having with Ms. Beaumont are yours—not mine."

"Oh, they're your problems all right. Aren't all of Booth Fortier's troubles your troubles, too?"

"And just how is Ms. Beaumont Booth's problem?"

"Tell Fortier he'd better start looking for a traitor in his midst. Somebody in his organization or in the Miller camp sent Grace a very informative letter."

Ollie's stomach knotted painfully. "Just how informative?"

"The message stated plainly that Dean Beaumont and Byram Sheffield's accident had been murder, ordered by Fortier because Beaumont had discovered Fortier's connection to our esteemed governor."

"God damn!"

"Grace has hired a private investigator to look into the matter. She's determined to unearth the truth—the whole truth."

"We've got ourselves a mess…a holy mess. Booth will have conniptions. He'll be fit to be tied when I tell him." Oliver knew exactly what Booth would do after he exploded—he'd give Grace Beaumont a couple of warnings, then he'd eliminate her, just as he had gotten rid of her husband and father nearly four years ago. "By the way, who's the P.I.? Is he local?"

"Not local. He's out of Atlanta. From the Dundee Private Security and Investigation Agency. His name is Jed Tyree and he's originally from Louisiana."

"Tyree." Jed Tyree. Oliver turned the name over in his mind several times. It sounded familiar. He knew he'd heard it before…somewhere, sometime. He couldn't recall right this minute, but it would come to him. Sooner or later. "So far, what's he done in the way of investigating?"

"I'm not sure. He took a look at the accident report and he's set up an office at Sheffield Media. And he has the entire Dundee Agency network at his disposal. I figure you can find out more. Make a few phone calls. Hell, call the governor."

Oliver heard more smug chuckles, the kind that said *I'm amused with myself.* Damn infuriating bastard. Dealing with self-serving amateurs was always a pain in the butt.

"Don't call again unless you have invaluable information," Oliver said. "It's safer for both of us."

"I understand. The ball is definitely in your court. And I don't envy you the task of reporting this news to Fortier."

"Good night." Oliver placed the receiver in its cradle, then walked across the den to the bar set up on a rolling cart in the corner. He undid the lid on the Crown Royal, lifted the bottle and poured the whiskey into a glass.

He wondered if Grace Beaumont realized that by her actions she had probably signed her own death warrant. Hell, no probably about it. He'd heard she was a smart lady, that to everyone's surprise she'd turned out to be as shrewd in business as her father had been. So did her life mean so little to her that she'd risk death to seek revenge on Booth Fortier?

Damn! He didn't want to make that call to Booth. And he wouldn't. Not tonight. Booth was in New Orleans at an exclusive brothel, his sickest, most vile pleasures being catered to around the clock. Tonight he was probably drunk or drugged and sated from hours of S&M titillation.

Oliver knew it was best to wait for morning to call Booth. Wait until he'd had a good night's sleep, eaten breakfast and was thinking clearly. Even at his best, Booth was a real son-of-a-bitch.

The earth glistened with morning dew, and puddles of rainwater, only partially evaporated from last night's thundershower, rippled ever so slightly in the morning breeze. As Jed paced himself to Grace's fast walk, he observed everything around them: the tall, ancient trees that lined the long, winding driveway to Belle Foret; the thick, verdant springtime grass, not yet dried out by summer's relentless heat; the quiet approach of daylight as the sun began its daily climb over the eastern horizon. At six o'clock there was no more than a hint of the day's upcoming humidity and high temperature.

But what he paid closest attention to was Grace herself. Fresh out of bed, not a hint of makeup, her long blond hair tied in a ponytail and bobbing up and down as she walked, the woman was beautiful. Born beautiful. And would no doubt be beautiful till the day she died. Her type of beauty didn't fade with age; it simply matured.

Jed hadn't slept well last night and he suspected Grace hadn't either. There was a slight darkness under her eyes and when he'd joined her downstairs just as she started out the door for her morning walk, she'd been a bit testy.

"What are you doing up?" She'd practically snapped his head off. She'd taken one look at his seen-better-days shorts, T-shirt and running shoes and said, "I don't need for you to go with me. I don't—"

"I'd like to go with you," he'd told her. "It will give us a chance to talk while we get some exercise."

She'd snorted, opened the door and made no further protest when he'd followed her.

They had walked to the end of the half-mile drive at a quick, steady pace, but they hadn't talked. He'd been waiting for Grace to acknowledge his presence, which she finally did when she came to a halt at the high, wrought-iron gates separating her estate from the road leading into St. Camille.

Staring pointedly at him, she placed her hands on her hips. "What do we need to talk about?"

He inspected her from head to toe, taking particular note of her long, slim legs, shown off to perfection in her jogging shorts, and the swell of her breasts beneath the matching cotton cropped top.

While she tapped her foot on the driveway, she narrowed her gaze and gave him a warning glare. "Take a picture, it'll last longer."

Jed laughed. "Sorry, but it's your own fault for looking so damn good first thing in the morning."

Grace crossed her arms over her chest and cocked one hip higher than the other. "You don't know when to give up, do you?"

Jed shrugged. "Look, Blondie, I apologize. I promise I'll behave myself from now on." He held up two fingers in a salute. "Boy Scouts honor."

"You were never a boy scout. A juvenile delinquent, maybe, but not a boy scout." She looked away from him and began walking back up the driveway.

He fell into step beside her. She'd been right on the money when she'd said he'd never been a boy scout; and she hadn't been far wrong when she'd suggested he'd been a delinquent. He'd been a damn rowdy teenager, and had known that any trouble he got into, his uncle Booth would get him out of at a snap of his fingers. There had been a time when he'd looked up to his uncle, had even admired him. But that had been before he'd found out exactly how ruthless Booth Fortier really was. If he hadn't learned about Booth's part in Lance Tyree's death, he might now be his uncle's right-hand man, in training to take over as head of the crime syndicate. The very thought that he might have chosen to follow his uncle's path in life sickened him.

"By the way," Grace said, "do you call all the blond women you know Blondie?"

She didn't look at him or slow her pace, so he followed her lead and kept walking and looking straight ahead. "Funny you should ask. I'm not sure why the term popped into my head. I've never called anyone else Blondie. Why, what difference does it make?"

Grace picked up speed, getting several feet ahead of him.

"It doesn't make any difference. I was just curious. But I'm not sure I like your referring to me with a pet name. It seems a bit too familiar."

She'd slapped him down again. Put him in his place. He'd have to keep in mind that calling her Blondie annoyed her. And maybe it bothered her because she liked the familiarity more than she'd ever admit.

Jed caught up with her. "We should discuss the five million you're picking up from your banker today. I want my two Dundee associates with us when you transport that much cash from the bank to your house."

"Fine. You work out the particulars with your people. Mr. Dotson will call me at work as soon as he has the money ready for us."

"I hope you're right about Dotson being a hundred percent trustworthy. If he's not, then we might have a problem."

"He's the president of St. Camille Savings and Loan," Grace said as she slowed her pace a bit. "Daddy always trusted him, so I see no reason why I shouldn't."

"Five million is enough money to make the most trustworthy person consider becoming untrustworthy for the first time in his or her life."

"Isn't there anyone you trust implicitly or do you automatically distrust everyone?"

"I trust people who have earned my trust," he told her. "I learned at a rather young age how devious and conniving people can be."

Just as Grace started to reply, the cell phone he'd stuffed into his shorts pocket rang. When he stopped to answer the phone, Grace continued without him. "Wait up, will you?" he called to her.

She stopped about fifteen feet from him, glanced over her shoulder and frowned. But then she nodded, moved off the drive and braced her back against the nearest tree.

Jed hit the On button. "Tyree here."

"Jed, it's Rafe. You were right about the warehouse

where Troy Leone is working. It's owned by Garland Industries. And it's a sure bet that there are drugs going in and out of there on a regular basis, covered up with a legal wholesale business. Supposedly Garland Industries imports all kinds of goodies from South America.''

''Yeah, I was afraid the Leone kid had gotten himself involved with the wrong people.''

''One more thing…'' Rafe hesitated.

''What?''

''I spoke to Sawyer before I called you and it seems when I had Dundee's do some online checking for me, Sawyer got in touch with Dante Moran.''

Jed glanced at Grace and lowered his voice. ''Don't tell me—the Feds already know about Garland Industries and are simply waiting for the right moment to pounce.''

''Hell, man, you're good. Ever thought of taking up fortune-telling?''

''The Feds don't want to make a move on the warehouses now, not until I help them trap Fortier. They don't want the small fish without the big fish. Right?''

Grace glared at him, then shoved herself away from the tree and came toward him. ''I'm heading back to the house for a shower.''

He held up his index finger, indicating for her to wait. ''Anything else?'' Jed asked Rafe.

''The guy overseeing things at the warehouse is Curt Poarch. Ever heard of him?''

''Curt Poarch, huh? Yeah, he was working for Fortier before I left Louisiana. If he's like he used to be—and my guess is that he is—he'd do anything my uncle asked him to do. And I mean anything.''

''Moran told Sawyer that Poarch is Fortier's number two man.''

''Let me guess—Jaron Vaden is number one. Right?''

''Right.''

''Anything else I need to know?'' Jed asked.

"That's about it, for now. Except Dom and Kate should arrive before noon today. They'll be in touch."

"Thanks. Later, okay?"

Jed hit the Off button and shoved the small phone into his pocket, then met Grace in the middle of the driveway.

"Troy Leone is working at a Garland Industries warehouse," Jed said. "Garland Industries is a front for a major portion of Booth Fortier's illegal activities."

Grace clenched her teeth together and shook her head. "Damn. This is just the kind of news Elsa doesn't need."

"What she needs is to get her brother out of there...and soon."

"Yes, of course, she should, but—" Grace eyed him quizzically. "What do you know that you aren't telling me?"

"When Fortier goes down, his fall is going to cause some mighty big ripples that will reach far and wide."

"What do I tell Elsa?"

"Tell her what she already knows," Jed said. "Tell her that if Troy continues working at the warehouse, it's only a matter of time before he'll wind up in prison."

Grace nodded, then without another comment, they fell into place side by side and returned to their morning walk, heading for the antebellum mansion Grace had called home her entire life.

"Jed?"

"Mmm-hmm?"

"How long do you think it will be before Booth Fortier finds out that I'm having the accident looked into and that Dundee's is digging into any connection he might have with Governor Miller?"

"A few days, a week at most. Sooner if what I suspect is true."

"What do you suspect?"

"I've been looking at what happened the night of the accident from several different angles and there's something I can't figure out."

"What's that?" she asked.

"How did Booth's hit man know in advance that your family—you, your father and your husband—would be in a car together that night? And how did he know the particular route you'd take?"

"I don't know." Pausing when they reached the front veranda, Grace slumped down on the steps. "I'd never thought about it, of course, because I'd always believed the accident really was just that—an accident. But I suppose he could have been tailing Dean and just waiting for the right opportunity."

"Possibly, but if his orders were to eliminate your entire family all at the same time—Dean, your father and you— then he might have had to wait for weeks. That's not Fortier's style. He gives a couple of warnings, then if they go unheeded, he strikes."

"Well, actually, I wasn't supposed to go with Dean and Daddy that evening. I'd been in bed with the flu and was just barely on the mend, but that afternoon I'd started feeling a lot better, so I decided to join them. I'd never missed any of the St. Camille Annual Charity Auctions, not since I was sixteen, and I desperately wanted to go.

"Did anyone know about the change in your plans, that you were going?"

Grace shook her head. "No, I don't think so. No. Only Laverna and Nolan. I didn't even take the time to phone Joy and tell her."

"Then if someone were keeping tabs on your husband's and father's activities and plans, they would have assumed the two men would be alone in the car that night, right?"

"Yes, I suppose so, but I don't see—"

"Nothing to see at this point," he said. "I was mostly just thinking out loud."

"Well I'm heading into the house. By the time we shower and dress, Laverna will have breakfast waiting for us."

"You go on, I'll be there in a few minutes."

Jed waited until Grace went inside before he punched in

Sawyer McNamara's private home number on his cell phone. The man answered on the third ring.

"It's Jed. I need Dundee's to poke around and see what, if anything, can be found on a couple of guys—Willis Sullivan, lawyer, and a Beaumont and Sheffield family friend. Then check out Hudson Prentice, the senior VP of Sheffield Media, Inc.''

"And you suspect them of what?" Sawyer asked.

"I don't actually suspect them of anything. Let's just say I'm curious as to whether either man would have had a reason to want to see both Dean Beaumont and Byram Sheffield out of the way.''

"I thought Booth Fortier was the suspect.''

"He is. Fortier gave the orders. I'm just wondering if someone was feeding Fortier information. Someone close to either Beaumont or Sheffield. After all, we don't know who told Fortier that Beaumont knew about his connection to Lew Miller and that Byram Sheffield was set to expose the proof by using all the radio and TV stations Sheffield Media, Inc. owned. And someone knew Beaumont's and Sheffield's plans the evening they were killed. Knew where they were going, at what time and which route they'd probably take.'' Jed cursed softly under his breath. "While you're at it, run a quick check on Laverna and Nolan Rowley. It's a long shot and I don't think it'll pan out. They're the household staff. Been with the family over thirty years. And might as well add Elsa Leone to that list. I'd say she's loyal to a fault, but the lady has big-time family responsibilities and probably money problems.''

"Willis Sullivan, Hudson Prentice, Laverna and Nolan Rowley, and Elsa Leone," Sawyer recited the names. "Is that it?''

"Yeah, for now.''

"I planned to call you later," Sawyer told him. "I wanted to give you a message from Moran. He wants you to make a move to get in touch with Fortier sooner than expected.''

"What's up?''

"They need to get word to their inside man at the Fortier house to let him know they've moved up the timetable on their sting operation inside Fortier's business empire. Things have progressed there faster than expected."

"I'll get in as soon as I can. But tell Moran that I won't do anything to jeopardize Grace Beaumont's life."

"Of course not. The lady is Dundee's top priority. She's our client and she comes first."

"Just remind Moran of that fact."

"Can and will do." Sawyer paused. "I'll run a check on those names and see what we come up with."

"Yeah. Call me when you find out something…if you find out something."

Jed shoved his phone into his shorts pocket, then bounded up the front steps and onto the veranda. When he opened the door and entered the foyer, he nearly ran smack-dab into Nolan. He grabbed the old man's shoulders to steady him.

"Sorry, I didn't know you'd be standing there," Jed said.

"It's quite all right, Mr. Tyree. It was my fault entirely. I heard you coming in, but I'm afraid I couldn't get out of the way in time. My reflexes aren't quite what they used to be."

Jed patted the old man on the back. "Glad we avoided a fatal collision. I'll be more careful myself from now on."

Nolan nodded solemnly and when Jed started to walk away, he called to him. "Mr. Tyree, me and Laverna know what's going on, at least pretty much know. We reckon Miss Grace could be in danger real soon, if she's not already."

Jed nodded.

"We love that gal. She's been mighty good to us, just like her daddy before her." Nolan's faded blue eyes misted with tears. "You just take good care of her, you hear? Don't let nothing bad happen to her. We want to see her happy again, but somebody's got to protect her, keep her alive, so she can get her second chance."

Jed felt guilty for having asked Sawyer to run a check on Nolan and Laverna. He'd spent so many years seeing the world's underbelly that he didn't trust anyone. Now his gut instincts told him that, apparently, he'd been dead wrong to have ever suspected the Rowleys.

"It's only a matter of time before Grace is under fire," Jed said. "But I plan to stand between her and whatever comes her way."

He added silently, *I've been trained to protect and I'm ready to lay my life on the line. Whatever happens, I'm prepared to kill to protect Grace—and I'm prepared to die for her.*

For some unfathomable reason, he wanted Grace to have a second chance at happiness just as much as Laverna and Nolan did.

Chapter 8

It was hot. A lot hotter than yesterday. Summertime hot, despite the fact that it was only the last week of May. But Charmaine didn't mind the heat. Never had. She'd been a summertime kid, loving the water, sunbathing and running wild through these woods. Despite the absence of caring parents, she'd had a fairly decent childhood, mostly thanks to Jaron. Her big brother had always looked after her, worrying about her the way a parent should. His only mistake had been introducing her to Booth Fortier. The first time she met her future husband, she'd been impressed. Impressed with his good manners, his fancy clothes, his sleek sports car and his large, beautifully decorated house. But it had been his teenage nephew she'd fallen in love with, practically at first sight. Jed Tyree had been the handsomest boy she'd ever seen. Thick curly black hair and smoky hazel eyes that had studied her body with hungry passion whenever they'd made love. And it had always been making love with Jed. But never with Booth. Not even on their wedding night.

"Stop the car," Charmaine ordered Ronnie. "I want to go inside and see what it looks like, see if anything is the way I remember.

Without responding verbally, Ronnie turned off into the driveway and killed the BMW's motor. He sat beside her, stiff as a poker, not speaking, not even glancing her way. She knew he was scared—scared of her. He realized she intended to try again today to seduce him, and he wasn't sure whether he could resist her again.

She sat there for a couple of minutes, basking in the fiery Louisiana sunshine. Maybe she was as crazy as Jaron said she was for even contemplating an affair with Ronnie. Hell, with any man. She understood all too well the penalty they'd both pay if Booth ever found out. But after all these years of enduring Booth's cruelty, death might be a blessing. One thing she knew for sure—she couldn't go on the way she had. Without love and tenderness. Without mutual passion. She hadn't cared for a man the way she did Ronnie since she'd been in love with Jed. Seventeen years ago. She wanted that again—that sweet, glorious feeling; she needed it as desperately as she needed air to breathe. If loving Ronnie cost her her life, she didn't care.

But what about him? an inner voice asked. *Does he want you enough to risk his life to be with you?*

"I'm going inside," she said as she flung open the car door. "You can stay here and wait on me…if that's what you want. Or you can come inside with me. Your choice."

She waited a minute, hoping he would respond, praying that he'd get out with her and follow her inside. But he sat there, looking straight ahead, silent and unmoving.

So be it, she thought, and jumped out of her BMW and raced across the knee-high grass and weed-infested yard. She maneuvered the rickety front steps and carefully made her way across the sagging wooden porch to the front door, which stood partially open. Instead of touching the rusty doorknob, she punched the center of the old wooden door. The hinges creaked as the door opened fully to reveal the shadowy interior of the living room. Charmaine stepped inside carefully, uncertain if the floor beneath her feet was sturdy, and wondering if any animals were using the place as a home.

When she glanced around, her heart sank. Things looked even worse than she'd imagined they would. The room was bare of furniture, which had probably been stolen years ago. Dirty, tattered wallpaper covered the walls, but the once colorful pattern was now indistinguishable. She remembered the day she and Jaron had put up the wallpaper—a print of stripes and flowers in sunny yellows and vivid greens, with a white background. She'd been fourteen. And life had still been filled with possibilities. At that age she'd still possessed the ability to dream.

With each cautious step she took as she explored her old home, more and more memories of the past assailed her. Flashes of sights and sounds, powerful emotions ranging from girlish happiness to abject misery. But God in heaven, what she would give to go back to those days, to know the freedom of choice, to live a life without fear. Why was hindsight always twenty-twenty? she wondered. If only...

She entered her old bedroom, the one she'd shared with her mother before she died. Often as not, Ma would pass out drunk and sleep for hours, snoring like a freight train. Luckily Ma hadn't been a mean drunk, just a sad, pathetic one. And on the nights when she'd brought home a man, Ma had sent her scurrying into Jaron's room. Time and again, he'd given her his bed and made himself a pallet on the floor. Even as a kid, he'd been reliable and responsible, always trying his best to look out for her.

After Ma died, she and Jaron had spruced up this room—with money he was earning working for Booth Fortier, back when they both thought Booth had hung the moon.

They'd painted the walls a pale pink and put up frilly white curtains, making it look all girly and sweet. At the time, they hadn't been able to afford a new bedroom suite, so they'd painted the old iron bedstead and the cheap nineteen-fifties dresser and chest. And Jaron had bought her a tape player/radio combo. She'd spent hours listening to her favorite pop music. The walls in her bedroom were now faded and dirty and the only piece of furniture remaining was the iron bed, devoid of mattress or box springs.

Charmaine closed her eyes and let the memories wash over her. Hearing inside her head the steady rhythm of the music that had once filled this room, she began to dance as if she were in a partner's arms. Her body swayed. She hummed an old familiar tune. If only she could go back in time. If only she could erase the years with Booth.

Suddenly strong arms encompassed her and turned her slowly into a tender embrace. She didn't open her eyes at first, almost afraid that she was dreaming, that the arms she felt around her were a figment of her imagination. As she continued humming, he danced her slowly around the room, holding her close, his cheek against hers.

Finally, garnering her courage, she lifted her eyelids and looked up into the face of the man she loved. Ronnie Martine smiled down at her. She sighed contentedly and returned his smile.

"I've been trying to seduce you," she told him. "I've used all my feminine wiles on you."

"I know." He pressed his cheek to hers and glided her around the room.

The temperature inside the old house had to be in the nineties and the humidity made it feel like a hundred. But the external heat was nothing to compare to the fire burning inside Charmaine. Hot, raging hunger boiled through her veins, peaking her nipples and moistening her femininity. She wanted…needed…craved…some good loving from a good man.

"I'm in love with you," she said.

His smile widened. "Yeah, I know." His large hand splayed across the center of her lower back and urged her closer—close enough so that she felt his arousal. "I love you, too," he whispered in her ear.

The world outside Ronnie's arms ceased to exist, magically shrinking to encompass only the two of them. Happiness exploded in the very depths of her soul. Whatever price she had to pay for this moment in time, she would gladly pay. But did she have the right to ask Ronnie to risk everything—his very life—to love her?

She gazed up at him through half-closed eyes and said, "You realize that if Booth ever finds out, he'll kill us both."

Ronnie halted the dance, but didn't release her. "I'll make sure he doesn't find out. I promise. I'll keep you safe."

"Booth is dangerous...very dangerous. Are you sure you're willing to risk—?"

Ronnie kissed her. Tenderly. Possessively. And it was all she'd ever dreamed it would be. There was no way to describe how he made her feel—all hot and cold at the same time. She had loved Jed Tyree with the raging hormones passion of a teenager; but that love had burned itself out long ago. What she felt for Ronnie was a woman's passion, a love that could last a lifetime.

When he deepened the kiss, slipping his tongue into her open mouth to taste and probe, she sampled his mouth in the same fashion. They kissed; they touched. She whimpered; he groaned. Sweat trickled between her breasts, over her belly and into the triangle of red curls between her legs. Ronnie cupped her hips and lifted her up and against him, pressing her mound against his erection.

"I want to make love to you," he told her.

"Yes, yes," she sighed the words against his neck, then licked the perspiration from his throat.

He glanced over her shoulder, exploring their surroundings. "You should have silk sheets and sweet music and candlelight."

"I've had all those things and they mean nothing." She clung to him, wanting to never let go. "All that matters is being with you. Anywhere. Anytime."

"Charmaine, honey, you've been driving me crazy. But you know that, don't you?"

"Come with me." She took his hand and guided him through the house. He followed as she led him onto the back porch, which was, surprisingly, still intact, although the roof sagged. "It's cooler out here."

She released his hand and backed away from him. When he reached for her, she grinned, then pulled her sleeveless tank top over her head. He watched her intently as she undid the hooks of her bra, slipped the straps down her shoulders and tossed the red silk onto the dirty floor. During her little striptease, she kicked off her expensive leather sandals, yanked off her designer slacks and twirled around in her bikini panties.

She had stripped for Booth on numerous occasions, but not by choice, not because she'd wanted to, but because he'd made her. And whenever he touched her, she cringed because she knew the things he would do to her.

Lifting first one leg and then the other, she took off her panties, added them to the pile of clothes on the gray wood plank floor and stood before him in all her naked glory. He held out his hand to her; she went to him. He kissed her again…and again…and again. She tore at his shirt, but he grabbed her hands to still her frenzied attack. He pushed her at arm's length, then undid the buttons on his shirt, removed it and tossed it atop her discarded clothing. He jerked her to him. She rubbed her breasts against his smooth, muscular chest. A deep rumble erupted from his throat. He lowered his head and took one tight nipple into his mouth. He sucked, nibbled, licked. She reached for his belt, undid it, and then unzipped his pants. Within minutes, he was as naked as she. Their hands went wild, touching each other all over. Their mouths mated, then their tongues explored. They couldn't get close enough. If she could have, Charmaine would have crawled into Ronnie's skin and shared it with him.

When she didn't think she could bear not having him

inside her, he lifted her up, hoisting her by the hips, then settled her over and down onto his sex. He filled her completely, spreading her wide. Her legs circled his hips as he pumped her up and down, gliding his sex in and out, putting friction on all the right places. While they mated in a frenzy, he maneuvered her around until her butt was shoved against the outer wall. When she felt her climax approaching, she claimed it fully, and cried out as the incredible sensations flooded through her. Within seconds Ronnie came. Shuddering. Moaning. Jackhammering into her.

"I love you...love you...love you..." She buried her face against his shoulder and knew that if she died this very second, she would die gloriously happy.

Jaron Vaden's hands perspired so much that he had to stop the car to wipe his hands dry with his handkerchief. While pulled off on the side of the road, he rehearsed his upcoming telephone speech, the details of the exchange—the documents he would take from Booth's safe tomorrow and swap for the five million dollars. Everything depended on Grace Beaumont. Jaron rubbed the smooth leather seat on each side of his hips in an effort to calm his trembling hands. He couldn't remember a time in his life when he'd been so afraid. If one thing went wrong, it could screw up all his plans. He couldn't allow a bad case of nerves to stop him. He had to get Charmaine away from Booth. It was something he should have done years ago.

A highway patrol car came whizzing by, its lights flashing in warning. Jaron's heart stopped for a millisecond. *Get hold of yourself. You can't fall apart. Not now when you're so close to accomplishing your goal.*

He was half an hour away from the phone booth he'd used before, but he wasn't sure if he should use one in such an isolated, out-of-the-way place. Maybe he should drive all the way into New Iberia and find a phone booth in a heavily populated area; that way, if the call was traced, he could simply disappear into the crowd. After all, he had no way of knowing if he could trust Grace Beaumont. She could have already called in the police.

When Elsa announced the arrival of the Dundee agents, Jed rose from his seat across the conference table from Grace, where they were sharing a takeout lunch. He'd almost finished eating a super-size meal and cola. Grace was still picking at a Caesar salad. Hudson, who had been included in their lunchtime plans and had finished his BLT, rose from his chair and took a speculative stance directly behind Grace.

Right when Grace had suggested to Jed that they eat in today, her cousin Joy stopped by, as had Willis Sullivan, both eager to meet Jed; so Grace had asked Elsa to order for them, too. Joy had declined, stating she was dieting and wanted only a glass of iced tea, but Willis had requested a steak sandwich. After half an hour with the threesome, Jed decided he liked Joy, despite the fact she talked incessantly about nothing and didn't seem to have a serious thought in her pretty head. And perhaps because she seemed to dislike Hudson Prentice even more than Jed did. He knew he had nothing more than gut instincts on which to base his unfriendly attitude toward Prentice. And maybe it was nothing more than the fact he'd picked up instantly on the guy's romantic interest in Grace. Not that Grace's love life was any of Jed's business, but he'd sure hate to see her settle for a guy like Hudson Prentice.

Then there was Uncle Willis. Jed's personal verdict on him was still out—to be determined on better acquaintance. He didn't actually like or dislike the man, although Uncle Willis's superior attitude—similar to, but much more annoying than Grace's—grated on Jed's nerves.

As Domingo and Kate entered the conference room, Jed met them just inside the door. "Did you have a good flight?" Jed asked, making idle chitchat, alerting the agents that the group assembled might not be a hundred percent trustworthy. Jed had no real reason to distrust any of them, including Elsa, who stood on the other side of the open door. Grace had already shared much too much with these people. *Yeah, but they're people she trusts, no matter what you think of them,* Jed reminded himself.

"Yes, the flight was fine," Kate replied as she glanced past Jed and studied the group congregated around the table.

Jed didn't know Kate all that well; they'd never shared an assignment. She was damn good-looking. Blond, brown-eyed, with a nice body and a pair of great boobs. He'd thought about asking her out, but had never gotten around to it. When she'd first come to work at Dundee's, he'd been seeing someone on a fairly regular basis and since his breakup with his last lady friend, he'd been playing the field. Something told him that Kate Malone was the serious type, who definitely didn't put out on a first date.

"Have y'all checked into the hotel yet?" Jed asked.

"We went by there first and left our luggage," Dom said. "Are you tied up here—" Dom glanced around the room "—or are you free for a few minutes?"

"Grace…everybody…" Jed plastered his best good-old-boy smile on his face. "This is Domingo Shea and Kate Malone, two of Dundee's finest. They're here to help me with the investigation." No need to mention to anyone that Rafe Devlin and J.J. Blair were already working undercover. Even Grace didn't need to know that particular fact. At least not yet.

Willis eyed Dom seriously, as if studying a specimen under a microscope. And Joy scrutinized him just as thoroughly, but with a romantic twinkle in her eyes. He'd seen women look at Dom that way plenty of times. The guy possessed the kind of Latin lover looks that appealed to most women.

"Grace, if you'll excuse us, we'll head for my office so we can go over a few things," Jed said. "Y'all enjoy the rest of your lunch."

Before he made it outside the door, Grace called to him,

"Don't you think I should take part in any discussions you have with your fellow agents?"

Jed halted. "Sure thing." *Just as long as you don't invite the masses to join in,* he added silently. Grace was too trusting. And despite the exterior sophistication and her business acumen, he suspected that, at heart, she was a still a naive girl.

Willis Sullivan cleared his throat loudly. "I'm Grace's attorney. Perhaps I should—"

"That won't be necessary, Uncle Willis," Grace said.

Hudson gripped the back of Grace's chair with white-knuckled tension. "If you'd like, I can—"

"No." Grace rose from her seat, patted Hudson's clutched fists curled around the chair and bestowed her most charming smile on her devotees. "I love each of you for being concerned, but from here on out, I don't want any of you involved. Things could get very dangerous and I couldn't bear it if any one of you was harmed because of me."

"Grace, sweetie, I wish you wouldn't..." Joy let her sentence trail off into oblivion when Grace gave her a disapproving stare.

"I have Jed to depend on now," Grace told them. "Y'all stay out of this, stay uninvolved, and let Jed do his job. He'll protect me...if it comes to that."

When Jed put his arm protectively around Grace's shoulders, she allowed him to escort her from the conference room, down the hall and into his office. Dom and Kate followed them, came inside and closed the door behind them.

"Just how many people are aware of what's going on?" Kate asked, her gaze moving from Jed to Grace.

"Too many," Jed said.

"Four people." Grace frowned. "Four people I trust implicitly. My cousin, who has been my best friend since we were children. My father's friend and attorney, who is like an uncle to me. The senior vice-president of Sheffield Media, Inc., a man who...well, who's probably in love with me. And my assistant of three years, who is loyal and trustworthy.''

''Kate didn't mean to upset you, Ms. Beaumont.'' Dom flashed her his irresistible smile. ''But the more people who know, the better the chances that something will leak out and—''

''Are you implying that Joy or Hudson or Uncle Willis or Elsa would betray me?'' Grace asked indignantly.

''Not willingly betray you, but perhaps unintentionally.'' Kate unzipped her briefcase, removed a computer CD and handed it to Jed. ''Here's the information you asked for.'' She glanced at Grace. ''You might want to look at it later.''

Jed laid the CD beside his laptop. ''Thanks, I'll do that.''

''What information?'' Grace eyed the CD. ''I hired Dundee's. I'm paying your salaries. But I get the feeling you're keeping me in the dark about something. Just what's going on?''

''Nothing's going on,'' Jed assured her, hating himself for lying to her. But he couldn't tell Grace about the FBI's involvement. It wasn't that he didn't trust her—he simply didn't know her. Not really. They'd met thirty-six hours ago, certainly not long enough to trust her completely. Besides, the Feds wouldn't look kindly on him sharing confidences with anyone outside the circle of Dundee agents involved in the case.

Jed clamped his hand onto Grace's slender shoulder. ''Let us do our job. And that job is to find the information you need and to keep you safe.''

Grace stiffened her spine, squared her shoulders and glowered at him, then glanced pointedly at his hand still clutching her. He removed his hand.

''All right,'' Grace said, and he could tell she was reluctant to agree. ''I'll leave y'all alone and get back to the business of running Sheffield Media.'' Without further ado, she nodded to Kate and Dom, then marched out of the room.

''Whew…'' Kate's expressive brown eyes spoke plainer than any words.

"What's going on with you and Ms. Beaumont?" Dom asked.

"I don't know what you mean, there's—"

"Cut the crap," Dom said. "There was so much tension between the two of you, I could cut it with a knife."

Jed shrugged. "I rub her the wrong way, that's all."

Dom grinned. "And you'd like for *her* to rub *you* the right way, huh?"

Kate cleared her throat.

Both men winced, then looked at her sheepishly.

"Sorry," Dom said.

"Yeah, sometimes we forget you're a woman," Jed said.

"Now, I wouldn't go that far." Dom winked at Kate.

Kate rolled her eyes upward and shook her head. "There's not ten cents worth of difference between boys and men." She sighed. "Okay, Jed, you take a look at the info we brought while Dom and I set up shop. Who do we ask about getting another desk and a couple of comfortable chairs moved in here?"

"Elsa Leone, Grace's assistant."

As if the mention of her name conjured up the lady, Elsa called from the other side of the closed door, "Mr. Tyree, please come quickly. Grace just received that phone call she's been expecting."

Instantly Dom's and Kate's gazes locked with Jed's; then Jed swung open the door and broke into a full run.

Elsa caught up with him just as he reached the door to Grace's office. She grabbed his arm and pointed to the portable phone he'd ordered she use to answer incoming calls today. He nodded understanding, then picked up the phone and placed it to his ear before entering Grace's office.

"Do you have the five million?" the disguised voice asked.

Grace glanced up when she saw Jed entering her office. He nodded. It had been arranged for them to pick the money from her bank later today, after Dom and Kate arrived. He

wanted backup when they transported that kind of cash.
"Yes," she replied. "I have it."

"Good. Now listen carefully. We'll make the exchange
tomorrow. You'll come alone. No cops. Nobody else."

Jed came over to Grace's desk, picked up a notepad and
pen and scribbled instructions. Grace read the message hurriedly.

"I've hired a bodyguard," Grace told her caller. "He
comes with me tomorrow for the exchange or it's no deal."

Silence.

Grace looked up at Jed, her eyes asking him if they'd
made the wrong move.

"Okay," the voice said. "You and the bodyguard. But if
you try to double-cross me, you won't get the evidence you
need. Do you understand?"

"Yes, I understand."

"Tomorrow morning, come to Terrebonne Park. Come in
on the south side, near the carousel. At precisely twelve
noon, get on the carousel, sit in the swan seat—just you.
I'll join you and we'll make the exchange."

Grace looked at Jed. He nodded. "All right," she said.
"Tomorrow. Twelve noon, on the carousel, the swan seat."

Chapter 9

The moment Jaron saw Booth's car pull up outside, he broke out in a cold sweat. The timing couldn't have been worse. He'd already telephoned Grace Beaumont and set up the exchange for noon tomorrow—no way to change the particulars now. Besides, he had to move as fast as possible. Time was running out. When Aric Luther, Booth's chauffeur and bodyguard, had called while they were en route to alert the household staff of Mr. Fortier's return, Jaron had taken full advantage of the advance notice. Curt had slept all morning and left directly after lunch to tend to some business in Baton Rouge. Charlie Dupree, who also lived at the house, had driven into Lafayette to visit his eighty-year-old mother, who was in a nursing home there. And Ronnie had taken Charmaine into town on yet another shopping excursion that would last for hours. With all three of Booth's flunkies out of the house, he'd been able to get into the safe where the documents he needed were kept. He'd hidden the papers in his room, in his bed, between the mattress and box springs. Tomorrow morning, he'd put the papers into his briefcase and use the excuse of making some spot checks on several of their businesses located in various nearby towns; then he'd keep his date with Ms. Beaumont. If anyone spotted him at Terrebonne Park—anyone who would report back to Booth—he'd say he'd stopped there for lunch. He'd be sure to arrive well before noon so he could pick up a sandwich and Coke at the refreshment center in the park. Cover all your bases, he told himself.

Jaron swung open the front door, rushed out onto the porch and down the steps to meet Booth as soon as Aric opened the limo door. Whenever Booth made a trip to New Orleans, he always used the black limousine. He liked playing the big man. Hell, there was no playacting to it—Booth Fortier was *the* big man in Louisiana.

Aric, a six-six black guy with a wrestler's body, had been in service to Booth since he'd been a kid and his mama had worked here at the house as one of the maids. Rumors abounded that Aric was Booth's illegitimate son, but there was no physical resemblance and Booth treated Aric the same way he treated his other employees.

"Welcome home." Jaron forced a wide smile as he greeted his boss. "You're back a couple of days early. I hope nothing went wrong."

"Something's gone wrong, all right." Booth's small black eyes glistened with fury. Jaron knew that look; he'd seen it on more than one occasion when Booth was out for blood. "I want a meeting with all of you as soon as possible, by no later than seven this evening. Wherever the hell everybody is, get them back here immediately."

"Yes, sir." Jaron followed behind Booth like an obedient puppy dog, while Aric popped the trunk and unloaded the luggage.

"Where's Charmaine? Didn't you tell her I was on my way home?" Booth stormed across the porch and into the house, where Nola stood waiting to take his hat and cane.

"Ronnie drove Charmaine into town to do a little shopping. They should be back any time now."

"Call her on her cell phone and tell her to get her ass back here. When I come home, I want my wife waiting for me right here." Booth emphasized the word "here" by stabbing his index finger into the air.

"I'll contact Charmaine and the others right away."

When Booth halted outside his office-cum-study, Jaron was so close on Booth's heels that he almost ran into him. Coming to a screeching halt only a few inches behind Booth, Jaron froze to the spot.

"What's the matter with you? You seem unusually jumpy. And you're sweating." Booth studied Jaron, as if sizing him up for a coffin.

Jaron shuddered inwardly, but managed to grin. "Hell, Booth, it's hot weather. That's why I'm sweating. And I guess I had too much coffee this morning. A lot of caffeine makes me jittery."

"Humph."

"Anything you want before I make those calls?" Jaron asked.

"When you've contacted the others, call Oliver Neville and tell him I'm home and for him to come on over this evening and join us."

"Yes, sir. I'll call Mr. Neville. Should I say what it's about?"

"He knows."

A sick feeling hit Jaron in the pit of his stomach. If Ollie Neville was involved, that meant some sort of legal problem. And legal problems for Booth meant problems for everyone in the organization.

When Jaron headed down the hall, intending to use the phone in his room to contact the troops, Booth called, "You ever hear from Jed?"

Jed? Jed Tyree? Why would Booth be asking about his nephew after all these years? "Nah, I haven't heard anything from him. Why would you think he'd get in touch with me?"

"You two used to be big buddies. Before he decided he

was too good for the likes of us. I thought maybe you knew where he was and what he was doing these days.''

''No, sir. I don't have any idea.''

''What about Charmaine? Has she heard from Jed?''

A sour bile rose up Jaron's esophagus at the thought of what Booth would do to Charmaine if he suspected she'd had any contact with Jed. ''I swear to you that Charmaine hasn't seen or heard from Jed since he left here seventeen years ago.''

''I think about him sometimes, you know. I wonder what it would be like if he'd stayed. Despite our differences, that boy was my blood kin. My only sister's only child. Everything I've spent a lifetime building could have been his.''

''Jed was ungrateful. You did so much for him.'' Jaron understood now why Jed had fled, why he'd escaped his uncle while he'd had a chance. If only he'd been that smart and taken Charmaine away before it had been too late.

''Jed wasn't strong enough.'' Booth's eyes got that faraway, almost glazed look that actually made him seem more human than he was. ''He had some of his mama's weakness in him.''

''Yes, sir, that he did.''

''Get going. Make those calls. And when Charmaine comes home, tell her I want to see her alone for a few minutes.''

Jaron tried not to think about why Booth wanted to see his wife alone, even for a few minutes. He couldn't do anything to stop Booth's tyranny. Not today. Not yet. But soon. Very soon.

The moment Ronnie headed the BMW up the driveway and Charmaine saw the limo parked out front, she knew her brief afternoon of happiness was over. Booth was home. Two days early.

''I can't bear the thought of him touching you,'' Ronnie said. ''I know how he treats you. You don't know how many times I've wanted to beat the hell out of him.''

"No, you mustn't. Don't even think that way." She gazed lovingly at Ronnie—for one last time today. "I can endure anything now that I know you love me. I'll live for our stolen moments. But we have to be very careful."

"One of these days, I'll take you away from here. I swear I will."

He wouldn't. He couldn't. No more than Jaron could. Both men loved her. Both promised to take her away from Booth Fortier. Neither would ever be able to fulfill that promise. The only thing that would ever free her from her husband was death. She knew that as surely as she knew cats had kittens. There were some things in this life that were inescapable.

Jaron stood on the front porch, rocking nervously back and forth on his heels. What the hell was wrong with her brother? He'd been acting like a whore in Sunday school lately. Fidgety. Nervous. He was up to something and hiding it from her. But what?

When Jaron saw them drive up, he came running. "Booth's home and something's wrong. Something big." The words flew from Jaron's mouth in a breathless rush. "He's building up to a fine rage. He's calling a meeting. Everybody's on their way in, including Ollie Neville." Jaron looked at Ronnie. "Stay out here with me, do you hear?" He glanced at Charmaine. "He wants to see you. Alone."

"No!" When Ronnie reached for Charmaine, Jaron stepped between them.

"It's all right," she said quietly. "Nothing will happen that hasn't happened before. I'll be all right. Just don't give us away by saying or doing anything to make Booth suspicious."

Jaron blocked Ronnie's path until after Charmaine entered the house. Once inside, she took a deep breath and hurried down the hall toward her husband's office. She knocked.

"Enter," he said gruffly.

She eased open the door. He sat behind the massive, elaborate antique desk, his head bent over as he snorted coke. In the past several years, Booth Fortier had become a drug addict. He couldn't make it through a day without his fix.

She closed the door, crossed the room and stood in front of the desk. "Welcome home."

He sniffed several times, lifted his head and grinned lasciviously. A shudder of apprehension fluttered along her nerve endings.

"Did you miss me, baby?"

"What do you think?"

His smile vanished. "I didn't miss you. I've been having me a real good time with some of the best trained whores in Louisiana. They know when to scream, when to cry, when to beg for mercy. It's your own fault that I have to hurt you more. You make it harder on yourself by being silent."

She knew. And that's the very reason she tried so hard to stay as quiet as possible, no matter what he did to her. Crying out in pain would give him too much satisfaction. And always in the back of her mind was one thought—if I scream and beg for mercy, Jaron might hear me. Now she had to worry about Ronnie, too.

"Come here." Booth waved his hand in a beckoning gesture.

Charmaine swallowed hard, then went to him, stopping when she was within arm's reach. He grasped her wrist tightly and tugged. The pain shot up her arm as his fingers bit into her flesh and he jerked her down onto his lap. He grabbed her face, his fingers digging into her cheeks; then his bleary black eyes focused on her.

"Have you been a good girl while I was away?"

"Aren't I always?"

His fierce grip on her face loosened. He slid his hand down her neck and tightened his fingers around her throat. "I got business to take care of this evening, but once that's done, I'll be free to spend some time with my loving wife. How does that sound to you?''

She knew how Booth loved to intimidate people, how he got his jollies from frightening others, but even more so from inflicting pain. Her husband was a sick—a very sick—bastard. A monster with the power of a god.

When he eased his ferocious grip on her throat, Charmaine gasped in air. She wasn't afraid he'd kill her, at least not quickly; slow torture was Booth's trademark.

As she sat on his lap, showing no sign of fear or pain, he ran his hands over her breasts. ''These are mine.'' His palm skimmed her belly and moved downward to cup her mound. ''This is mine.'' She managed to keep the shudder of revulsion inside her. ''Every damn ounce of this luscious hundred and ten pounds is all mine. Isn't that right?''

''Yes, that's right.''

He laughed. She waited. He shoved her off his lap, sending her toppling. Her left hip hit the floor with a hard thud; pain radiated through her hip and down her leg. She clamped her mouth shut to stop herself from crying out. He would ignore her now, as if she were a piece of trash he'd tossed aside. He'd forget she even existed…until later. Until he needed his daily fix of sadism. He was as hooked on cruelty as he was on the cocaine.

Charmaine went up on her knees, then grasped the edge of the desk for leverage so she could stand. Despite the pain in her hip, she didn't favor her left side as she walked across the room, straight and tall, showing no sign that his actions had injured her. She had to make it to her room without limping, without crying, in case Ronnie or Jaron saw her. She had been able to control Jaron's outrage over the years, reminding him that if he confronted Booth, it could cost both him and her their lives. But Ronnie wasn't like Jaron. She had no idea whether or not he would actually try to defend her against her husband; but her feminine instincts told her that he might. No matter what it cost her, she couldn't let Ronnie ever realize the extent of Booth's inhumane abuse.

Tonight when her husband brutalized and humiliated her, she would think of Ronnie and the joy of being in his arms. She would shut out what was happening to her, withdraw into herself, as she always did. To a safe place. But tonight would be different. She wouldn't be alone in that safe place. Ronnie would be there, holding her, comforting her.

Elsa parked her white Honda Civic in front of the first warehouse on the long row of warehouses along the riverfront. Looking the building over as she stood on the cracked sidewalk, she noticed faded lettering above the huge double doors facing the street. Garland Industries. She'd come to the right place. Ordinarily she would never come to this part of town. One, because she'd have no reason to be here; and two, although the crime rate in St. Camille was relatively low, everyone knew East Fifth Street wasn't really safe after dark. But it isn't dark, she reminded herself. It's barely six-thirty. She'd stopped by to see Milly after work, as she did almost every day. The staff at St. Camille Haven often told Elsa how much Milly looked forward to her big sister's daily visits, so no matter how difficult her day had been or how bone-tired she might be, Elsa did her best to not miss their evening visit. Today, she had needed to see Milly for her own sake. She needed to believe in her heart that she'd done something right in caring for her siblings. Sherrie didn't live close by, not close enough to drop in on at a moment's notice. How was it, she asked herself, that she had succeeded so well in mothering her two sisters and had failed so miserably with Troy? He'd been the sweetest little boy; but sometime around puberty, he'd changed, become rebellious and angry. What he'd needed then—and now— was a father. When a boy was coming of age, he needed a man's strong, steady influence. A father's firm hand and loving guidance.

When Jed Tyree had spoken to her today and confirmed

her worst fears, she'd been able to think of little else. Troy was working in a warehouse owned by Garland Industries, which was nothing more than a front for one aspect of Booth Fortier's illegal activities. Mr. Tyree had told her to do whatever she had to do to terminate her brother's employment.

"Booth Fortier doesn't give a damn about the guys who work for him," Jed Tyree had said. "He has sacrificed people all his life to protect himself, to punish others or just on an illogical whim. If your brother continues working at the warehouse, he'll wind up either doing time in prison or six feet under."

God, help me, Elsa prayed as she straightened her shoulders, took a deep breath and marched toward the small office door at the side of the warehouse. Usually she was logical and levelheaded, never a risk-taker. But desperate times called for desperate measures. She intended to speak to Troy's boss, this Curt Poarch he'd mentioned. And if the man was uncooperative, she'd wait and talk to Troy. She had to make him understand the danger he was in, the horrible chances he was taking by working for Booth Fortier— for the Louisiana branch of the Southern Mafia.

Halfway to the door, Elsa paused, opened her shoulder bag and glanced down at the small can of Mace she carried. She didn't own a gun, was in fact uneasy around them. And she didn't usually carry Mace because in a town like St. Camille she really didn't need it. But on the way here this evening, she'd made a stop to purchase a can of Mace and a whistle.

She chuckled silently, laughing at herself and her silly precautions. All the safety paraphernalia in the world wouldn't make her an equal match for a real criminal. After closing her purse, she headed straight toward the warehouse. When she reached the door, she didn't hesitate to knock, loudly and repeatedly. She waited several minutes for a response, but received none. The door remained locked. She tried again, knocking again and again, until her knuckles tingled with pain. Still no response. After that, she tried knocking on the huge double doors. Nothing.

Maybe there's another entry, around back, she thought. But in order to reach the back of the building, she'd have to go down the alleyway. Okay, just do it, she told herself. After all, it's still daylight. There aren't any boogey men waiting to jump out in the dark. But what if something did go wrong? These warehouses and the area around them seemed unusually quiet, not a single soul stirring. If she screamed, would anyone hear her?

Don't chicken out now, an inner voice goaded her into action. She walked up the street, rounded the building on the end and found the alley that ran between the warehouses and the river. Pausing briefly, she garnered her courage and headed down the alley. Suddenly, from out of nowhere, a couple of guys sprang out at her. Gasping, she jumped back and began trying to unlatch her shoulder bag. She made eye contact with first one man and then the other; and realized they weren't much more than boys. A couple of kids about Troy's age. One black. One white. Both scruffy-looking. Both smiling fiendishly.

"What's a fine thing like you doing down here on the wharf?" the black teenager asked, his ebony eyes raking over her insultingly.

"She's come to see me, haven't you, baby doll?"

The redheaded, freckle-faced white boy came toward Elsa. She backed away...slowly...as her fingers circled the can of Mace in her purse.

"Go away and leave me alone," she warned them.

"You got a gun in that purse?" the redhead asked.

Just as Elsa jerked the Mace from her purse, the black teen pounced, knocking the can out of her hand. When he snatched her purse away, she managed to clasp the whistle and close it up in her hand before he shoved her to the sidewalk. Hitting the sidewalk on her knees, she winced in pain. Oh, God, what a fine mess she'd gotten herself into this time. While she struggled to stand, the two boys emptied her purse, dumping the contents on the sidewalk.

"She ain't got no gun," the redhead said. "Just a can of Mace."

They rummaged through her wallet, pulled out the cash and tossed the wallet back on the ground. "All she's got is forty bucks," the redhead complained.

"Yeah," the black teen agreed, then zeroed in on Elsa, who was trying to back away from them. "Maybe she's got something else she can give us to make up for not having no real money."

Fear surged through her body; adrenaline pumped wildly through her veins. Elsa turned and ran, and in the process managed to get the whistle in her mouth. She could hear the boys laughing as they ran after her. She kept blowing the whistle, kept running. She made it to the end of the alley before they caught up with her. What now? she asked herself when she felt one of them latch his hand onto her shoulder. She knew one thing for sure and certain—she was going to give them the fight of their lives!

Just as the redhead whirled her around, a deep baritone voice coming from behind her said, "Let her go."

Both boys shifted nervously, but the redhead didn't release her. Elsa wondered who her rescuer was and if he could truly save her from these hoodlums.

"Yeah, who's going to make us?" the black teen asked.

"I am," the man replied.

"So you got a gun. Big deal. We got guns, too." The redhead tightened his hold on Elsa.

A gunshot splintered the concrete as it hit the sidewalk half an inch from the redhead's right foot, letting the boys know the big deal was that his gun was in his hand. The redhead jumped when the bullet hit so close, and in the process, released Elsa, who didn't waste any time turning and running. A tall, muscular man, in jeans and T-shirt, a baseball cap covering part of his shaggy brown hair, held a large, sinister-looking pistol in his hand. When the black teen took a step forward, as if he was going to come after Elsa, her hero fired his weapon again, this time sending the shot a hairbreadth from the other guy's foot.

"You win, man. We're outta here." The redhead backed away.

"Toss the lady's money on the ground by her purse," the man told them. "Then you can go."

The redhead jerked the bills from his pocket, dropped them on top of Elsa's empty purse, then started backing away again. The black youth followed suit; when they'd backed up about ten feet, they turned and ran down the alley.

Elsa released a pent-up breath and made direct eye contact with her rescuer. "Thank you."

"What the hell were you doing back here in this alley?" He scanned her from head to toe. "You don't look like you belong anywhere around here."

"I—I was trying to find someone inside one of the warehouses," she said, realizing as she spoke that her statement probably didn't make any sense to this man. "My brother works down there—" she pointed to the Garland Industries warehouse "—and I wanted to talk to his boss."

Narrowing his gaze, the man studied her, as if he was wondering whether he knew her. "You made a big mistake coming down here. Go home and don't come back. Whatever trouble your brother's in, you can't fix it with his boss."

"How do you know—"

He grasped Elsa's upper arm, dragged her up the alley to where her purse and its contents lay. "Gather up your things and I'll walk you back to your car."

She knelt, raised the flap on her handbag, shoved the contents inside and picked it up.

After she hung the strap over her shoulder, she turned to him. "Do you work around here? Is that the reason you—"

He grabbed her arm again and marched her up the alley, toward the end of the street. She quickened her pace in order to keep up with him. When they rounded the corner onto East Fifth Street, she stopped and dug in her heels.

"Please, if you can, help me." She gazed pleadingly up at him, but his hard expression didn't soften. "My brother's life could depend on my getting him to quit his job."

"What's your brother's name?"

Elsa hesitated. She didn't know this man, had no idea if she could trust him. But he'd rescued her, probably saved her from being raped or perhaps even killed.

"Troy Leone."

"You promise me you won't come back down here to the warehouse, and if there's anything I can do to keep an eye on your brother, I will."

"Do you know Troy?" she asked.

He didn't reply.

Realizing she'd lost the battle, she nodded. "I'm Elsa Leone. I want to thank you again for saving me."

"You're welcome." His lips twitched, but he didn't smile.

"And you're…?" she asked.

He looked at her quizzically.

"Your name?"

"Rafe," he said softly, his deep voice little more than a whisper.

When he tightened his grip on her arm and prodded her into action, she allowed him to escort her to her car. He waited for her to get inside, lock the doors and back out of the parking place. As she drove away, she glanced into her rearview mirror and saw him watching her departure.

Who was he? she wondered. Her mysterious hero. Did he work on East Fifth in one of the warehouses? Was he just a dock worker or was he employed by Booth Fortier? He'd reacted to Troy's name as if he recognized it. So did that mean they had the same boss? If so, would it be possible for him to actually keep an eye on Troy? She'd probably never know because there was little chance their paths would ever cross again.

Rafe. He'd said his name was Rafe. No last name. No real identity. Why was it that when she finally met a guy who made her blood pound and her heart race, he turned out to be someone she'd never see again, someone who might be a criminal?

As she zoomed her little Honda along the twilight streets of St. Camille, her thoughts jumbled wildly. With concern about her brother. And with visions of a shaggy-haired knight in shining armor.

Chapter 10

Charmaine waited in her room until everyone had assembled in Booth's office, with the door closed and perhaps locked. She didn't know; didn't care. Once—and only once—she had dared to enter Booth's office uninvited. During the first year of their marriage. He had taught her a lesson that day, one she never forgot. When she was certain nobody other than Nola might spot her, she left her room and tiptoed down the hall. After glancing around to make sure she was alone, she opened the door to the room directly above Booth's office—a large storage closet. While exploring the old house one day while Booth was away, she had discovered something very interesting about that closet, something she knew Booth knew nothing about, that perhaps only Nola and the housekeeper before her knew existed. There was a peephole in the floor between the closet and Booth's office. Who had cut through the layers of flooring and why, she had no idea, but someone, long ago, had found a way to spy on the lord and master in his study—perhaps in Booth's father's day. At first glance in the closet, the peephole appeared to be nothing more than a light spot in the dark floor. Since first discovering the hole, Charmaine had kept it covered with a large cardboard box. Downstairs in Booth's office, the peephole really wasn't noticeable because the ceiling was high and the hole itself was located near the hundred-year-old chandelier, which actually blocked the view from below but not from above.

Charmaine eased the box aside, being careful that her actions created no sound; then she maneuvered herself down onto the floor and placed her eye directly over the peephole. She tilted her head right and left, searching the room for its occupants. She saw Jaron first, standing near the door, his arms crossed over his chest. Booth sat behind his massive desk, a lit cigar in his mouth, the smoke curling up and over his bald head.

"Sit," Booth ordered.

Hurriedly she scanned the chairs scattered about the room, all forming a semicircle around the desk. Oliver Neville sat closest to Booth. She noticed a black leather briefcase propped beside his chair. Aric, Curt, Ronnie and Charlie Dupree filled the other chairs. Her gaze lingered on Ronnie. Her lover. Her love.

She sensed the tension in the room as everyone waited for the big boss to speak, to explain why he'd called the top-secret meeting. It had to be something important to have cut short Booth's trip to New Orleans. And it had to do with something legal—or rather illegal—to require Ollie's presence.

"We've got ourselves a snitch in the organization," Booth said.

A palpable silence filled the room, as if each man was holding his breath. Oh, God, Charmaine thought, some poor fool is going to die.

"The guy's either one of ours or he's one of Lew Miller's group—either way, he signed his own death warrant when he screwed with me." Booth squinted his eyes menacingly as he puffed on his big, expensive Cuban cigar.

Charmaine knew Booth was waiting to see if anyone in the room dared to respond. No one did. Booth grinned.

"Somebody sent Grace Beaumont, former attorney general Dean Beaumont's widow, a letter telling her that I had her hubby and dear old dad bumped off because Dean was on the verge of securing evidence that proved a connection between our governor and me." Booth nodded to his lawyer.

"We're relatively certain that no one in the governor's immediate circle knew about the hit on Dean Beaumont and Byram Sheffield," Ollie said. "That means the traitor is someone privy to Booth's most confidential business. Knowing that narrows down the possibilities and will help us discover the traitor's identity quicker."

"You aren't implying that it's one of us, are you?" Charlie Dupree ran two fingers under his tight collar.

"No one is implying anything," Booth said. "Ollie's telling y'all that each one of you is under suspicion, as are half a dozen other guys who have worked here at the house in the recent past."

"I think everyone knows what happens to anyone who betrays you," Jaron said. "Why would any of us be that stupid?"

"Damn good question," Ollie remarked.

"I wasn't working for Booth four years ago," Ronnie reminded them. "I don't even know who these people—the Beaumonts—are."

"We're aware of everyone's work history." Ollie directed his attention to Ronnie. "However, once inside the inner circle, like y'all are, you learn things, see things and become privy to all sorts of information. Sorry, Ronnie, but we can't rule you out entirely."

"How are you going to find out who it is?" Aric asked. "I know it's not me—hell, I'd die to protect you, Booth, and you know it."

Grinning like a Cheshire cat, his white teeth shimmering

against his dark skin, Booth flicked the ashes from his cigar into a sterling silver ashtray on his desk.

"What none of you knew is that we had an informant who gave Ollie the information we needed about Beaumont and his father-in-law the night they were run off the road...an informant who had reason to want both men out of the way. That informant is still working for us."

Not by choice, Charmaine surmised. Once you did a job for Booth Fortier, you were never free from him, not ever. She wiggled to loosen the tension in her body, then switched from her right eye to her left eye as she continued gazing through the peephole.

"Our very helpful informant let us know about the letter to Grace Beaumont," Booth told them. "It seems our traitor has now telephoned the lady and wants to exchange proof of my connection to Lew Miller for five million dollars."

A hushed rumble reverberated around the room. Ronnie, Curt, Aric and Charlie shifted uncomfortably. Charmaine glanced at Jaron. He was sweating. *Oh, Jaron, please, please, don't let it be you.* But somehow in her heart she knew it was. Why would he risk his life for the money? Didn't he know Booth would catch him? Hadn't he learned anything after nearly twenty years with Booth? While she kept her gaze on her brother, he removed a white handkerchief from his pocket, wiped his face, then his hands, and returned the handkerchief to his pocket.

"We'll find our man before he can make the exchange," Booth said, "but that won't eliminate our problem. It seems Mrs. Beaumont has hired herself a private investigation team to dig into the accident that befell her family, as well as any connection between the governor and me."

"Grace Beaumont has to be stopped." Ollie looked directly at Booth.

"I want the lady warned. Tonight." Booth took a couple of puffs on his cigar, laid it in the sterling tray, then shoved back his chair and stood. "Charlie, I'm putting together a little package for the young widow and I want you to deliver it. Tonight.''

"Yes, sir.''

Charlie Dupree wasn't the sharpest knife in the drawer, but he was loyal to a fault and he hero-worshiped Booth. Although he was good to his elderly mother and had a soft spot for his pet parrot, Feathers, the guy had a vicious streak a mile wide. Like Booth, he actually enjoyed inflicting pain.

"That's it for now,'' Booth said. "Y'all can go. And whoever our traitor is had better enjoy his last days on earth.''

When Jaron's trembling hand grasped the doorknob, Booth called to him. "Jaron, wait up. I want to talk to you. Privately.''

Charmaine held her breath. Did Booth already know that Jaron was the traitor? Was he going to question him, grill him, until he confessed? She couldn't just stand by and do nothing. But what could she do? Think, Charmaine, think!

You could kill Booth, an inner voice advised her. Yes, she could kill Booth. She had dreamed of murdering the bastard in his sleep, had planned and plotted his demise numerous times.

"Yeah, Booth, what do you need?'' Jaron asked, and Charmaine marveled at how calm her brother's voice sounded.

Booth walked over to Jaron, gripped his shoulder tightly and said, "Jed's back in Louisiana.''

"What?'' Jaron's gaze darted up from the floor to meet Booth's steady glare.

At the mention of Jed, Charmaine's heart missed a beat. She hadn't been in love with Jed in a long, long time, but she'd never forgotten him. And a part of her had never forgiven him for leaving Louisiana without her.

"It seems my nephew works for the Dundee Private Security and Investigation Agency, out of Atlanta.'' Booth loosened his hold on Jaron's shoulder. "He's the one heading up the investigation for Mrs. Beaumont.''

"Jed is? I can't believe... God, Booth, why would he—"

"Look me square in the eye, Jaron, and tell me the God's honest truth—have you or Charmaine heard from him since he came back?"

Jaron shook his head. "I swear on my life, neither I nor Charmaine knew Jed was back, that he was working here in Louisiana."

Booth slapped Jaron on the back. "You can stop sweating. I believe you. You've always been loyal, always knew your place. I like a man who realizes when I own him. And you know that I own you and your sister. Always have."

"Yeah, Booth. I know."

Booth laughed. The sound sliced through Charmaine like razor-sharp blades, creating deep, agonizing wounds. She hated his laughter because when Booth was happy, it usually meant he had just inflicted pain on someone else.

If Jed was back, if he was working against Booth, was it possible that he could help Jaron? Help her? If as she suspected, Jaron was the traitor, could Jed save him from Booth? There was no way she could contact Jed from the house, no way to get a message to him. If Ronnie would take her into town and allow her to make a phone call... But on what pretense could she leave the house again tomorrow when everyone knew she'd gone into town two days in a row?

Charmaine eased up on her knees, scooted the cardboard box over the peephole, then stood up and opened the door just a fraction. She peered out, looking up and down the upstairs hall. Empty. Good.

She opened the door all the way, hurried out of the closet and closed the door very quietly behind her. With her heart racing wildly, she tiptoed down the hall to her room. Once inside, she rushed to her dressing table, sat down and picked up her silver brush. She brushed her hair, counting the strokes as the bristles glided through her thick, curly mane. It was only a matter of time until Booth came into her room through the door that connected her room to his. She wanted him to find her sitting here waiting for him. Calm. Cool. Controlled. She glanced at the nail file lying atop the mirror-topped silver tray on the table. Could she kill him with the nail file? It wasn't very big, but if it went into his jugular vein…

Charmaine's hand trembled so badly that she dropped the brush. Oh, God, what was she thinking? Unless Booth was unconscious, passed out drunk or drugged, she'd never be able to overpower him. Besides, if she killed him, his syndicate associates would kill her, if his household entourage didn't do the job first. And that meant Jaron and Ronnie would die, too, because she knew both men would lay down their lives for her.

Restless, Jed meandered around in his room at Belle Foret, probably wearing a hole in the antique Persian rug beneath his feet. He had grown up in a nice home, surrounded by expensive things, but Booth Fortier's decor had nothing to do with good taste and everything to do with how much things cost. In Grace's home, the decor whispered timeless elegance, the very essence of what was once referred to as gentility. It was there in every room, in every stick of furniture, every painting. A style that had taken generations to cultivate. Just as Grace was quality, pure and simple, so was her home. Yeah, quality, that was the big difference between the two of them. She was; he wasn't. And the funny thing was, money had nothing to do with it. If Grace didn't have a penny to her name, she would still be quality.

He'd done everything he could to convince himself that he'd be a fool to approach Grace on a personal level again. The kiss they'd shared had only whetted his appetite for more. But the lady had said no. If he was smart, he'd listen to her, and take her refusal to heart.

Think about business, he reminded himself. There's five million dollars sitting in the safe at Sheffield Media, Inc., with Dom and Kate staying overnight at the office to assist the nighttime security guards. Of course, none of the employees were aware that a small fortune had been deposited in the company's safe. But Hudson Prentice knew, as did Elsa Leone. And Grace's uncle Willis and cousin Joy knew. They were four trusted friends, but Jed suspected one of them had betrayed Grace in the past, so what was to keep him or her from doing it again? Had the traitor told Booth exactly what was going on? Did Booth already know he had a Benedict Arnold among his most trusted associates?

The person who had helped Booth destroy Dean Beaumont and Bryam Sheffield would still be under Booth's thumb. He or she would still be reporting to Booth. That meant what the informant knew, Booth knew. Not only would his uncle be aware of a traitor in his midst, he would know Grace was having his association with Governor Miller investigated. And he'd also know that Jed was working for Grace. "The Plan" had been set in motion. It was only a matter of time before he could have an excuse to go to his uncle, confront him and ask him to disprove the allegations against him, all a guise to put Jed in contact with the federal agent working in Booth's camp.

Jed stood at the windows, pulled back one curtain and looked down at the dark, sprawling backyard lawn. Glancing up he studied the few stars visible tonight. Partial cloud cover shielded a section of the moon and half the stars.

If Booth already knew that Grace was having him investigated, if he suspected a traitor in his midst, then Grace was in danger. And when Booth discovered the traitor's identity, he was a dead man. But if Booth knew, why hadn't he made a move? Why hadn't he issued a warning? It wasn't like his uncle to bide his time. Just as soon as the first threat against Grace occurred, Jed could put their plan into action. He would have an excuse to visit his uncle and find a way to make contact with the FBI's undercover agent who apparently was trapped within the organization and kept under such close scrutiny recently that he had no way to exchange information with his superiors within the Bureau.

"Jim Kelly is one of our top agents," Dante Moran had told Jed. "He infiltrated your uncle's organization over two years ago and up until six months ago was able to keep in touch on a regular basis, then his job duties changed and it has become increasingly difficult for him to get any word out to us."

Jed chuckled. Booth Fortier not only had a traitor in his midst, but he had a spy, too. And if either man was found out…

A telephone rang. He heard the echo coming from Grace's room. Jed picked up the portable phone he'd requested to be kept in his room, then rushed out the door and across the hall. Grace's door was closed, but he didn't think twice about entering without knocking. He'd given Grace orders to answer her own phone from now on, now that the trace had been placed on her telephones, both at home and at work.

When Grace looked up at him, she nodded, her cue to him that he should listen in. He put the phone to his ear.

"There's a gift waiting for you, Mrs. Beaumont," the disguised voice said. "It's been left at the front gate. You might want to send someone down to get it."

"Who is this? What sort of gift?"

The dial tone hummed in their ears. Damn! Jed thought. No way was the guy on the phone long enough to trace the call. Besides, it didn't really matter if he'd used a pay phone or a cell phone that could be traced only to the nearest tower.

Grace hung up the receiver. "What do you think?" she asked.

"I don't think this was our guy, the one who's expecting five million dollars tomorrow at noon. I think this is someone else."

Grace's blue eyes rounded in surprise. "Who do you think…" she gasped. "You think Booth Fortier already knows about—"

"I'm going to make a quick phone call and have someone check the front gate for your gift."

"Who are you going to call and why not just go get it—" Grace paused as realization dawned. "Do you think it's a bomb? Are you phoning the sheriff?"

"Do you want the local law involved?" he asked.

Her shoulders lifted and fell as she sighed deeply. "Not unless it's absolutely necessary. Since we have nothing but our suspicions to go on...no solid proof. Not yet."

Jed punched in a series of numbers, then lifted the portable phone to his ear.

"Who are you calling?" she repeated her question.

He held up his index finger in a signal for her to wait. She nodded agreement.

"This is Jed. Ms. Beaumont just received an interesting phone call. It seems someone has dropped off a gift for her at the front gates and I need you to pick it up. Understand?"

"Yeah, I understand," Rafe Devlin replied. "I'll get some of Moran's boys to check it out and if it's not lethal, I'll bring it up to the house."

"Thanks. I'll be waiting to hear from you."

"Will do."

Jed turned to Grace. "Why don't you stay up here and I'll go downstairs and wait. If there's a bomb or anything else, he'll call back. If not, he'll leave the package."

"Are you taking one of the Dundee agents away from guard duty at Sheffield Media to check out whatever was left at the gate?"

"No." He turned and walked away, hoping that would end it, at least for the time being.

Grace followed him into the hall. "Jed, what are you not telling me?"

Pausing, he kept his back to her. "There's a third Dundee agent working this case. I called him."

"A third person? Why didn't you mention this before? I swear to goodness, Jed Tyree, you're the most aggravating man I've ever met. Why all the secrets? If I'm paying for four Dundee agents, don't you think I'll find out when the bill comes in?''

''Yeah, sure. Sorry I didn't mention it.'' When her bill came in, she'd be charged for three agents—Dom, Kate and himself. He supposed you could say the others—Rafe and J.J.—were working pro bono, without pay, for the public good. Over the years, the Dundee agency had formed a co-operative relationship with the Bureau. As with all relationships it often resulted in a you-scratch-my-back-I'll-scratch-yours policy. And now that the CEO of Dundee's was a former Fed himself, it cemented an already strong bond.

Jed left Grace standing in the hall, then galloped down the long, winding staircase and into the marble-floored foyer. He sat in one of the two antique armchairs flanking a ornately decorated chest that rested against the right entrance wall. He figured he'd be waiting no more than thirty minutes before he heard from Rafe, letting him know the package had been examined and either destroyed or was on its way up to the house.

While he waited, he went over several different scenarios. He was ninety-nine percent certain the ''gift'' was from Booth. And whatever it was, it would be an unpleasant surprise. If he could, he wanted to protect Grace as much as possible from the ugliness. She was a strong, brave woman, but she'd suffered more than enough for two lifetimes. He had no intention of letting her become another of Booth Fortier's victims.

''Want some company?'' Grace asked as she floated down the staircase, her movements fluid and unhurried.

He glanced up and watched her as she descended, her yellow silk pajamas only a shade darker than her shoulder-length hair. Looking at her, he couldn't see a flaw. Not one tiny imperfection. But then, he hadn't explored every inch of her.

His sex reacted instantly to the thought of his hands caressing Grace's naked body. *Down, boy, down!* he ordered a particular part of his anatomy. Okay, so he was a red-blooded American male, and what guy in his right mind wouldn't be attracted to a woman as beautiful as Grace? But it wasn't like him to react so strongly to a woman he barely knew—one who'd put up No Trespassing signs all around her. Yes, he got as horny as the next guy, but he had never hurt for female companionship. If he wanted to get laid, he didn't figure he'd have a problem once this assignment was over and he was free to indulge in some extracurricular activity. But the problem was he didn't just want to get laid. He wanted Grace. He wanted to make love to her. Sweet, slow, all-night-long love.

"Jed?" she called to him when she reached the foot of the stairs.

"Huh?"

"Are you all right?"

No, honey, I'm not all right. I'm hurting in the worst way, but you don't want to hear it. "Yeah, sure, I'm fine. Just thinking."

"Mind if I wait with you?" she asked, but didn't pause long enough for him to reply before she sat in the matching armchair on the opposite side of the chest.

"Look…whatever the gift is, it's not going to be anything you want to see." Jed leaned over slightly, so that he could look around the huge chest that separated them. "Take my word for it. My guess is Booth Fortier has sent you a warning. Why don't you just go back upstairs and let me handle this."

"You're trying to protect me and I appreciate it, but—"

"That's my job, isn't it?"

"To protect my life," she told him. "Not protect my heart."

Jed huffed, then leaned back in the chair and crossed his arms over his chest. "Stay. We'll wait together."

"How long—"

"I'm not sure. Thirty minutes. Maybe longer."

She kicked off her yellow satin house slippers, curled her legs up under her and placed her hands in her lap. He kept stealing quick glances at her in his peripheral vision. Once or twice, he caught her doing the same. Minutes ticked by. The grandfather clock on the landing struck the half hour. Neither of them said a word.

After about fifteen minutes, Grace eased her feet down to the floor, slid her feet into the slippers and readjusted her position in the chair. "Would you like a sherry or brandy? I could get us something."

"No, thanks, but you—"

"No, I really don't want anything."

Time dragged. Jed checked his watch every couple of minutes, more for something to do than anything else. The grandfather clock struck eleven times. Just as the vibration from the last dong ended, Jed's cell phone rang.

"Tyree here."

"Yeah, the package is clean, but it's not something you want to let the lady see," Rafe said.

"I understand. I'll open the gates and be waiting on the veranda for you."

"Take a look at the pictures for yourself first, then tell her what they are, if you have to. But I'm telling you—do not let her see them."

Jed's gut tightened.

"I'm going to open the gates and disarm the security system while I go outside on the veranda and take the package," Jed told Grace. "You stay in here. And you need to know now that you aren't going to see what's inside your gift package."

"What is it?"

"Just do as I ask, will you? Stay in the house and let me handle this." She nodded. Damn, that was too easy, Jed thought. She'd agreed too quickly. "Go back upstairs, will you?"

"I'd rather wait here." She didn't budge from the armchair.

Jed got up and walked over to the controls hidden in a panel behind the staircase, punched in the code to deactivate the security system, then used another code to open the massive wrought-iron gates. When he opened the front door, he glanced over his shoulder to check on Grace. She didn't move or even look at him. He closed the front door behind him and waited for Rafe. In just a few minutes, the rental car Rafe was using pulled up in the circular drive. Jed went down the steps to meet his fellow Dundee agent. Rafe got out of the car and joined Jed. He held out a large manilla envelope. Jed took the envelope, loosened the clasp, then removed the contents. Photographs. Police shots from the accident scene. A few of the shots were particularly gruesome and Jed wondered what sicko cop had taken them. Closeups of Dean Beaumont and Byram Sheffield, both dead and bloody. And a shot of an unconscious Grace. More photos. Some taken at the funerals. And one of Grace in her hospital room. Rage burned through Jed's veins.

Yeah, this was definitely Booth Fortier's handwork. It had his fingerprints all over it.

Jed shook his head. "This was a mild warning for Grace. The next one will be far worse."

Just as Jed started to slip the photos back into the envelope, intending to give them to Rafe, Grace came running out of the house and directly toward them.

"Hell," Jed cursed under his breath. He shoved the photos into the envelope and held them out to Rafe.

"Wait," Grace called. "Whatever it is, I want to see it."

"No, you don't," Jed told her and handed the envelope to Rafe.

She marched straight to them, planted herself between them and held out her hand. "Give me the envelope."

Rafe grunted. "Ma'am, you really don't—"

"Give them to her," Jed said.

Rafe hesitated for a couple of seconds, then gave Grace the envelope. "Call if you need anything else," he told Jed, then got back in the rental car and drove off.

Grace stared at the envelope for a couple of minutes before slipping the photos out and looking at them, one by one, studying them carefully. Watching her for a reaction, he waited for her to say something, but she said nothing. After she finished with the lot, she turned away from Jed and started walking back toward the house, the envelope loosely clutched in her hand.

"Grace?"

One by one, the photos dropped from her hand and floated onto the driveway, as if she were scattering rose petals. The envelope sailed downward and landed at Jed's feet. He ignored them as he followed Grace. When she reached the steps, she faltered. Damn! Was she going to faint?

Jed rushed toward her just as she staggered, her feet searching for the first step. When he put his arm around her waist to support her shivering body, she pivoted slowly around and laid her head on his chest. Tears streamed down her cheeks. He pulled her into his arms and held her while she wept.

Chapter 11

Grace lifted her head from Jed's chest and looked up at him through teary eyes. Hating herself for falling apart the way she had, she pulled back, disengaging herself from his strong, comforting arms. During those first few unbearable months after she'd lost her family, she had almost lost her mind, too. Once she had gone through her own personal trial by fire, she'd emerged a woman of steel. At least for the most part. She prided herself on not allowing her emotions to control her actions. But tonight, seeing those horrific photographs, she had reverted to that mentally fragile place she'd been right after the accident.

No, not an accident. After Daddy and Dean were murdered, she told herself. *After Booth Fortier killed my husband, my father and my baby.*

Emotion lodged in her throat. She swallowed hard and willed herself under control. "I'm sorry," she said. "I don't usually…" Her voice cracked. Damn!

"Grace, it's all right," Jed told her. "Anyone would have

reacted the same way." He held his hands in front of him, palms up, as if he wanted to reach for her.

She glanced down at the scattered photos and manilla envelope in the driveway. Quivering, she closed her eyes, but instead of blocking out the sight of the pictures, she simply visualized them in her mind. Her eyelids flew open.

"I never want to see them again," she said.

Jed nodded.

"I should have listened to you." Grace wiped her damp face with her fingers. "Both you and the other Dundee agent tried to tell me, but I wouldn't listen, would I?"

When she swayed slightly, Jed reached out to steady her. So strong was the physical reaction he created within her that his mere touch seared her, as if his hands were on fire. She tensed. Their gazes met and froze. Her heart pounded, loud and fast, rumbling in her ears.

"Don't try so hard to be brave," he told her. "You're only human. If you need somebody to lean on right now, lean on me."

She lifted her hand and placed it over his where he gently gripped her arm. "I want to go inside my house, up to my bedroom and shut out the world. I want to find a way to forget what I saw, to erase the memory of those pictures from my mind."

"I understand." He released her arm. "You go on. I'll gather up everything and take care of it, then I'll come upstairs and check on you."

"Just leave them," Grace said. "They'll still be there in the morning. Please, come with me...I don't want to be alone. Not just yet." She hadn't meant her words to translate into an invitation, but seeing the hunger in Jed's eyes, she wondered if he had misinterpreted. Although a part of her wanted Jed, the saner part of her kept telling her that getting emotionally involved with her bodyguard would be a major mistake. "I didn't mean...I'm upset and confused and—"

Jed reached down and slipped her hand into his. "It's all

right. I understand. I didn't think you were inviting me into your bed.''

A relieved sigh escaped her lips. She couldn't remember the last time she'd felt so weak, so utterly exhausted. Emotional stress could quickly deplete the body's physical energy.

Leaving the horrible photos where they had cascaded onto the brick driveway, Grace and Jed walked up the steps, onto the veranda and into the house. He held her hand securely, but didn't touch her in any other way; nor did he say a word. His silent strength supported her, the touch of his hand comforting beyond measure. Jed paused in the foyer to reactivate the security system and close the gates, but he accomplished both with one hand, not breaking the physical contact with Grace. She wasn't sure exactly why, but she felt as if she'd be lost, as if she'd drift away into nothingness, were Jed to let go of her.

Side by side, hand in hand, they made their way up the spiral staircase. When they reached the open landing, Grace glanced downstairs and caught a glimpse of Laverna and Nolan standing together in the foyer, both with concerned looks on their faces. She offered them a weak smile. No explanations. Not now. All she wanted was to forget. Forget the photographs. Forget the pain that tore her apart inside when she remembered lying in Dean's arms, knowing the security and love he provided. Forget how difficult life was each day without her husband, without her wonderful father…without the hope of a child. Instinctively her hand went to her belly, to that spot where Emma Lynn had lain, nurtured and protected from the outside world. Until one deadly night…

Jed looked directly at Nolan and said, ''Would you mind picking up some photographs Grace left in the driveway.''

''No, sir, I don't mind.''

''Just put them away for safekeeping tonight and I'll collect them from you later.''

''Yes, sir. I'll take care of it immediately.''

Realizing Jed was simply doing his job—making sure any evidence of the threat against her life was retained and at the same time taking care of her—Grace sighed. While she wanted nothing more than to forget those photographs, she understood that Jed couldn't leave them lying outside where they could be stolen or blown away in the wind.

Trusting Nolan to carry out Jed's instructions, Grace led her bodyguard into her bedroom and closed the door, then reluctantly released his hand. "I don't think I'll sleep a wink tonight. Would you mind staying up with me? We can talk or play cards or listen to music or…" Fueled by nervous agitation, she paced around the room. "God, I feel as if I'm losing my mind."

Jed came up behind her and stopped her in mid-stride by placing his arms around her and pulling her back against his chest. After crossing his arms to encompass her, he lowered his head just enough so that his chin rested on the top of her head.

For half a second she thought about breaking free, but instead she melted against him, surrendering to the pleasure of being held. His was not her father's protective embrace nor was it Dean's loving embrace, but rather it was comfort. The comfort of another human being, of another warm body, on a night when the worst thing for her was to be alone.

"What were you like as a little girl?" Jed asked.

She breathed in the unique scent that was Jed Tyree. Soap and water. Sunshine. A hint of some subtle aftershave. No expensive colognes. Nothing to mask the pure masculinity he exuded.

Her head lolled back to rest comfortably against him as she lifted her chin. "I was spoiled rotten because I was an only child. I was Daddy's little darling. What about you— what were you like as a little boy?" She felt him tense and wondered if she'd mentioned a sensitive subject.

"My father died when I was small. And my mother…" Jed lowered his head and rubbed his cheek against her temple. "My mother was sick and spent most of my life in an institution. I lived with my uncle."

"Oh, Jed, how terrible for you." Grace gazed at him sympathetically. "I thought losing my mother when I was sixteen was tragic, but at least I had both her and my father while I was growing up. You must have been a very sad little boy without a mother."

"Yeah, I think every little kid needs a mama. Probably more than anything else, even a father or brothers and sisters. But I survived."

Sensing Jed's uneasiness at discussing his childhood, at appearing vulnerable to her, Grace changed the subject.

"I always wanted a brother or a sister. What about you? Did you have brothers or sisters?" Jed was so close, his arms surrounding her, capturing her with his gentleness.

"I was an only child, too. I had a buddy who had a younger sister and she looked up to him. They were very close. I guess I envied that, would like to have had it for myself."

"I mostly wanted a brother," Grace admitted. "A sister would have been too much competition. You know how we spoiled little rich girls are."

Jed chuckled. "Did you always get everything you wanted?"

"Most of the time, but not always. Believe it or not, Daddy did expect me to behave myself, even though I usually had a difficult time sharing. What was mine was mine…that sort of thing."

When Jed nuzzled the side of her face, tingles of awareness radiated through her. Her nipples peaked. No, she couldn't allow this to happen. She jerked away from him, desperately needing to put some distance between them. When she crossed the room and stood by the double French doors that led out onto the upstairs porch circling the entire house, Jed didn't follow her. Not at first. She opened both doors and stepped outside into the moist nighttime air. Although the temperature had dropped, the humidity remained, making it feel warmer than the thermostat indicated.

"Come back inside, Grace," Jed told her. "You'd make a perfect target standing out there on the porch with the bedroom light silhouetting your body."

She whirled around and stared at him. "You think someone could be on the grounds with a rifle right now, that I'm a target?" She came back inside and closed the doors.

"I doubt there's anyone on the grounds, but an expert marksman with a high-powered rifle could be outside Belle Foret and still hit a target here at the house."

"I see. I suppose I didn't realize how easy it would be for a professional to kill me." A chill of fear shuddered through her.

"Booth Fortier has sent you a warning," Jed told her. "He'll send one or two more before he attempts to kill you. At least that's his usual MO. Two or three warnings, then go in for the kill."

"I hate to even think about that type of life, a criminal's life, where killing comes so easily and revenge is counted in dead bodies."

"Then don't think about it. Not tonight." Jed glanced around the room, his gaze lingering over the huge armoire that housed her bedroom entertainment center. "We could watch TV, maybe find a movie. Or listen to music. Or play cards. It's your call. What do you want to do to pass away the time?"

What did she want to do? She wanted to lie down in her bed...with Jed. She wanted to lie in his arms all night and know she was safe. But she could hardly ask him for that. After all, he was a man, not some sort of robot. He had feelings, desires. *And so do you, Grace,* she told herself.

"Music," she said, then crossed the room, opened the entertainment center and punched the buttons on her CD player. A light, bluesy tune filled her bedroom suite. She closed her eyes, allowing the instrumental rendition of a cool jazz standard to caress her senses. She hummed softly along with the music and began to sway with the rhythm. "I haven't danced in years." Lifting her head, she focused her gaze on Jed, then held out her hand to him. "Will you dance with me, Jed Tyree?"

"It's been a while since I danced the night away," he told her as he came forward, a lazy, sexy grin lifting the corners of his mouth. "But I can't think of a better way to kill some time."

His arms went around her with gentle ease, his movements non-threatening and not sexual in nature. He kept several inches between their bodies as he took charge of their first dance. Surprisingly he was a good dancer. Some big men seemed to have two left feet. But not Jed. He moved her about the room in a slow, sweet flow. She felt light and free. But the comfort of being close wasn't there; and a part of her desperately needed that closeness.

The first tune ended and another began. A silky clarinet mourned as the brush of drums accented the song's melancholy. Inadvertently Grace leaned toward Jed, her body seeking contact with his. As if sensing her need, he pulled her closer, just close enough for their bodies to touch. But not close enough. Grace made the move on her own when she laid her head on his shoulder and pressed herself against him. She felt a slight pause…a hesitation…but he kept moving to the music. After several minutes, he leaned down and pressed his cheek against her temple.

"You're very good at this," she told him.

"At dancing?"

She sighed. "Yes, at dancing. And at giving comfort."

"Grace…" He spoke her name as if it were a prelude to a comment, but he didn't continue.

"Do you know what I want?"

"What?" His hand at her waist glided downward and splayed across the base of her spine.

"I want to stop thinking." She snuggled against him. "I want to forget about those damn photographs and I want to stop thinking about Daddy and Dean and…"

Jed slowed, released her hand and cupped her chin, urging her to look up at him. The minute she did, he lowered his head and planted a light, elusive kiss on her mouth. Her lips parted on an indrawn breath as tingles of awareness shot through her nerve endings. It had been such a long time since she'd felt sexual excitement, since she'd felt anything except pain and grief and loneliness. Even on the best of days, she existed, never actually lived.

"I want to stop thinking," she repeated. "All I want to do is feel alive. Alive with good feelings and not bad. For just a little while. Is that too much to ask?"

Standing there in the middle of her bedroom suite, soft music playing in the background, Jed gazed longingly into her eyes. "I've never become personally involved with a client. And it's probably not a good idea for us…for me…to…" He ran the back of his hand over her cheek. "But I can help you stop thinking. I can help you feel alive." His big hands cupped her face. "Is that what you want? Be very sure, Grace."

She knew what he was asking her. Was it what she wanted? If she said yes, he wouldn't stop with comfort, with tender loving care. He would expect more. "Yes, it's what I want." *It's what I need!*

Her permission sent him into action. He forked his fingers through her hair and gripped the back of her head, then took her mouth in a ravenous yet remarkably tender kiss. Every muscle, every nerve…the very essence of her being reacted, loving the way he made her feel. When he deepened the kiss, she whimpered and her lips parted to allow him entrance. Her body arched and stretched, lifting up to meet his kiss, giving itself over to the passion. Jed cupped one hip, then rubbed his hand over her buttocks. He pushed her closer so that she felt his obvious arousal.

Her nipples hardened, her femininity moistened. It had been years since she'd felt anything like this. And if she were honest with herself, she'd have to admit that no other

man's kiss had ever aroused her so intensely or so quickly.
Not even Dean's and she had loved Dean dearly.

Desire swept over her like a tidal wave, obliterating everything but pure physical hunger. Her body clenched and
unclenched; a sexual ache pulsed between her legs. She
wanted…oh, how she wanted…

Jed eased his tongue from her mouth and slid his lips
away from hers. Before she could tell him not to stop kissing
her, his tongue drew a spiraling line from her chin to her
throat. He pushed aside the collar of her pajama top then
licked and mouthed her collarbone. Grace clung to him,
aware that tonight this man was her lifeline; and for a few
brief hours he would be her lover.

Easily, gradually, Jed began touching her. A caress on
her shoulder, down her arm. His hands petting her hips and
buttocks. Gentle. Non-threatening. And yet so very sensual.

He took her hand in his and began a slow, leisurely dance,
keeping their bodies pressed intimately together. Odd,
Grace's dazed mind thought, very odd that he should start
dancing again instead of taking her straight to bed. When
his hand slipped between them to fondle first one breast and
then the other, she accepted his touch with pleasure. Working quickly, he undid all the pearl buttons on her silk top,
then tugged it free from her pajama bottoms and guided it
down her shoulders, down her arms and off. The garment
dropped to the floor in one swift, fluid move.

He lifted her hand and laid it on his chest. "Your turn."

Her turn? Oh, yes, of course, he expected her to remove
his shirt now. When she tried to undo the first button, her
hands were shaking so badly that she couldn't. Jed grasped
her hands and held them between their bodies.

"Here, Blondie, let me help you."

He unbuttoned his shirt, then took her hands and placed
them on his naked chest. She spread her palms out over his
chest, loving the firm, masculine feel of his pectoral muscles
and the thick curling hair that formed a *T* shape from nipples
to down inside his jeans.

He danced her across the room, then turned the dimmer switch that lowered the lighting to a romantic glow. He stroked her naked back, first with the entire palm of his hand and then with his fingertips. Her skin tingled. Her body begged for more. When he reached out and cupped her breasts in his big hands, she tensed for a moment, a hint of uncertainty making her question her sanity.

She'd been sane and sensible for over three years now. Always in control, never indulging in lengthy bouts of self-pity. But the depth of her despair lay just below that cool, aloof surface she presented to the world. Inside she was still grieving, still tormented by what had been and could never be again. And once she'd learned the truth about the night her husband and father had been killed, all the pain and anguish she'd pushed deep down inside had come rushing to the surface.

Let Jed help you forget. Just for tonight. Don't be sane and sensible. Don't be the woman of steel.

She closed her eyes and sighed as he gently massaged her flesh. His thumbs skimmed across her nipples. He lowered his head and flicked his tongue over the puckered tip; she sucked in a deep breath as sensation radiated from her breasts to the core of her body. He took turns, giving each breast equal attention. And just when Grace thought she couldn't bear another second of his arousing fondling, he lifted his head, clutched her hips and brought her up against him, her breasts to his chest. Then he rubbed their bodies together intimately and began dancing again.

Was he trying to drive her mad? she wondered. He was seducing her with every touch. Didn't he realize she wanted him now? He didn't have to continue the seduction.

"Jed?" She tilted her head just enough so she could see his face. He was so handsome, in a very rugged way.

He gazed down at her, desire bright in his hazel eyes. "Yes, Grace?"

How did she tell him that she wanted him to make love to her now? Show him. That's the best way. She inched one hand between them and struggled to unbuckle his belt. Failing at that, she glided the palm of her hand over his erection which strained against the zipper of his jeans.

He reached between them and grasped her hand. "Not yet."

"But—"

He brought her hand to his mouth, turned it palm up and licked a circle in the center with the tip of his tongue. Grace shivered.

"I'm not going to rush...we have all night," he told her. *All night?*

He paused, unbuckled his belt and removed it, then said, "That should make it easier for you."

She responded with action, not words, and undid his zipper. He shimmed his hips as she pulled his jeans down his legs. When they hung on his boots, he dragged her across the room, then sat on the edge of her bed and held up one foot. She stared at his boot, then took hold of it, yanked it off, and followed up with the other. Jed kicked off his socks and removed his jeans. When he stood, he wore nothing but a pair of low-riding navy blue briefs. Grace stared at him, her gaze focused on his bulging sex pulsating beneath the scrap of material.

Jed quickly removed her pajama bottoms. Now, she thought, now he's going to make love to me. But she was wrong. He pulled her into his arms and began dancing again. His hairy legs rubbed against her smoother legs, the friction unbearably erotic. Her aching breasts flattened against his hard chest. Without any barriers separating their sexes, they practically made love as they danced.

Grace didn't know how much more of this she could endure. She was already wild for him, wanting him more than she could remember ever wanting a man. Such overwhelming passion was new to her, this raging hunger so powerful it frightened her. And for a man who was little more than a stranger to her. How was it possible?

He knew he was prolonging her agony, was doing it on

purpose. She could tell by the way he watched her, the way he studied her. He was waiting until she was begging him for it.

Jed nuzzled her ear, then whispered, "I want you hotter than you've ever been. I want you hurting so bad for release that you'll do anything for it." He slipped his hand between her thighs and fondled her mound.

She gasped for air. "Can't you tell I'm already at that point."

He eased his fingers between her feminine lips and rubbed back and forth, touching just the right spot. She undulated against his fingers.

"Tell me," Jed said. "Tell me what you want."

"I…I want you to take me. Now. Please…please…"

He inserted his finger inside her. Moisture gushed around his hand. "You're wet…and hot. Very hot."

She grabbed his forearms and tried to pull him with her toward her bed. "Now, Jed."

He scooped her up in his arms, carried her across the room and laid her on her bed, then gently spread her legs apart. She held her breath, crazy with anticipation.

And then he did the unexpected. He kissed the inside of each thigh. Suddenly she realized his intent. *Yes, yes, yes,* her body screamed. *Do it. Give me relief.*

His mouth came down over her as he held her legs apart. He kissed, then sucked, then licked, his tongue working magic. She thrust her hips forward, exposing herself completely as he continued putting pressure on her most sensitive spot. When she complied without reservation, spearing her fingers through his hair to hold his head in place, he reached up to her breasts. The moment he pinched her nipples, she moaned. She was on the verge, so very close. Tension wound tighter and tighter inside her. And then with one final stroke of his talented tongue, Jed sent her over the edge, into complete and utter fulfillment. Her climax splintered her into a million shards of pure pleasure.

Before she could cry out, he came up and over her and

covered her mouth with his. It was several minutes later that she realized he still wore his briefs. She tugged on them as she spread kisses all over his face. He grabbed and stilled her hand.

"I don't have any condoms," he told her.

"Oh, Jed…no…"

"I never anticipated this happening between us."

"No, I don't suppose you did." She knew what she wanted to do, what she intended to do if he'd let her. "Let me do for you what you did for me."

He shook his head. "You don't have to."

"I want to."

"Are you sure?"

"Very sure," she told him.

He removed his briefs, tossed them on the floor, then scooted into the middle of her bed. "I'm all yours, Blondie."

She positioned herself between his legs and studied his impressive sex. Renewed arousal rippled through her at the thought of touching him, tasting him, giving him release. First she stroked him with her fingertips, then she lowered her head and licked him as if he were a lollipop. He groaned. She opened her mouth and surrounded him, taking him as deep as she could. He groaned again. Harder. Louder. And when she used her tongue to add just a bit of pressure, he gripped the back of her neck and urged her into action.

Within minutes he came apart, release hitting him hard. The salty, musky taste assailed her senses as she removed her mouth and licked her lips. He grabbed her and hauled her up to his side, then kissed her with lingering passion, each tasting the other on their lips.

"Thank you," he said quietly.

"No, thank you," she replied. "I needed sex. I needed sex with you."

"Did I help you stop thinking?"

Yes, he had stopped her from thinking, but he'd made

her feel far more than she'd intended. Of course she couldn't admit that to him. "I didn't think about anything, not the past, not my present problems...nothing. I simply felt alive for the first time in years."

Jed glanced around the room. "Want me to stay all night or should I dress and go back to my room?"

She hesitated before replying. "Stay. Please."

"All right." He ran his hand down her neck and across her shoulder. "How about a shower together before we hit the sack?"

"I'd prefer a bubble bath," she told him. "Are you interested?"

"Yeah, Blondie, I'm interested. Very interested."

"I'll scrub your back and you can scrub mine."

He jumped out of bed, grabbed her arm and pulled her to her feet. "What are we waiting for?"

She laughed. Amazing, she realized, she was laughing, having fun...with a man. And not just any man...with Jed, who had pleasured her and whom she had pleasured in return.

Oh, dear God, please, she thought suddenly, *don't let me care too much for him. Don't let me fall in love.*

Chapter 12

Jed had gotten out of bed over thirty minutes ago, slipped
on his jeans and gathered up his clothes and boots; then he
sat in a chair across the room and watched Grace while she
slept. The beauty and elegance of her bedroom paled in
comparison to the naked woman. The covers rested midway
down, just enough to reveal her naked shoulder blades. With
her back to him, she continued sleeping. During the night
he had become acquainted with every inch of her body. He
remembered the location of every mole, every freckle and
the faint scars left from the car wreck that had almost killed
her. He had caressed and kissed and licked those long, luscious legs and those slender arms. Every touch had elicited
a reaction from her and prompted her to reciprocate, giving
as well as taking. He had wanted to make love to her in
every sense of the word, but he wasn't in the habit of keeping condoms in his wallet while he was on assignments like
this one, where bodyguard duties were required. He planned
to rectify that today. If he couldn't find a way to pick up
some himself, he would—albeit reluctantly—ask Dom or

Rafe to do it for him. The next time Grace invited him into her bed, he would be prepared.

How do you know there will be a next time? he asked himself. Grace had needed sex last night. She'd been hurting in a bad way. She hadn't been with anyone in nearly four years. She was sated now, brought to climax half a dozen times during the night. So maybe that's all she needed, all she'd want. God, he hoped not, because he wanted more. He wanted her again right this minute. Despite how good it had been between them, nothing would fully satisfy him until he'd buried himself deep inside her. And there had been a couple of times when Grace had been so consumed with passion that he could have taken her completely and she wouldn't have protested. It hadn't been easy for him to hold back when what he'd wanted more than anything was to delve hard and deep inside her.

What was it about this woman, Jed wondered, that made her so special? He'd known his fair share of women over the years, had even thought himself in love a few times, but no other woman had ever affected him the way Grace did. Except for the fact that she was exceptionally beautiful, she really wasn't his type. Not that he didn't like the cool and sophisticated Hitchcock blonde type. Who wouldn't? But his tastes usually ran more to earthy women. Wild, big-breasted redheads. Raunchy, fun-loving brunettes.

His first love had been Charmaine Vaden, a voluptuous seventeen-year-old redhead, and the little sister of his best buddy, Jaron. He and Charmaine had been young lovers, hormone-driven and experimenting with sex and with life. Over the years he'd wondered what happened to Charmaine and wished her well. Then about ten years ago, he'd found out that she had married his uncle Booth. God help her!

Jed's most recent serious relationship had been with a fiery Hispanic lawyer. They'd come damn near close to making a commitment. That had been nearly five years ago. Since their breakup Marta had married a colleague of hers and they were expecting their first child.

Sex was an essential part of Jed's life; and even love wasn't new to him. But he'd never fallen so hard, so fast, and for a lady who was all wrong for him. Grace was a blueblood through and through; he was a mongrel with a scandalous heritage. She was definitely class; he definitely wasn't. He liked fast cars, fast women, football and beer. She was the chauffeur-driven type, the marrying kind, and he'd bet his last dime she preferred the opera to sports and a glass of Moet's Dom Perignon to a bottle of Budweiser.

So knowing all this, why was it that after just one night together, he already realized he couldn't get enough of her. One night wasn't enough—a dozen wouldn't be enough. God, he was hooked, seduced by her beauty, her strengths and weaknesses, her intelligence, her vulnerabilities. He wanted to ravish her and protect her at the same time. And the thought of another man ever touching her made him feel violent. Sometime between last evening and this morning, he had taken possession of Grace Beaumont. As illogical as it sounded, even to him, Grace belonged to him now.

Hell, he'd lost his mind. What made him think he had a right to lay claim to this woman? They'd had sex. Nothing more.

Grace turned over onto her back and sighed. Her eyelids fluttered. Jed scooted to the edge of the chair. Should he get up and leave before she woke or should he stay?

"Jed?" she called his name just as she opened her eyes.

"Yeah, Blondie, I'm here."

She rose up in bed and looked around the room to find him. When the sheet slipped below her breasts, she gripped the edge and lifted it high enough to cover her. "Good morning."

"Good morning yourself." Why the hell did she have to look so good at this time of day. It wasn't quite seven o'clock. They'd stayed awake half the night, tossing and tumbling in the throes of passion. Her hair was disheveled and her face void of makeup. And yet the sight of her took his breath away.

"Since last night was my first one-night-stand, perhaps you can tell me what the proper etiquette is in a case like this." Grace's gaze met his boldly, but a slight flush colored her cheeks.

"Was it just a one-night-stand?" he asked, and hated that her answer was so damn important to him.

Grace pointed to the closet. "Would you mind getting me a robe? There are several on the first rack to the right. Anything light will do."

She had neatly evaded his question and he knew better than to push her for an answer. Without saying anything, he got up, went to the closet and found a short, pale blue silk robe. When he took it to her, she looked up at him and smiled as she grabbed the garment.

"Thank you."

"You're welcome."

She slipped on the robe, careful to expose as little of her nakedness as possible, then she tossed back the covers and got out of bed. Jed picked up his boots and clothes and headed for the door.

"Don't go. Not yet." She followed him across the room.

He turned and faced her, then waited for her to continue.

"I don't know what last night was," she admitted. "I've had two lovers. I was engaged to one and married to the other. So I lack experience when it comes to…what would you call it? An interlude? An affair?"

"Why call it anything?" Jed shrugged. "If it was just a one-night-stand and if that's the way we both feel about it, then no big deal, right? I don't think there's any protocol or guidelines for how we're supposed to act the morning after."

"Are you angry?" she asked.

"Why should I be angry?"

"I don't know, but there's a sharp edge to your voice and you're acting…well, you're behaving as if I've said or done something wrong."

"Sorry." His gaze bored into hers, daring her to look

away. "But you know what? You're a first for me, too. I've never slept with a client. I've never slept with a multimillionaire or a Southern aristocrat with a pedigree she can trace back to Adam and Eve. So I'm as dumbfounded as you are by what happened between us. I can't say I didn't want it—and a lot more—but I didn't plan it, didn't expect it. I have no idea how we're supposed to act this morning or where we go from here."

She reached out and caressed his cheek. "Why don't I just say thank you very much for what you did for me? I needed you. More than you could possibly know. And you were there for me."

"Sure, that sounds good to me." If she kept looking at him with those soulful blue eyes, he was going to dump his clothes and boots on the floor and carry her back to bed. And this time, he wasn't going to care that he didn't have a condom.

"I know we can't pretend it didn't happen," Grace said. "I don't want that. But maybe we should just get on with what has to be done today and let whatever's happening between us take care of itself."

"If that's what works for you, I can handle it." He turned around, walked to the door and opened it. Before he entered the hall, he glanced over his shoulder and said, "Next time—if there is a next time—I'll be prepared."

By the expression on her face, he knew she understood his meaning. They both realized there would be a next time. Tonight. Tomorrow. The day after that. And when he took her to bed again, it would be to make love to her fully and completely.

Jaron removed the documents from the hiding place between the mattress and box springs, stuffed them into his briefcase and carried his briefcase outside to his car. He checked his watch. Seven-thirty. Except for the servants, the household was still asleep. Everyone except Ronnie, with whom he'd shared breakfast in the kitchen around six.

Booth coming home a day early complicated things, but since the boss slept late as a general rule, it should be simple enough to leave on some pretense of syndicate business before Booth awakened. During the past few years, Booth's addiction to drugs and alcohol had lengthened the hours he spent in bed. If not for the training and working precision of the team surrounding Booth, the demigod's crime empire would have already begun crumbling.

Before he left the house, Jaron knew he needed to see Charmaine. She'd sent him a message last night telling him they had to talk. He suspected she wanted to finally admit to him that she and Ronnie were lovers.

Jaron went upstairs, knocked softly on his sister's bedroom door and waited. Booth seldom stayed the night in Charmaine's room; he preferred for her to come to his, then would dismiss her when he'd finished with her. Jaron's stomach knotted. Charmaine had never confided in him, so he didn't really know the extent of Booth's brutality to her. But he had a good idea how bad it was.

The door eased opened and Charmaine, hidden behind the door, said, "Jaron?"

"Yeah, it's me. Are you alone?"

"Yes."

"Let me come in. I got your message and we do need to talk, but I've got business this morning and have to leave soon."

She backed up and turned away from him before he saw her face. Jaron came in and closed the door. When he walked up behind her and grasped her shoulders, she winced.

"Turn around," he said.

She did. And what he saw made him want to kill Booth. But it wasn't the first time that the sight of his sister's battered face had instilled murderous rage in him. God forgive him, he'd been such a coward all these years, so afraid of Booth that he'd let him get away with repeated brutish cruelty to Charmaine. But that was all about to change.

Once he had Grace Beaumont's five million dollars safely tucked away in an island bank account, he would quickly move on to Stage Two of his plans. Setting up his and Charmaine's deaths. He'd already come up with a couple of possible scenarios he thought would work.

"Dear God, look at you." He lifted his hand to her bruised cheek, but didn't touch her. He stared at her cracked, swollen lip. "I'm going to get you out of this hell. I swear I will. If you can endure it just a few more days…"

"Don't do it," Charmaine whispered. "I know you're the one and if you follow through with your plans, he will find out. And when he does, he'll kill you."

Jaron's heartbeat stilled for a millisecond. Charmaine knew he was the traitor Booth was trying to find. But how did she know anything about what had been discussed in Booth's private office last evening, unless Booth himself told her.

He grabbed her shoulders and shook her, paying little heed when she whimpered in pain. "Did Booth tell you he suspected me of betrayal?" Jaron got up in her face, talking low so no one could overhear him. "Tell me, damn it, tell me what he said."

She jerked away from Jaron and sat on the edge of her bed. One bruised leg peeked out when her robe parted slightly. "Booth didn't tell me anything," she said softly. "I have no idea what he suspects, but I know you're the one who sent the letter to Grace Beaumont and called her asking for five million dollars. You're trying to get enough money so we can escape from Booth, aren't you?"

"How do you—Ronnie! Ronnie told you about what was said in the meeting."

"It doesn't matter how I know, I just know."

"Then Booth doesn't suspect me?"

"No, but it's only a matter of time before he finds out. Whatever you're planning, don't go through with it. You'll be signing your death warrant."

"I can get it done and we can be long gone, out of the

country, before Booth figures it out. Neither of us can go on living this way. One of these days, when Booth beats the hell out of you, he's going to kill you.''

''Yes, I know.''

Jaron paced the room, guilt and regret riding heavily on his shoulders. ''This is all my fault. Everything. I got you into this living hell and I'm going to get you out. You just sit tight and wait it out. A few more days. A week at most.''

''Jaron…don't.''

He kissed her forehead. ''I've let you down over and over again, but this time I'm going to make it right. I promise.''

She smiled weakly. ''Can't I say anything to change your mind?''

''I've got to go. Wish me luck.'' He strode to the door, doing his best to appear far more confident than he actually was.

''You could go to Jed, ask for his help.''

Jaron stopped abruptly and looked back at her. ''You know about Jed, then, know he's working for Grace Beaumont.''

Charmaine nodded. ''Talk to Jed.''

''Too late for that. Now you take it easy today and think good thoughts.''

Jaron hadn't counted on Jed Tyree being Grace Beaumont's bodyguard, but he couldn't switch gears and change plans now. Jed was sure to recognize him when he showed up at the park, but maybe, for old times' sake, Jed wouldn't rat him out. Jed hated Booth, as much, if not more than he did, so he had to be wanting to get his hands on solid proof against his uncle. Why would Jed care that it cost Ms. Beaumont five mil? She'd have what she wanted—and so would Jed. Revenge. Sweet, sweet revenge.

When Jaron opened the door of Charmaine's bedroom, he nearly ran into Ronnie, who asked, ''Is Mrs. Fortier up yet?''

Jaron closed the door before Ronnie could see inside the

bedroom. "She's probably going to stay in her room all day today, so don't disturb her unless she calls for you."

"Yes, sir."

"And, Ronnie?"

"Sir?"

He wanted to ask Ronnie to take care of Charmaine if anything happened to him today. But he could hardly do that without making Ronnie suspicious.

"Nothing. Just take care of my sister the way you always do."

"Yes, sir. I intend to do just that."

Jaron made a beeline for the front door, then once outside breathed a sigh of relief. He'd make a few stops along the way just to give the appearance that the trip was on the up-and-up. But he wanted to arrive at Terrebonne Park no later than eleven-thirty, grab a bite to eat and be on the lookout for any sign of trouble.

He realized that a lot of things could go wrong, that he was taking a big risk, that Booth might find out or Jed might turn him in once he recognized him. But if he succeeded, he and Charmaine would be free. That alone was worth any risk.

The satchels containing five million dollars rested in Jed's lap. He sat in the passenger seat of Grace's Mercedes as she drove them along the road leading out of town toward Terrebonne Park. Dom and Kate followed at a discreet distance. Rafe and J.J. had arrived at the park before eleven and by now had thoroughly inspected the place. Dante Moran had been given the details of the exchange so that he could put his men in place. The Feds wanted to know the identity of the guy who had betrayed Booth and get their hands on the proof of the governor's involvement with the syndicate. But for the most part, the federal and Dundee security at Terrebonne Park wasn't set in place to capture one of Booth's underlings, but to protect Grace and retrieve any evidence that would incriminate the head of the Louisiana Mafia. The traitor could be useful to the Bureau, only if he was willing to testify against Booth.

Jed wondered if Grace truly had any idea how much danger she was in? Once this deal went down and she had the proof against Booth she needed, that wouldn't be the end of it. Not by a long shot. Even if Booth were arrested, he could and would issue orders from his jail cell—and one of his first commands would be to eliminate Grace Beaumont. But Jed had no intention of letting that happen. When he'd taken this assignment and had agreed to work with the FBI, his main objective had been to find a way to bring his uncle down. Working for Grace had simply been a means to an end. But in a few short days, a great deal had changed. He hadn't expected to get personally involved with the client, hadn't thought her welfare would matter more than anything else.

"You're awfully quiet." Grace stole a quick glance in his direction.

"I was just thinking." *Thinking about how I'm going to keep you safe, and why the hell you mean so much to me.*

"Having the other two Dundee agents at the park won't cause a problem, will it?" she asked. "I mean, what happens if he suspects we didn't come alone?"

"Take my word for it—he won't be aware that we have any type of backup. Dom and Kate are professionals. They know what they're doing."

"I'm nervous," she admitted. "We're so close to getting our hands on the evidence that Dean and Daddy paid for with their lives."

"You have every right to be nervous. We don't know who we're dealing with, and there's every likelihood that this man is dangerous. He's probably one of Booth's henchmen. And all we have is his word that he's got the documents he claims he has."

"If he doesn't have the documents, I'm not giving him the money. Right?"

"Right. Just demand to see the evidence first."

"Yes, of course."

"I'll be where I can see you at all times and if I think you're in trouble, I'll either come in after you or I'll take him out."

"You'll kill him," Grace said.

"If it's necessary to protect you."

She grasped the steering wheel so tightly that her knuckles turned white. He knew how difficult this was for her. The ugly, sordid, sinister side of life had been alien to her, but now she was getting a hefty dose of harsh reality.

"Doing the dirty work isn't easy and it's not pleasant," Jed told her. "But the fact is that in order to keep a balance between the right and wrong side of the law—between good and evil, if you want to put it in those terms—then someone has to enforce the law. Despite the fact that I have killed people in the line of duty, in the army and as a Dundee agent, I consider myself one of the good guys."

Yeah, Tyree, just how much of a good guy would she consider you if she knew Booth Fortier was your uncle? How would she feel about you if the truth ever came out about your family history? A crazy mother who died in a mental hospital and her deranged mob boss brother. He had tried numerous times to convince himself that there wasn't a hereditary mental defect in the Fortier family, that environment had played a major role in warping his uncle and in driving his mother insane.

"I know you're one of the good guys," Grace said. "You don't have to convince me of that fact. If I implied otherwise, I'm sorry."

What was wrong with him? He'd never thought it necessary to explain himself to anyone. Yeah, but Grace wasn't just anyone. She was a Dundee client who was depending on his protection, on his expertise. And she had become important to him personally in a very brief period of time. What she thought of him mattered. It mattered a whole hell of a lot more than it should.

"No matter what happens out there today, believe one

thing—I'm going to take care of you. That's my number one objective."

Grace breathed in and out on an internal sigh. "I think someone up there was watching out for me and sent you into my life right when I needed my own personal guardian angel."

Jed chuckled. "Blondie, you're the first person who's ever thought of me as an angel of any kind."

She smiled. "I suppose most women consider you a real devil, huh?"

"Now that would be kissing and telling, wouldn't it? And that's something I don't do."

"Jed?"

"Mmm-hmm?"

"Thanks."

"For what?"

"For everything."

Their conversation ended on that last comment. What could he say in response? She saw him as her guardian angel, her knight in shining armor; but that was only temporary. Once she learned the truth—the whole truth—how would she feel then? When she discovered that the Dundee agency was working with the Feds to bring down Booth Fortier and that Booth was his uncle, she wouldn't be thanking him. She wouldn't see him as a hero. The best he could hope for was that she'd try to understand…and that she wouldn't judge him.

Fifteen minutes later, Grace drove her Mercedes into Terrebonne Park, coming in on the south side, as instructed. The park had been built around a small lake, fed by an underground spring, and over the years had evolved into a picnic area, playground and a miniature amusement park. On any given day during the spring and summer months, the place was filled with people…anywhere from a couple of dozen to a couple of hundred. And on holidays, like the Fourth of July and Labor Day, the park swelled beyond capacity, sometimes recording nearly a thousand people.

As they emerged from the car, Jed noted it was a slow day, maybe twenty-five or thirty people stirring about, most of them picnicking from baskets brought from home or lunches purchased at the dairy bar. Dom and Kate pulled up and parked several slots down from them, then waited inside the car.

Grace glanced at her wristwatch; Jed took a look at his. Eleven-forty. A twenty-minute wait, if their man showed up on time. As they made their way toward the carousel, Jed surveyed the area, seeing if he could spot Dante Moran's men. He picked out a couple of guys, but wasn't a hundred percent sure about them.

"Isn't that the Dundee agent who came by the house last night?" Grace whispered as she nervously shifted the briefcase she carried from one hand to the other.

Jed followed her line of vision to where Rafe Devlin and Jenifer "J.J." Blair were frolicking about on a nearby set of swings, for all intents and purposes nothing more than a young couple having fun.

"Yeah, that's Rafe," Jed replied, keeping his voice low. "And the woman with him is an agent, too."

"That's two extra Dundee agents. The number seems to be growing, doesn't it?"

"It takes as many as it takes. Okay?"

"Okay. I trust you, Jed. If you think we need a dozen of Dundee's finest, then it's all right with me."

A pang of guilt hit him square in the gut. She trusted him. And just by being who he was, he was betraying her trust. Nothing could ever change the fact that he was Booth Fortier's nephew, that they shared a gene pool and an ancestry of cutthroats and criminals. His pedigree—or lack of one—had never mattered to him or to any of the women in his life. But it would matter to Grace. She might be able to deal with him being a mongrel, but she'd never be able to accept the fact that his mother had been a Fortier.

"Do I wait until noon to get on the carousel?" she asked.

"Yeah. No need putting yourself on display until the very

last minute." He nodded to the dairy bar. "How about something to drink? A cola? Iced tea?"

"Come to think of it, my mouth is as dry as cotton. Besides, I suppose getting something to drink will kill some time, won't it? I need something to do while we wait. I'm so nervous." Jittery laughter bubbled from her lips. "I said that already, didn't I?"

"Take a few deep breaths," he said. She did. "Now, let's see what's on the drink menu."

They bought iced tea, sat together at one of the concrete picnic tables and waited. The minutes seemed like hours, each one longer than the one before, until finally twelve noon arrived. Jed scanned the area around the carousel and noticed J.J. and Rafe paying their fares and hopping up on a couple of side-by-side wooden horses. They were laughing and playing around, nothing the least bit suspicious about them. In his peripheral vision he saw Dom and Kate eating ice-cream cones about twenty-five feet away. There was a guy picking up trash and another trimming hedges, both not more than thirty feet from the carousel. He pegged them for Feds, but only because he knew Moran had people here.

Jed handed Grace the other briefcase, the one he'd been carrying around. Each case contained two and a half mil. After Jed paid her fare, Grace boarded the carousel. She made her way to the swan seat, eased down and placed both briefcases in her lap, then crossed one hand over the other on top of the cases. Jed's stomach rumbled as tension knotted his muscles. Even with more than a half-dozen sets of eyes trained on Grace, anything could happen. She understood that if he called her name, she was to take a nosedive under the swan seat. He just hoped to high heaven that this whole thing wasn't some sort of setup. But his gut instincts told him it wasn't, that someone wanted out of the organization and needed cash fast. And whoever this guy was, he was willing to risk Booth's wrath.

Noon came and went. Five after. They waited. Ten after. Still no sign of anyone approaching Grace. She paid the fare

again, as did several other people, including Rafe and J.J.
He could tell that with each passing minute, Grace grew
more nervous. Who could blame her? She'd been holding
up remarkably well. So far. By twelve-thirty, Jed was beginning to doubt the guy would show. But they'd wait until
one, the time he and Grace had agreed on before coming
here today. They'd wait one hour, that was all.

At twelve-forty-five, a car backfired. Grace cried out and
inadvertently knocked one of the suitcases to the wooden
floor of the old carousel. Four Dundee agents and two FBI
agents came to full alert, but no one made a move. A tall,
blond man jumped down off the wooden horse in front of
Grace and knelt to retrieve the case. Jed watched carefully,
wondering if this could be their man. But the guy, not much
out of his teens, placed the case back in Grace's lap and
flirted outrageously with her, then when he saw he wasn't
making any headway, he walked around to where a teenage
girl sat alone on a brightly painted wooden horse. He got
up on the horse beside her and started talking.

Jed let out a relieved sigh. What was going on? Where
was their man? If he didn't show, that meant something had
gone wrong. Had Booth found out he had a traitor in his
organization? Or had the man simply chickened out at the
last minute? Maybe he hadn't been able to get his hands on
the documents. Anything was possible.

At one o'clock, Jed motioned to Grace and she nodded,
then when the carousel finished that round, she got off, a
briefcase in each hand. Jed took one briefcase from her, put
his arm around her waist and led her toward the parking
area.

"What happened?" she asked. "Where is he?"

"If he's lucky, he's still alive and just ran into a hitch of
some kind. If that's what happened, he'll be back in touch
with us," Jed told her. "But if he's not so lucky, then he's
dead and Booth Fortier will make another move very soon."

"Another move against me," Grace said with utter certainty.

"And when he makes his move, I'll be right there with you, standing between you and whatever he sends your way."

"Oh, Jed, I couldn't bear it if anything happened to you."

He tried not to react to her revealing statement. Didn't she realize that you didn't say something like that to a man unless he meant something special to you?

"I'm your bodyguard. It's my job to be in the line of fire."

"You're more than my bodyguard and we both know it."

Chapter 13

Charmaine pushed the food around on her plate, the prime rib unappetizing. Booth preferred his meat rare and everyone was forced to eat it the way he liked it or not eat at all. As she gazed at the thinly sliced, pink beef, surrounded by bloody juice, she barely controlled the overwhelming urge to vomit. Even if she were hungry, she'd find it difficult to chew with a swollen lip and bruised jaw. No one had mentioned her bruises, not even Ronnie; but they hadn't been alone all day. Either Booth or Curt or Aric had been around since she'd ventured from her room a little after two this afternoon.

Booth and Curt were laughing about something. Charmaine hadn't been paying attention, had tuned out their conversation. A trick she'd learned years ago. Sit there, look as pretty as possible, smile occasionally and always respond instantly when Booth spoke to her. A few times during the course of the meal, she'd stolen a quick glance at Ronnie, who remained silent unless responding to Booth. She liked that about Ronnie, that he was a man of few words. The strong, silent type. She loved Ronnie with all her heart, but she wasn't sure how much she could trust him. If it came down to the nitty-gritty, would he remain faithful to Booth? She wanted to tell Ronnie about her fears for Jaron, but what if Ronnie went to Booth?

Her brother had left the house early this morning and hadn't returned. She knew where he'd gone and what he'd intended doing. If he'd been successful, if his scheme had worked, why wasn't he home now? Her imagination had gone wild, producing several vividly gruesome scenarios. What if at the exchange site, the police had been waiting? Jaron could be in jail right now. If he was, did Booth know? And on the other hand, what if Booth had suspected Jaron? If that was the case, then Jaron was dead.

Charmaine barely managed to stifle a frightened whimper. Fear for Jaron's life, fear for her own consumed her thoughts. If Booth had ordered Jaron killed, then it was only a matter of time before he'd come to the conclusion that she had been involved in Jaron's plot. And then he would kill her, too—or worse. She knew only too well what he was capable of, knew what he'd done to his own sister.

Oh, God, Jaron, I begged you not to do it. You can't betray Booth and get away with it. Somehow, some way, he always knows…and he always takes revenge.

"What seems to be wrong, my dear?" Booth looked pointedly at Charmaine. "You don't look well."

"I—I'm afraid I don't feel well." Tears misted her eyes. Don't you dare cry, she told herself. Show him any weakness and he'll use it against you. "May I please be excused?"

"I'd be glad to see Mrs. Fortier to her room." Ronnie was halfway out of his chair when Booth motioned for him to sit down. He sat.

"You're excused." Booth's black gaze studied her, as if waiting for her to make a misstep where he could pounce on any small error. "You can make it to your room alone, can't you? There's no need to ruin Ronnie's meal just because you aren't feeling sociable this evening."

"I'll be quite all right alone." She laid her linen napkin on the table, shoved back her chair and stood. Although she was sore from Booth's brutal beating the night before and every movement was painful, she pretended otherwise.

When she reached the doorway leading from the dining room into the hall, she looked back at Booth and said, "When Jaron comes in, please, ask him to stop by my room and say good-night."

Booth cut a huge hunk of meat and stuffed it into his mouth. Bloody juice dripped down on either side. He dabbed his chin with his napkin, then chewed slowly. After he swallowed, he looked at her and grinned. Her heart sank.

"Oh, yes, I forgot to tell you, Jaron won't be home tonight," Booth said.

Stay calm. Don't overreact, she warned herself. "Why is that?"

"I sent Charlie to join Jaron this morning. They're attending to some important business for me. I don't expect either of them back for a while."

Charmaine swallowed, trying to control her distress. It was all she could do not to look at Ronnie, not to scream aloud that Booth had probably sent Charlie to kill Jaron.

Without another word, she turned and walked away. She almost made it to her bedroom before the tears overcame her. The minute she got behind closed doors, she threw herself across the bed and muffled her cries in a pillow.

She knew in her heart that Jaron was dead. It was only a matter of time before his body would show up somewhere and Booth would lay the blame on someone else.

Rafe wasn't in the habit of sticking his nose into other people's affairs, but he knew what it was like to be a kid in trouble, going down the wrong path, headed straight for a life of crime. Anybody who knew him would tell you that Rafe Devlin was a bad-ass, a guy who didn't take any guff from anybody, a man who minded his own business and expected others to do the same. But a few of his friends were aware of another side to Rafe and even suspected his one weakness. His Achilles' heel was kids in trouble. Looking back now, he realized that if Detective Roy Dutton of the Knoxville PD hadn't interceded in his life when he was eighteen, he'd probably be in the pen by now. Either that or dead.

Before hunting down Troy Leone in the apartment he shared with his twenty-six-year-old waitress girlfriend, Rafe had put in a call to Sawyer McNamara to okay it with him. After all, Rafe was on an assignment and Dundee's wouldn't look kindly on him doing anything that screwed up his undercover work in St. Camille. And the Feds would hang him out to dry if he messed up their well-laid plans.

He wasn't sure why he felt compelled to have a talk with a boy he didn't even know. Hell, admit it, man, he told himself. It's because of the sister. Elsa Leone. And it really had nothing to do with the fact that he was attracted to the woman. After all, he'd probably never see her again. But knowing she had practically risked her life just to talk to her little brother, to try to persuade him his new high-paying job was a first-class ticket to the world of organized crime, reminded him of Sandy. His big sister had done her level best to help him, but all he'd given her was grief. God, what he'd give to be able to do that relationship all over again. But he'd never have the chance. He'd lost his only sibling just as he'd begun turning his life around.

Rafe parked two blocks away and strode through the run-down neighborhood on the east end of town. The citizenry was a mixture of black, white and Hispanic. 1212 East 7th Street was a two-story house, probably at least seventy-five years old, with peeling white paint on the exterior and a few cracked windows. From the row of mailboxes near the front entrance, Rafe surmised there were six apartments. Damn small apartments would be his guess just from looking at the building. The minute he entered the foyer, he smelled cabbage cooking, a none-too-pleasant odor. He checked the numbers on the three downstairs apartment doors. 1212-E was, as he'd figured, upstairs. As he made his way up the rickety, scuffed staircase, he heard the loud shouts of a couple fighting in one of the downstairs apartments.

1212-E was on the left. Rafe raised his hand and knocked loudly several times. A long-haired, barefoot boy in tattered jeans and no shirt came to the door.

"Yeah, what do you want?" The kid glowered at Rafe.

"Troy Leone?"

Giving Rafe his I'm-a-tough-guy glare, Troy said, "Who wants to know?"

There was only one language a cocky, smart-mouthed kid like this knew. Rafe punched Troy in the middle of his chest, pushing him backward as Rafe moved into the apartment and, using his foot, slammed the door shut behind him.

"Hey, man, what's this all about?" Troy took a defensive stance. One hand slid into the pocket of his jeans.

"If you've got a knife, let it stay in your pocket," Rafe advised. He whipped the Beretta 8000 Cougar from its resting place beneath his belt, shoved Troy up against the wall and rammed the nose of the pistol under the boy's chin. "You've got a nosy sister, Leone. The boss doesn't like nosy women. She's gonna cause you trouble."

"I'm not responsible for my sister. I've told her to stay out of my life, but she's been like a mama to me, so she won't leave me alone."

"There's no place for mama's boys in our organization."

"I ain't no mama's boy."

"You willing to prove it?" Rafe eased the gun away from Troy's face, but kept it in his hand.

Troy puffed out his skinny chest. "Yeah, I'm willing. Aren't I a good worker? Just ask Mr. Poarch."

"Mr. Poarch isn't involved in this. I'm bringing you word from Booth Fortier himself."

Troy's eyes widened in shock, and if Rafe interpreted his

expression correctly, a healthy dose of fear. "*The* Booth Fortier."

"That's right. Mr. Poarch didn't tell you who his boss was, did he?"

"Hey, look, my sister isn't involved in any of this. I don't want Mr. Fortier to go after her or nothing. Okay?"

There might be hope for this kid, Rafe figured. He was scared at the thought of working for Fortier and he still cared about his sister.

"Mr. Fortier has a little job for you to do. If you're interested, it'll mean some extra cash," Rafe said. "But if it's not your thing, then we need to know now so we can terminate your employment."

"What—what sort of job?"

"Have you ever killed anybody?"

Troy Leone turned chalk-white. "Nah." He shook his head.

Rafe figured the kid was shaking like a leaf inside.

"If you're interested in being part of the organization, you've got to be capable of following any order you're given. Now's the time for us—" Rafe pointed his Beretta at Troy "—and you to decide if you're in or out."

"And if I'm out?"

"As long as you keep your mouth shut, then we're square. You go your way and don't look back." Rafe gave him a few minutes to consider his only two options. "Well, kid, what's it gonna be?"

"I—I'm not sure I could kill somebody."

"Okay." Rafe put away his gun, then reached into his jacket pocket and pulled out an envelope that held five hundred dollars in crisp, straight-from-the-bank, hundred-dollar bills. This wasn't the first time he'd used his own money to help out a kid in trouble. "Consider this severance pay. And don't show up at the warehouse ever again."

"And that's it? You'll leave my sister alone? And you won't come after me?"

"That's it. Keep your nose clean, kid." Rafe saluted

Troy, then left him standing there with his mouth gaping open and a stunned look on his face.

Rafe's con wouldn't have worked with a tougher, meaner kid. Making a boy decide immediately whether he was willing to kill, willing to become a murderer, separated the redeemable from the hopeless. Once a boy had no qualms about murder, he was usually lost forever. Rafe was glad that Troy still had a conscience, not only for Troy's sake, but for Elsa Leone's sake.

Getting anything accomplished at the office this afternoon had been impossible. Every time Grace had heard a phone ring, she'd tensed. Why hadn't *he* called back? She knew what Jed thought—that the man had been found out and silenced. After all, if he was still alive, why hadn't he shown up at the designated time and place? After hours of waiting, trying desperately to hold on to the least bit of hope that the opportunity to get her hands on documented proof against Booth Fortier wasn't lost to her forever, she'd finally given up and let Jed drive her home.

They had eaten a late supper of tossed salads and cold cuts, but she hadn't had much appetite. The adrenaline rush she'd experienced at Terrebonne Park had depleted her energy and left her stomach tied in knots. After nibbling at her food, and assuring Laverna that everything was delicious, all she'd wanted to do was take a long soak in her bathtub and go to sleep.

Jed had hovered over her, as if he thought she was so fragile that the day's disappointment might shatter her. He had offered her his strength, but she'd turned him away. She didn't dare chance a repeat of last night's intimacy. Not that the idea of making love with Jed didn't appeal to her—it did. But she'd never been a woman for casual affairs, for going-nowhere relationships. Until Jed, she'd never had sex without being in love, and something told her that, given half a chance, she'd fall head over heels for her big, rugged bodyguard.

Jed Tyree wasn't her type, of course. He was a little too rough around the edges. Marty Austin had been a sweet man, gentle and easygoing. Although not worldly-wise, he'd been schooled in good manners and was, to his very core, a gentleman. Dean had possessed many of her father's personality traits—strong, dependable, sophisticated, aggressive. No rough edges. And her father had adored him almost as much as she had.

What would Daddy think of Jed? she wondered. Oddly enough Grace believed her father would have liked Jed because Jed wouldn't have been the least bit intimidated by Byram Sheffield.

Jed…Jed… Why is it that if you're Mr. Wrong, being in your arms feels so right?

Grace sat at her dressing table in her large, luxurious bathroom and looked at herself in the mirror. Just thinking about Jed affected her. Her cheeks were slightly flushed. Her nipples stood at attention. And a sexual ache pulsed between her thighs. Her body would never forget being loved so thoroughly. But not as thoroughly as she and Jed had wanted.

Stop thinking about him! She snatched up the hair dryer, turned it on, tossed her long hair over her head and let the hot air style her natural waves. The only thing she should have on her mind was getting justice for Dean and her father. Her first priority—her only priority—should be proving the connection between Fortier and Miller. She couldn't allow her attraction to Jed to sidetrack her.

Once she finished with her hair, she went into her massive walk-in closet and chose a pair of pink silk pajamas, with shorts instead of pants. She slid her feet into matching slippers and tossed the matching robe over her arm. When she neared her four-poster bed, she halted and stared at the turned-down covers. Her mind revisited last night's events and the early hours of this morning…and all she could see was a mass of tangled sheets and Jed Tyree's big naked body. The sound of his voice, deep and sultry, echoed in

her ears. The erotic phrases he'd whispered to her. The sat-
isfied groans and moans that had excited her beyond all
reason.

If she wanted him, all she had to do was walk across the
hall and knock on his door. If she wanted him? Mercy!

Stop this right now, she told herself. Go to bed, go to
sleep and tomorrow you'll return to square one with the
investigation and back to a friendly business relationship
with Jed.

Grace crawled into bed, turned off the light and closed
her eyes. Images of Jed flickered through her mind. Her
eyelids popped open. Damn! She punched her pillows,
flopped over and peered through the windowpanes at the
slice of moon high in the dark sky.

She kept telling herself to go to sleep, to think about work
or about going with Joy on her next shopping spree to New
Orleans. Her body relaxed. She inhaled and exhaled several
times. See, that was easy, wasn't it? she told herself.

An hour later, Grace was not only still awake, but she
had tossed and turned so much, she'd worn herself out. She
had checked the digital lighted clock on her bedside table
every five minutes. And no matter how hard she tried, she
couldn't stop thinking about Jed Tyree.

Maybe a brandy or some sherry…or even warm milk—
yuck—might soothe her into sleep. She'd try anything.
Well, not anything, she amended. Just as she got out of bed
and reached for her robe lying on the nearby armchair, the
telephone rang. She stared at the antique-style, crystal contraption as if she'd never seen it before. Who was calling
at nearly midnight? she asked herself. Please, let it be the
man who has the Fortier/Miller documents. Let him explain
why he didn't show up at Terrebonne Park today and make
arrangements for another meeting.

On the fourth ring, Grace reached out and picked up the
receiver. By the time she had it to her ear, her bedroom
door swung open and Jed stormed in, the portable phone in
his hand. Their gazes met for one brief moment.

Gripping the phone, Grace said, "Hello."

"How are you, Mrs. Beaumont?" The voice was disguised, so she wasn't sure who he was. Was it the man who had missed their appointment today? Or was it someone else? Maybe it was the same person who'd called to tell her about the gift waiting outside the gate last night.

"Who is this?"

"I'm the gift-giver."

Grace's jaw clenched; her gaze darted to Jed. He walked over to her and put his hand on her shoulder, squeezing reassuringly.

"What do you want?" Grace asked.

"I have another present for you."

If the next present was anything like the first one, she didn't want to see it. "I don't like your kind of gifts."

A rumbling chuckle vibrated through the telephone line. "Like it or not, I've delivered another little gift and you can find it in the same spot where your other gift was left."

"You can take your gift and—" The dial tone trilled in her ear.

Grace slammed down the receiver and turned to Jed. "Whatever it is, I don't want to see it."

"Good girl." He kissed her on the tip of her nose, then when she leaned toward him, he slipped his arms around her and held her. "I'll call in a couple of Dundee agents to pick up the package. There's no need for you to even go downstairs."

She lifted her head. "I don't want to see whatever it is, but I need to know what he's left this time. You can just tell me what it is. Okay?"

He grasped her shoulders. "I'll go in my room to make the necessary calls. I want you to stay here in your room."

"I don't think I can stay up here alone. I want to go downstairs with you, but I promise I'll stay in the house and not go outside to look at whatever sick present he's sent me."

* * *

Jed phoned Dom and Kate and explained the situation, then he waited downstairs in the foyer with Grace, just as they'd done last night. What he knew that Grace didn't know was that this gift would be much worse than the first one. Escalating cruelty was Booth's trademark style. Jed had a sick feeling in the pit of his stomach. His gut instincts kept warning him about tonight's present, but he tried to shut out the all-too-real possibility.

"What's taking so long?" Grace asked.

"It's been only fifteen minutes."

Grace sighed. "This is driving me crazy."

Yeah, and seeing her like this—a bundle of nerves—was really getting to him. He didn't like this helpless feeling. Waiting. Not knowing. Certain and yet uncertain. The torment Booth was putting Grace through, the hell he'd made of her life four years ago, was another reason to hate his uncle.

"Why don't we go in the kitchen and fix you something to drink," Jed suggested. "If you've got some ice cream and cola, I'll make you a float. How does that sound?"

"It sounds like you're trying to take my mind off what's happening."

"I guess my strategy isn't working."

Grace smiled and his gut tightened. She was just a woman, like so many other women, but nothing more than her fragile smile turned him inside out.

"Has anyone ever told you that you're a good man, Jed Tyree?"

"No, ma'am. You're the first."

"I can't believe that."

Jed grinned. "Well now, a few ladies have told me that I'm good," he said jokingly. "But they were referring to certain talents that—"

"That I've been privileged to experience firsthand." Her gaze locked with his. "Those ladies were right, you know."

Jed felt as if his racing heart was going to jump out of his chest. God help him, if Grace didn't have him tied in knots. How did a man react when a woman told him that it had been a privilege to be his lover?

"Ah, Blondie, you sure know how to make a man speechless."

"That'll be the day." Her smiled widened, reaching her eyes and putting a sparkle in them.

He reached out to touch her, to skim the back of his hand over her cheek. His cell phone rang. His hand froze in midair, then he retrieved his phone from the clip-on holder and punched the On button.

"Tyree here."

"Jed, it's Dom. I'm sending Kate up to the house to stay with Ms. Beaumont. After she gets there, you'd better come on down here. I've already put a call in to the sheriff, so they should be here soon."

"Damn!"

"You already know, don't you," Dom said.

"I've got a pretty good idea."

"Fortier's gift to Ms. Beaumont weighs in at about one-seventy-five. He's got his hands and feet bound, hogtied actually, and he's got so many stab wounds in him that his body looks like a knife thrower was using him for target practice."

"I'll be on down as soon as Kate arrives."

"Yeah, you do that," Dom said. "And in the meantime, I'll get in touch with Sawyer and he can handle the Feds."

"Send Kate on up."

"Open the gate and she'll be on her way."

Jed punched the Off button and replaced his phone, then turned to Grace. "Kate Malone is coming to the house to stay with you. When she gets here, I'm going down to the gate to wait with Dom until the law arrives. He's already called the sheriff's department."

"The law?" Grace paled instantly. "It must be truly horrible if Mr. Shea has contacted the sheriff. What did Booth Fortier send me this time?"

Jed looked at her point-blank. "He sent you the body of the guy who betrayed him."

Chapter 14

Jed headed down the driveway at a fast trot, then ran the last few yards over to where Dom stood just beyond the open gates. Security lights beamed brightly on either side of the brick pillars and illuminated a good twenty-foot circle. The hogtied body waited for him, undisturbed since it had been dumped—several feet off the main road and directly in front of the entrance to Belle Foret. When Jed approached, Dom moved away from where he'd been standing near his rental car.

"I looked him over, but didn't touch anything," Dom said. "I'd say this guy was tortured for hours before he finally died. He's a bloody mess. But there's something odd."

"What would that be?"

"He's covered with stab wounds, but there's not even a bruise on his face." Dom snorted. "It's as if whoever ordered the killing wanted to make sure this guy was recognized without any problem."

Jed glanced at the lump of human flesh, neatly tied with

rope—like a gruesome gift. "It's a fresh kill. There's no rotting odor, only the smell of recent death. And some of the blood on his wounds looks like it hasn't dried out. Hell, he could have been finished off right here."

Jed moved closer. The body lay on its side, so the man's back was to him. Black hair, cut short. Jed circled the body, then bent down on his haunches and took a closer look. He felt as if he'd been poleaxed. He shot to his feet instantly.

Jaron! Jaron Vaden. Older. A mask of torment on his face. But there was no mistaking those dark Creole looks.

Why, damn it, man, why? What the hell were you thinking trying to double-cross Booth? You were probably his right-hand man. What would possess you to do something so stupid?

"What's the matter?" Dom asked. "You've got an odd look on your face."

Jed walked a few feet away from the dead man and kicked the fence so hard a sharp pain shot through his foot. A string of curses burst from his mouth as he curled his hands into fists.

"Hey, what's going on?" Dom took several steps toward Jed. "You know this guy?"

A shot of salty bile zipped up Jed's esophagus. It had been years since the sight of a dead body had caused him to puke. But then, it wasn't every day a man got a look at the end results of an old friend's life. There had been a time, back in their teens, when Jaron had been his best buddy. God, but they'd shared some good times.

"I knew him," Jed admitted. "He's Jaron Vaden. One of Booth Fortier's personal entourage. And Booth's wife's brother."

"He ordered his own brother-in-law killed?"

Jed snorted, then chuckled. "Yeah, it isn't the first time he's murdered a brother-in-law. When Booth sets out for revenge, no one is safe." Hadn't Booth killed Jed's own father? Why did it surprise him in the least that he'd have no qualms about killing Jaron?

"Look, if you'd rather not be here, I can handle things with the sheriff. You can go on back up to the house and—"

"I'll stay. I want to see the sheriff's reaction or the deputy's, whoever the hell shows up. I should be able to tell just by the way they handle things if Booth's got the law around here in his hip pocket."

"You think he's got somebody on his payroll?"

"Maybe. But it could be someone in the St. Camille police department, since the Garland Industries warehouse is in the city limits," Jed said. "No way to know for sure."

"So, you think Fortier ordered his goons to leave the guy's face untouched so that you'd recognize him? If that's the case, then it means your uncle knows you're back in Louisiana and that you're working for Grace Beaumont."

"Yeah, it looks that way, doesn't it?"

The distant sound of a siren told them the law wasn't far away. Jed wished there was some way to protect Grace from being questioned, but since she was directly involved, that wouldn't be possible. He could shield her from only so much, despite his desire to save her from more pain.

"So, how dumb do we play?" Dom asked. "Just how much information do we share with the sheriff?"

"Almost everything. No reason not to. After all, it's obvious that Booth knows almost everything."

"You still think someone close to Ms. Beaumont is feeding Booth info?"

Jed nodded. "I've pretty much ruled out the Rowleys and I don't think Joy Loring is bright enough. Besides, she has no motive. My gut instinct tells me that Elsa Leone would never betray Grace."

"So that leaves the uncle and the rejected suitor."

"The report Sawyer sent on both of them didn't give me a clue." Jed had hoped a red flag would pop up in either Willis Sullivan's or Hudson Prentice's life, but that wasn't the case. "Uncle Willis is a solid citizen. He's respected and admired by all who know him. And Prentice is a golden boy, with an almost genius IQ. The guy's never gotten so much as a speeding ticket.''

"They both sound too good to be true, if you ask me.''

Before Jed had a chance to respond, two patrol cars pulled up in front of the open gate. Three men emerged from the vehicle. One, older, dressed in civilian attire, issued orders, then walked over to Jed and Dom.

"I'm Sheriff Adams. Want to tell me what happened here?''

"Are you sure I can't get you anything, Miss Grace?'' Laverna asked for the fourth time in the past thirty minutes.

"Nothing, but thank you.'' Grace peered through the window in the front parlor, wondering how long it would take Jed and Dom Shea to finish up with the sheriff's department. "Why don't you and Nolan go on back to bed. There's really nothing you can do for me.''

Kate Malone cleared her throat. Grace looked at her questioningly.

"They might want to stay up a bit longer,'' Kate suggested. "My guess is the sheriff or one of his deputies will come on up to the house and ask all of us some questions.''

"Oh, my!'' Gasping, Laverna clutched the neck of her cotton housecoat.

"Don't fret,'' Nolan told her. "We don't know anything and we'll tell them so.''

"Perhaps I should put on some coffee.'' Muttering to herself, Laverna meandered out of the parlor and down the hall.

"If you don't need me, Miss Grace, I'll go with Laverna. This whole murder thing, right at our doorstep…well, almost at our doorstep…has rattled her something awful.''

Grace patted Nolan's shoulder. "You go on with Laverna. I'm all right. And after she fixes coffee, go to your quarters. If the sheriff needs to speak with y'all, I'll come get you.''

"Yes, ma'am.''

Once the elderly couple was out of earshot, Kate said, "They seem to be very devoted to you."

"They've been with our family for over three decades. They were here at Belle Foret before I was born." When she moved, Grace swayed slightly, her equilibrium momentarily unbalanced. Stress, she thought. The calm, orderly world in which she'd existed for over three years now had abruptly exploded into danger and violence.

"You look a bit unsteady on your feet. Why don't you sit down? If you'd like a drink, just point me toward the liquor cabinet."

"You've been so kind." Grace glanced out the window. Again. "But I don't think I can sit. And if Sheriff Adams is going to question me, I don't want him to smell liquor on my breath."

Kate laughed. Grace gave her an inquisitive stare.

"Sorry," Kate said. "I've lived in Atlanta for so long that I've almost forgotten what it's like to live in a small town and be concerned with what everyone thinks."

Grace smiled. "One's good reputation is priceless."

"I suspect that's a direct quote from your mother or grandmother."

"My grandmother," Grace said. "My mother's mother. I barely remember her. She died shortly after my sixth birthday, but I distinctly remember her imparting little pearls of wisdom whenever she came to visit."

"With me, it was my aunt Bernice. Pretty is as pretty does was one of her favorites."

"Where did you grow up?"

"A little town called Prospect. It's in Alabama, but it's not thirty miles from the Georgia border. A lot of the Old South remains, you know. Kind of like here in St. Camille."

"Sounds like we may have some things in common," Grace said.

"We probably do, only I've never been as rich as you are, Ms. Beaumont." Kate grinned. "My husband's family had money, but after our divorce I had to return to work to make a living."

"Do you have children?" Grace asked, then when she noted the sad expression in Kate's eyes, she regretted having asked. "I'm sorry. That was a personal question and none of my business."

"It's a perfectly normal question." Kate eyed one of the twin sofas that faced each other in front of the fireplace. "Let's sit down. Okay?"

When Kate sat, Grace joined her. But the nervous tension dancing along her nerve endings made her antsy. She felt as if a thousand tiny feet were jitterbugging inside her. It was all she could do to simply sit still.

"I don't have any children," Kate said.

"Nor do I."

Kate hesitated, as if she were uncertain she should reveal anything more personal about herself. Finally she said, "You and I do have something else in common. I lost a child, too. Years ago."

Grace studied Kate Malone and surmised that the woman was near her own age of thirty. "You must have been very young."

"I married at twenty-one, gave birth to my daughter when I was twenty-two and lost her before I turned twenty-three. That was eleven years ago. I'm thirty-four now."

"My daughter was stillborn." Grace placed her hands in her lap. The pain was still there, only dulled slightly by time and by sensing Kate's true understanding—the type that only another woman who had experienced such a loss could know.

"I guess people are always telling you that you should marry again and have another child," Kate said. "I heard that for years. I still get that type of advice every once in a while, from some well-meaning acquaintance."

Grace sighed. "Ms. Malone…Kate…I was wondering…?"

"What were you wondering?"

Kate faced Grace, who saw only compassion and caring in the other woman's honey-brown eyes. She knew why this shrewd Dundee agent had begun talking to her about personal things—it was to get her mind off the fact that a man had been murdered and deposited at her front gate. Her motives didn't really matter, although they were completely kind, because Kate had, for a few brief moments, succeeded. But she'd done more than that, she'd shared a painful part of her past, which couldn't have been easy for her.

"Is the reason you've never remarried, never had another child, because you're afraid of being deeply hurt again?" Grace watched Kate closely, hoping to see the truth in her expression. She believed that she wasn't alone in her fear; that her thought process wasn't totally irrational.

"That's one of the reasons," Kate admitted. "I'd like to think that if the right man ever came along, I'd deal with the fear. To be honest, I don't know what I'd do. I'm more afraid of having another child than I am of loving another man, but…" Kate's voice trailed off. She glanced away, then cleared her throat.

"I appreciate your sharing your feelings with me. I don't suppose you meant to get so personal when you decided to try to take my mind off what's going on down at the front gate tonight. But if it makes you feel any better, your being here and our talking has helped me a great deal."

"Service with a smile." Kate turned around and offered Grace a fragile smile.

"You know, I think I'd love a drink now. Do you like cappuccino? If you do, I'll fix us some."

"I love cappuccino. My absolute favorite is the flavored kind."

"Name your poison."

"You wouldn't happen to have raspberry flavoring, would you?"

Grace grasped Kate's hand. "Vanilla, cinnamon, caramel, cherry and…raspberry."

"Ms. Beaumont, I'm your friend for life," Kate said.

"Please, call me Grace."

Twenty minutes later when Jed and Dom walked into the kitchen, with Sheriff Adams in tow, Grace and Kate were seated at the table, just finishing off their cappuccinos.

Jed didn't know what he'd expected, but it hadn't been this. Grace and Kate appeared to be best buddies, acting as if they'd known each other for years. He was surprised to find Grace so calm. When he'd left her over an hour ago, she'd been a nervous wreck.

"Sorry to bother you, Ms. Beaumont." Sheriff Adams removed his baseball cap. "Sure am sorry to hear about what's being going on. Mr. Tyree here explained things and I must say I'm mighty shocked."

Grace rose to her feet and held out her hand. "Thank you, Sheriff. I suppose we should have let you and Chief Winters know what was happening, but I thought it best to try to handle things on my own until we had some sort of evidence."

He shook hands with Grace, then said, "Yes, ma'am, I understand." Adams shuffled nervously, and once again Jed was amused by the way even the law in LaDurantaye Parish kowtowed to Grace. "But now we've got ourselves a murder, and a damn brutal one at that."

Jed cleared his throat. Adams turned beet red. "Sorry, ma'am."

"That's all right. Now, may I offer you some coffee?"

Adams's eyes rounded in surprise. "No, thank you, ma'am."

"Well, perhaps you'd like to get straight to your questions."

"Just got a couple. Mr. Tyree and Mr. Shea have filled me in on just about everything. And we already got us an ID on the dead man."

Grace paled instantly; her lips parted and her gaze flashed to Jed. "Who is...was he?"

"Booth Fortier's right-hand man," Adams replied. "Mr. Jaron Vaden himself."

"Fortier's right-hand man betrayed him?" Grace asked, a dubious tone to her voice.

"It's a nasty business." Adams scratched his head. "So, I gotta ask—did you know Mr. Vaden?"

"No," Grace replied. "I'd spoken to him…or at least I think it was him…on the phone. Twice. But I never knew his identity."

"Mmm-hmm. And you were here at your house with Mr. Tyree when somebody called to tell you there was a present waiting for you at the gate?"

"Yes."

"And you and Mr. Tyree have been in all evening?"

"Yes."

"Sorry, ma'am, but I had to ask."

"Believe me, Sheriff Adams, I wanted that man alive. Neither I nor Mr. Tyree had any reason to kill him."

"Oh, I know that, Ms. Beaumont. Like I said, I had to ask."

"Is that all, Sheriff?" Jed took a solid stand beside Grace.

"Yeah, that about covers it. For tonight. Guess there's no reason to question your staff."

"No, there isn't. The Rowleys are elderly and I assure you they know nothing."

Adams looked pointedly at Jed. "I want to be kept informed from now on."

"Certainly," Jed agreed.

"I'll see the sheriff out." Kate stood, then motioned to the kitchen door with a sweep of her hand, and Adams followed her without a backward glance.

Grace released a pent-up breath and turned to Jed. "What happens now?"

Before Jed could reply, Dom interrupted. "Kate and I will head on back to the hotel."

"Thanks," Jed said. "I'll talk to y'all in the morning about that other matter."

As soon as Dom left the kitchen, Grace asked, "What other matter?"

Should he come clean with her now? Jed wondered. Should he confess everything? At least about his personal life? "I'm going to pay a visit to Booth Fortier tomorrow and I also plan to attend Jaron Vaden's funeral."

"What?" Grace glowered at him, disbelief and a hundred questions in her blue eyes.

"If I asked you to take me on faith, to not question my motivation, would you?" When he reached for her, she sidestepped his grasp. "Yes, I'm keeping things from you. And yes, there's more to this situation than you know about, but—"

"But what? Don't ask any questions, don't expect to be fully informed by the agent and the agency I'm paying—and paying damn well—and take you on faith? Why? Because we slept together last night?"

"Damn it, Grace, can't you just trust me to take care of things, to take care of you?"

"No, I can't. I let Dean and Daddy do all my worrying and a lot of my thinking. I let them take care of things. But that was the old Grace." She tapped her index finger on her chest. "This Grace Beaumont takes care of herself."

"I'll have to get permission from my boss—" he didn't mention the FBI or Dante Moran "—before I can explain."

"Then get permission."

"I'll call him in the morning."

"Call him now."

"Now?"

"Yes," Grace said, a determined expression on her face. "Now."

Charmaine lay in bed, wide-awake. She had spent all evening wondering when Booth would come to her room, waiting for him to tell her Jaron was dead. The sadistic bastard would take great pleasure in detailing every moment of her brother's last hours on earth. Oh, Booth hadn't done the deed himself, but he had watched. Watched and enjoyed. Fresh tears sprang free; she didn't bother wiping them away. No doubt her eyes were swollen and bloodshot. Along with her bruises and cracked lip, she probably looked like hell. But what did that matter? With Jaron gone, it was only a matter of time before Booth killed her, too. He would try to beat the truth out of her, try to make her confess that she'd been involved in the plot all along.

Oh, God, what would Ronnie do? He was a strong, rugged man, but he was no match for Booth's unparalleled power. She had to find a way to protect Ronnie. She couldn't let Booth kill him, too.

As she racked her brain trying to think of some way to protect the man she loved and coming up with nothing short of killing Booth herself—a well-worn fantasy of hers—she heard a ruckus downstairs. The doorbell rang, then loud voices filled the house and the sound of footsteps, walking hurriedly, running. She crept from the bed and tiptoed to the closed door that connected her room to Booth's. She tried the knob, and when she found the door unlocked, she eased it open. Before even entering the room, she heard Booth snoring. Aric had no doubt carried him to bed after he'd passed out. Drugged to the gills. It would take a damn tornado to waken him.

Kill him now! an inner voice commanded. *You're going to die anyway,* she told herself. *Do the world a favor and get rid of Booth Fortier. It would be one way to save Ronnie.*

A weapon. She needed something more than her nail file. A knife? A gun? She stood at the foot of the bed and watched Booth. Suddenly she noticed the pillows stacked all around the head of the bed. Smother the bastard! Filled with a courage she'd never before possessed, Charmaine walked quietly toward her sleeping husband. Just as she reached out to grab a pillow, she heard someone calling her name. Nola was in her room!

Charmaine backed away from the bed, then whirled

around and fled. By the time she returned to her room, Aric had joined Nola.

"You've got to come downstairs right away, Mrs. Fortier," Nola said. "The sheriff's here and he wants to talk to you."

Charmaine's gaze linked with Aric's. "If they want to see Booth, you'd better tell Sheriff Long that Mr. Fortier is sick and on medication and can't be disturbed."

"Ronnie's handling things with the sheriff right now," Aric said. "But the sheriff's wanting to see you. He says it's about Jaron."

Yes, of course it was about Jaron. Undoubtedly his body had been found. The law had come here to tell her that her brother was dead. Strange. Everyone in this house probably already knew that Booth had ordered Jaron's execution.

"Is Charlie back yet?" Charmaine asked, amazed at her calmness.

"No, ma'am. We're not expecting him back for a while," Aric replied.

"Is Curt here?"

"Curt's at the warehouse tonight."

Charmaine nodded. "I'd appreciate it if you stayed up here to keep an eye on Booth. We can't have him waking up and making a scene in front of the sheriff." Charmaine looked directly at Aric and saw from his expression that he understood her meaning.

"Yes, ma'am, I'll see that Mr. Fortier stays put. And you let Ronnie handle things with the sheriff."

She caught an odd look in Aric's black eyes. Sympathy? Yes, that was it. Aric knew the sheriff was going to tell her Jaron was dead and Aric felt sorry for her.

"Nola, get me my robe, please." Charmaine allowed Nola to help her into her robe, then she belted it tightly, put on her house slippers and marched into the hall. She took her time, bolstering up her strength as she made her way downstairs. She found Ronnie in the living room with Sheriff Long. Both men turned to face her when she entered the room. Ronnie watched her intently and she could tell that he wanted to hold her, comfort her. The sheriff's eyes widened when he noticed her battered face. If he asked, she knew what to say. I tripped over a stool and fell into the door. Wasn't that the standard response for abused wives?

"What brings you out to our neck of the woods, Sheriff?" Charmaine asked, as if she didn't have a clue.

"I hate to be the one to deliver bad news, Mrs. Fortier, but I don't suppose bad news is anything you haven't heard before...considering..."

"Please, deliver your news and forget about preaching a sermon on the evils of crime. It's wasted here."

"Yes, ma'am, you got that right." Eugene Long removed his hat and held it at his side. "No easy way to say it, so I'll just tell you straight. Your brother, Jaron Vaden, is dead. He was knifed to death and his body dumped outside the Belle Foret estate belonging to Ms. Grace Beaumont, over in La Durantaye Parish."

The words bounced off her heart, like arrows off a shield. She had already cried, already mourned her brother. And she would again. In private. And in Ronnie's arms, if that was possible. She closed her eyes for a split second and allowed the reality of Jaron's death to sink in fully.

"Ma'am, are you all right?" the sheriff asked.

Before she could respond, Ronnie was at her side, a strong, steady hand on her shoulder. "Would you like to sit down? Or do you need a drink or—"

"I'm all right." She looked directly at the sheriff. "When may we have the body? I'll need to plan a funeral."

"Can't say for sure, but it could be a few days. Maybe a week or more. Gotta do an autopsy and all."

"You said Jaron was knifed to death...could they tell by looking at his body if he'd been tortured?"

Sheriff Long swallowed hard. His forehead dotted with perspiration. "Hell, Mrs. Fortier, what do you think?"

Ronnie grasped Charmaine's arm. "Mrs. Fortier, maybe I should call a doctor for you."

"No, that won't be necessary." Why did she suddenly feel faint?

"Any chance of me talking to Mr. Fortier tonight?" the sheriff asked.

"My husband has been ill—"

"I've already explained that Mr. Fortier is under doctor's orders to stay in bed and he's been given a sleeping pill," Ronnie said.

"Well, that's it then, folks." The sheriff plopped his hat down on his head, knowing it would be useless to pursue the matter tonight.

Ronnie lowered his head and whispered in Charmaine's ear. "Wait right here." Then he walked the lawman to the door.

Charmaine felt nothing, only a blessed numbness. Jaron was dead. She soon would be. But before she died, she intended to find a way to save Ronnie.

"He's gone," Ronnie said as he returned to the living room and closed the pocket doors in order to give them a little privacy.

She looked at him. Could he see inside her, deep inside her? Did he realize she was a soulless creature, that a part of her spirit had died tonight along with Jaron?

Ronnie pulled her into his arms and held her. "Go ahead and cry."

"What if someone comes in and sees us?"

"Just act like you've fainted and I'll pretend I'm catching you."

She lifted her hand and caressed his cheek, then brushed a kiss across his lips. "I've already cried. Can't you tell. Just look at me. I'm a mess."

"I'm getting you out of here as soon as I can," Ronnie whispered, as if he suspected the walls had ears. "Booth had Jaron killed, didn't he?"

"You didn't know—I mean before the sheriff came to-night?"

"No." He shook his head. "But you knew, didn't you?"

"Jaron was the traitor. I didn't know what he was doing, not until it was too late to stop him. I begged him not to go through with it. I told him Booth would find out."

Ronnie cradled Charmaine's face with his hands. "Play dumb, do you hear me? Tomorrow when Booth sees you, act like you're shocked about Jaron. Put on a real show. Pretend you had no idea Jaron would do such a thing."

"I don't understand...."

He squeezed her face gently. "I can't explain more. Just trust me, will you, Charmaine? I love you and I'm going to take you away from all this very soon. Do you believe me?"

She smiled. Tears misted her eyes. She'd been wrong when she thought she could no longer feel anything. Ronnie made her feel, but he couldn't give her hope, no matter how much he wanted to.

"I trust you," she told him. "I believe you."

But she didn't believe. She knew he meant what he said about taking her away from Booth, but Jaron had made her the same promise. And look where that had gotten him. She was trapped, more so than ever. With no way out.

"Promise me something, will you?" She laid her hand over his heart. "Don't risk your life for me. I want you safe, no matter what."

"Charmaine, I can't—"

She placed two fingers over his lips to silence him. "Promise me that even if you can't save me, you'll save yourself."

"How can I promise you such a thing?"

"If you love me as much as I love you, you'll do it."

"I promise that I'll save us both."

"Oh, Ronnie, no..."

"Yes. It's both of us or neither of us."

In that moment, she knew that Ronnie Martine truly loved her. She knew she could trust him. But she also knew that it was only a matter of time before Booth would have them killed...just as he'd had Jaron killed.

Chapter 15

"What do you mean you want to tell her everything?" Sawyer MacNamara growled the question. Jed's having phoned him in the middle of the night and wakened him from a sound sleep might have something to do with his less-than-pleasant attitude.

"She has a right to know what's going on," Jed said. "Her life is in danger. She had a dead body dumped at her gate tonight."

"What's going on there with you two?" Sawyer asked. "You sound as if you've gotten personally involved with Ms. Beaumont. Tell me you haven't."

"Whether I have or not isn't the issue, the issue is—"

"Damn it, man, you've known her only a few days, just how serious could things have gotten in that length of time? And you're right—the issue isn't whether you've got the hots for Grace Beaumont. It's that Dundee's, and therefore you, are part of a major operation involving the Federal government. There's a hell of a lot more at stake than just proving Dean Beaumont's and Byram Sheffield's deaths were murder.''

"Don't you think I, of all people, know that," Jed snapped. "I'm telling you that Grace can be trusted with the truth."

"The Bureau isn't going to see it that way."

"Screw the Bureau."

"Look, we're going to keep Ms. Beaumont safe—you, Dom, Kate, Rafe and J.J. When this is all over, she'll be alive and we'll have Fortier behind bars for the rest of his life. What more could she want?"

"Grace wants to know whatever I'm not telling her. It's not the information that's so important to her, it's the fact that I'm keeping something from her. She's the type who doesn't like being kept in the dark—about anything. Besides, she's smart. She'll probably start figuring it out pretty soon."

Sawyer groaned. "Use some of that good-old-boy charm of yours and feed her a line of bull. You've charmed many a woman, haven't you? This wouldn't be any different."

"I'm not going to lie to Grace. I won't fabricate some story to pacify her."

"There's no way Moran will give you permission to share secret information with her. Too much is at risk, including the life of the agent working undercover."

"Maybe I won't ask Moran."

"Don't you go off half-cocked and do something stupid," Sawyer said.

"Get this straight—I'm telling her something, even if it's only half the truth. I've already told her that I'm going to see Booth tomorrow and that I'm attending Jaron's funeral."

"Did you tell her that you're Fortier's nephew?"

Every muscle in Jed's body froze. He wanted to tell Grace everything—everything except that. "No, I haven't."

"She'll find out eventually," Sawyer reminded him. "Maybe your personal history with Fortier is what you should share with her, not the details of a highly confidential and potentially deadly FBI operation.''

''Yeah, you're probably right.'' Jed knew he wasn't going to tell Grace that he was Booth's nephew. Not yet. Not until he had no other choice. ''The other reason I called is so you can tell Moran that if he wants to give me a last-minute briefing, he should call before nine. I'll be leaving then for Beaulac to pay a visit on my uncle.''

''I'll let Moran know that you're set to make contact with his agent tomorrow. And as far as the other, don't let your dick do your thinking,'' Sawyer warned. ''If you do, you could wind up in trouble with the Feds and you could also lose your job at Dundee's.''

''Mmm-hmm. Sounds like a win-win situation.''

Sawyer harrumphed. ''You're going to do whatever the hell you want to do, regardless of what I say. Why bother even asking me?''

''I don't know what I'm going to do,'' Jed said honestly. ''But I do know that my first priority is Grace Beaumont.''

''Bringing Booth Fortier down will be in Ms. Beaumont's best interest. Just remember that.''

''Yeah, I'll remember.'' Jed hit the Off button on his phone.

He'd pretty much known before he called Sawyer what Dundee's CEO would say. Hell, the guy was a former Fed. And Jed knew that as much as he wanted to come clean with Grace, he couldn't. If by keeping silent, he had to face her wrath, he could handle it—even if she stayed angry with him until this assignment was completed. But it sure would make things easier for him if he could tell her something. Anything to appease her curiosity. *Okay, Tyree, just how much can you tell her and not jeopardize the operation?*

Of course the wise thing would be to tell her nothing. He could just go to bed right now, get a few hours of sleep before leaving for Beaulac, and then face Grace later in the day. As much as he hated to leave her under someone else's protection, he trusted Dom and Kate to keep Grace safe. But by not coming clean with her, all he was doing was putting off the inevitable.

He paced the room in his sock feet. Sometimes avoiding an issue was a solution. A temporary solution. He sat on the edge of the bed, yanked off his socks, then unbuttoned his shirt. If he told Grace that Booth Fortier was his uncle, would that satisfy her curiosity? If he swore to her that he hated the man as much as she did, would she believe him? Or would she distrust him, turn against him, fire him as her bodyguard?

Jed removed his shirt and hung it on the cannonball bedpost of the Colonial style oak bed, then flopped down across the top of the bedspread. Lying there his hands cupped behind his head, he tried to stop thinking about Grace…about the trip to his uncle's house tomorrow…about Jaron. He had no idea what sort of man Jaron had become, how many crimes he'd committed for Booth, for the syndicate. But he figured his old friend had been guilty of just about every offense on the books. What Jed couldn't figure out was what had made Jaron so desperate to escape Booth's hold that he'd risked everything for Grace's five million.

A soft rapping on his door abruptly ended his speculation. He started to get up, but didn't. Instead he said, "Yeah, come in."

The door eased open. Grace peeked inside. "Jed, may I speak to you?"

"You should be in bed trying to get some sleep." So much for putting off a confrontation, he thought.

"I can't sleep." She opened the door all the way, walked in and shut the door behind her. "We need to talk."

Why was it that just the sight of this woman made him soft in the head and hard everywhere else?

"Can't it wait?" he asked.

"Did you telephone Mr. MacNamara?"

"Yeah. And the answer is no. No way in hell."

She nodded. "I figured as much."

"If it was my decision to make, I'd tell you." Jed sat up

and slid over to the edge of the bed. "But I work for Dundee's and—"

"I understand."

Standing in the muted light from the one bedside lamp, she looked like an angel. A golden angel, all shimmering beauty. And he could tell that the fiery indignation with which she'd confronted him an hour ago downstairs in the kitchen had burned itself out. She seemed quite calm, even a bit subdued.

"You don't have to tell me anything," Grace said. "I think I've figured it out. You're working for Dundee's, but you're cooperating with the FBI. They're interested in proving that Fortier and Lew Miller are in cahoots."

"Grace…"

She signaled him to say no more. "Don't worry, I'm not sharing my theory with anyone else. I promise."

"Look, Blondie, you should go to bed. It's been a rough night." Jed stood, but made no move to go to her. "If you've got a sleeping pill, take it. You're the boss over at Sheffield Media. You can take the morning off if you want to. Stay home tomorrow. Before I leave for Beaulac, Dom and Kate will come over here and stay with you. They'll act as your bodyguards while I'm gone."

Grace nodded; then suddenly an odd look appeared in her eyes and her mouth opened on a surprised gasp. "Booth Fortier lives in Beaulac? Didn't you tell me that you're originally from Beaulac? Did you know Fortier years ago when you lived in the same town?"

The inevitable had arrived sooner than he'd expected. *What are you going to tell her?* he asked himself. *The truth? Or a lie?*

Troy Leone sat in a chair near the window where the old air conditioner chugged out cold air as it rattled and rumbled. He reached over and picked up a pack of cigarettes off the table, knocked a fresh one from the pack and lit it with the butt of the one he'd finished. Josie had fallen asleep right after they'd had sex. She was a wild thing in bed, but she wasn't one for cuddling afterward. Hell, neither was he. It wasn't like he was in love with Josie or anything. She was red-hot and couldn't get enough, which suited him just fine. But now that he'd decided not to return to the warehouse and wouldn't be making big bucks, he figured Josie would tell him to get lost. She liked pretty things; and without money, he couldn't buy her clothes and jewelry and whatever else she wanted. He knew what she wanted more than anything—to quit her waitress job.

Troy scratched his chest, then glanced over his shoulder, back into the bedroom where Josie slept. He sure wished she'd let him stay. He liked having a place of his own and a willing woman in his bed; but mostly he dreaded the thought of tucking his tail between his legs and crawling home to Elsa. Okay, so his sister cared about him, worried about him, wanted what was best for him. But God Almighty, she smothered him. Couldn't she get it through her head that he was a man now, not some snot-nosed kid? So he'd made a mistake taking the warehouse job. He'd thought he was tough, that working for the mob wasn't such a big deal. But after that guy had paid him a visit today and he'd found out he really was working for none other than Booth Fortier, Troy had known he was in way over his head. He wasn't interested in a life of crime, in becoming a career criminal. All he'd wanted was some easy money.

Puffing on his new cigarette, Troy leaned his head back against the wall as the front legs of the straight chair lifted off the floor. If he moved home—when he moved home—Elsa would be onto him again about his smoking. If it wasn't one thing with her, it was another.

So, don't go home, he told himself. Go back to the warehouse tomorrow night. But if he did that, he'd knowingly be working for Booth Fortier and that guy would show up again and ask him to do a job for the big boss. Fortier would expect him to kill somebody. He just didn't think he had it in him to be a murderer. Ask him to lie, cheat or steal and he'd do it. But kill another human being in cold blood? No way.

He took a last draw on his cigarette, ground it into a nearby ashtray and headed back to the bedroom. He stood over the bed and watched Josie sleeping. She wasn't pretty, but she was built good. He crawled into bed beside her, draped one arm over her and cuddled to her back.

She had no idea he'd quit his job at the warehouse. Tonight he'd stayed at a bar on East Sixth Street until the place closed down, then he'd come back to the apartment and told Josie he'd gotten off work early. He'd have to tell her the truth before tomorrow night, but he wasn't going to mention it until then. Since tomorrow was her off day, he figured they could spend most of the day in bed. If she needed a little incentive, he'd just show her the five hundred bucks Booth Fortier's man had given him.

Troy kissed Josie's ear. She grunted. He licked her neck. She slapped at him as if she were swatting a fly. He chuckled.

"Wake up, honey. Wake up just enough to say yes."

She growled, then flopped over, but kept her eyes closed. "What time is it?"

"Early. Not quite four."

Josie groaned. "I'm too sleepy to—"

He kissed her, stuck his tongue in her mouth while he whipped the covers off her. When he rubbed his erection against her belly, she started kissing him back. God, he was going to miss getting sex all the time like this. But as soon as Josie found out he didn't have any big money coming in, she'd sure as hell kick his ass out the door. *Just get it while you can, man,* he told himself. *You'll miss it—miss her—but you can always find another woman. But if you let yourself get in too deep with Booth Fortier, you could wind up in the pen for life or end up dead.* He didn't intend for either to be his fate. He loved money and he loved sex, but not enough to die for either.

* * *

Grace wondered why Jed didn't answer her, why he wouldn't allow his gaze to meet hers. There was something he didn't want to tell her, something too painful to share. Had, as she suspected, Jed lost someone to Booth Fortier's ruthlessness?

"Jed?" She took a few hesitant steps toward him, wanting to put her arms around him and offer him comfort.

He held up a restraining hand. She stopped immediately. Oh, her poor Jed. What could be so horrible that he couldn't tell her? And she knew from the pained expression on his face that his experience with the infamous Mr. Fortier had been horrible.

"Jed, whatever it is, you can tell me. I'll understand."

He took a deep breath, then faced her, his mossy hazel-brown eyes searching for the understanding she'd promised. "I knew Fortier." He paused. "I'd rather not go into too many details. Not tonight."

"All right." Grace kept her distance, despite the overwhelming desire to rush to Jed.

"He had my father murdered."

She could tell that the bold statement hadn't been intentional. It was as if Jed's very soul needed to make a confession, to share a painful secret.

When Jed turned his back on her, she wondered if he was crying. "Oh, Jed, I'm so sorry. I felt it was something like that. No wonder—"

"Don't!" He snapped around and glared at her, his face etched with anger. "I don't want or deserve your sympathy."

"Jed, please…what is it? What's wrong?" She rushed toward him, but when he backed away from her, she paused. "You're frightening me. What—?"

"My family…" He swallowed. "The people I come from were criminals, part of organized crime here in Louisiana. Don't you see, don't you understand—when I was eighteen, I ran away from Booth Fortier and his kind."

For a moment she didn't know what to say, didn't know

how to respond. What he'd told her was certainly a surprise; she'd never expected to hear that Jed's family had worked for the syndicate. No wonder he knew so much about Booth Fortier.

"You aren't your family," she told him. "You aren't responsible for what they did. You didn't choose that type of life. You chose to be different. You're a good man, Jed." She walked over to him, lifted her hand and caressed his cheek. "You have nothing to be ashamed of—nothing!"

He shoved her hand aside, then narrowed his gaze and focused on her eyes. "I knew Jaron Vaden, the man who was dumped outside your front gate."

Grace gasped.

"We were friends as teenagers."

"How terrible it must have been for you to see him to-night. Murdered."

"Stop being so damn understanding!"

She stared at him, totally puzzled by his attitude. "If you're trying to make me dislike you—"

"You should, you know. You should hate my guts."

"Why?"

"Because I'm not a nice man, not a good man. And I've kept things from you. More things than you can imagine." He grabbed her shoulders and shook her. "I am the worst man on earth for you, but God help me, I want you so bad I ache with the wanting."

"Oh, Jed...I—I—"

"Get away from me." He released her. "And stay away from me."

"What if I don't want to...what if I can't?" Hearing herself say it made her realize it was true. She wanted Jed...the way he wanted her. The passion between them didn't make sense and they both knew it was crazy, knew they were all wrong for each other. And how was it that she could have such powerful feelings for a man she'd met only a few days ago?

"Damn it, Grace, you don't know me at all. I'm absolutely nothing like your rich, brilliant husband. I'm just a good old boy, without a college degree, who has a shady family history. All my edges are rough. I'm a crude, ornery ex-soldier who knows a hell of a lot more about danger and death than I do about living and loving.''

He sounded as if he was warning her off, but her heart recognized his admission for what it was—a plea for her to want him despite all the reasons she shouldn't.

''I loved Dean Beaumont and thought I'd spend the rest of my life with him. I know I'll never find another man like him.'' She sensed Jed's discomfort and noticed him wince at the mention of her husband. ''I'm not saying I've fallen in love with you...'' She smiled. ''In lust maybe.'' He reacted with a halfway smile. ''What I'm trying to say is that I don't expect you to be like Dean. I don't want you to be a replacement for Dean. I want you, Jed. I want you just the way you are.''

He grabbed her and pulled her into his arms so fast he took her breath away. With his cheek pressed firmly against hers, he held her close and whispered hoarsely, ''No past, no future. Just the here and now.''

''Yes, just the here and now.'' She stood on tiptoe so that their mouths were perfectly aligned. She understood that for this moment in time, they had no yesterdays and no tomorrows. They were simply two people wanting and needing each other.

He kissed her. A million butterflies danced wildly in her stomach. He deepened the kiss. Skyrockets burst inside her head. His big hands cupped and lifted her buttocks, then yanked her up against him so that she could feel his arousal. Her nipples peaked; her femininity moistened. A maddening ache throbbed between her legs.

He kissed her again and again and again. Her mouth, her face, her neck. She ran her hands over his hard pectoral muscles, loving the feel of him. He tore off her robe and tossed it aside, then ripped the buttons from her silk pajama top as he jerked it off her. She unzipped his jeans, which he shrugged off and onto the floor, then she helped him remove her pajama bottoms. And all the while they kept kissing and touching. When they were both naked, Jed swung her up in his arms and carried her to his bed. He flung her on the rumpled bedspread, then came down over her. They kissed wildly, passionately, as they tossed about on the bed. His lips were everywhere, tasting her skin from mouth to toes. Her hands grasped and plucked and explored. He pinched her nipples, then laved them with his tongue. While he tested her readiness, she circled his sex with her fingers and stroked him.

"I want you inside me," she told him. "I want you now."

He eased off her and got up. She reached for him.

"I'll be right back," he assured her. "The pack of condoms is in my shave kit." The pack of condoms Dom Shea picked up for him earlier today.

While he disappeared into the bathroom, she scooted the bedspread, blanket and sheet to the foot of the bed, then rested her head on one of the two huge goose down pillows. She stretched like a cat basking in the sun. Every fiber of her being was ready and waiting…and wanting. Jed had awakened her sleeping sensuality, making her feel brazen and sexy. And for one crazy moment, she wished Jed would make love to her without protection. Just for that one moment she wanted something she thought she'd never want again—to get pregnant. Pregnant with Jed's baby.

"Are you out of your mind calling me at this ungodly hour?" Oliver Neville yelled into the telephone.

"Too bad I woke you," he said. "But I was awakened by several phone calls myself. It seems that there was a news bulletin on our local Sheffield Media, Inc. owned station about a body being dumped in front of Belle Foret tonight. I've had four phone calls from Sheffield Media employees, all worried about Grace."

"You shouldn't have your phone number listed in the book," Oliver said.

"You promised me that nothing would happen to Grace. You swore to me that she'd be safe."

"No one has harmed a hair on Ms. Beaumont's head, have they?"

"Not yet, but—"

"Then stop worrying. And stop calling me."

"Swear to me that Fortier isn't planning to hurt Grace. If he hurts her, I'll—"

"You'll do what? Nothing. Absolutely nothing. Not if you want to stay out of trouble."

"I should never have agreed to help you four years ago, when Fortier sent you to make me an offer. You swore to me then that Grace wouldn't be hurt, that Fortier wanted to kill only Dean and Byram."

"We had no idea Ms. Beaumont was in the car that night. Even you didn't know."

"Tell Fortier that if he hurts Grace, I'll go to the police and confess everything. Do you hear me?"

"Yes, I hear you, you fool. Talk like that will get you killed. Is Grace Beaumont's life worth more to you than your own?"

He gasped. "Oh, God! Oh, God! He does plan to kill Grace, doesn't he?"

"Calm down. Booth will do whatever he has to do to stop Ms. Beaumont. If you can't persuade her to let matters drop, then I can't be held responsible for what Booth does."

"If I'd known how things would turn out, I'd never have helped you," he mumbled. "She wasn't supposed to get hurt. I thought she'd turn to me for comfort, but she didn't."

"Well, from what I hear, she's found all the comfort she needs from her bodyguard," Oliver said.

"That's a damn lie! Grace would never stoop that low. The man is an uncouth lout."

"Maybe her taste in men has changed."

"Shut your damn mouth."

"Pull yourself together," Oliver advised. "If you keep acting like this, yours will be the next body dumped on Grace Beaumont's doorstep."

Chapter 16

Grace lay in bed, shamelessly naked, waiting eagerly for Jed. The steady, uninterrupted rhythm of her daily existence had blown up in her face when she'd received the letter from Jaron Vaden. Now, the man was dead. Brutally murdered and deposited at her front gate as a warning. Her life was out of control and she was reeling from the aftershocks. For four years she had clung to the memory of her husband, loving him, grieving for him, needing him every day. She had been empty inside for such a long time, the loss of her family leaving her adrift, emotionally unconnected to anything other than anguish. She had clung to Sheffield Media, Inc. as if it were her only lifeline. Indeed, it had been her one reason for living.

But everything had changed when Jed Tyree walked off the plane from Atlanta a few days ago. Had it really been less than week since his arrival? Odd that it seemed she'd known him for years. Laverna would say the feeling came from the fact that Grace and Jed had known each other in another life and were simply reconnecting in this one. Although a devout Christian all her life, Laverna dabbled in the supernatural, a trait not uncommon for many Louisiana natives whose roots went generations deep in bayou soil. Grace wasn't a believer in reincarnation, yet she couldn't truthfully say she was a disbeliever. She did know one thing for sure—Jed Tyree was no stranger to her heart.

When Jed emerged from the bathroom, his fist closed tightly over a couple of square packets, Grace suddenly felt shy, but she forced herself not to reach for the sheet to cover herself.

"Lady, you're the most beautiful thing I've ever seen," he told her as he stopped in the middle of the bedroom and stared at her.

"You look pretty darn good yourself."

Oh, yes, pretty darn good, indeed. Drop-dead gorgeous might better describe the naked man standing before her. Tall, muscular, not an ounce of fat on his hard, lean torso. The type of man a woman dreamed of having for a lover.

"Like what you see?" he asked, a cocky grin curving his lips.

She stared directly at his rock-solid erection. "I like what I see very much."

"I'm thinking this time should be fast, to give us both some much-needed relief," Jed said as he walked over and laid one of the condom packets on the nightstand. "And then later, we'll take it slow and easy…and make it last." He ripped open the packet in his hand.

Flushed with excitement, Grace watched as he sheathed his sex. Her femininity tightened and released, throbbing, sending sexual longing through her whole body. What was it about Jed that made her want him all the time? She was aching so much she didn't think she could stand it another minute. Getting up on her knees, she crawled to the edge of the bed and reached out for him. She grasped his hands and tried to drag him into bed with her.

"Eager, aren't you, Blondie?" His voice was husky, exuding a mixture of amusement and desire.

"Didn't you say we'd do it fast this time?" She yanked on his hands. "Let's see some action, big boy." Her gaze settled on his impressive erection.

Jed grinned. "You want action?"

He reversed roles by grabbing her and flipping her around so that her back faced him.

When she yelped in surprise, he slid her to the edge of the bed and pressed his sex against her buttocks. His arms went around her waist, clenching her tightly. As she rested back against him, letting her body melt into his, he kissed her neck. One hand slid down her belly and covered her mound. She rubbed against him, slowly, sensuously. He groaned. She sighed. When he nudged her thighs apart, she cooperated fully, giving him full access. Two fingers glided inside her moist feminine lips and across her sensitive nub. She whimpered when he eased his fingers inside her and brought his thumb down to caress her intimately. She rode his hand, undulating against the friction as he petted her.

While she lay back against him, one of his hands worked magic between her legs and the other rose to her left breast, cupped it, lifted it, then stroked the tight, tender nipple. She cried out when hot, clawing sensation shot from her breast to her core, then rippled along her nerve endings. She was on the verge of climaxing. So close she could do nothing to prolong the pleasure. Giving her simultaneous attention above and below her waist, Jed bit her neck with tender passion. And Grace unraveled, coming apart like a tightly wound ball of yarn. She whimpered as Jed manipulated her body so that those orgasmic sensations continued…on and on, until finally he'd drained every ounce of sexual tension from her body.

Or so she thought….

Suddenly, Jed dragged her backward so her knees rested on the edge of the bed. Before she realized his intent, he positioned himself to align his body to hers, then he took her from behind, ramming himself to the hilt inside her wet, welcoming depths. When he jackhammered into her, she clutched the bedspread and braced herself for the onslaught. His big hands held her hips, keeping her in place. Unbelievably, her body responded, awakening anew to a hunger she had thought already appeased.

With one hand on Grace's hip, holding her steady as he thrust in and out, Jed slipped his other hand between her thighs. He increased the speed of his lunges and his fingers stroked repeatedly until she heard him groan and knew he had reached his limit. His release came quickly, wildly, and the last few thrusts jolted her with the force of a body slam. But what she felt—all she felt—was fulfillment claiming her once again. Within seconds after Jed came, she did, too. A second time.

He toppled her into bed, the two of them still joined, his sex still hard and hot between her legs. He nuzzled her neck.

"I'd like to stay this way until we fall asleep," he whispered hoarsely. "But…" He pulled out of her, got up, then leaned over to kiss her before he headed for the bathroom.

Grace felt lost without him. She wanted him back in her arms, back in her body. Now.

In the sweet, dark hours of predawn, it was easy to believe that nothing and no one existed outside this room. The whole world had shrunk to encompass this sixteen-by-sixteen bedroom, this big oak bed and the man who had given her unparalleled pleasure.

Gone only a couple of minutes, Jed came out of the bathroom carrying a damp washcloth. When he sat on the bed, he spread her legs apart and cleaned her, then planted a kiss just below her navel. Before she could say thank you, he left her again. But within seconds he reemerged from the bathroom.

"You're not leaving to go back to your room, are you?" he asked as he stood by the bed.

"Not unless you want me to." Her heartbeat hummed inside her head.

Jed lay down beside her and pulled her into his arms. He

kissed her temple and said, "What I want is you to stay right here, as close to me as you can get."

"That's what I want, too."

She cuddled against him, feeling more alive in her sated, drowsy state than she'd ever felt in her entire life. And in that moment she knew—she couldn't deny it any longer, at least not to herself. She was in love with Jed Tyree. Head over heels, madly, passionately in love.

Jim Kelly sat alone in his room in the Fortier house gazing out the window at the dawn sky. He couldn't sleep, couldn't even rest. He'd wanted to do more to help Charmaine Fortier after the sheriff had informed them of her brother's death. But he couldn't go to her, couldn't stay with her without arousing suspicion.

He had been part of the Louisiana Mafia for nearly two years, his credentials forged, his identity falsified. He'd been able to stay in contact with the Bureau without any problems, up until six months ago when he'd been assigned to Booth Fortier's inner circle of bodyguards. A real stroke of luck, but with definite drawbacks. With his movements restricted, his every waking hour spent with others, he had little or no opportunity to even make a phone call or mail a letter. He was determined to do nothing to jeopardize his position, because when the time came, his firsthand knowledge of Fortier and the syndicate he ruled would prove invaluable. He'd managed to make a few phone calls when he was away from the house, but he'd been tied to his bodyguard duties twenty-four-seven for months now. All he could do was wait for the Bureau to come to him. And he knew they would. Moran would send in an agent—whether Federal or independent—to make contact. They'd have to let him know when they were ready to strike, ready to bring Fortier and his crime empire down.

But lately things here had gotten really complicated. Ever since he'd moved into Fortier's private residence, he had suspected that Booth abused his wife. Now he knew it for sure. The most recent beating had left Charmaine horribly battered. Jim wondered how her brother had been able to stand by all these years and watch Booth use her like a punching bag. Then again maybe he did understand. After all, what had he done to help her? But he couldn't help her—not yet. He didn't dare do anything to jeopardize his undercover work. More than his life or Charmaine's depended on the success of his mission. He couldn't take the chance Jaron Vaden had taken—taken and lost. But when the operation came to a close, when Fortier was arrested, Jim intended to make sure Charmaine was protected.

Jed kissed Grace's shoulder, then ran his tongue up her neck to her ear. She roused from sleep and moaned softly. His open palm skimmed over her belly, past her navel and covered her mound. She turned and draped her arm across his chest, pressing her body to his side.

"What time is it?" she asked, her eyes still closed.

"Almost daylight." He lifted himself over her just enough to kiss her lips.

Her eyelids flew open instantly. He was nose-to-nose with her, smiling seductively.

"Did you wake me for a reason?" she asked, humor in her voice.

He bent his head over and caught one peaked nipple in his mouth. He nipped, then sucked, and followed up by laving it with his tongue. While her hips arched, he moved to the other breast, then lifted his head and said, "Why waste time sleeping when we can be making love?"

She flung her arm around his neck and brought his mouth back down to hers. "My sentiments exactly." She kissed him.

They were as wild for each other this time as the first time. No slow loving. No lingering foreplay. But Grace didn't care. They tossed and tumbled on the bed, touching and tasting, hungry for sex. Jed donned another condom and took the dominant position. He grasped her hips, lifting her to meet his first deep, powerful thrust. He filled her completely—her body, her mind, her heart.

Jed showered and dressed. All the while, Grace slept. As he eased his Beretta into its holster, he turned toward the bed and looked at her. He was about as hung up on her as a guy could be. And as much as he'd like to tell himself that it was just the great sex, he knew better. Yeah, the sex was incredible, but that was only part of it. He cared about Grace in a way he'd never cared about another woman. He wanted to please her, make her happy. And he wanted her to be proud of him, needed her to think well of him.

You damn idiot, he told himself. *You've gone and screwed up big time. You've let yourself get emotionally involved with a woman who is bound to hate you once she discovers you're Booth Fortier's nephew. Why the hell didn't you just tell her the truth? If you had, you could have saved yourself and her a whole lot of heartache.*

Although he'd told Grace he'd come from a family of criminals and she hadn't judged him or condemned him, he couldn't count on her understanding when she learned that he was the nephew of the man responsible for her father's and husband's deaths. Would she ever be able to look at him again and not think about the fact that he was the nephew of the man who had taken away those she had loved the most dearly, including her precious unborn child?

His instinct was to kiss her goodbye before he left, but he squelched that desire. He removed his jacket from the hanger, put it on and quietly left the room. When he got downstairs, he found Dom and Kate had already arrived and were sharing coffee in the kitchen.

"Is Miss Grace not up?" Laverna asked, her wise old eyes studying Jed speculatively.

"She's sleeping in this morning. Don't disturb her." Jed turned to Kate. "Call her office and tell Elsa that Grace is taking the morning off."

Kate nodded.

"Do they know you're coming?" Dom asked quietly as he walked up beside Jed.

Jed shook his head. "That would eliminate the element of surprise. I plan to just show up."

"And you think they'll invite you in?"

"I know they will," Jed replied. "Booth will be curious as hell about why I'm paying him a visit." Jed caught both Laverna and Nolan looking at him curiously. "Yes, Miss Grace knows my plans. She knows I'm going to see Booth Fortier this morning."

Laverna looked away hurriedly. Nolan cleared his throat, then said, "I'm sure you're doing what you think is best for Miss Grace."

Laverna handed Jed a cup of coffee—just the way he liked it. Black. "Thanks," Jed said.

Dom placed his hand on Jed's shoulder. "Why don't I walk you out? It'll give us a chance to go over a few things."

Jed nodded, took several quick sips of the hot coffee, then set the cup on the table. "I'm trusting you and Kate to take care of Grace."

Dom followed Jed out into the hall. "Moran called me. He said he'd tried to reach you, but your cell phone was off."

Jed cursed under his breath. "I didn't recharge the battery last night. I forgot." He tapped the phone he'd left on inside his coat pocket.

Dom gave Jed a speculative glance, but made no comment, although Jed figured Dom suspected why he'd forgotten to recharge his phone battery. After all, Dom had been the one who'd gotten the condoms for him.

"I got distracted," Jed admitted.

"It happens." Dom whipped his phone from his pocket and handed it to Jed. "Swap phones with me. You need to call Moran on your way to Beaulac."

The men exchanged phones, then once they were outside

near the rental car Kate had driven over for Jed this morning, Dom recited Moran's number.

"Good luck," Dom said.

"Keep watch over Grace."

"You know we will. Stop worrying. The way you're acting, you'd think she was your—" Dom grinned, then grimaced. "Holy shi— What am I saying? I realize she's not
just a client to you."

"Yeah, yeah. I know I've screwed up. But save the name-
calling. I've already called myself every name in the book.
And don't think I don't know how she'll react when she
finds out that Booth is my uncle."

"She's a smart lady. Give her time and she'll understand.
She won't blame you for the things your uncle has done."

"I just hope you're right."

Jed opened the car door, slid behind the wheel, started
the engine and drove away. When he reached the gates at
the end of the long drive, they already stood open. Nolan's
doing, no doubt. He pulled the car just beyond the gates,
then punched in Moran's number on Dom's phone and
waited. On the second ring, Moran answered.

"Jed Tyree here. I'm leaving Belle Foret right now. I
should be in Beaulac in about forty-five minutes."

"Our agent's name is Jim Kelly," Moran said. "He's
been undercover for two years. Fortier and everyone in the
syndicate know him as Ronnie Martine. He's been Charmaine Fortier's personal bodyguard for six months."

Chapter 17

The Fortier home was located toward the back of twenty acres, along the riverfront outside the small town of Beaulac. Although at first sight no one would suspect the extent of the security surrounding the place, Jed knew. No one got near the house without being watched like a hawk. Booth had guard points set up all around the property and underlings manned those inconspicuous stations. When he'd stopped at the front gate and announced himself, he'd been allowed entrance, without hesitation. Whether Booth had given the okay or one of his flunkies had, Jed didn't know. But it seemed Booth's nephew was welcome. And that's just what Jed had been counting on. Booth was a ruthless man, a true killer at heart, but he considered blood relatives different from other people. Jed had heard his uncle say more than once that a man didn't eliminate his own blood kin. Besides, Booth had to be curious about why Jed would come to see him, especially since his uncle no doubt already knew he was working for Grace Beaumont. As he drove up the road toward the house, he mentally prepared himself for what was to come. He hadn't seen his uncle in seventeen years, but the closer he got to the house, the hotter the rage inside him. Being at the old homestead brought back memories—both good and bad. Foremost in his mind was the fact that Booth had ordered his father's death, something Booth hadn't denied when Jed confronted him.

From the moment he'd been conceived, Jed's life had been affected by his uncle's actions. As he parked the rental car in front of his grandparents' old house, he realized that despite having separated himself from Booth, putting time and distance between them, he hadn't been able to escape his heritage. He was part of the Fortier family; and just as Booth had, Jed had inherited a legacy of criminal activity that went back generations.

He'd grown up in this house, the privileged nephew of a powerful man. His childhood had been less than perfect, but he'd learned at a young age to be tough and resilient. A boy without a mother, with only a ruthless dictator as an adult role model, Jed had been a cocky, smart-ass kid. And Booth had allowed him unlimited freedom, more than any teenager should have had. He had both feared and admired his uncle, and in an odd way he'd loved Booth. But all that had changed when his mother had told him the truth—Booth had ordered his father's murder.

After parking the car and getting out, he was met by Aric, who had changed very little in seventeen years. His uncle's chauffeur and private bodyguard stood on the veranda, his arms crossed over his massive chest, his black eyes narrowed to a warning glare.

"Morning," Jed said as he slammed the car door. "Uncle Booth around?"

Aric uncrossed his arms and dropped them to either side of his body. The sunlight reflected off the gun riding inside his shoulder holster. "He's not up yet. But you're welcome to go on inside and wait for him."

"What about Charmaine, is she up?"

"Mrs. Fortier is having breakfast by the pool this morning."

"Then maybe I can see her first, pay my respects and give her my condolences."

Aric stepped aside as Jed walked up the steps and onto the veranda. "You know the way, Mr. Tyree."

"Sure do."

Aric hadn't even flinched at the mention of giving Charmaine condolences. Jed had thought maybe the big black man would respond by saying what a tough break it was that Jaron had been killed. But he said nothing more. Jed moved past Aric, who stood ramrod straight; then he opened the unlocked front door and went into the foyer. As he looked around, he realized the place had been redecorated. He glanced up the staircase and wondered what Booth had done to his old bedroom—a teenage boy's bedroom. Burned the furniture and had the room fumigated? Inwardly Jed laughed, but it was a bittersweet emotion.

A big, rugged guy with dark hair and a pensive glare came down the hallway and met Jed. "Mr. Tyree?"

"Yeah." Jed nodded. "And you're…?"

"I'll have to ask you for your weapon. Mr. Fortier doesn't allow anyone who doesn't work for him to carry a weapon on the property."

Jed shoved back his jacket, undid the holster and removed his Beretta. He had to admit that he felt naked without it. Whenever he was at work, he carried a gun. And during his life, he'd spent more time working—for Booth, for the U.S. Army and for Dundee's—than doing anything else. Jed was surprised this guy hadn't frisked him. If he had, he would have discovered Jed's backup weapon strapped just above his ankle.

"I understand Booth isn't up yet." Jed studied the guy who still hadn't told him his name. From the description Moran had given him of Jim Kelly, Jed figured this man was the undercover agent.

"He sleeps late most mornings."

"Then I'd like to see Mrs. Fortier and give her my condolences...."

"She's in pretty rough shape. Mrs. Fortier cared a great deal about her brother and his death has hit her pretty hard."

Jed knew genuine concern when he heard it. This guy cared that Charmaine was grieving. What Jed didn't know was whether it was simply sympathy for another human being or a sentimental attachment. Had Jim Kelly fallen for Charmaine? If so, heaven help him, because if the FBI agent was in love with Booth Fortier's wife, then he was in a worse situation than Jed was with Grace.

Jed patted his coat pocket. "Damn, I forgot my cigarettes. You don't happen to smoke do you? I'm a Lucky Strikes man myself."

The guy held out his hand as he studied Jed. "I'm Ronnie Martine, Mrs. Fortier's private bodyguard." Jed and he shared a firm handshake. "Sorry, but I don't smoke anymore. But I still carry around my old cigarette lighter." Ronnie pulled a red-and-silver lighter from his pocket, flipped open the lid and flicked the striker. An orange-red flame shot half an inch high.

"I should give up smoking," Jed said. "It's a nasty habit."

Ronnie closed the lighter and returned it to his pants pocket. "If you'll follow me, I'll take you to Mrs. Fortier."

Jed followed Ronnie down the hall, but refrained from saying more than the code phrase he'd used—I'm a Lucky Strikes man myself. In this house, the walls often did have ears. He'd wait for Ronnie to make the next move. At least now, they knew each other. The contact had been made.

When they entered the patio, Ronnie stopped abruptly before alerting Charmaine of their presence. "Everything is set here," Ronnie said low and soft.

"That's good."

"I need to know when it's coming down. There are preparations I have to make."

"All I know is soon. Things have escalated since Grace Beaumont became involved."

Charmaine, who reclined on a chaise longue halfway across the patio, lifted the wide-brimmed straw hat from her head, removed her sunglasses and stared at Jed and Ronnie.

"Mrs. Fortier," Ronnie called to her. "Your husband's nephew, Jed Tyree, is here to see you and your husband. He's come to pay his condolences."

Charmaine shot up off the chaise, tossed aside her hat and glasses and came running toward Jed. Her long, wild red hair bounced on her naked shoulders. Jed watched her as she came to him, still gorgeous at thirty-five, her figure displayed to perfection in the slim-skirted, strapless sundress. When she reached Jed, she threw her arms around him and hugged him, then pulled back, grabbed his hands and smiled. He noticed the bruises on her face and the slightly swollen lip. A pain of regret and remorse shot through him. He knew without asking that Booth had done this to her. Even when he'd hero-worshiped his uncle, he'd known the man had a mean streak, had even seen several demonstrations.

"Lord help me, it's good to see you, Jed." Tears misted her eyes. "You've heard about Jaron." She lowered her voice to a whisper. "He would have loved to see you. He missed you when you went away. We both did."

Jed brushed his hand across Charmaine's discolored cheek. She drew back, suddenly embarrassed, and her gaze connected with Ronnie's. Jed recognized the look that passed between them, a silent explanation of why it was all right for another man to touch her so gently, with tender concern. Heaven help them both, Jed thought, Charmaine and Jim Kelly were lovers. Apparently Booth didn't know; otherwise, they'd both be as dead as Jaron.

"I'm really sorry about Jaron," Jed told her.

Charmaine motioned to the umbrella-shaded table several feet away. "Come on over and sit down. Talk to me. Tell me all about yourself. Are you married? Do you have kids? Where do you live? What do you do for a living?"

Jed sensed her nervousness, noted the way she kept staring back at the house. She was playing a game. But why?

"Not married. No kids." Jed followed her to the other side of the patio and sat with her at the table. "Booth's up, isn't he?" Jed whispered.

"I guess you know I married your uncle Booth," Charmaine said, then mouthed the word yes.

"I live in Atlanta," Jed told her, then asked softly, "is he watching us?"

"Atlanta, huh? What brings you back to Louisiana?" Charmaine busied herself pouring them both a glass of orange juice. She handed Jed his glass, then whispered, "He knows you're working for Ms. Beaumont."

"Thanks." Jed accepted the juice, then said in a normal voice, "I work for the Dundee Agency. I'm here on business, working for Grace Beaumont. She's hired our agency for some investigative work and to act as her bodyguards."

She pointed to Ronnie. "Booth sees that I'm well protected at all times. He rotates my personal guard once a year."

"Booth always was a man who looked after his own."

Robust laughter echoed from the open French doors. Jed glanced over his shoulder and saw his uncle, smartly dressed in white slacks and navy shirt, standing in the doorway. Charmaine blanched when she saw her husband, then forced a smile.

"Booth, darling, come see who's paying us a visit. He— he's here in Louisiana on business and heard about Jaron." Although Charmaine's voice was syrupy sweet, the look in her eyes told Jed of her true feelings. Anger. Bitterness. Hatred. But above all else, fear.

Head high, shoulders straight, Booth Fortier marched toward Jed, then when he drew near, he sized up his nephew and said, "It's been a long time, boy."

"Yes, sir, it has. Seventeen years." Jed stood to greet his uncle, showing the respect Booth demanded.

"You're looking well."

"So are you," Jed lied. Even though his uncle appeared quite fit, there was something not quite right about his appearance. It was in the eyes. Just a hint of illness. What plagued the old buzzard? Jed wondered.

Booth walked over and stood behind Charmaine's chair. Jed noticed how she tensed when Booth placed his hand on her shoulder. "Our Charmaine is still a beauty, isn't she?"

"Yes, she is." Jed glanced behind Booth to where Ronnie stood in the background, his stance rigid, as if he were struggling to keep himself in check. If Ronnie—Jim Kelly— cared about Charmaine, it must have killed him seeing the results of Booth's handiwork on her body.

"Guess you never figured when you left us that Charmaine would wind up being mine." Booth caressed her throat, his fingers circling her windpipe as his thumb stroked the side of her neck. "Yeah, our girl moved right to the top. She went from being the heir apparent's woman to become the king's wife."

"And what did Jaron become, other than your brother-in-law? Was he the new heir apparent?" Jed asked.

Charmaine gasped.

Booth frowned. "Jaron was my right-hand man, always at my side to do my bidding. But he was never in line to inherit my throne." Booth released his hold on his wife, then motioned with a sweeping hand gesture toward the house. "Come into my study for a drink and you can tell me why you're really here."

Jed nodded, got up, walked over to Charmaine and said, "I really am very sorry about Jaron." With his uncle watching closely, he leaned over and kissed Charmaine's cheek.

"Thank you." She swallowed her tears.

Jed followed Booth into the house, down the hall and straight into his study. Booth closed the doors behind them, then went to the liquor cabinet. "Whiskey for me. What will you have?"

"The same," Jed replied.

"Neat or on the rocks?"

"Neat."

Booth served as bartender, something Jed couldn't remember his uncle doing in the past. He held a glass in each hand as he approached Jed. Booth held one out to him, which he took.

"Sit."

Jed sat in an overstuffed chair to the right of Booth's desk. Booth braced his hips on the edge of his desk, lifted his glass to his lips and downed a hefty swig.

"Why are you here?" Booth asked. "And don't tell me it's simply to tell us how sorry you are about Jaron." Booth grinned. "By the way, how did you hear about Jaron's death?"

Jed took a sip of whiskey, then eyed his uncle over the rim of the glass. "I guess you already know Jaron's body was dumped at the front gates of Belle Foret, Grace Beaumont's home."

"So I was told."

"I'm Ms. Beaumont's bodyguard. She hired the agency I work for to investigate an allegation she received in a mysterious letter." When Booth didn't respond, simply sat there sipping his liquor, Jed continued. "Why don't I cut to the chase and just ask you out right—did you put out a hit on Dean Beaumont and Byram Sheffield four years ago?"

Booth finished his drink, set the glass down on his desk and looked right at Jed. "Now why would I have done something like that?"

"Because Dean Beaumont was gathering evidence against Lew Miller...evidence that would have proved you controlled the governor."

Booth laughed. "Hell, boy, I've been friends with every governor for the past thirty years and my daddy before that. But I don't control Lew Miller and there's no way Dean

Beaumont could have come up with any evidence proving I do.''

"Then you're saying you didn't order a hit on—''

"You go back to Ms. Beaumont and tell her that Booth Fortier gives her his word that he had nothing—absolutely nothing—to do with her husband's and father's deaths.''

Jed stood, set his glass beside Booth's on the desk, then stared into his uncle's cold, black eyes. "I'll tell her, but you should know she probably won't believe you. I'm sure she'll expect us to continue the investigation. She's determined to prove the allegations to be either true or false.''

"Let me give you some advice.'' Booth grinned, his expression pure evil. "Do what you can to persuade Ms. Beaumont that it's in her best interest to let the matter drop. It's not healthy for a young widow to dwell on her husband's death. Who knows, an obsession like that could kill her.''

Jed barely restrained himself. He wanted to grab Booth by the throat and choke the life out of him. How dare he threaten Grace right to Jed's face! He wanted to warn his uncle that if he tried to harm Grace, he'd have to answer to him personally. He wanted to shout at the top of his lungs that Booth was on the verge of being arrested by the FBI.

"My job is to protect Ms. Beaumont. I'll do whatever it takes to make sure no harm comes to her.''

"Yes, I'm sure you will. But I'd hate to see the two of us on opposite sides. After all, you are my nephew. Your rightful place is here with me. Don't you ever regret having given up the chance to inherit my empire?''

"I regret a lot of things.''

"It's never too late to right the wrongs of the past.'' Booth eased off the edge of the desk, reached out and placed his hand on Jed's shoulder. "But before I could trust you again, you'd have to prove yourself.''

Jed glared at his uncle's hand resting on his shoulder. Booth squeezed his shoulder, then released it. "You're in a unique position to be of service to me.''

"How is that?''

"You're Grace Beaumont's bodyguard."

"You want me to kill her, is that it?"

Booth smiled. "Just persuade the lady, by whatever means necessary, that digging into the past is dangerous."

"You made two mistakes," Jed said and chuckled when his uncle's smile vanished. "First, you assumed that I might be interested in inheriting your crime empire. I'm not. Second, you assumed I'd be willing to kill an innocent woman. I'm not." And what Booth didn't know was that Grace Beaumont's life was worth more to Jed than his own.

"Headstrong and stubborn as always," Booth said. "And just a bit weak. Like your mama. I thought maybe you'd gotten tougher, but I see you haven't."

Jed walked to the pocket doors, opened them, then said, "I'll say goodbye to Charmaine and let her know I'll be at Jaron's funeral."

"If you have any ideas of renewing your relationship with my wife, I advise against it. You must remember how possessive I am of my personal property."

Yes, Jed remembered all too well the beating he'd taken at the age of ten when he'd dared to borrow one of Booth's diamond rings. Booth had caught him taking it from the jewelry case in his bedroom. It had been the one and only time his uncle had physically abused him, but Booth had beaten him so badly that he'd learned a lesson he never forgot. Never steal from Booth. Never lie to Booth. Never double-cross Booth.

"Take care of yourself, Uncle Booth," Jed said sarcastically. "And enjoy what you've got…because you never know when it's all going to come tumbling down around you."

Booth waited until Jed said goodbye to Charmaine, retrieved his gun from Ronnie and got in his car before he picked up the phone and called Curt Poarch.

Curt answered on the third ring. "Yeah, Poarch here."

"Curt, there's something I'm going to need you to do for me."

"Yes, sir. Name it."

"I want you and Charlie to get together and come up with a plan to ensure that Grace Beaumont isn't a problem for me anymore."

"All right. I'll get with Charlie later today and—"

"Get together with him now. I want it taken care of this afternoon."

"You want us to handle it personally or bring in an outside man?"

"I'll leave the particulars up to you. Just be sure that by tonight, the lady is no longer a thorn in my side."

Chapter 18

Grace straightened the collar on her beige blouse and re-arranged her pearls so that they lay in the center of her chest. After hurriedly applying peach-tinted lip gloss, she donned her brown silk jacket and picked up her brown leather clutch purse. As she headed for the stairs, she checked her wristwatch. Ten-thirty-five. When she'd awakened an hour ago alone in bed, she had glanced at the clock on the nightstand and realized Jed had already left for Beaulac. After their heated confrontation, she hadn't questioned him any further about his mission, his reasons for making a personal call on Booth Fortier, but when she'd told him she'd figured out the FBI was somehow involved, he hadn't denied it.

As she made her way downstairs, she thought about the hours she had spent in Jed's arms this morning and a fluttering sensation tingled through her body. She was in love. Crazy in love. Unexpectedly in love. After Dean's death she had thought herself incapable of ever loving again, of finding someone who made her heart sing.

"Morning, Miss Grace," Laverna met her as she came down the back stairs into the kitchen.

"Good morning," Grace replied. "I don't want breakfast this morning. Just coffee and juice. I'd like to go to the office as soon as possible."

"Yes, ma'am."

Kate Malone stood by the bay window, a cup of coffee in her hand. "Jed should be back by noon, if you'd like to wait for him."

"He can meet us at the office." Grace placed her purse on the counter, accepted the small glass of orange juice Laverna held out to her, downed it in one long gulp, then handed the glass back to the housekeeper. "We're in the process of acquiring TV and radio stations in Newport, Arkansas, and in Corinth, Mississippi. I'm expecting updates on both negotiations today and I'm sure we'll have something to celebrate. Plus, we have a company picnic coming up in a few weeks and I always help Elsa plan the event."

"When do you want to leave?" Kate asked.

"In five minutes." Grace accepted the coffee cup Laverna handed her and said, "Please, ask Nolan to bring the car around." She looked directly at Kate. "You can ride with me, and Mr. Shea can follow. Will that be satisfactory?"

"It should be. Just as long as one of us is with you at all times."

Grace took several sips of hot coffee, then placed the cup on the saucer sitting on the counter. "Ask Mr. Shea to contact Jed and tell him to meet us at Sheffield Media headquarters."

"While you finish your coffee, I'll tell Dom. He's in the den."

The minute Kate left the kitchen, Grace lifted the telephone from the wall, dialed her office number and picked up her cup.

"Sheffield Media, Inc.," Elsa said. "Ms. Beaumont's office."

"Hi, Elsa. I'll be coming in late this morning. We're leaving here in five minutes."

"Yes, ma'am."

"Have we heard anything from Newport or Corinth?"

"I received a call from Mr. Sullivan. He's still negotiating terms with the lawyers representing both affiliates, but he said to tell you to pop the champagne. He's sure it'll be a done deal by this afternoon."

"Wonderful." Grace sipped on her coffee. "Since a celebratory lunch is in order, please, make reservations for two…no make that for six, at Rudy's. I want you and Hudson to join us—Jed and I and the other two Dundee agents. Mr. Shea and Kate have become my second and third shadows. By the way, when you call Rudy's make sure you speak personally to Rudy. I want our lunch prepared by Rudy himself. And be sure to ask him to chill a couple of bottles of Krug Grande Cuvee."

"Yes, ma'am. I'll see to it immediately."

Grace knew Elsa was probably dying to know all about the corpse that had been dumped at her gate, but was too circumspect to boldly inquire. "I suppose you've heard about the gangster that was dropped off in front of the house last night."

"Yes, everyone's heard. It's front page news this morning. And Hudson approved having our radio and TV stations cover the story. He felt that you wouldn't want Sheffield Media to shy away from the story just because…well, because you're involved. And he chose not to bother you at home with making the decision."

"Hudson did the correct thing."

"The man who was murdered, the police identified him as Jaron Vaden, one of Booth Fortier's top henchmen," Elsa said. "They say Fortier is married to Vaden's sister."

I knew Jaron Vaden, the man who was dumped outside

your gate. We were friends as teenagers. Grace heard Jed's voice inside her head.

"Grace?"

"Mmm-hmm?"

"Are you all right?" Elsa asked, concern in her voice. "You sound a bit strange."

"Yes. Yes, I'm fine."

"It must have been terrible for you last night. I mean having a dead body…you didn't see it, did you? The police didn't make you—"

"Jed took care of everything," Grace said. "I did have to speak to Sheriff Adams, but he asked me only a few questions."

"If you'd rather not come into work today—"

"I'll be there shortly. I'm not letting Booth Fortier scare me so badly that I can't function normally. I have a team of bodyguards to keep me safe." As safe as it was possible to be when a man like Fortier decided he wanted you dead, Grace thought.

"We'll expect you soon." Elsa paused. "And Grace… Troy called me a few minutes ago. He asked if he could come by the house this evening."

"That's good news, isn't it?"

"Yes, I think it is. He actually apologized for acting so badly the day he moved out. I'm hoping I can persuade him to give up the job at the warehouse."

"I certainly hope you can." Grace wondered if she should mention her idea of a major job promotion to Elsa. It would mean Elsa moving from St. Camille and uprooting Milly, but if she could persuade Troy to go with them, it might give the kid one more second chance. Better wait, Grace decided. Selfishly she wanted Elsa here at Sheffield Media, Inc. headquarters until this nightmare with Booth Fortier was over. Then she'd offer Elsa the type of job she knew her assistant longed for—managing affiliated radio and television stations. Grace intended to give Elsa her choice of Newport or Corinth, then when she'd done her apprenticeship in a small town, Elsa could move to a larger city when a managerial position came open.

"Inform Hudson that he's invited to lunch to celebrate. And phone Uncle Willis and see if he can join us. If he can, make the reservations for seven."

"I'll handle everything. Have a safe trip into town," Elsa said, then hung up.

Grace finished her coffee, set the cup down and picked up her purse. "Laverna, let's have dinner in the sunroom tonight. Make it really nice. Linen tablecloth and napkins. And Grandmother's china and silver."

"Candles and fresh flowers, too?" Laverna asked.

"Mmm-hmm. Yes. The works." Grace waltzed over and hugged Laverna, whose dark eyes widened in surprise. "I want music, too. Something romantic."

"Yes, ma'am." Laverna smiled timidly.

Jed waited in a long line of cars backed up on the highway between Beaulac and St. Camille. He'd decided to take the shortest route to Sheffield Media, Inc. headquarters, not realizing a road crew would have a section of highway blocked and was making the eastbound traffic take turns with the westbound traffic on the narrow strip of old road.

Jed thumped his fingers on the steering wheel as one foot patted nervously on the floor mat. Dom had phoned to let him know Grace had insisted on heading to the office immediately and wanted him to meet them there. Mentally he knew Grace was as safe with Dom and Kate as she would be with him; but on a possessive male, gut level, he didn't want Grace going anywhere without him.

Just as he started to call the office to let them know he'd be late, his lane of traffic got the go-ahead, so he shifted gears and moved forward, but only at a snail's pace.

An hour later, he parked at Sheffield Media, Inc. headquarters and strode into the main building. When he arrived at Grace's office, he was told by one of the secretaries that Ms. Beaumont had already left for lunch.

"Where did she go?"

"Rudy's. It's on Main Street. You can't miss it. Ms. Beaumont asked that you join them as soon as possible."

"Them? Do you mean the Dundee agents?"

"Yes, sir, they were with her, along with Ms. Leone and Mr. Prentice."

Oh, great, just great, Jed thought. Lunch with Hudson Prentice. He didn't like the guy. And it wasn't just because the man was in love with Grace. Jed's gut instincts told him Prentice couldn't be trusted. If he had to choose between Prentice and Uncle Willis to be the bad guy, the informant who had betrayed Dean Beaumont and Byram Sheffield, he'd pick Prentice. After all, what had Willis Sullivan gained by the two men's deaths? Nothing. On the other hand, Prentice had believed he would be named CEO of Sheffield Media, Inc. after Grace's father died. And with Dean Beaumont out of the way, he'd probably thought Grace would fall into his waiting arms.

Of course Jed had no real proof. And gut instincts wouldn't hold up in court. Nor would his gut instincts persuade Grace that her senior vice-president was a two-faced, conniving bastard. Besides, Jed told himself, there was always the off chance he could be wrong.

"How long have they been gone?" Jed asked.

"They just left. Less than ten minutes ago. Rudy's doesn't open until twelve-thirty during the week and there's always a crowd."

Jed dashed into the parking lot, jumped in the rental car and screeched out onto the road. As he zipped from red light to red light in the business district of downtown St. Camille, he asked himself why the hell he was in such a rush. What did he think would happen to Grace without him at her side?

As soon as he turned onto Main, he saw the restaurant at the end of the street, the last building on the left. Like so many establishments in town, Rudy's was housed in an old building that had been renovated and yet maintained a Louisiana antebellum ambience. Black wrought-iron banisters lined the upstairs porch as well as the downstairs one. Glistening black shutters flanked two sets of long, narrow windows across the front of the old whitewashed redbrick exterior. As he crept slowly along the street—the speed limit was fifteen miles an hour—he spotted Grace's Rolls parked out front, with Nolan sitting inside; then he saw a line of people slowly entering Rudy's. When he drew nearer, he recognized Kate and Dom standing in line and to their right Prentice stood beside Elsa Leone. Undoubtedly the others blocked his view of Grace. When Jed drove up in front of the restaurant, he hunted for a parking place, then noticed a sign pointing to parking in the rear. Grumbling under his breath, he eased the rental car onto the narrow alleyway that led to the back of the restaurant.

When he got out of the car, locked it and headed toward the sidewalk, some odd sixth sense kicked in, alerting him to danger. His steady walk turned into a hurried trot and then broke into a full run. As he turned the corner, he comprehended several different events occurring simultaneously. In his peripheral vision he caught a glimpse of a car crash at the intersection. One vehicle ran through the red light and rammed straight into the side of the other car. Looking directly ahead, he noted the customers entering Rudy's had stopped, turned and gaped in surprise at the nearby accident scene. Dom and Kate, flanking Grace, took defensive positions, blocking her body with theirs. And for some unknown reason, Hudson Prentice froze in place, closed his eyes and looked as if he was praying.

Jed hurried toward Grace. Two of the men in the crowd raced across the street toward the accident site, presumably going to offer assistance. When Grace saw Jed, her face lit up. Nothing had prepared him for the way her reaction made him feel. The woman had him turned inside out, her every look tightening his gut, her every touch arousing him.

"Jed…" She turned to him, but stopped herself before actually reaching out to him.

He knew what she felt because he felt it, too. He wanted

to haul her into his arms and kiss her senseless. But Grace Beaumont wasn't the type of lady who would go in for public displays like that.

Before he could say anything, one of the men who'd rushed from Rudy's to the accident site, called out, "Hey, there's a guy over here who's having some kind of convulsions. We need a doctor or somebody with medical training."

The crowd buzzed with concern and curiosity. Jed knew what he had to do, but that nagging feeling in the pit of his stomach cautioned him not to leave Grace. He grasped her arm and said, "I've had medic training. I should—"

"Go…go," she told him.

Most of the people in line at Rudy's went inside for lunch, but a few decided watching an accident scene was preferable to eating. Grace instructed Elsa and Hudson to go on into the restaurant, then she turned to Kate and Dom.

"Mr. Shea, why don't you go with Jed and see if you can help out. Kate and I will go in and order, then y'all can join us later."

Jed looked squarely at Kate. "Take care of her."

"You know I will," Kate replied.

Reluctantly Jed headed toward the car crash at the intersection, Dom at his side, as Grace and Kate followed Elsa and Hudson into the restaurant. *Just go do what has to be done to help out,* Jed told himself. Kate will look after Grace. After all, what could happen to her in Rudy's?

Jed and Dom parted the crowd hovering around the two wrecked vehicles—a shiny red Toyota convertible and a black Ford Windstar minivan. It appeared the man driving the convertible had run the red light and smashed into the side of the minivan—probably at no more than twenty miles an hour. The woman driving the Windstar had two toddlers in regulation child safety seats in the back. She was crying, but she seemed to be physically all right, as were her two squalling babies. The young man behind the wheel of the sports car was in the throes of a convulsion and since Jed couldn't see how he could have been badly injured in what appeared to be just a major fender bender, he figured the guy had some sort of medical condition.

"You look after the lady and her kids," Jed said. "I'll see what I can do for this guy."

By the time Jed checked the guy over and decided he hadn't received any injuries and that he possibly suffered from epilepsy and had gone into a seizure which had no doubt caused the accident, the police showed up and an ambulance siren could be heard several blocks up the street. Jed discovered a medical emergency bracelet on the man's wrist which verified Jed's suspicions that he had epilepsy. Since Jed and Dom were firsthand witnesses to the collision and the lady was too hysterical to give the officers a competent report on how the accident had occurred and the other driver would soon be on his way to the hospital, Officer LeBeck asked the Dundee agents to fill him in on what had happened.

All the while they were being held up doing their duty as responsible citizens, Jed kept getting that uneasy feeling in the pit of his stomach.

He leaned over and said quietly to Dom, "I can finish things up here. I want you to check around the block. Just look for anything suspicious. I'm getting some odd vibes."

"Danger signals?" Dom asked.

"Call me crazy, but I can't shake the notion that something is fixing to happen."

"You think Fortier is going to strike out at Grace today? Is that it?"

"Maybe. I don't know. All I know is that my gut instincts are telling me something's wrong. Bad wrong."

"I'll check the block, then keep watch outside. I can grab a late lunch later." Dom shot across the street and disappeared around the corner beside Rudy's. Jed completed his report to Officer LeBeck, then went straight to Grace's Rolls. He pecked on the window to gain Nolan's attention.

The old man opened the door and started to get out, but Jed motioned for him to stay put.

"Have you stayed with the car every minute since leaving Belle Foret earlier today?" Jed asked.

Nolan gave Jed a puzzled look. "Yes, sir. Miss Grace told me to wait and not return home since she had made plans for lunch in town." He pointed to the CD and tape player. "I listen to books on tape while I wait."

"So there's no way anyone could have tampered with the Rolls today?"

"No, sir, not unless he was invisible."

Jed released a relieved sigh. He could rule out a car bomb. But his relief was short-lived. He just couldn't shake this nagging sense of unease.

"Is there something wrong, sir?" Nolan asked.

"No. You go back to your book on tape," Jed told him. "I'm just being cautious."

Nolan closed the car door. Jed turned around just as Dom came around the building.

"Anything?" Jed asked.

"Nothing obvious," Dom said.

"Damn!"

"Go on in and have lunch with Ms. Beaumont and the others," Dom suggested. "I'll keep watch out here."

Before Jed could reply, the front doors to Rudy's swung open and Grace came rushing outside, Kate at her side. Holy hell. His mind screamed, "Go back inside!"

"She wouldn't stay put," Kate said. "She was concerned because y'all were taking so long."

"Jed, is everything all right?" Grace asked.

Suddenly, from out of nowhere a shot rang out. Kate knocked Grace to the sidewalk, covered Grace with her body and pulled her 9 mm, all in record time. Simultaneously Dom pulled his weapon and took cover, while Jed rushed toward Grace. Another shot rang out.

"Second story window across the street," Dom hollered. "Man with a rifle."

"Go after him," Jed ordered as he went down on his knees beside Grace and Kate. He lifted Kate up and when he did, he saw that both she and Grace were covered in blood. Bright red, fresh blood. Grace lay flat on her back on the sidewalk, her face chalk-white, her beige blouse and brown silk jacket soaked in blood.

"Grace? God damn it, Blondie, why didn't you stay inside and wait for me?"

Chapter 19

The waiting room of St. Camille Hospital's surgery unit
held an assortment of concerned men and women. Dom
Shea paced the floor in a circle, then went into the hall and
tromped restlessly up and down the long corridor. J.J. Blair
stood gazing out the row of windows overlooking the rear
parking lot. Hudson Prentice sat alone in the corner, practically comatose, not saying a word nor responding to anything said to him. Elsa Leone perched precariously on the
edge of the vinyl sofa right beside Grace, while Jed kept
guard on the other side. When Jed had first realized that it
was Kate who'd been hit and not Grace, he'd been thankful,
relieved that Grace wasn't hurt, then felt guilty because of
Kate. She'd taken a bullet in the shoulder, which had gone
clean through and cut out a chunk of flesh as it exited. All
the blood on Kate and Grace had belonged to Kate, who'd
risked her life to save the client, as she'd been trained to
do. Dom blamed himself. Jed blamed himself. Hell, even
Grace said it was all her fault. In a case like this, there was
always enough blame to go around.

Even now, four hours after arriving at the hospital, Grace's face was still pale and her hands, which she held tightly in her lap, still trembled. And despite Elsa's best efforts to wash off the blood from Grace's clothes when she'd taken her employer into the ladies' room shortly after they'd arrived, her jacket, skirt and blouse still held the copper-red stains, slightly faded and smudged, but plainly evident. Kate's blood had splattered Grace's face and hair, which Elsa had managed to clean quite well.

"What time is it?" Grace asked.

"Six-twenty-five," Elsa replied, her gaze focused on the electric wall clock above the door.

"Kate's been in surgery over four hours," Grace said. "Why is it taking so long? Why hasn't someone come out and told us how she's doing?" Although Grace's eyes remained dry, her voice quivered with emotion.

Jed put his arm around Grace's shoulders and pulled her to him, then he reached down and covered her tightly clasped, shaky hands with one of his hands, then squeezed. "Let me take you home. You're exhausted and filthy and—"

"After Kate comes out of surgery. Not until then." She looked at him, a strained expression on her face, and he realized she was doing her level best not to cry.

"Sure thing. We'll stay right here."

"I wish Dom had been able to find the rifleman before he got away," Grace said. "If he was a hired killer, the police won't be able to find him, will they?"

"The guy who pulled the trigger isn't all that important," Jed told her. "It's the man who hired him that we want. And even if the police were to apprehend the shooter, he won't give up the name of his employer."

"Booth Fortier."

Jed nodded.

"It could have been me. It was supposed to be me. If Kate hadn't—" Grace's voice cracked.

Rafe Devlin showed up in the doorway, a wild look in

his eyes. "How's Kate? I just got word that she'd taken a bullet for Ms. Beaumont."

Before Jed could respond, Elsa stared at Rafe and asked, "Who is that man?"

"Another Dundee agent," Grace replied.

"Oh…yes, of course," Elsa said. "I should have known."

Jed wasn't sure why Elsa fixed her gaze on Rafe, but he got the feeling that she knew him…or thought she knew him.

J.J. came away from the window and met Rafe at the door. "Kate's in surgery. We're just waiting to hear something."

"How bad was it?" Rafe asked.

"Bad enough," J.J. said. "But probably not lethal."

"Thank God."

A cell phone rang. Everyone glanced around trying to figure out whose phone was ringing.

"Mr. Prentice, I believe that's your phone," Elsa said.

Hudson Prentice nodded, then reached into his jacket and pulled out the phone, hit the On button and placed the phone to his ear. "Yes?"

All eyes were on Sheffield Media, Inc.'s senior vice-president.

"It's a business call," Prentice said, speaking for the first time since arriving at the hospital. "I'll take it in the men's room."

A couple of minutes after Hudson disappeared into the rest room, Dr. Williamson came to the waiting area and asked for Kate Malone's family. All four Dundee agents went straight to him.

"Ms. Malone came through surgery without any complications," the doctor said. "She's young and strong and the bullet didn't hit any vital organs or sever a major artery. Barring any unexpected problems, I anticipate a full recovery. Of course, as with all cases of this type, the first twenty-four hours are crucial."

"When can we see her?" J.J. asked.

"She'll be in Surgical Intensive Care for several days. Check with the SIC nurses about a visiting time."

Dom followed up with half a dozen more questions, which the doctor answered, then when Dr. Williamson left, Dom said, "I'll stay here tonight. I can bunk out on the sofa." He looked at Jed. "Is that okay with you?"

"Yes, it's fine." Jed glanced from Rafe to J.J. "You two will stay with us at Belle Foret, then the three of you can take shifts here at the hospital until we know Kate's out of the woods. And you will also be able to provide backup protection for Grace."

"Sounds like a plan to me," J.J. said. "Should we ask for a replacement agent for Kate?"

Jed grimaced. "I don't think that will be necessary." He glanced at Rafe and then at Dom. "Do we all agree we can handle things with the team that's in place?"

"Yeah," Rafe replied.

Dom nodded.

"I'm taking Grace home now," Jed told them.

"Do you need me to go home with you?" Elsa asked Grace.

"Thank you, but no. You should go home. Troy's coming by this evening, isn't he?"

"Oh, God, in all the hullabaloo I'd forgotten."

"You go see your brother. I'll be all right," Grace said. "Jed will take good care of me."

"You can count on that." Jed helped Grace to her feet, then led her from the waiting room. As he passed J.J. and Rafe, he said, "J.J., you come with us now. Go to the parking area and ask Nolan to bring the Rolls around." J.J. nodded, then hurried down the hall. Jed looked at Rafe. "Check on Prentice." Jed caught the look of understanding in Rafe's eyes. "When you find him, tell him to go home."

"Will do."

A few minutes later when Jed, Grace and J.J. emerged from the elevator on the first floor, Grace stopped abruptly.

"Oh, mercy. I didn't think to call Laverna and tell her not to follow through with our special plans for dinner."

"Don't worry about it," Jed assured her. "Nolan's been in touch with her. I'm sure she realized whatever dinner plans you'd made needed to be canceled."

"Yes, I'm sure she did."

While J.J. left to instruct Nolan, Jed remained alert to every sound, every movement, taking nothing for granted, least of all Grace's safety. A couple of minutes later, J.J. motioned to him and he hurried Grace through the hospital lobby and straight to the Rolls parked at the curb. J.J. waited by the door, her violet-blue eyes scanning the area all around the car. When the three of them were encased in the back seat, Jed gave Nolan the go-ahead and the chauffeur eased the car from the circular drive onto the street. Jed put his arm around Grace. She laid her head on his shoulder and sighed heavily. And it was in that one moment he realized exactly how much Grace meant to him. Everything. Absolutely everything.

"I told you that I wouldn't stand for Grace being hurt," Hudson Prentice said into the phone. "Somebody tried to kill her today and shot one of her bodyguards instead. You tell Fortier that I'll go to the police and tell them what I know. I swear I will."

"Go to the police," Oliver Neville told him. "You have no evidence. I've been the go-between for you and Booth and if you tell the police some wild tale, I'll simply deny it."

"You egotistical son-of-a-bitch, do you think they'd take your word over mine? They know you're as crooked and underhanded as Fortier is."

"What they know and what they can prove are two different things."

"Damn you. Damn Fortier."

"Calm down, shut up and listen. Grace Beaumont is a liability. She has to be eliminated. I know you have a thing

for her, but she hasn't reciprocated your feelings in four
years, so it's a good guess that she never will.''

"You don't know that!''

"Look, you hang in there, play ball with us and you'll
be running Sheffield Media, Inc. in a few weeks. After all,
with Ms. Beaumont out of the picture, who else but you
would the board choose to become the next CEO?''

Hudson became silent as he weighed his options. He
loved Grace. She was the woman he longed to possess. But
Ollie was right—Grace didn't return his feelings. She would
never be his. But Sheffield Media, Inc. could be his to control.

"What do you want me to do?'' Hudson asked.

"Now, that's more like it. Booth likes cooperation. He
rewards team players.''

Hudson shuddered. He didn't want to be on Booth Fortier's team. He never had. He should have thought about
that sooner—like four years ago, when Ollie first contacted
him and dangled the carrot in front of his nose, promising
him Grace and Sheffield Media, Inc. in exchange for cooperation and information. He had made a deal with the
devil and lived to regret it. But once a man made a blood
pact with Fortier, he could never again he free. He was
doomed for life.

"Like I said, what do you want me to do?''

"What do you know about a kid named Troy Leone?''
Ollie asked.

"Leone? He's Elsa's kid brother, but I don't know anything about him except he's given Elsa a lot of trouble.''

"How close are Elsa and Grace Beaumont?''

"How close? Elsa is Grace's assistant.'' Hudson wondered where this game of Twenty Questions was leading.

"What about their personal relationship, Grace and
Elsa's?''

"They're friends.''

"Good friends?''

"Yes, very good friends.''

"How far would Grace go to save her good friend Elsa's little brother?"

"Damn, is that what this is all about? You plan to use the kid to get to Grace."

"Maybe."

Hudson felt awful, felt like the lowest pond scum. How had he sunk so low? He loved Grace, didn't he? How could he betray her this way? How could he offer her head on a silver platter to Booth Fortier? "Is that it? Is that why you called me?"

"That was one thing...but there's something else."

"What?" Hudson dreaded to even consider Ollie's response.

"Is Grace Beaumont still at the hospital?"

"She was a few minutes ago."

"If she's still there, then give her this information now. If she's gone home, pay her a visit this evening and inform her that the man she trusts so implicitly, her big, tough bodyguard, Jed Tyree, is none other than Booth Fortier's nephew."

"The hell you say! Tyree is Fortier's nephew?"

"That's right. Booth told me so himself."

"I don't understand any of this. You said you thought Tyree's name sounded familiar, but you didn't know who he was. Now you tell me—"

"Tyree left the organization seventeen years ago. I didn't go to work for Booth until several years later and he never mentioned his nephew."

"Why tell Grace? If Tyree is working for—"

"He's not Fortier's ally. Jed Tyree is his uncle's enemy and he poses a problem for Booth, being Ms. Beaumont's protector. Once she learns who he is, she'll dismiss him, maybe even dismiss the whole Dundee force. But at the very least, she'll distrust him completely."

"And you want me to be the one to deliver the bad news? Well, tell me this—how is it that I'm supposed to have come by this revealing information? I'm sure you don't want me to tell Grace that it came straight from Booth Fortier, do you?''

Ollie chuckled. ''Tell her you got an anonymous phone call. That will explain this call and give her an explanation as to how you found out about Tyree.''

''Once she fires Tyree, what if I can persuade her to forget about the investigation? Would Fortier allow her to live?''

''You really are hung up on the bitch, aren't you?'' Ollie sighed dramatically. ''Hasn't anybody ever told you that they're all alike in the dark? Start looking for another woman. Grace Beaumont is history.''

As the massive wrought-iron gates to Belle Foret opened for them and the Rolls entered the long driveway, Jed's cell phone rang. Grace glanced up at him, but didn't lift her head from his shoulder.

He grabbed the phone, hit the On button and said, ''Tyree here.''

''Listen very carefully,'' Dante Moran told him. ''We need you to get a message to Jim Kelly and since you have a good excuse to go see your uncle tonight, we figure this is the right time.''

''What excuse would that be?'' Jed felt J.J. and Grace watching him.

''An attempt was made on Grace Beaumont's life. A Dundee agent was seriously wounded. You should be outraged,'' Moran said. ''You should want to tell your uncle that it's war between the two of you, that you'll kill him if he comes near Ms. Beaumont again.''

''That excuse would work if I was a hotheaded idiot.'' Jed paused, considering the possibilities. ''Oh, I see. The hotheaded idiot is the part you want me to play.''

''You got it. And while you're visiting your uncle, find a way to let Jim know he should be ready in seventy-two hours. It's all coming together and he needs to be prepared.

We don't want Booth Fortier slipping through our fingers at the last minute.''

"I understand."

"Contact me if anything goes wrong. Otherwise I'll know the stage is set on that end."

Jed hit the Off button, then looked from Grace to J.J. "I'm going to pay Booth Fortier another visit. Tonight."

Grace gasped. "No. Why would you—"

"J.J. will stay with you," he said. J.J. nodded. "And Rafe should be on in a little while."

"I'm not worried about me." Grace lifted her head from his shoulder, her gaze focusing tenderly on his face. "I'm concerned what may happen to you if you go see that despicable man again."

Jed cupped her face in the cradle between his thumb and forefinger. "This is all going to be over soon. And you'll be safe. I promise."

"Will you be safe?"

"Don't worry about me, Blondie. I always land on my feet."

Instead of the romantic dinner that Grace had planned, she shared sandwiches in the kitchen with J.J. Blair. She liked the other female Dundee agent, whose effervescent personality was a contrast to Kate Malone's gentle, demure manner. J.J. moved quickly, talked fast, exuded an aura of frantic energy. Petite and vivacious, she looked nothing like a person's idea of a bodyguard. But in their dinner conversation, Grace had learned that this little ball of fire was not only a weapons expert, but she had mastered several martial arts. How deceptive that pretty face, that Elizabeth Taylor black hair and violet eyes were, Grace thought.

To pass the time, they decided to settle into the den and watch a documentary about ancient Egypt on the Discovery Channel. Rafe had phoned to tell J.J. he'd be arriving in about an hour, that he'd gone out and gotten supper for Dom and him. Both Grace and J.J. were concerned about Kate, although Rafe had said that the nurses had allowed them to go into the SIC unit to see Kate at seven and she was resting peacefully. And they were both worried about Jed. J.J. as his friend and Dundee comrade. Grace as his lover.

A soft rap on the door gained Grace's attention. "Yes?"

Laverna eased open the door. "Mr. Prentice is here to see you, Miss Grace. Shall I have him wait in the parlor or would you like for him to come to the den?"

"Ask him to come back here, please."

"Very well."

Grace turned to J.J. "I can't imagine what brings Hudson out here tonight." She wondered if he'd been upset because she'd left the hospital without saying goodbye. "I've never seen him in the condition he was in right after Kate was shot. But then, we were all half out of our minds."

"Seeing someone shot like that isn't easy for anyone," J.J. said. "But it had to have been more difficult for you, since you knew you were the intended victim."

"Kate saved my life. How do you ever repay someone for that?"

"It's our job," J.J. said. "Although it isn't that often we actually get wounded in the line of duty, we're always aware that it's a possibility."

Hudson cleared his throat as he stopped in the doorway. "Excuse me. Grace, may I see you alone, please."

"Sorry, but that won't be possible." J.J. rose to her feet and glared at Hudson. "Whatever you have to say to Ms. Beaumont, you'll have to say with me present."

"Grace, really…is it necessary for her to be here?" Hudson tilted his nose haughtily.

Grace glanced at J.J., then smiled at Hudson. "Please, come in and have a seat. And don't mind J.J. Just pretend she isn't here. I'm afraid Jed left specific instructions for me not to be alone until he returns." Well, that wasn't exactly true, but Grace understood that J.J. had no intention of leaving, so to avoid a ruckus, a little white lie was in order.

"Very well, but…I have something to tell you. Something you're not going to like."

Grace watched the peculiar expressions on Hudson's face, changing from indignation to excitement to concern. She had the oddest feeling that the concern was fake. "Mercy, you're being awfully mysterious. Whatever is it?"

"I received an anonymous phone call…at the hospital. If you'll recall, I went to the men's room to take the call."

"And…" Grace prompted.

"And what I was told is terribly upsetting. I hate to be the one to tell you, but you have every right to know. You should have been informed before you took Jed Tyree into your home and put your trust in him."

J.J. tensed as she scrutinized Hudson, her narrowed gaze and rigid stance a warning.

"Be specific," Grace said. "What are you talking about?"

"Jed Tyree!" Hudson's cheeks flushed bright pink.

"What about Jed?"

"God help us, Grace, you've been harboring this man in your home, putting your trust in him to protect you, to help you unearth evidence against—"

"Damn, Hudson, whatever it is, just say it."

"Very well, I will. Jed Tyree is Booth Fortier's nephew."

Chapter 20

Aric met Jed at the door, but made no attempt to stop him as Jed shoved Aric out of the way and stormed down the hall toward Booth's office.

"Mr. Fortier has already retired for the evening," Aric said, his deep voice utterly calm.

Jed spun around and glared at Aric. "Does the old bastard still have the same bedroom upstairs?"

"Mr. Tyree, if it's urgent for you to see your uncle, perhaps it would be better if I announce you."

Jed slung back his jacket to reveal his Beretta. "Shall I give it to you or do you prefer to take it from me?"

Aric came over and removed the 9 mm from its holster. "Come with me. I'll show you to your uncle's room."

Jed nodded, then followed the chauffeur/bodyguard up the stairs. "Wait out here," Aric said, before disappearing inside the bedroom. When he returned a minute later, a frown wrinkled his forehead. "He's willing to see you." Aric's glare issued Jed a warning. "Mr. Fortier isn't feeling well. Please, keep that in mind when you see him."

"He'll see me now? I don't have to wait or beg or humble myself?" Seeing Booth was only an excuse for the real reason he'd come here and he didn't look forward to another confrontation with his uncle. Where's Jim Kelly? Jed wondered. Would he get a chance to make contact with the FBI agent or would this trip turn out to have been for nothing? "Is Booth alone?"

"Quite alone," Aric replied. "Alone and...not quite himself."

Jed opened the door and marched in, but stopped dead still when he saw his uncle sitting on the edge of his bed, stooped over the nightstand's inlaid wood surface, brushing away something from the top and sending white dust floating in the air. Booth looked up at Jed through bloodshot eyes and grinned.

"To what do I owe the pleasure of this visit?" Booth asked, as he tried to sit up and wound up falling backward into the bed. He chuckled softly, then righted himself and waved Jed forward with a sweeping hand gesture.

Jed realized that Booth was either drunk or drugged—maybe a deadly combination of both. An almost-empty glass of what appeared to be whiskey sat on the nightstand. His uncle had always been a heavy drinker, but hadn't been an alcoholic. And although he'd bought and sold drugs, he hadn't touched the stuff himself back when Jed had lived under his roof. Apparently all that had changed.

"You're a sorry sight, old man." Jed came around the foot of the bed and stood there staring at his uncle. "No wonder you have to beat the hell out of your wife in order to feel anything. You probably haven't been able to get it up in years."

Growling like a wounded bear, Booth tried to stand, but didn't manage to get to his feet before dropping back down on the bed. "You're treading on thin ice, boy." Booth stuck his index finger out toward Jed. "You may be my nephew and I might have loved you once, but that doesn't give you the right to—"

"And you don't have the right to murder people." Jed rushed right up to Booth and looked him square in the eyes. "Somebody tried to shoot Grace Beaumont today, but then you already know about it, don't you? Well, your guy missed. He shot a Dundee agent instead. Grace is alive and well and more determined than ever to nail your sorry ass."

"If you'd been more like me and less like your mama, you'd have had the guts to stay with me, to learn from me, to take over my empire." Booth reached out and grasped Jed's shoulder. "But you're weak, just like she was weak. I tried to help her, tried to fix her mistakes..."

"By killing the man she loved!"

Booth squeezed Jed's shoulder. "I take care of my own. I did what I thought was right. She never understood, never forgave me. I had no choice but to have her locked away and to keep her drugged so she wouldn't try to go to the police. Hell, boy, she was my sister. I couldn't kill her, could I?"

Jed stared at his uncle, who used Jed as a crutch to support himself as he stood. "Are you saying my mother wasn't crazy, that she didn't have mental problems?"

"Surely you understand why I did it? Why I kept her locked away from you and kept her from running her mouth off to the police. It was either keep her in that sanitarium or kill her. I made the right choice, didn't I, Jed?"

Bile rose to Jed's throat and for just a minute he thought he might throw up. All these years he'd thought his mother was crazy, when she'd actually been sane. God in heaven. What had it done to her being sane and locked up and held a prisoner in a mental hospital for most of Jed's life? Had the drugs she'd been forced to take been what had finally killed her?

Jed put his hands around his uncle's neck. Booth's head snapped up and he stared into Jed's eyes. Before he realized what he was doing, Jed tightened his hold. Booth gasped as Jed strangled him. He wanted to kill Booth. God, how he wanted to kill the man.

Suddenly Jed released his uncle, who dropped to his knees, coughing and spluttering.

"You aren't worth killing." No, he wouldn't murder his own uncle. He could wait for legal justice. The FBI was closing in on Booth; his days were numbered. Besides, there wasn't much left of the man Jed had once known. Apparently Booth Fortier had almost succeeded at self-destructing.

The door to the adjoining bedroom flew open and Ronnie Martine barged in, with Charmaine hovering in the doorway behind him.

"Mrs. Fortier heard loud voices and was concerned," Ronnie said. "Are you all right, Mr. Fortier?" Ronnie rushed over and helped Booth to his feet.

Booth cleared his throat, and through bleary eyes, glared at Jed. "If you were anybody else, I'd kill you."

"Don't you mean you'd have me killed, old man? You haven't got what it takes to do the job yourself and we both know it."

Booth clung to Ronnie's huge arm. "Get him out of my house. And issue an order to Aric and the others that Jed Tyree isn't welcome in my home." Booth focused on Jed. "You leave now, boy, while you still can. And if I ever see you again, I'll forget you're my nephew."

Ronnie eased Booth down on the side of the bed. Charmaine came running into the room, hovering about, fussing over Booth. Putting on a damn good show of concern. Ronnie walked over to Jed, grasped his arm and marched him out into the hall.

"Walk straight down the stairs," Ronnie said. "I'm seeing you to your car and making sure you're off Fortier property once and for all."

When they reached the front door, Aric blocked their path. They paused and watched while the big black man unloaded the clip from Jed's Beretta, then tossed the gun to him.

"Why did you throw it all away, man?" Aric asked. "He would have given you everything. Even after all these years, if you'd come back and told him you wanted in, he'd have given you a second chance.''

''A second chance to turn out just like him? No thanks!''

''I'm seeing him to his car and making sure he leaves,'' Ronnie explained to Aric as he shoved Jed out the door.

Once outside, Jed began talking fast, keeping his voice low so that only Ronnie could hear him. He'd burned all his bridges tonight. He wouldn't be coming back here ever again.

''Tell Moran I know the combination to the safe here at the house,'' Ronnie said. ''But most stuff is kept in safety deposit boxes, enough evidence to put Booth and other big-wigs in the syndicate away for life. And to have Governor Lew Miller impeached. Charmaine can and will help us once Booth is arrested and I get her away from here. Tell Moran I want immunity for her and we'll both need to go into the Witness Protection Program when this is all over.''

Jed realized just how serious the undercover agent was about Charmaine Fortier. ''You're in love with her, aren't you?''

''Yeah. And it's mutual,'' Ronnie said. ''That lady has lived in hell for a long time. All I want is a chance to make her happy. I'd do just about anything to see that happens. Can you understand?''

Jed allowed Ronnie to shove him behind the wheel of his rental car. He looked up at the big, rugged FBI agent and said, ''Yeah, I understand. There's a lady I feel the same way about.''

''Don't tell me—it's Grace Beaumont?''

Ronnie grinned, then sobered instantly in case anyone was watching them closely. ''Hell, Tyree, you're as big a fool as I am.'' Ronnie slammed the door, crossed his arms over his chest and watched while Jed drove away.

Yeah, Jed thought, he was a fool. A fool in love.

Troy Leone packed all his belongings into black plastic garbage bags, took them out to his pickup and dumped them into the truck bed. Just as he'd thought—once he told Josie he'd quit his job at the warehouse, she'd told him to get lost. Maybe he should have waited and told her after he'd talked to Elsa. After all, he couldn't be a hundred percent sure his sister would let him move back in with her. Not after the way he'd acted, after all the things he'd said. He wouldn't blame her if she'd washed her hands of him for good this time. But when he'd called her, she had agreed to see him tonight. That was a good sign, wasn't it? He checked his watch. Damn, he was running nearly two hours late. Josie had insisted he take all his things tonight. Screwy bitch!

As Troy dumped the last bag in the truck, he started rehearsing his speech, the one he'd give to Elsa. He'd have to be humble and not lose his temper no matter what she said to him. And he'd have to agree to pretty much anything she asked. She had already given him so many second chances that he'd lost count. But he bet she hadn't.

Just tell her you're sorry. Yeah, sure, like she hasn't heard that before. *Promise her you'll get your act together for real this time.* After all he wasn't doing drugs and that should please her. What the hell would he do if she turned him away? She won't do that, he told himself. *She's your sister. She loves you.*

Troy opened the door and started to hop up in the cab when a big hand clamped down on his shoulder. He froze, then glanced back to see Curt Poarch grinning at him. Troy's heartbeat accelerated at an alarming speed.

"Mr. Poarch." Troy's voice quivered. "What—what are you doing here?"

"I came to see you."

"Me? About what? You know I appreciated the job at the warehouse, but—"

Curt jerked Troy backward and put his arm around his shoulder. "This isn't about the warehouse job. It's about something more important. My boss wants to see you. He thinks you're just the man we need."

"Me? But I'm not. I told you people already that I'm not the right guy for—"

"Why don't you let us be the judge of what you're the right man for."

Oh, God, help me, Troy thought. Who the hell are they going to want me to kill?

Jed drove around for a while before he returned to Belle Foret. He needed some time to cool off, to think about what he'd almost done. He'd come damn close to strangling his uncle tonight and that knowledge scared the hell out of him. Was he, like many of the Fortiers before him, a murdering bastard at heart?

Once he had himself under control, he'd called Moran and Sawyer MacNamara with updates from Jim Kelly. The FBI's main concern was that Booth would find a way to escape before he was arrested. Their second biggest concern was that Booth would find a way to get rid of any evidence against him. But Moran had been pleased to learn that Charmaine Fortier was willing to betray her husband.

"Kelly has promised her immunity from prosecution and a new identity under the Witness Protection Program," Jed had told Moran.

"If the lady can provide enough evidence to put her husband away for the rest of his life, we'll give her anything she wants."

Jed didn't bother telling Moran that Jim Kelly intended to disappear along with Charmaine, once Booth had been prosecuted and found guilty. He'd let Kelly tell his superiors that he'd fallen in love with the Mafia don's wife.

Jed pulled up in front of the gates that separated Belle Foret from the rest of the world. A little kingdom all to itself, once ruled over by a king and his princess, now held for posterity by the new queen. And Grace *was* a queen. Elegant. Refined. Cultured. All the things he wasn't and never would be. Hell, his mother had been a Fortier. Nothing could ever change that fact. Okay, so she'd been a Fortier, but she hadn't been insane the way Booth was. And he'd never heard anything about either of his grandparents being mentally deranged, despite his grandfather's mob ties. He'd heard the old man had been unscrupulous, devious and mean, but not certifiable. Apparently insanity didn't run in the family as Jed had thought...as he had feared all these years. He had been so afraid that one day he'd snap and go mad the way his mother had done. He'd kept that secret fear locked away inside him, refusing to deal with it, but he had never married, never fathered a child, in great part out of fear he would pass along defective genes.

When the gates opened, Jed drove the rental car up the driveway. There in the distance he saw the exterior and interior lights shining, welcoming him home. Home? Who was he trying to kid—Grace Beaumont might enjoy having him as a sex partner, but she knew as well as he did that at least six generations of Sheffields would roll over in their graves if she were to make a lifetime commitment to a man like him.

The minute he parked the car and got out, Rafe Devlin walked onto the veranda to wait for him. Instinctively Jed knew something was wrong. When he stepped up on the veranda, Rafe motioned him away from the front door. Not a good sign.

When they'd walked to the end of the sprawling porch, Rafe looked out at the vast front lawn, then stuffed his hands in his pants pockets. "We had a visitor earlier this evening."

Jed's heart lodged in his throat. "Grace—"

"Physically, she's fine," Rafe said.

"Just spit it out. What happened?"

"Before I got here, while J.J. and Ms. Beaumont were here alone, Hudson Prentice stopped by and dropped a bombshell on our client."

Jed's heart stopped for a split second. He knew what Rafe was about to say.

"He claims he received an anonymous phone call," Rafe

said. "And he couldn't wait to get here to share the big news with his boss lady."

"Just say it, will you."

"He told her that you're Booth Fortier's nephew."

The whole world caved in on Jed, the weight resting heavily on his chest, making breathing impossible. Numbness set in. Then suddenly the air rushed into his lungs and he let out a long, shuddering breath. Feeling returned to his limbs and torso...and to his brain, and with it came excruciating pain.

"How did she take it?" Jed managed to say.

"I wasn't here, but J.J. said it hit her pretty hard. It seems she struck out at Prentice, called him a liar and ordered him to leave. But later, when she'd had time to calm down, she came right out and asked J.J. That happened about the same time I arrived."

"You told her the truth, didn't you?"

"Yeah, I did. I knew you wouldn't expect us to lie for you. After all, it was only a matter of time before she found out." Rafe cut his eyes in Jed's direction, then glanced away hurriedly. "Hell, man, you should have already told her."

"Where is she?"

"She went upstairs to her room, locked herself in and not even the old housekeeper can get her to come out or respond in any way."

"I have to talk to Grace, try to make her understand."

When Jed turned and headed for the front door, Rafe caught up with him and grabbed his arm. "Maybe you should wait until morning. Give her a chance to digest the information."

Jed shrugged off Rafe's grip, shook his head and kept walking. He heard his fellow Dundee agent huff loudly. Okay, so Rafe thought he was making a mistake. He got the message. What Rafe didn't understand was that he couldn't risk letting Grace decide she neither wanted nor needed him, as a bodyguard. If she rejected him personally, he'd find a way to live with it. But he couldn't allow her to fire him as her personal protector. He knew in his gut that Booth had pulled Hudson Prentice's strings. Booth wanted Jed off this case. He wanted Grace vulnerable and exposed.

Once inside, Jed took the stairs two at a time. When he reached Grace's bedroom door, he stood there, hesitant, and said the first real prayer he'd uttered in he couldn't remember when. *Don't let her hate me. Please, let her understand.*

Jed knocked on the door. No response.

"Grace?"

He knocked again.

"Grace, please, let me talk to you. Let me explain."

He leaned over and pressed his head against the door. Of all the women on earth, why did she have to be *the one?* Most women wouldn't give a damn that he was Booth Fortier's nephew. But Grace cared. It mattered to her in a way it couldn't matter to anyone else.

"Grace, I'm sorry. I should have told you."

Jed grabbed the crystal doorknob, and much to his surprise, it turned and the door opened. Had she unlocked it for him? He eased the door back a little bit at a time until he could see inside the dark room. She hadn't bothered turning on a light; only the pale, shadowy glow from the moonlight drifting through the windows saved the area from total darkness.

"Grace?"

Moving slowly and carefully, he entered the bedroom and began searching for Grace. Within moments he saw her sitting in one of the two chairs flanking the fireplace. All he could make out was her silhouette. He flipped the switch that activated the wall sconces on either side of the mantel and a soft, creamy blush washed over Grace. She sat staring off into nothingness, her hands folded neatly in her lap. When Jed approached, she didn't move or speak. He went down on his knees beside her chair, but didn't touch her.

"I didn't mean for you to find out the way you did. I'm sorry. I should have told you myself."

"Yes, you should have," she said in a soft, low whisper.

"I know you probably hate me." His hand hovered over her arm. He wanted to grab her, hold her, never let her go. "Hell, I hate myself. I've spent seventeen years trying to run away from the fact that I'm Booth Fortier's nephew and I thought I'd succeeded. Until this case. And even then, I had no idea how much it would cost me to be that monster's blood kin."

Grace turned to him, and when he saw her red, puffy eyes and the tears still clinging to her eyelashes, he felt as if his heart was being ripped from his body. He knew he didn't deserve this woman, knew he was all wrong for her, but knowing the facts didn't stop him from wanting her—wanting her more than he'd ever wanted anything in his entire life.

"Hate me if you must," Jed said. "Don't forgive me for lying to you, for keeping a horrible secret from you, but do not fire me. Don't send me away. Please, Grace, allow me to remain your bodyguard. Keep me and the Dundee agents on the job."

Grace reached out and rubbed her fingertips across his cheekbones and it was only when she touched him that he realized he was crying. He didn't understand what was happening. He didn't cry. Not ever. Not since his mother died when he was a teenager. Nothing and no one had ever mattered that much to him. Not until Grace.

"I won't go," he told her. "Do you hear me? I won't leave you!"

"My poor Jed." Grace caressed his cheek.

Emotion choked him. He swallowed hard, then grabbed Grace's hand, brought it to his lips and turned it palm up to kiss. He was so overcome by her gentle touch, by her kind heart, that he couldn't speak.

Grace turned around, leaned over and pulled Jed to her. He pressed his head against her bosom as she wrapped her arms around him. When she laid her cheek against the top of his head, he slipped his arms around her and held on for dear life.

"How can you be so kind to me?" he asked, his voice harsh because he was trying so hard to conceal how emotionally vulnerable he was. "My uncle is the man who ordered your husband and father murdered."

"He ordered your father's murder, too," she reminded him. "It isn't your fault that your mother was Booth Fortier's sister. None of us chose our families."

Grace cupped Jed's face with her hands and urged him to look at her. When he did, what he saw surprised him beyond belief. Although crying, Grace smiled at him. Her face blurred quickly through the mist of tears in his eyes. She lowered her head and brushed her lips over his.

"I've had a couple of hours to think about you and me and why you didn't tell me about your relationship to Booth Fortier," she said. "My emotions have pretty much run the gamut. But I realized something a few minutes ago when I heard your voice outside my door." Holding his breath, he stared at her. Praying. Hoping beyond all reason. "When all is said and done, you're as much a victim of Booth Fortier's viciousness as I am. Perhaps even more so."

"Ah, Grace...Blondie—"

She kissed first one cheek, then the other. "I love you, Jed. Knowing who your uncle is doesn't change that fact."

"But do you trust me?" he asked.

"Yes, of course, I trust you."

"Enough to put your life in my hands?"

"Yes. Now and forever." She kissed him with a passion born of desire and uncertainty.

Jed returned her kiss, deepened it, took it to its furthermost reaches. When she curled her arms around his neck, he lifted her into his arms and carried her to bed. And they made slow, sweet love to each other, savoring every moment, understanding how precarious and unpredictable life can be.

Chapter 21

Elsa finished checking e-mail, then rose from her swivel chair and picked up her empty coffee mug. Grace had asked her to send out for lunch, so Elsa had included her order with the others. The delivery boy from Café Continental should be here in the next five minutes, giving her just enough time to refill her coffee mug and drop off a couple of file folders to Mr. Prentice's office. Odd that she hadn't seen him this morning. Customarily he made up excuses to frequent Grace's office. Maybe he'd finally realized he was never going to get to first base with Grace, especially now that Jed Tyree was in the picture. Although Grace hadn't confided in Elsa about her personal relationship with her bodyguard, it didn't take a genius to figure out they were crazy in love. It was all they could do to keep their hands off each other. What a time for Grace to fall in love, Elsa thought, then sighed. She was twenty-eight and had never been in love. When had she ever had time to form a serious relationship with a man? Being both mother and father to her three siblings hadn't afforded her the luxury of even dating all that much in the past ten years.

When Elsa approached Mr. Prentice's outer office, his secretary Terrie, who stood with her ear to her boss's door, saw Elsa and put her finger to her lips in a Be Quiet gesture.

"What's going on?" Elsa asked.

"Sh...Mr. Prentice just arrived a few minutes ago and I notified Mr. Tyree, as I'd been told to do. Then Mr. Tyree came storming down here and marched right into Mr. Prentice's office and has been giving him a tongue-lashing. It seems he's accusing Mr. Prentice of betraying Ms. Beaumont." Terrie leaned back against the door and listened. "Oh, my gosh, I believe Mr. Tyree just fired Mr. Prentice."

"I don't think Mr. Tyree has that authority," Elsa said.

"Uh-oh, it's gotten awfully quiet in there." Terrie scurried away from the door and barely made it into her chair before Jed barreled out of Hudson Prentice's office.

"Morning, ladies." Jed grinned as he glanced from Elsa to Terrie. "Why don't you take an early lunch today, Terrie? Mr. Prentice will be leaving for the afternoon. He has an appointment with Chief Winters, who will be here shortly to pick him up for questioning."

As soon as Jed disappeared down the hall, Terrie leaned over and gushed with information. "Mr. Tyree accused Mr. Prentice of being in cahoots with Booth Fortier. I didn't believe it, but now I do. If the chief of police is coming to get Mr. Prentice, then it must be true. Mr. Prentice claims that Mr. Tyree has no evidence against him, but he sounded scared. And Mr. Tyree said that the Dundee Agency has Mr. Prentice's personal telephone records that show he recently made several phone calls to a man named Oliver Neville."

Elsa dropped the file folders on Terrie's desk. "Don't spread this type of gossip around the office. Wait until Ms. Beaumont makes an official announcement. If Chief Winters isn't going to arrest Mr. Prentice, only question him, then perhaps it's all a big misunderstanding."

"Oh, yeah, sure thing. But I heard Mr. Tyree tell Mr. Prentice that things would go easier for him if he told the truth instead of waiting until the police had more evidence against him."

Elsa nodded, then turned and headed back toward the kitchenette area near her office, knowing the minute she was out of earshot, Terrie would be spreading the news throughout the complex. Elsa wasn't sure why the thought that Mr. Prentice might be involved with a mobster didn't surprise her. Perhaps it was because she'd never really respected Hudson Prentice, although she'd often felt sorry for him. What did surprise her was that he would betray Grace. She'd been so sure he was in love with Grace.

No sooner had Elsa returned to her desk, with a full coffee mug in hand, than her telephone rang. As she placed her coffee on a coaster atop her desk, she picked up the receiver.

"Sheffield Media, Inc. Grace Beaumont's office. How may I help you?"

"To whom am I speaking?" The voice was disguised, making certain Elsa couldn't identify it later.

"This is Elsa Leone, Ms. Beaumont's personal assistant."

"Miss Leone, I have someone here with me who'd like to speak to you."

"Who is this?" Elsa asked as she buzzed Grace's office, per Jed Tyree's instructions, were she to receive a suspicious call. "What do you want?"

"Elsa, it's Troy." Her brother sounded scared to death. His voice quivered. "Please, sis, you've got to help me. If you don't do what they say, they're going to kill me."

"Troy, who has you? Where are you?"

Jed rushed out of Grace's office, an extension phone to his ear. When Elsa looked up at him, he nodded and motioned for her to keep talking.

"Troy? What's going on?" Elsa asked.

"Troy's a little tied up right now," the voice said. "But he sends his love."

"What do you want?"

"Your cooperation."

Elsa's stomach knotted painfully. "I'm listening."

"How much do you love your little brother? Enough to exchange your boss's life for his?"

Elsa closed her eyes as the painful realization hit her—someone connected to Booth Fortier had kidnapped Troy. "I don't understand—"

"Now, don't play dumb with me, Miss Leone. Not when I know what a smart girl you are. So listen up. Here's the deal—you find a way to bring Grace Beaumont to us and we'll give you back your little brother all in one piece."

"But how do you expect me to—"

"That's your problem. Figure it out. I'll call you back in one hour to tell you where we'll make the exchange."

The dial tone screamed in Elsa's ear. The end. Finality.

Elsa glanced up at Jed, her frightened gaze meeting his troubled glare. "What—what am I going to do?"

"Don't panic," Jed told her. "We'll find a way to help your brother."

"But how? You heard what he said—they want Grace."

"Who wants me?" Grace walked out of her office into Elsa's just as the delivery boy from Café Continental arrived.

After Jed took the box lunches, then paid the boy and tipped him generously, getting rid of him as quickly as possible, he explained the details of Elsa's recent phone conversation to Grace.

Grace put her arms around Elsa. "We won't let them harm Troy." She looked to Jed. "Will we?"

"I don't want either of you trying to figure out a way to help Troy. Do you hear me?"

Jed's gaze went from Grace to Elsa and back to Grace. "I need to talk to the other Dundee agents, then contact my boss." He put his hand on Elsa's shoulder. "We'll figure out a way to save Troy without putting Grace in danger."

Elsa nodded, but knew in her heart that what Jed Tyree had promised them simply wasn't possible.

* * *

An hour later, after Elsa received the second phone call from the mystery man and Jed had been in contact with both Sawyer MacNamara and Dante Moran, the Dundee agents were assembled in Grace's office.

"No way in hell am I going to allow this," Jed bellowed.

"It's the only way to save Troy," Grace said.

Jed paced the floor like a wounded bull preparing to charge. Grace understood how he felt; if their roles were reversed, she'd feel the same. And it wasn't as if she was being noble or was fearlessly prepared to walk into the lion's den. She was scared senseless. But they truly had no other choice.

"I know it's not a foolproof plan." Dom Shea watched Jed moving about frantically. "But Moran has promised us that the Feds will be all over the place within fifteen minutes of Grace's arrival at the warehouse. They'll be as thick as flies on sh—" He cleared his throat. "They're moving up their timetable by forty-eight hours in order to take advantage of this situation."

"To hell with their timetable!" Jed spun around, leaned down and grasped the arms of Grace's chair on either side. "Don't you understand that there is no way either the FBI or Dundee's can guarantee your safety? I'm not willing to risk your life. Not to save Troy Leone or anybody else. And certainly not to catch Booth Fortier. A week ago you might have been willing to die to bring Booth to justice, but I thought…I thought you felt differently now."

Grace grasped both of Jed's wrists and looked up into his face, their gazes connecting. "I want to live now more than I've ever wanted to live. Everything in my life is different. You know that." Grace sensed a hush fall over the room and knew that Elsa and the three Dundee agents were all aware that Jed and she were lovers. "But neither of us could live with ourselves if we don't do all we can to save Troy and to put Booth Fortier behind bars for the rest of his life."

Jed pulled away from Grace and stood, then glanced from

one Dundee agent to the other. Dom, Rafe and J.J. "I'm going with her."

A rumble of protests arose from the agents, then Rafe said, "You can't do that and you damn well know it. For this thing to work, it's got to look as if Elsa and Grace slipped away from all of us without telling us what had happened with Troy."

"I'm not letting her go in alone," Jed told them.

"She won't be alone," Dom reminded him. "Not for long. She'll be wearing the homing device and we'll know where she is at all times, even if they move her from the warehouse. Once everything is in place, Moran's people will move in. And we'll be with them. I told Moran you had to be part of the rescue mission."

Grace stood, walked over to Jed and slipped her arm around his waist. "See, in the end, you'll be my knight in shining armor."

"Some white knight I am." Jed pulled her into his arms and held her fiercely. "If anything happens to you…"

"Whatever happens…" She glanced around the room. One by one, Elsa and the Dundee agents made hasty exists, leaving Grace and Jed alone. "Whatever happens, I want you to know that the time we've had together has been wonderful. You've brought me back to life, given me a reason to—"

He kissed her with all the passion and frustration he felt. And she gave herself over to the moment, pushing aside her fear. *Please, dear God, help us. I don't want to die. I want to live. I want a chance for a new life…with Jed.*

Two hours later Elsa drove her Honda Civic to the Garland Industries warehouse and parked out front as she'd been told to do by the mystery voice over the phone. Grace adjusted her blouse and glanced down at the cameo attached to the gold necklace the FBI agent had brought to Sheffield Media and placed around her neck.

"There's a small homing device inside the cameo," Special Agent Taylor had explained.

"We'll be able to track you as long as you're wearing the necklace."

Elsa turned to Grace. "I'll never be able to thank you enough for doing this. You're risking your life for Troy."

Grace patted Elsa's hand where she clutched the steering wheel. "Jed and the Dundee agents aren't going to let us get hurt. And don't forget that the FBI knows what's happening and they're going to arrest Booth Fortier today. To add to all his other crimes, they'll now be able to prove that he was behind Troy's kidnapping."

Elsa took a deep breath. "If only Troy hadn't gotten himself involved with these people, this wouldn't be happening."

"No time for worrying about all that," Grace said. "Now, come on. We're to go to the door over there—" Grace glanced in the direction "—and knock once, then they'll let us in."

Elsa nodded. "He said that they have Troy here and will make the exchange as soon as we arrive."

"Then let's get this over with."

Grace opened the passenger door, got out and waited for Elsa. They walked down the sidewalk and to the front door of the Garland Industries warehouse. Elsa knocked once. The door opened. They went inside the dark, dank, cavernous building, but didn't see anyone, not even whoever had unlocked the door for them. Grace's heartbeat thundered in her ears. Be brave. Show no fear, she told herself.

"You did a very good job, Ms. Leone," a man's voice said, but still they could see no one. "By now, Ms. Beaumont, you must know that your assistant has led you into a trap."

"What's going on here?" Grace asked. "Who are you? Elsa said Troy was in trouble and asked me to come here with her to get him. Where is Troy Leone?"

"Troy is safe," the voice replied. "For now."

Elsa called loudly, ''You promised me that if I delivered Grace, you'd free Troy.''

''Free Troy?'' Grace went into her astonished act. ''What do you mean, free Troy? What's going on here?''

''You may leave now, Ms. Leone. Your brother will be returned to you safely in a few hours.''

''No, that wasn't the deal,'' Elsa said, the nervous strain in her voice all too real.

''I demand to know what's going on?'' Grace planted her hands on her hips.

''Unless you want to die with Ms. Beaumont, then I suggest you leave, Ms. Leone.''

''Die?'' Grace gasped, then turned to Elsa and slapped her. ''You ungrateful little bitch! After all I've done for you, you hand me over to—whoever you are, you're working for Booth Fortier, aren't you?'' Grace stumbled around in the eerily dark building as she searched for the source of the voice; then she whirled around and glowered at Elsa. ''Go ahead and leave. Do it now, unless you're having second thoughts and are willing to die with me.''

Go, damn it, Elsa. Leave while you still can. Grace issued the silent warning. She didn't want Elsa to try to do anything heroic. If Troy Leone was still alive, these people could hardly let him go, not if he could identify them later. Elsa knew, as Grace did, that Troy's only hope was being rescued when Grace was rescued. Hopefully, they were holding Troy here at the warehouse. Otherwise…Grace didn't want to think of the alternative.

''I want my brother!'' Elsa held up her hand in a tight fist.

''Leave now and we'll send him to you. If you stay, you and he will both die with Ms. Beaumont.''

Elsa spun around and hurried to the door. Once Elsa was outside, Grace sighed with relief. But before she could say a prayer of thanks, a tall, hawk-nosed man came from out of the shadows; a short, stocky man, with an acne-scarred face followed him. Instinctively Grace began backing up.

Hawk-nose grabbed her by the arm. She thought about protesting, but knew it would be futile. *Are they planning on killing me now?* Grace wondered. *Or will they wait for Booth Fortier to come and watch?*

The man dragged her into motion, taking her through the warehouse, as the stocky guy guided their way with a flashlight. When they reached the rear entrance, Grace balked, realizing they were going to take her away. But where?

"Strip," Hawk-nose said.

"What?"

"Strip down to your slip," he told her.

"I'll do no such thing."

"Either you do it or I'll do it for you."

Reluctantly Grace removed her jacket, blouse and skirt, leaving her body covered by a beige silk slip. The cameo rested on her bosom, atop the heavy lace adorning the bodice of her slip. *Oh, Jed, please be close by. I'm being as brave as I can be, but I don't know for how long. I'm scared. I'm really, really scared.*

"The shoes, too," he told her.

She took off her leather pumps.

"All your jewelry."

"Why can't I keep on my—"

He ripped the necklace off her and threw it on the ground. "Want me to take off your earrings, too?"

Grace quickly divested herself of her earrings, watch and heavy gold bangle bracelet. The stocky guy opened the back door. Hawk-nose lifted Grace off her feet, tossed her over his shoulder, carried her outside and down to the loading dock. Within minutes Grace realized their intent. They placed her in a speedboat, tied her hands behind her back, gagged her with a foul-smelling rag and while Hawk-nose sat beside her, the other one started the boat's motor.

How would Jed ever find her now? The homing device was back at the warehouse, and she was being taken away to only God knew where.

Chapter 22

Jed and Rafe slipped into the warehouse, a silent, deadly operation to rescue Grace—and Troy Leone, if the boy was still alive. With the precision of trained soldiers, they moved about inside the dark cavern, searching for any sign of life. After a thorough survey of the entire place, they ended up with two flunkies who'd been left behind as guards to protect the illegal contents of the building. With both men tied up and left for the Feds, Jed and Rafe made their way to the doors that opened onto the loading dock at the back of the warehouse.

Jed spotted the pile of clothing lying just inside the door. He reached down and grasped Grace's blouse in his hand. "God damn it! They made her strip out of her clothes."

Rafe pointed to several shiny gold objects on the sidewalk, a few feet outside the door. "That looks like Grace's jewelry, including the cameo Special Agent Taylor gave her."

"That means she's not wearing the homing device." Anger and frustration surged through Jed. And fear. Fear like nothing he'd ever known in his life. Not even in battle. "They're taking her to Booth."

"You can't be sure—"

"I'm sure. Booth enjoys playing games. He'll want to toy with Grace first." Jed balled his hands into tight fists, the thought of Grace in Booth's hands unbearable to him.

"Don't go off half-cocked," Rafe said. "We'll find her. I'll call in Moran now and—"

"If we don't find her soon, it'll be too late." Jed stormed off toward the river, mumbling to himself. "I knew this wouldn't work. I tried to tell them. I begged her not to go through with it. But would they listen? No! Would she listen? Damn it, Grace, don't you dare die. Do you hear me? Don't you dare die!"

Within five minutes the entire block was swarming with FBI agents, covering every inch of the warehouse and the surrounding area, including the pier. Dante Moran sent a team down river in case Grace's captors had spirited her away by boat, as Jed suspected.

When Jed tried to get away, slip off so he could head for Booth's place in Beaulac, Elsa Leone ran up to him. "Where are they? Is Grace all right? Is Troy alive?"

"Neither of them are here," Jed told her. "Troy was probably never here, at least not in the past few hours. And I have no idea if he's alive. Maybe. And Grace—Grace is gone. Taken away. And we have no idea where."

"Oh, God, no!"

"If y'all had listened to me, this wouldn't have happened. At least Grace would be safe, but no, you and Grace were so eager to do what the FBI wanted that you didn't consider their scheme might get Grace killed." Jed glowered at Elsa.

Elsa gasped; her face paled. "I'm sorry...I...er...I—"

"Take it easy on her, will you. This isn't Ms. Leone's fault." Rafe came up behind Jed and gripped his shoulder. "She didn't want anything to happen to Ms. Beaumont anymore than you did."

Jed heaved a deep sigh. "Cover for me, will you? I'm

going to the source. If Booth isn't holding Grace at his house, then somebody there will know where they are."

"You can't go in there alone," Rafe said. "From what you've told me that place is overrun with guards. They'll shoot you before you get ten feet beyond the gate."

"I know the place like the back of my hand. I can probably get inside and make it to the house without being detected. Once I'm there, I'll kill anyone who gets in my way."

"I'll go with you," Rafe said. "And we'll call Dom and J.J. and have them meet up with us—"

A familiar voice called out to them, "Where do you two think you're going?" Dante Moran joined their threesome. Completely ignoring Elsa, he glanced from Rafe to Jed. "Look, Tyree, I know you're pissed about the screwup, but we'll find Ms. Beaumont. We have teams closing in on Booth Fortier right now. It's only a matter of time before we arrest him."

"Time isn't on Grace's side," Jed said. "If we don't find her soon, it'll be too late."

"What did you have in mind?"

"Finding Grace."

"You and Devlin were thinking about going to Fortier's home, weren't you?" When neither Jed nor Rafe replied, Moran continued, "Drive out there with me. By the time we get there, one of our teams will already be there and have cleaned out the place. If Fortier is there, we'll take him into custody. And either he or one of his employees will tell us where Grace Beaumont is being held."

Jed laughed sarcastically. "You don't know Booth Fortier if you think he won't kill Grace before you people take over his private domain. If she's in Booth's home, then you've signed her death warrant."

By the time the FBI team entered the Fortier home, Ronnie Martine had hurriedly told Charmaine about his true identity and enlisted her help in securing the house. The domestic servants surrendered without a fight and lined up in the hallway to wait for the Feds.

No one else was inside the house, except Charlie Dupree who had shown up early this morning and gone straight to bed. Aric had driven Booth away over an hour ago, without informing anyone of where he was going. But Charmaine knew. When Booth had informed Aric of his plans, she'd listened at the door connecting her bedroom to her husband's.

As Ronnie and Charmaine waited for the federal agents, Charlie Dupree came bounding downstairs, barefoot and wearing only his jeans and gun holster. Apparently he'd been asleep when he'd heard the ruckus outside.

"What the hell is going on?" Charlie asked as he noticed the servants lined up in the hallway. "Sounds like all hell has broken loose outside. Are we being raided or what?"

"The FBI has stormed the compound," Ronnie said. "They're arresting anyone who doesn't resist and killing those who do."

"Sons of bitches! What the hell are you doing holed up in here?" Charlie ran toward the front door. "Are you coming with me or not?"

"Don't open that door," Ronnie ordered.

Charlie glanced over his shoulder and noted that Ronnie's 9 mm was aimed directly at his back. "What's this? You turning traitor?"

"I'm giving you a chance to surrender," Ronnie told him. "Toss your gun aside, put your hands over your head and—"

Charlie whirled around and opened fire. Ronnie shoved Charmaine behind him, and as Charlie's bullets splintered the door facing to their right, Ronnie took aim and fired. His shot struck Charlie's hand, sending his gun flying. But that didn't stop Charlie, who hit the floor and rolled through the living room doorway, then snatched a knife from his jeans pocket, flipped it open and slung it toward Ronnie. When the blade pierced Ronnie's shoulder, he winced in pain and dropped his weapon, Charlie jumped up and came barreling toward him. Just as he pounced, Charmaine grabbed Ronnie's gun off the floor. She didn't give Charlie any warning. She just shot him. He staggered around and looked at her, his gaze plainly saying he couldn't believe she'd done it. Charlie slumped to the floor.

Just as Charmaine ripped open Ronnie's shirt to inspect the knife wound, the front door burst open and half a dozen FBI agents burst into the foyer.

Half an hour later, Jim Kelly, aka Ronnie Martine, was being treated by the paramedics. Jed paced the floor outside on the front porch shortly after he and Rafe arrived with Dante Moran. With each passing minute, the chances of finding Grace alive grew slimmer and slimmer. Although the Feds had rounded up a couple of dozen underlings, five household staff and a badly wounded Charlie Dupree, Booth was nowhere to be found.

When the paramedics carried Jim to the waiting ambulance, Charmaine followed them, then paused and looked at Jed. "Wait just a minute," she called out, "I'm riding in the ambulance with Ron—with Special Agent Kelly." She grabbed Jed's arm, leaned over and whispered, "Booth's at the old mill. There's no one there except him and Aric. I heard him tell Aric that he wanted to take care of Grace Beaumont personally."

"Thanks, Charmaine. You just might have saved Grace's life."

"I hope so." She kissed Jed's cheek. "Good luck."

Before the ambulance was out of sight, Jed pulled Rafe aside. "I know where Booth is holding Grace. Give me a fifteen-minute head start, then tell Moran."

"Don't go in there alone," Rafe said.

"I think I can handle Booth and Aric. Charmaine told me it's just the two of them." Jed gripped Rafe's arm fiercely. "I need to do this alone. If the Feds swarm the place, he'll kill Grace for sure."

"Ten minutes, but that's it," Rafe said. "Now, tell me where you're going?"

Booth Fortier was a sadistic monster. Grace clenched her teeth tightly as he struck her again, pain shooting through her stomach as his hand connected with her face. She couldn't believe that such an evil man was Jed's uncle.

"You're trying to be a brave lady, aren't you," Booth said snidely. "But I'll have you begging for mercy soon enough." He slapped her again. For the fifth time or the sixth? Grace didn't know. She'd lost count. She did know that the right side of her face was numb. If only the rest of her was, too, then she wouldn't be able to feel the pain. She hadn't cried, but she was screaming inside. How much longer could she resist the urge to scream aloud?

"Maybe you'd like to see me kill the kid first," Booth said. "Would that scare you enough to make you yell?"

Booth walked over to where Troy Leone lay on the floor, his hands and feet securely tied, his mouth gagged. Grinning with apparent delight, Booth kicked the boy in the ribs. Grace winced.

Booth rushed back to her and put his face down in front of hers where she sat strapped to a rickety wooden chair. "I can make you scream." He removed a small pocketknife from his pants, flipped it open and ran the tip across Grace's slip, from one breast to the other. "Talk to me, Grace. Tell me what you fear the most."

Grace swallowed hard and looked the devil in the eyes, doing her level best to show no fear. He was going to kill her. But he wanted to torture her fist. Torture her for his own sadistic pleasure.

"You know that I could kill you quickly," he told her. "But what's the fun in that?"

The big black man standing guard at the door called out, "I hear a car."

"Go check it out," Booth ordered. "I don't want anyone interrupting my fun. You hear me, Aric?"

Aric opened the door and went outside, while Booth continued to toy with Grace. Using his pocketknife, he sliced Grace's slip from bodice to hem. A couple of times the blade's tip nicked her flesh. One nick on her belly, the other on her thigh. When Booth pulled apart the silk garment and saw the two bloodstains on her flesh, he smiled, then wiped off the blood and licked his finger.

The door swung open and someone shoved Aric inside, then came in behind him. Grace blinked several times to clear the moisture from her eyes. Then she saw Jed. Jed! Oh, God, Jed had found her.

"Well, well, look here at what the cat's dragged in," Booth said, turning his attention to Jed. "How the hell did you find me, boy?"

"Let her go," Jed said.

"Now, why would I do that?"

"Because if you don't, I'm going to kill you."

Booth laughed as he glanced from Jed to the gun he held on Aric. "You can't kill both of us. If you shoot me, Aric will jump you. If you shoot Aric, I'll have my Ruger out of its holster before you get off a second shot." Booth eyed his shoulder holster, the rich brown leather gleaming against his sweat-stained, white shirt.

"Are you willing to bet your life on that, old man?" Jed asked.

"I could kill her right now." Booth held the knife under Grace's throat.

Jed growled. Booth eyed him speculatively.

"I know you'd hate to lose a client. Wouldn't look good on your record," Booth said. "Or is it more than that? You haven't been screwing Ms. Beaumont, have you?" Booth laughed. "Was she good, boy? Did she purr for you? Hell, I can't get her to say anything."

Jed glanced from Grace's badly bruised face to her eyes. She gazed at the boy lying in a pathetic heap on the floor. That's when Jed noticed Troy Leone. He cursed softly under his breath.

"I know you probably don't have the stomach to watch," Booth said. "You being weak like your mama, but if you leave now, you won't have to see her die."

Jed aimed his Beretta straight at his uncle. "Let her go or I'll shoot you."

"No you won't. I'm your mama's brother. Your uncle. That good guy conscience you inherited from your old man would torment you until the day you died if you kill me. I know you, Jed. You might want to kill me, but you won't."

"I will, if that's what it takes to save Grace."

"Grace, is it? You call her Grace and not Mrs. Beaumont. Then I was right. You did have her, didn't you?" Booth glared at her. "Did you think just because he screwed you, he loved you? We Fortier men don't love women, we use them. And if you think he'll kill me to save you, you're wrong."

"No, you're wrong," Grace said, finally speaking to the loathsome creature.

Just as Booth prepared to slit Grace's throat, two gunshots rang out within seconds of each other. One bullet hit Fortier between the eyes, the other entered his heart. The pocket-knife in his hand fell into Grace's lap. Aric cried out and rushed toward his boss, as Rafe Devlin and several other men stormed into the old mill. Jed dropped his gun and ran toward Grace. He squatted beside her and gently cupped her bruised face. Two men, whom Grace assumed were FBI agents, apprehended the big black man, then the tall, lanky agent in a dark suit who seemed to be in charge walked over and inspected Booth Fortier's body.

He glanced at Jed and said, "My bullet killed him. He was already dead when yours hit him."

"How can you be so sure it was your bullet that killed him, Moran?" Jed asked.

"Take my word for it. You didn't kill your uncle. I did."

"Yeah, sure." Jed hurriedly untied Grace and lifted her into his arms. "I'm getting you to the hospital as fast as I can."

She draped her arm around his neck. "I don't need to go to the hospital. I'm all right. Just a few bruises. Please, Jed, take me home." As Jed carried her toward the door, she called to the one Jed had referred to as Moran. "Please, take care of Troy." She glanced down at Elsa's bound brother lying in a heap on the floor. "I don't think he's badly hurt."

Jed carried her out the door and to his car. With such tenderness that his loving care broke her heart, Jed placed her in the front seat, then gently kissed her forehead.

"I'm sorry, Grace. God, I'm so sorry."

"You have nothing to be sorry for," she told him. "Don't you know that? You're my white knight, my protector, my hero."

Rafe Devlin herded a dirty, tattered and slightly bruised Troy Leone outside and over to Jed's car. "Mind if we catch a ride with y'all? You could drop me and the boy off at his sister's on the way to Belle Foret. Moran said the kid and Ms. Beaumont can answer questions tomorrow."

Jed grumbled.

"Yes, please, come with us." Grace glanced in the back seat after Rafe and Troy got in. "Troy, are you all right?"

"Yes, ma'am, I'm okay." He bowed his head. "Hey, Ms. Beaumont, I'm sure sorry about what happened. It was stupid of me to ever go to work at the warehouse. If I'd known what would come of it, I'd never...." He swallowed and cleared his throat.

"If you're truly sorry, go home to Elsa and prove to her what a good person you can be. You owe it to her to straighten up your act permanently."

"Yes, ma'am. I swear that's exactly what I'm going to do."

When Jim told her that Booth was dead, Charmaine didn't quite believe him. How was it possible for such evil to die so quickly and easily?

"I want to see his body," she said.

"Honey, you don't want to do that."

"I won't believe he's dead if I don't see him."

"All right," Jim said. "I'll see if I can arrange it. I'll go with you to the morgue, but once that's done, I'm getting you out of Louisiana as fast as my boss can arrange things."

"You're coming with me, aren't you?" She clung to him, knowing that without him, she couldn't make it, that her life wouldn't be worth living.

"Let them try to stop me." He kissed her temple. "I've already told my boss that I'm resigning from the Bureau as soon as possible. He told me that he'd allow me to live under federal protection with you until after the trials of Booth's associates are over, then they'll arrange for us to go into the Witness Protection Program. We'll have new identities and new lives."

"We'll be just ordinary people, with ordinary lives." She sighed, loving the thought of being Jim's wife. "I guess I won't have to get used to calling you Jim, will I, since you'll have another name when we relocate."

"If you can call me husband and lover and maybe the father of your children, I don't care what other name you call me."

"Children? You—you want children?"

"If you do. Maybe only one. A little girl who looks just like you."

Charmaine cried; tears cascaded down her cheeks. "Oh, Jim...my sweet, sweet darling. You really want me—" she thumped her chest "—me—to be the mother of your child."

"Of course, I do. I love you, Charmaine. I think you're beautiful and smart and brave...fun to be with and—I want to spend the rest of my life making you happy."

She laid her head on his chest and said the first real prayer she'd uttered since she was a kid, thanking God for bringing this fine, loving man into her life.

The lights inside and outside Belle Foret shone brightly, welcoming its mistress home. When Jed leaned over into the front seat of the car and scooped Grace up into his arms, Laverna and Nolan came rushing out onto the veranda. Jed carried Grace up the steps and into the house, the servants following, both making a big fuss over Grace.

"I'm all right," she assured them. "Really, I'm fine."

"Where are your clothes?" Laverna asked. "And your poor face."

"My clothes don't matter and the bruises on my face will fade in a few weeks."

"Should I go upstairs and run you a hot bath?" Laverna headed toward the staircase.

"Don't bother," Jed said. "I'll take care of Miss Grace."

"Yes, sir." Laverna backed away and gave her husband a knowing look.

Jed ignored everything and everyone, concentrating only on Grace. She clung to him, her head on his chest, her arm around his neck. He'd come damn close to losing her tonight. Although he would have killed Booth to save Grace— had actually pulled the trigger—he was grateful that Dante Moran had acted first, that he could tell himself it was the FBI agent's bullet that had ended Booth's life. As much as he hated Booth, the man had still been his uncle. And there had been a time he'd cared about him. Despite growing up as the heir to a Mafia kingdom and later having spent years as a member of the Delta Force, Jed found that he still possessed a conscience.

The minute Jed entered Grace's bedroom, he slammed the door closed with his foot, marched into the bathroom, set her on the vanity stool, then turned on the shower. He tended to her with the utmost gentleness, removing her tattered slip, her bra and panties, grimacing at the bruises on her body where she'd been manhandled by Booth's goons and struck repeatedly by Booth himself.

"Don't think about it," Grace said. "It's over. He's dead. He can never hurt me or you or anyone else ever again." Grace caressed Jed's cheek. "Not unless you allow him to continue to influence your life."

Not saying a word, Jed stripped, took Grace's hand and led her into the huge shower stall. She went with him. No second thoughts. No hesitation. She knew that she would follow this man anywhere. She would trust him now and forever—with her body, her heart, her very soul. Like a dutiful caretaker, Jed washed Grace, shampooing and rinsing her hair, lathering her body and taking special care to be gentle with her. As he sprayed away the soap bubbles, he kissed each bruise and each tiny knife prick; then when he had cleaned her, he helped her out of the shower and dried her body and her hair. As she sat on the vanity stool and watched him, Jed dried himself. She couldn't take her eyes off him.

He lifted her into his arms. "Let me make love to you."

She smiled softly. "I want that. I want us to make love." She kissed him. "I need you, Jed. I need you so very much."

He placed her in the middle of her bed and lay down beside her. She reached for him, but he grasped her hands and placed them on the pillow above her head, then leaned over and captured her mouth in a ravaging kiss. Her hungry response ignited his passion even more. Whispering hot, erotic words of urgency and expectation, Jed caressed and kissed her from forehead to the instep of each foot. It seemed he was trying to memorize every inch of her body. And when she knew she couldn't bear another moment of his arousing attention, she touched him intimately, which gained her his immediate attention.

"Make love to me now, Jed," she told him breathlessly. "I'm aching so. I need you inside me."

He pulled himself over her, bracing himself with his elbows, keeping part of his weight off her slender body. "Don't let me hurt you."

"The only way you'll hurt me is if you make me wait."

He took her in one fast, deep thrust, embedding himself fully inside her. She gasped as he filled her completely, his shaft large and hard. Lifting her hips, meeting him lunge for lunge, she gripped his large shoulders and gave herself over to the pleasure. They mated in a frenzy, both wild with need. And when she felt herself on the verge of release, she slid her hands down his back and dug her fingers into his taut buttocks, urging him to hurry. "Faster," she panted. "Harder and faster."

He jackhammered into her. "Like this." Sweat glistened on his forehead.

"Yes," she cried out as fulfillment claimed her. "Yes, yes."

Minutes later, he jetted into her, groaning in the throes of his own climax.

Jed slid off her and onto his back. He lay there beside her, staring up at the ceiling. Grace cuddled against him, then threw her arm across his waist and nuzzled his neck.

"We're good together," she told him. "You know that, don't you?"

"In bed, we're good together." He stroked her naked hip. "Great sex isn't a problem for us, but—"

She popped her index finger over his lips to silence him. "Do you love me?"

"Do I—how can you ask me such a question?"

"You've never told me you love me."

"And you want to hear the words, want to hear me say it." He rose up, leaned over her, looked her directly in the eyes and said, "I love you, Grace. More than anything."

She grinned. "That's what I thought, but I needed to know for sure. After all, when a woman is planning on spending the rest of her life with a man, she needs to know from the very beginning that he loves her."

"What do you mean—spending the rest of her life…the rest of your life with…Grace, you can't mean that you actually want me to be a part of your life."

Sighing contentedly, she lifted her arms around his neck. "Only for the next fifty or sixty years. Just until we have great-grandchildren running all over Belle Foret and they bury us side by side in the family cemetery."

"Are you by any chance asking me to marry you?" Jed's gaze locked with hers.

"Would that be so bad? You and me and two or three babies and—"

He kissed her.

When he lifted his head from hers, he said, "You know who I am, what I am, what I come from, and you still want to marry me and have my babies?"

"Uh-huh."

"Blondie, you must be crazy," he told her, humor in his deep voice.

"I am," she said. "Crazy in love with you."

"Then before you come to your senses, I'm going to accept your proposal." He flipped over, pulled her on top of him and held her firmly against him. "No big wedding. Something small and private. Something just for us. Okay?"

"Sounds perfect to me. How about a week from Saturday?"

"In a hurry?"

"Could be. After all, we didn't use any protection when we made love, so I could already be pregnant."

"In that case, let's get married right away and I'll forget all about buying that super-size box of condoms. If you're not already pregnant, you will be by the time our honeymoon is over."

Grace lay there in Jed's arms, happy beyond belief. Four years ago her life had changed drastically in the span of a few hours. Now once again her life had altered completely, but this time for the better. Nothing could have prepared her for falling in love with Jed Tyree. The passion she felt overwhelmed her.

"I love you, Jed. You're everything to me. For now and forever."

"I feel exactly the same way about you, Blondie. Now and forever."

Epilogue

Grace sat in the ornate white wicker rocker on the back veranda, the twilight sky a canvas of glorious color. She loved this time of day. Early evening. And she loved this season—springtime—when the world was fresh and alive, bursting with new life. She covered her protruding belly with her hand and caressed the mound that contained her precious daughter. Elizabeth Ann was due to arrive in less than three weeks. The pink nursery, filled with lace and frills and dozens of dolls, awaited the birth of Grace and Jed's third child.

Life was good. So very good. There wasn't a day that passed that Grace didn't thank the good Lord for her many blessings. She would never forget Emma Lynn and Dean. They would be a part of her heart forever. And to this day, she still missed her father. But in the six years she'd been married to Jed, she had known true joy. Happiness beyond measure.

Looking back—which she seldom did these days—she thought about those weeks and months following her kidnapping and Booth Fortier's death. Jed and she had married a few weeks later and he'd been at her side, sharing his strength with her, during the dark days that followed. Governor Lew Miller had been impeached, arrested and found guilty of numerous crimes. It was doubtful he'd ever be released from prison. The crime syndicate in Louisiana had taken a nearly fatal blow, but even she knew that nothing would totally eradicate the Southern Mafia. What had been the most difficult for Grace was accepting the fact that Hudson Prentice had been an accomplice in Dean's and her father's murders. She had trusted him, believed him to be a true friend, and he had betrayed her in the worst way possible. He had written to her from prison, begging for forgiveness. She had burned his letters and never responded. Hudson, who had confessed everything, was serving a life sentence, as was Oliver Neville.

Grace watched Jed romping in the backyard with their sons. Their firstborn, five-year-old Byram was tall and lean, with his father's hazel-brown eyes and the same white-blond hair Grace had as a child. Dark-haired, three-year-old Lance squealed with boyish laughter as Jed scooped him up in his arms and sat him on his shoulders. He waved at his mother, his big blue eyes sparkling with mischief.

During the past six years, Grace had spent a great deal of time on maternity leave and whenever she returned to work—even part-time—Lois, their nanny, accompanied her to Sheffield Media, Inc. headquarters with both boys in tow. Byram would start kindergarten in the fall, but by that time, Elizabeth Ann would be spending a great deal of time with her mommy at work. Of course, Grace never could have managed juggling motherhood with her CEO responsibilities without Jed's support. After a year of training at her side, shortly before Byram was born, she had nominated Jed for the presidency of Sheffield Media, Inc. and the board had wholeheartedly and unanimously approved.

With Lance on his shoulders and Byram holding his hand,

Jed marched Grace's men toward her, all three smiling as they approached.

"Daddy says we can make ice cream tonight," Byram said. "Can we, Mommy? Please, please, please."

"Please, Mommy," Lance added, not to be ignored.

Jed swung Lance around as he sat down in the wicker chair beside Grace, then planted his younger son in his lap. "Yeah, Mommy, we all want ice cream."

"Byram, go tell Nolan to get out the ice cream freezer," Grace told her elder son. "And ask Laverna to prepare the recipe for vanilla—" She paused when she noted Byram's frown. "Let's make that strawberry. I believe we have fresh berries, don't we?"

"Yea!" Byram jumped up and down. "Strawberry is my favorite!" He raced up the back veranda and inside through the kitchen door.

Jed leaned over and kissed Grace. Caught between them, Lance squirmed, then when they parted, he held out his arms to Grace, who grabbed him and hauled him over into her lap. His fat little hand patted her swollen stomach.

"Baby," Lance said.

"Baby sister," Grace replied and placed her hand over his.

With Byram at his side, Nolan brought out the old crank-style ice cream freezer and put it on the edge of the porch. "Go get your brother," Nolan said, "and you boys can help me bring out the ice and salt."

Lance scooted down off Grace's lap and ran to Nolan, who took the child's hand and headed back inside, with both boys in tow. He stopped in the doorway and said, "Miss Joy just telephoned. She's back from her shopping trip to New Orleans and said she's got a ton of baby clothes she wants to bring by. Wanted to know if tonight was all right."

"I'll phone her in a few minutes," Grace said.

Jed stood, held out his hands and lifted a rather awkward Grace to her feet, then he sat back down and pulled Grace onto his lap. "Have I told you today how much I love you and how happy I am being your husband?"

Grace draped her arm around his shoulders. He laid his open palm over her belly.

"That works both ways, you know. I love you. And I love being your wife."

"Who would have ever believed that you and I would be so perfect for each other?"

"We, my darling, were a match made in heaven. I've always believed that Daddy and Dean and Emma Lynn sent you to me." She kissed Jed. "I love you. You and the boys and this little girl—" Grace laid her hand over Jed's where it rested on her stomach "—are my life."

Jed cupped her chin in the valley between his thumb and forefinger. "It's all right, you know, that you still love Dean and Emma Lynn. Your loving them doesn't take anything away from me and our children. You have such a big heart that you have more than enough love for all of us."

Tears gathered in Grace's eyes. "Jed Tyree, see what you've done—you've made me cry." She laid her head on his shoulder and cuddled against him. "Have I told you lately what a wonderful man you are? The absolutely best husband and father in the world."

"Ah, Blondie…" Jed kissed her. Passionately.

A couple of minutes later, Byram and Lance came racing out of the house, then skidded to a halt beside the wicker chair.

"Shelby Lou Perkins, who's in my Sunday school class, says that's how babies get here," Byram said. "When mommies and daddies do all that kissing and hugging and stuff."

"We're getting a baby sister," Lance said proudly.

"Yeah, I know," Byram replied. "That's because our Mommy and Daddy do a lot of that stuff. I guess we're going to wind up with a whole bunch of baby brothers and sisters."

It was all Jed and Grace could do not to laugh out loud. With two little Mr. Know-it-alls, life was never dull at Belle Foret. As a matter of fact, Grace thought, life was just about perfect.

* * * * *

AN HONOURABLE WOMAN
by
Lindsay McKenna

For Michael Burdet of Switzerland, friend,
shaman, healer and inspiration…

I cherish our friendship.

Dear Reader,

I'm proud to introduce Chief Warrant Officer Cam
Anderson's story to you. I'm sure you will love reading
about her adventures, her challenges and her growth as an
individual and a woman.

Cam is a combat pilot and a very good one at that. She's
seen combat, had close calls, and, in her most harrowing
mission, she crashed a helicopter after it was fired on and
hit. She is still struggling to come to terms with this
traumatic event when her commanding officer, Major Maya
Stevenson, chooses her for an even more daunting mission:
Maya asks Cam to become a commanding officer of a small
contingent of Apache helicopters stationed in Mexico, just
below the border with the US.

More than anything, Cam wants to impress her
commanding officer—and she wants to atone for the
mistakes she believes she made on her last mission. But she
learns that it is one thing to be a combat helicopter pilot
and completely another to be a leader and manager of
people—especially a squadron of male pilots, who don't
want to be 'bossed around' by a woman. Cam has her work
cut out for her and then some! Will she make the grade?
She wonders about that—and whether she should give her
heart to one of those pilots, Chief Warrant Officer Gus
Morales. Gus is too intriguing and charismatic to resist,
and Cam finds herself in a battle to maintain her
command—and keep her heart safe from being hurt again.
Will she be able to salvage her honour on both fronts?
Read on and find out!

Warmly,

Lindsay McKenna

Chapter 1

"Hey!" Wild Woman hissed as she stuck her head around the door of the ready room. "Have you heard yet, Cam?"

Cam halted her pacing and quit gnawing on her fingernails, which were almost nonexistent at this point. "Er, no…not yet." Turning toward the door, she watched as Jessica Merrill, U.S. Army CWO2, otherwise known as Wild Woman, entered the room, dressed in her close-fitting black flight uniform. "You got the duty?"

Cam had had flight duty for the last twenty-four hours and was waiting to be relieved by another crew.

Wrinkling her nose, Wild Woman said, "Yeah. Me and Snake are taking over from you." Hooking a thumb across her shoulder toward the door of the Quonset hut, which stood inside the massive cavern where the Black Jaguar Squadron had its base of operations, she added, "Snake'll be along any second now." Looking at her watch, she uttered darkly, "Geez, 0600 comes so early. What I'd give to have a day off and sleep in. No such thing as 'beauty sleep' around here, is there." She patted her cheek. "I'm still good-looking despite that handicap."

Chuckling, Cam nodded. Sitting down at the picnic table and picking up her cup of coffee, she said, "Yeah, I know what you mean. But you're right—we're such gorgeous girls we don't need beauty sleep."

Going to the coffee dispenser that sat on a dark green army-issue desk, Wild Woman laughed. "But isn't that why you volunteered for this new mission coming up, Cam. So you'd get to sleep in?"

"Oh, sure!" Cam snorted. Running her fingers through her shoulder-length reddish-chestnut hair, she muttered, "I'm on pins and needles. I don't think I'll get it."

"I saw Morgan Trayhern a few hours ago. He just flew in from Agua Caliente, piloted by Storm Queen." Grabbing a chipped white cup, Wild Woman poured herself some of the strong coffee. "He looked serious."

"Yeah," Cam said unhappily, "I saw him. He's with Major Stevenson and Major York, reviewing the short list of possible pilots for this mission." Shrugging, Cam watched her colleague walk confidently to the table and sit down opposite her. Jessica had short blond hair with a bright red streak dyed in it. Major Maya Stevenson, commanding officer of the BJS, allowed Wild Woman this unique expression of herself. It went well with her pilot handle, Cam thought with an inward smile. And all you needed to do was take one look at Jessica's square face and frosty blue eyes filled with feral intelligence to understand why she was one of the best Apache gunship pilots here at the squadron. She was competitive, rebellious, and never afraid to break rules and regulations over the skies of Peru or Bolivia when it came to stopping the drug trade.

"You'll get it," Wild Woman said confidently, sipping her coffee.

"I dunno," Cam muttered worriedly. She gnawed again on her index finger.

"You don't have any nails left, Cam."

Chuckling, Cam looked at her fingers, then at her friend. "You're right about that."

"You always do that when you're nervous—No Nails Tree Trimmer!" Jessica chortled.

"Tree Trimmer" was Cam's nickname. Every pilot got one after graduating from flight school. She'd earned hers by dropping the Huey helicopter she'd been flying into the jungle in Peru. Of course, at the time she was being shot at by a Kamov Black Shark helicopter, piloted by a Russian mercenary hired by a drug lord to shoot her out of the sky.

Feeling heat rush into her cheeks, Cam grinned. "I look forward to the day when I can earn a new and better handle."

Laughing huskily, Wild Woman turned her head as the creaky door to the ready room opened and closed. "Hey, Snake! My, don't you look bright-eyed and bushy-tailed, girl."

Snake glared at them as she entered the hut. Pushing her straight, dark brown hair off her shoulders, she headed for the coffee urn. "Shut up. I haven't had my java yet," she growled.

"And a dreary good morning to you, too," Cam murmured, a grin crawling across her mouth. "Depriving Snake of her coffee is like stepping on the rattles of her tail...."

"Yeah, and she bites," Jessica giggled. "Forget any hissing. This girl just sinks her fangs into you."

Cam saw that Vickey Mabrey—Snake—was dressed into her combat uniform, too. She was all set for her twenty-four-stint duty with Wild Woman. The Velcro fastening of her uniform collar was open at her throat, exposing the dark green cotton T-shirt she wore beneath. The body-fitting uniform, made of special fire-retardent materials, hugged her tall, lean figure.

"Both of you can it. Gawd, I need my coffee." And Vickey reached for the pot.

Cam grinned across the table at Wild Woman, who had a twisted, evil smile on her own face. "No one walking into this place could tell you two were the best of friends, could they?"

"Military friendships are like that—full of verve and content," Wild Woman murmured sagely, sipping her coffee.

"Humph," Snake said, pouring herself a mug of coffee.

"So, you're worried about getting this assignment, Cam? You're cut out for it, you know," Wild Woman stated.

Shrugging, she muttered, "I don't even know what the assignment *is,* so why am I sweating it?"

"Who's in the running?" Snake asked as she sauntered over and sat down at the end of the table near her friends. Stirring creamer into her coffee, she breathed in the rich scent as she lifted the cup to her lips.

"Storm Queen and Pele," Cam replied. She truly admired Pele—Lieutenant Mirella Gallardo, one of the first two women helicopter pilots in the Peruvian Army. Pele was the Hawaiian goddess of volcanoes, and Mirella had gotten the handle because of her hair-trigger temper and in-your-face attitude. Mirella was a take-no-prisoners kind of woman on the ground and in the air. She'd fought hard to become one of the first Peruvian women to fly helicopters and her competitiveness was legendary. Here at BJS, she was competent, aggressive and combative in the air—the exact qualities a gunship pilot needed in order to survive.

"Humph. You'll get it, Cam," Snake said, huddling possessively over the coffee, her long, thin fingers wrapped around the mug in a death grip.

"Yeah? Why?" Cam asked.

"Because it's your turn for something good to happen to you." A sly grin edged her full mouth. "I mean, there was nowhere to go but up after you gave that poor jungle a haircut with the runners of that Huey."

Wild Woman burst out in raucous laughter and slapped her knee. "Snake, you have deadly humor at 0600."

"Thanks, ladies," Cam growled good-naturedly. She saw a glimmer of humor dancing in Snake's narrowed green eyes. Vickey was half Navajo and half German—an unusual blend, Cam thought. She was

quiet like her Indian father, and meticulous like her
mother, a college professor of botany who hailed from
Cologne. Snake's skin was a golden color, hinting at
her mixed heritage. Cam had seen a photo of her
friend's parents, and knew she favored her father
physically. She had taken after him in many ways,
from what Cam could tell. She was a good listener,
but when she spoke, everyone stopped jabbering and
paid attention.

In the air, Snake was a deadly gunship pilot. She
was absolutely lethal and had no qualms about facing
off with drug runners in a game of sky chicken, where
whoever blinked first turned back. Snake never
blinked. As she'd wisely pointed out one time, snakes
don't blink at all. She was proud of her handle and
lived up to it daily.

"How long have Maya and Morgan been confab-
bing?" Jessica asked, heading to the coffeepot for her
second cup of coffee.

"At least an hour," Cam answered glumly.

"You don't even know what this mission is and
you *want* it?" Snake wrinkled her nose and then
shook her head. "That's why I didn't volunteer to be
interviewed. I want to know going in what I'm volunteering for. Not after the fact."

Cam saw an evil grin spread across Snake's oval
face. "You know the major wouldn't throw us to the
wolves," she retorted. "I figured it would be fun to
get out of here for a while. Three years is a long
time."

"And leave us?" Wild Woman cried in a pitiful,
dramatic voice as she poured more coffee into her
cup. "I mean, we're *sisters!* You love us, Cam. You

know you do! Hell, we've spent three years of our lives down here, hangin' out in this cave, chasin' bad guys together. We're bonded.''

"More like welded," Snake added dryly.

"Yeah, that, too. Thanks, Snake, that says it better." Wild Woman sat down and gave Cam a mock serious look. "You'd actually run out on us? Who says this new mission has any women on it? Look what Akiva got into," she exclaimed, referring to one of their colleagues. "She got chosen for that Gulf of Mexico black ops with Joe Calhoun, along with three enlisted women from BJS."

"That was a great mission," Cam said fervently. "I'd have given my right arm to take part."

"Well," Snake counseled in a soft, husky tone, "Akiva and Joe are doing well out there...now. At first it was rocky for Akiva, until she settled into her job as a C.O. Big difference, being just a pilot versus commanding officer of an operation, you know?"

"But," Wild Woman said, "she did it. She rose to the challenge."

"Do you think that because Akiva and Joe made it a success, another mission like that might be on the table?" Cam wondered.

"Don't count on it," Snake advised. "Maya isn't known to duplicate operations. She keeps things hot and lively. That way—" she grinned "—we don't grow bored around here."

"No one from personnel gave a peep about this covert mission," Jessica muttered with a frown, more to herself than to them. "I tried pumping Sergeant Prater the other day for info, but got nada. Nothing. She's buttoned up tighter than a clam about it. She works directly for Major Stevenson, so she knows what it's all about. But she ain't sharin'.''

Chuckling, Snake stated, ''Prater's got more sense than you, then. She knows if she gossips about it to us, Maya will have her red head on a platter, pronto. She's smart to keep her mouth shut in front of the likes of you while you're nosin' around like a curious coyote.''

Wild Woman grinned. ''Hey, I gave it the ol' college try, didn't I? I wasn't born to understand the word *no*.''

''I don't think I'll get it,'' Cam muttered, running her fingertips across the roughened surface of the table. ''Storm Queen and Pele are both wonderful pilots.''

''You're always cutting yourself down, Cam. Don't you see yourself as equal to those two gals?'' Snake demanded, her voice hardening.

Shrugging, Cam said in a painful whisper, ''I guess not. I mean…after I deserted Maya out there in the jungle and left her to be captured by the druggies…'' She sighed.

''Quit chewin' on that, will you?'' Snake shook her head in disgust. Taking a rubber band out of the thigh pocket of her flight suit, she gathered up her straight hair and fastened it in a ponytail at the back of her head. ''You made the *right* decision, Cam, not the wrong one. The Peruvian jungle is damned near impenetrable. You couldn't have carried Maya, wounded and unconscious, anywhere. You had to escape.''

''Yeah,'' Wild Woman interjected, ''and if you hadn't gone to get help, how would we have known what really happened? It was only when Major York found you and got you back here that we knew Maya had been captured.''

''Not that Maya needed any rescuing,'' Snake chuckled darkly. ''She took care of that drug lord dude right and proper. Buried the bastard in the Canyon of Death. Yeah, that was a right fine burial ground for the likes of him.''

''Well, we got there in the nick of time,'' Wild Woman said.

Sighing, Cam slowly got up. ''I need a third cup of coffee like a hole in my head,'' she muttered unhappily, heading for the dispenser along the wall, ''but I'm in dire need today....''

''After two cups we can't scrape you off the ceiling,'' Snake complained. ''You're maxing out at three.''

''High-wire act, Cam the Tree Trimmer.''

''Funny, girls. Very funny...''

The door to the Quonset hut opened. ''Chief Anderson?''

Jumping as her name was called, Cam whirled around. Sergeant Prater, dressed in her dark green cammies, stood expectant in the doorway, a serious look on her freckled face.

''Yeah?''

''Major Stevenson wants to see you, ma'am.''

''Er, thanks...yeah, I'll be right there, Sergeant. Thank you.''

Prater smiled and nodded. ''Yes, ma'am.'' The door closed.

''Ohh,'' Wild Woman teased, ''you're gonna get this mission, I got that feelin'!''

Frowning, Cam set her empty cup on the counter. "Maybe, maybe not. Maybe the major is callin' me in to tell me Pele or Storm Queen got it, instead."

"You're such a die-hard pessimist," Snake groaned. "Gawd, gimme another cup of coffee...." Gracefully she unwound herself from the chair, a grin lurking at the corners of her mouth.

"You think?" Cam asked, heading for the door. "That I got it?"

Waving her hand, Wild Woman chortled. "Oh, honey, you're such a widget at times! My gut says yes. What does yours say, Snake?"

"That I need another cup of java."

Laughing, Cam headed out the door and waved goodbye to them. "I hope you two have a quiet shift."

"Oh, yeah, right. That's just what I want," Snake growled.

"I'm bored already," Wild Woman griped. "Don't wish that on us, Cam!"

"Okay, ladies, may the Sharks come out and hunt your butts, then. See you later! I'll let you know what happens!" Cam couldn't keep the hope out of her voice. Closing the door, she turned to her right and hurried across the black lava floor of the cave. All around her, the noise of women's voices as well as the clang of tools being used on the Apaches in the rear of the cave echoed and reechoed.

Wiping her mouth in a nervous gesture, Cam barely paid attention to the activity on the wide lip of the cave, their landing and takeoff point. At this time of morning the clouds were thick, hiding the cave entrance. The sun hadn't come up yet so the fog hadn't burned off. Hurrying across the mammoth cave complex to the two-story headquarters building on the other side, Cam felt her heart racing. Had she gotten the secret mission? Had Jenny Wright, the psychologist who worked for Perseus and who had interviewed her awhile back, chosen her to head this one up? Cam hoped so with all her heart and soul. Trying not to run, she hurried toward the steel grate stairs that wound up to the second floor of H.Q., where Major Maya Stevenson, her boss and commanding officer, had her office.

More than anything in the world, Cam wanted this mission. She *had* to prove to Maya that she was worthy, that she could be counted on not to run from a situation, as she'd run from the crash, leaving her superior behind to be captured.

Wiping her mouth again, she rapidly climbed the steps two at a time, her heavy black boots shaking the staircase in the process. She entered the door at the top, which led to a long passageway lined with open doors. The army personnel who ran the black ops base—those in charge of communications and planning—were all here. Cam hurried down the hall, nodding to various enlisted women as they came and went from their offices.

Cam headed to the last door on the right, Maya's office. The C.O. was a woman of incredible ability and leadership. Many times Cam wished she had some of the confidence and wisdom her boss had. To Cam, Maya was a role model, someone she nearly worshipped. Though she'd been born in Brazil, Maya had been adopted by an American colonel and his wife early in her life, and had grown up in the United

States. But rumor had it that Maya had a very mysterious background. Even her name suggested the mystery inherent in her birth, and pilots of the Black Jaguar Squadron were always whispering about her almost uncanny powers and abilities.

Maya had single-handedly fashioned this black ops out of nothing. She had been one of the first women to take Apache helicopter training at Fort Rucker, Alabama, getting badly burned by gender prejudice in the process. Afterward, she had contacted her father, a U.S. Army general by that time, and gotten him to help her set up the BJS base—a covert operation dedicated to stopping cocaine shipments from leaving Peru, one of the main producers of the drug. He'd agreed, and the rest was history. Now Maya was C.O. of the all-female Black Jaguar Squadron.

Cam had joined Maya when she'd graduated from the next class at Fort Rucker, volunteering to come down to the all-woman base. She'd never for a second regretted her decision.

Halting at Maya's door, which was open as usual—part of her open-door policy so that anyone who needed to could see her—Cam nervously smoothed the fabric of her black uniform. Then she knocked briefly. ''Major Stevenson? You sent for me?''

Maya lifted her head from her desk, which was covered with paperwork. ''Yes, come in, Cam.''

Entering, Cam stood at attention. ''Reporting as ordered, ma'am.''

''At ease, Cam. Have a seat.'' Maya gestured toward a chair in front of the desk. ''Oh…close the door?''

Feeling her heartbeat speed up, Cam gulped, did an

about-face and closed it. Only rarely did Maya ask that her door be closed. It meant she was going to say something that she didn't want to be overheard. Was she going to announce that Cam wasn't getting the mission? Dying inwardly, Cam kept her expression carefully neutral and sat down gingerly in the chair. Placing her hands on her thighs, she waited, holding her breath as Maya placed a bunch of signed orders into her out basket for Sergeant Prater to distribute.

Smiling warmly, Maya set her pen aside and folded her hands in front of her. "I'm sure it hasn't escaped your eyes or ears that Morgan Trayhern flew in this morning?"

Grinning a little and feeling like a kid caught with her hand in the cookie jar, Cam said, "No, ma'am, it hadn't escaped me."

"You know why he's here?"

"I think so. The new mission is on the table?"

"Very good," Maya murmured. "I've been in conference with Mr. Trayhern and Major York about it."

Cam blinked. Maya's large, emerald-green eyes glimmered with mirth. "Yes, ma'am?"

"You know," she said, pulling a few files off a teetering stack to her right and placing them in front of her, "that three of you were interviewed by Jenny Wright, the Perseus psychologist, for this mission?"

"Yes, Storm Queen and Pele were interviewed, too."

"Right." Maya slowly opened Cam's file, revealing a color photo of her stapled on the left side. "We've reviewed everything, Cam. I know none of you knew what the mission was about, and that was done on purpose. Ms. Wright knew the schematic on it, and conferred with Morgan and myself about the three of you. You were all good, strong candidates for the position.''

Heart sinking, Cam knotted her hands on her thighs. Maya was going to tell her she hadn't gotten the mission. Straightening her spine, she tried to hide her disappointment. It was so important to her to have Maya look upon her as trustworthy once more. Since that horrific crash landing, Maya had never again flown with Cam. Which was unusual, because she routinely flew missions with all her pilots from time to time.

Lifting her head, she pinned Cam with her gaze and smiled. ''We've chosen you to head up this mission, Cam. We felt you were the best qualified for it. Congratulations.'' Maya rose and extended her hand.

Blinking, Cam stared at her superior. Then she leaped to her feet and thrust out her own hand.

''Thanks, Major! Thanks so much! You have no idea what this means to me,'' she whispered, her voice raspy with sudden, unexpected tears. Cam quickly pushed them away by taking several gulping swallows. Pumping Maya's hand rapidly, she continued, ''You won't regret your decision, ma'am. I *promise* you you won't. Thanks for the chance…the opportunity… I won't fail you this time. I swear I won't….''

Easing her hand away, Maya stood there looking at Cam. The pilot's face glowed with relief, with joy. Her green eyes swam with tears she was desperately trying to force back. Maya knew Cam needed to prove herself again.

"Listen to me, Cam," she murmured gently, "this mission is not about you proving yourself to me or anyone else. If I didn't think you had what it took in the first place, I'd have chosen someone else, so let's get over that hurdle, okay?"

Choking back her tears, which she knew were not appropriate, Cam nodded. "Yes, ma'am. I understand." Her heart was soaring. She felt giddy, almost dizzy, and so relieved. She saw respect in Maya's eyes, sincerity in her expression, and Cam was so surprised and delighted she could barely sit still in the chair. Opening and closing her hands, she whispered, "Thanks for letting me do this. It means so much to me...."

"I know it does," Maya said gently. Giving her a brief smile, she looked down at a red-and-white-striped folder labeled Top Secret. Picking it up, she handed the folder across the desk to Cam. "Here's your mission. Everything you'll need to know."

Feeling like an exuberant puppy, Cam laid the file in her lap and opened it with trembling hands. Immediately the text blurred before her eyes, and she self-consciously wiped away the tears. She didn't dare cry in front of Maya. Not now. Cam had to show her C.O. that she was up for this assignment, no matter what it entailed.

"This mission is going to be the hardest one you've ever said yes to," Maya warned in a dark tone. "Let's go to the briefing room. Morgan Trayhern is waiting to talk to you about it."

Chapter 2

"Cam, I want you to meet Morgan Trayhern. He owns Perseus, a top secret company that interfaces with the CIA and many other agencies around the world."

Cam smiled and gripped Morgan's hand. "Mr. Trayhern, this is an *honor*," she said, meeting his warm blue gaze and his smile. Morgan Trayhern was a living legend. He had been a marine captain in the closing days of the Vietnam War. Since then, he had risen to heady heights within the secret, black operations world by his success with his covert agency, which provided much-needed assistance to democratic countries all over the world. He had a knack for employing some of the best men and women from the military as mercenaries to help people in trouble. And now Cam was gripping his firm, powerful hand. She was giddy with excitement.

"It's a pleasure to meet you, Cam," Morgan said, releasing her hand. "And congratulations on being chosen for this mission. Have a seat." He gestured toward a row of chairs that faced a blank white wall.

"Yes, sir."

Maya sat next to Cam. She handed her a folder that had been sitting on the table in front of them. "You'll need this, too. Morgan? You ready?"

"Yep." Moving to one end of the table, he flipped open a laptop computer and pushed a button. The wall became a viewing screen for a slide presentation.

Cam's heart raced with excitement. She had gotten the mission! She'd been chosen! Joy warred with anxiety within her chest. More than anything, she wanted to prove that she was worthy of her C.O.'s belief and trust in her. Compressing her lips, she listened as Morgan's low, deep voice filled the small room.

"Major Stevenson has given you two files," he said. "The first is an overview of the mission. The second has photos, biographies and fitness reports of the three Apache pilots you're going to be responsible for training in interdiction in northern Mexico."

"Mexico?" Cam said, looking at Maya.

"Yeah, northern Mexico," she repeated with a smile. "Right on the border with California. Lucky you. Maybe when things iron out, you can head to San Diego and kick up your heels. Do a little partying in your spare time." Maya knew that many of the BJS pilots longed to go back to the U.S. from time to time. Living in the humid Peruvian jungle year in and year out, in constant combat mode, took a heavy toll on each of them. Maya started to enforce a thirty-day vacation for her pilots each year so they wouldn't get too homesick. Three years of duty with no down-time wasn't good.

Looking at Cam's face, lit up now with a glow of pleasure, Maya smiled. "And your home state of Oregon isn't that far from there," she added, reading her mind.

"I know!" Cam exclaimed happily. She gripped the open folder on her lap. "It's *real* close!"

"Well, first things first. Congratulations, you're going to be the commanding officer of this mission, so who knows? When things are quiet, you might put one of your other pilots—your executive officer probably—in charge, and you can take off for a weekend and visit your family in Oregon. Anything is possible once you get this mission on track."

Morgan smiled. "Major Stevenson, who is used to commanding, makes this sound easy, Cam. Leading is the hardest work you'll ever learn how to do."

"Yes, sir," Cam said, looking at him. Morgan was tall and broad-shouldered. He wore civilian clothes—charcoal-gray slacks, hiking boots, a red polo shirt. His black hair was cut military short, the silver at his temples lending his handsome face a frame for those lively blue eyes that didn't miss a thing. She smiled at him as he cocked his head and gazed at her almost as if he were looking through her. Ordinarily, Cam would have felt invaded, uncomfortable, but she didn't now. Maya had that same ability, and Cam never felt threatened by it, either. Maybe good leaders had that quality of being able to look into the heart and mind of their people in a nurturing way, to see what they were made of.

"You said 'commanding officer'?" Cam asked in surprise.

"Yes, that's you," Morgan murmured with a smile. He pressed a button on the laptop. "You may recognize this place. It's Tijuana, Mexico—a huge, sprawling city on the U.S. border, right across from San Diego. This is where you're going." He pressed the button again.

"There's a small Mexican Air Force base just beyond the southern outskirts of Tijuana. Two Apache Longbow helicopters are going to be flown in from the States for your use. Your mission, Cam, is to be C.O. for a small contingent of Mexican helicopter pilots who are just now graduating from flight school at Fort Rucker."

Her brows rose in surprise, but she tamped down her desire to ask questions.

"Two of the three pilots are Mexican nationals. The third—" Morgan pressed the button "—has dual citizenship, from the USA and Mexico. He's Chief Warrant Officer Gustavo Phillipe Morales."

Cam looked up as a color slide flashed across the wall. The man who stared back at her made her heart thump hard. About six feet tall, medium-boned and athletic, he was dressed in a dark green, one-piece army flight uniform. Looking deadly serious, he stood in front of an olive-green Apache helicopter, his helmet dangling loosely from his long, tanned fingers.

Gulping, Cam quickly perused the man's photo. There was something arresting, beckoning and frightening about him, all at the same time. His face was square, his jaw set and his mouth thinned into a hard, single line. Thick, straight brows sat over his cinna-

mon-colored eyes. It was his eyes, with their huge
black pupils, that drew Cam the most. The eyes of a
predator. But then, she reminded herself, all gunship
pilots had to have that "look." If they didn't, they
weren't going to cut it in combat. Morales's eyes had
that gleam of a hunter looking for its prey.

Her pulse raced momentarily. His black hair was
cut short, with a few rebellious straight strands dipping over his broad, unwrinkled brow. With his high
cheekbones and hawklike nose, he definitely had the
face of an Indian, and he reminded Cam of an Incan
god she had seen carved in stone on some ancient
frieze somewhere. Gustavo Morales had sharp angles
and rough edges, giving Cam the impression that he'd
been around the block and taken a lot of beatings, but
learned from each experience. She saw confidence
and pride radiating from him. Just the way Morales
stood, with one hand propped on his narrow hip, his
helmet in the other, spoke of his certainty about himself and his abilities.

"Warrant Morales," Morgan intoned, "is U.S.
Army, Cam. Though his mother was Yaqui Indian,
from northern Mexico, his father is a colonel in the
U.S. Army, currently stationed in Afghanistan with a
top secret contingent of Apache pilots working behind
the lines to hunt down the Taliban."

"They're over there?"

Morgan nodded grimly. "Yes. But that piece of
info goes nowhere."

"Of course not, sir."

"You should consider Morales as executive officer
material, Cam. He's twenty-five years old, and he's
been in the army for four years. He's an ace helo

pilot—he grew up flying with his dad. He speaks
Spanish as fluently as you do. I believe, as does Major
Stevenson, that he'll be a key player in making this
mission work, even though you're in charge.''

"How so, sir?''

"Let's put it delicately, Cam,'' Morgan said, giving her a droll look. "The other two officers, both
lieutenants with the Mexican Air Force, are...well,
for lack of a better word, somewhat biased about
women having a lead role. In the Mexican military,
there are no women combat pilots.''

"These two Mexican pilots are supposed to be the
cream of the crop,'' Maya added. "At least, that's
what their general is telling us.''

Morgan pressed the button and their pictures were
projected on the wall.

"Lieutenants Antonio Zaragoza and Luis Dominguez did okay at Fort Rucker and learned to fly the
Apache,'' Maya assured her.

"But,'' Morgan warned, "these men come from a
country where most women are still kept barefoot and
pregnant. The only way they relate to females is as
mothers and lovers.''

"Yeah,'' Maya growled. "So you've got your
work cut out for you, Cam. These two dudes are not
going to want to accept you as C.O. or even listen to
your wise counsel, no matter how much more experienced you are as a combat pilot.''

"I see….'' Cam murmured. "And Warrant Morales? He's been raised in a gender-neutral environment, where women are accepted in leadership
roles?''

"Yes,'' Morgan said. "Which is one of the many

reasons Chief Morales was chosen for this duty. He isn't aware of *why* he was chosen. He'll find that out from you once you arrive at the base in Tijuana.''

"Yaqui Indians," Maya told her, "have a matriarchal society, and women are considered equal to men. Morales has been steeped in a tradition where women are accepted as being just as strong, smart and effective as any male.''

"That's good," Cam said, relieved.

"You're going to have your hands full," Morgan warned her gravely. "These are green students who have just learned the basics of day and night flying techniques. They know nothing of interdiction duties, especially in the dark. That's where you come in. We want you to build a schooling program around them, starting with day flights, and then working in night operations. We all know night flying is more dangerous, but unfortunately, the president of Mexico does *not* want Apaches flying around where people can see them. He's afraid it will scare the populace.''

"So," Maya said, pointing to the screen as a picture of high-desert terrain was shown, "during the day, you're going to fly your boys into the hills along the Baja coastline and out over the Pacific. There're plenty of mountains and hills for you to play hide 'n seek in, to train them on the finer points of interdiction.''

"And then you'll train them in on night interdiction, once they've got the basics and you're confident of their skills," Morgan said.

"So bottom line, I'm running an advanced interdiction flight school.''

"Yes," Morgan said. "You're going to create that

template. And if you're successful, we'll take on other Mexican Air Force pilots, train them at Fort Rucker and then get them flying interdiction in their own country, instead of U.S. pilots always putting their lives on the line to do it.''

"Sounds like a good plan to me," Cam said. She was in awe that they'd choose her for such a mission. Still, fear threaded through her. Could she do it? She would have to. Never had Cam wanted anything more than this. It was a plum—a huge one. And if she was successful, Maya would surely forgive her past error….

Her C.O. was watching her with an assessing expression on her face, Cam noted. "It's a wonderful opportunity," Maya said, "but I think this is going to be the roughest mission you've ever agreed to, Cam. Those Mexican pilots aren't going to sit still for your mother hen ways." She smiled slightly. "You're a nester, a nurturer by nature, Cam—you appear so warm and easygoing, even though inside there's a jaguar. You're just as competitive and cool as any of the other women pilots who fly the Apache, but you come across as soft. You can't let that happen on this mission. Those pilots see soft and they'll eat you alive.''

Nodding, Cam gulped and said, "I understand."

"Down here," Maya said, "we love your mother hen ways. You're the one who makes chicken soup if one of us gets a cold or the flu. You're the one who sits down and listens when someone has a problem and needs to talk it out. You have a natural instinct for caring for others.''

"Those are all good attributes in a leader," Morgan

said quietly. "But you lack the management skills, the firmness and decisiveness setting required in a leader. But you can develop those abilities."

Nodding, Cam said, "I understand, sir. I'll do my best to learn to be tough."

"Well," Maya said, cocking an eyebrow, "you won't have much time or space to do it in, Cam. I'm hoping Morales will like you, side with you and act as a natural buffer between you and those two dudes who are going to rain hell on your head every day." Her mouth quirked. "I've experienced more than my fair share of those redneck, good-ole-boy attitudes in the past. I don't look forward to you cutting your teeth on them, but under the circumstances, they are the cloth we have to work with. That's the way it is."

"I'll handle it, Maya. I swear I will."

"Oh," Morgan said, chuckling, "you'll be swearing, all right. Apache pilots aren't the tamest people to begin with. They're edgy, alert, tense and combative by nature. We're all hoping that Chief Morales will be the great leveler here between you and the others."

"Because," Maya predicted grimly, "if he isn't, it's going to be three to one—them against you—and this mission could grind to a halt in a hurry."

"I won't let it happen," Cam promised fervently. She gave them a grateful look. "I know it's going to be a challenge. But I know I can do it. Just let me have the chance...."

"You've got the chance," Morgan murmured. He flipped off the projection program and shut down the laptop. Walking to the other end of the table, he picked up an object and handed it to Cam.

"This is going to be your most precious possession, Cam. It's an iridium satellite cell phone. There
are sixteen satellites circling the globe, and this phone
is hooked up to them. You can call from anywhere
in the world and reach someone at the other end."

Cam examined the slender but heavy device.
"Okay…"

Maya got up. "The iridium is a very expensive toy,
but one you're going to need."

Cam looked up in confusion as Maya came and
stood in front of her, with Morgan at her shoulder.
"Why?"

"Because if you need help, you can call Morgan
or myself. We suspect you're going to need advice
from time to time, and with that phone you can reach
us."

"Good leaders ask for help when they get their
backs to the wall," Morgan told her. "Good leaders
are forged in the fires of hell, they aren't born. You've
not had the privilege of college level management
courses, Cam. We're throwing you into this mission
without any background education. Being a good pilot is one thing. Being a leader is a whole other ball
game."

Nodding, Cam murmured, "I realize that from talking to Akiva."

Maya smiled. "Yes, Akiva became C.O. of a covert black ops base on the Gulf of Mexico, and she
found out about it the hard way, too."

"She did it, though," Cam said firmly. "And so
will I." She held up the phone and said, "I'll be
calling often."

Grinning, Morgan patted Cam's shoulder. "Excellent. That's what we want to hear. No one knows everything. If I don't miss my guess, Morales will be your ace in the hole. Use his knowledge and listen to him, too. Take what he says under consideration.''

''Cam's a good listener. She always has been,'' Maya murmured.

''We're throwing you to the wolves,'' Morgan said worriedly. ''You're a helluva good Apache pilot, Cam. You're the best. The Black Jaguar Squadron has more time in grade in drug interdiction efforts than any other aviation group in history. That's why you're being chosen to run this mission—because of your three years of hard-earned experience.''

''She's still alive. That says it all.''

Cam grinned up at Maya. ''Yes, ma'am, you taught us well.''

''Take that training up north, Cam, and use it to help educate these pilots.''

''I will,'' she promised, a catch in her voice.

''I only hope,'' Morgan said, ''that when you meet these macho Mexican pilots, they don't think you're breakfast, to be eaten alive.''

Rising, Cam grinned. ''Mr. Trayhern, I may *look* like a cream puff, but in here—'' she pointed to her heart ''—I'm a black jaguar. They just don't know it yet.''

Chapter 3

"I can't believe they're sending a *woman* to teach us," Lieutenant Antonio Zaragoza muttered, his long legs stretched out in front of the door to the barracks room where they waited for their C.O. to arrive.

Gus Morales, who stood at the window, peering through the venetian blinds, glanced over his shoulder at his schoolmate, who sulked like a petulant child. Zaragoza was five foot nine inches tall, only average height for a helo pilot. He made up for his lack of stature by being arrogant and brazen. Lifting his mouth in the ghost of a smile, Gus said, "I think it's ironic."

Lieutenant Luis Dominguez, who sat at the table smoking a cigarette, twisted to look in Morales's direction. "I think it stinks." He flipped ashes into the ashtray in front of him.

Chuckling, Gus looked at the two Mexican Air

Force pilots, who, like him, were dressed in dark green, single-piece flight uniforms. Each of them had the Mexican flag sewn onto his right shoulder. On his own uniform, Gus had the American flag, reflecting the fact that he was in the U.S. Army.

"They want us to fail," Zaragoza said flatly, his black brows dipping, his arms wrapped across his chest in defiance. Staring down at his highly polished black flight boots, which blocked the entranceway, he glowered. "Women have nothing to teach men!"

"*Sí,*" Luis agreed. "Their place is in bed, with us."

"Yes, they are good for pleasure," Antonio stated darkly. "But not as Apache instructor pilots, teaching us the finer points of drug flight interdiction."

"Where I come from," Gus told them lightly, a cockeyed grin on his face, "women are not only teachers, but equals. I guess you two need to square away your attitudes on that one. Otherwise, you won't learn a thing from Chief Anderson."

Snorting vehemently, Luis took a deep drag of his cigarette, then blew the smoke out—an eloquent, if silent, reply.

Gus turned and looked out the window again. He and the others were on the second floor of the barracks, waiting for their new commanding officer, C.R. Anderson. They'd been informed she was an Apache gunship pilot who had been on duty in Peru for three years, flying drug interdiction on a black ops combat mission. That's all they knew. He was curious. And anxious to learn what she knew. At Fort Rucker, they were given basic Apache training, but time did not allow for them to learn the finer points of certain types of missions, such as drug interdiction.

Outside, the air base was quiet. It was small in comparison to other Mexican military bases. Gus saw two dark green Boeing Apache Longbow helicopters, their blades tethered, sitting in the revetment area, waiting like they were. Hungry to get in the air again, to feel the power and surge of the world's most lethal and deadly gunship, Gus shifted position. He was eager to get this show on the road.

"I don't see why our *presidente* would allow us to be taught by a mere woman," Antonio drawled in frustration. "This is mano a mano—hand to hand fighting in the air. No woman can fly a combat helicopter."

"Women in the U.S. Navy and Air Force fly fighter jets all the time," Gus reminded him. "And they're just as good, some of them better, than their male counterparts. I don't see the difference."

Luis glared at him. "You wouldn't. You're still tied to your mamacita's apron strings, amigo." He chuckled indulgently.

Gus allowed the insult to slide off his broad shoulders. He knew both pilots well enough from their time at Fort Rucker. Both used to bluster and fluff their feathers like bantam roosters when the flight instructors at Fort Rucker challenged them on their lazy attitudes toward flying. In Gus's opinion, neither one really had the competitiveness needed, that primal urge, to hunt down sky predators. Both pilots came from rich families. Zaragoza came from new money, his father being quite a phenomenon in the computer world. Dominguez's father, from old money, was mayor of Placido, a suburb of Mexico City.

His colleagues' condescending attitude throughout flight school had been amazing to Gus. And instead of making them buckle down and do the work, the U.S. Army instructors had let these two pilots slide, not pushing them to work to their potential. Morales figured it had to do with politics and the fact that they were "foreign exchange" pilots that they didn't get their chops busted like the rest of the class did.

Looking down at his watch, he saw that it was nearly 1400, or 2:00 p.m. Chief Anderson was due to arrive at their newly designated H.Q.—this small room on the second floor of the only barracks at the base—momentarily. None of them knew how she would arrive. Smiling to himself, Gus wondered obliquely if she'd ride in on an Apache in a thunderous display of her power and skill. Probably not. The president of Mexico didn't want the Apaches seen by the local people, for fear it would frighten them. The helos were lethal looking monsters, for sure, decked out with an awesome array of weapons that included rockets, a cannon and missiles.

His mind wandered back to C.R. Anderson. What did she look like? How old was she? If she'd been flying drug interdiction in an Apache for three years, and was a CWO2, she was most likely around twenty-five or twenty-six, like himself. Was she married? Did she have children? What was her husband like? What events in her life had shaped her, to make her what she was today?

Gus laughed at himself, and at his curiosity, which often got him into trouble. He enjoyed people, enjoyed figuring out how and why they worked the way they did. He glanced at his cohorts, who thought they were the best Apache pilots in the world—despite the fact that they'd just graduated from school, at the bottom of their class with barely passing grades. Gus thought the instructors must have padded their grades to pass them, so as not to embarrass the Mexican military. It would have been better if two far more hungry, less rich applicants had been selected. Hunger made a person want to prove himself in the eyes of his peers. These two had everything money could buy and wore their considerable egos like royal coats to make up for what they didn't have internally.

Sooner or later, Gus felt, they would be exposed. During training, neither had had that competitive zeal that characterized the other Apache gunship students. When he sat in the seat of an Apache, he felt like a hungry jaguar on the prowl looking for his quarry. That was the way it should be. Gus found himself wondering if Chief Anderson was the same.

The door to the rear of the barracks, just down the hall, opened and closed.

Gus looked at his watch. He gazed at the other two pilots, who lifted their heads to listen. "Fourteen hundred hours, guys. That's her. Our new C.O., Chief Anderson."

"Humph," Luis snorted, "no woman is *ever* on time."

"Not the ones you know," Gus said, barely able to hold back a smile. He pinned his gaze on the olive-green-painted door. Any second now she would come through it.

"It's just a soldier entering the barracks," Antonio said in a bored tone, waving his hand languidly.

The door opened.

Gus immediately came to attention, his arms at his side—standard procedure when a C.O. entered. He saw with shock that neither of his fellow pilots moved.

Cam Anderson stood in the doorway. The first thing she saw was a thick, choking cloud of cigarette smoke. The second thing that struck her was the malevolent stares of the two pilots sitting before her. Heart pounding, she kept her face carefully arranged. Determined to learn how to be a good leader, Cam had decided to let Maya Stevenson, her C.O., be her role model. Maya never looked harried, pressed or anxious. She walked with a confident, quiet and commanding presence that automatically demanded respect. She never raised her voice, but no one mistook that as a sign that she didn't mean exactly what she said. At all costs, Cam was going to try to be like Maya and not melt into her usual warm, motherly self.

Her gaze snapped from the pilot whose legs barred her way to the one smoking at the table, his dark brown eyes alive with distaste—for her. Lastly, Cam looked across the room. The man standing at attention at the window wore an American flag on the right sleeve of his flight uniform. That was Chief Morales. He knew that when a C.O. entered, one came to attention until told otherwise.

Realizing with a sinking heart that her career as a leader could be over right now depending on how she handled this insubordination by the Mexican pilots, Cam allowed the anger she felt to flow through her.

"Lieutenant—" she peered down at the pilot whose feet barred her path "—Zaragoza. I know the Mexican military has different protocols, but I do believe one of them requires that you stand at attention when your commanding officer enters the room. Get off your butt and on your feet, mister. Right now."

Gus choked back a laugh as Zaragoza's head snapped toward the woman. Gus saw the firm, quiet look on her oval face. Even though her thick, shoulder-length chestnut red hair gave her the look of an angel, he saw the devil in her narrowed green eyes which were now focused like a laser on the hapless pilot.

"Get up, Lieutenant. And if you can't make it to your feet, then crawl out of here and get out of my sight forever. Because that tells me you really aren't serious about training for drug interdiction."

Cam swallowed hard. She'd never been so brazen before, but her career depended upon it. Would Maya have said the same thing? Would she have handled this situation differently? Cam wavered inwardly, but refused to show her fear and indecision.

Zaragoza slowly retracted his legs and stood up in a semblance of attention, his eyes ahead, staring at the light green wall opposite.

Cam fixed her gaze on the second pilot, who was grinning down at the table, cigarette in hand. He had a lean, narrow face, short black hair, thick brows and a smirk across his full lips.

"And you...Lieutenant—" she peered at the leather patch sewn above the left pocket of his flight suit "—Dominguez. This is a nonsmoking zone. It will always be a nonsmoking zone, from here on out. Put out the butt, mister, and come to attention."

Lazily, Luis smashed out his cigarette in the glass ashtray. The smirk never left his features as he pushed back the chair and got to his feet.

They thought this was a game, Cam realized with a sinking feeling. The only pilot here who had shown respect was the U.S. Army chief.

"With your permission, ma'am," Gus said, "I'll open the window to let in fresh air?"

"Good idea, Chief Morales. At ease." Cam looked at the two Mexican pilots. "Sit down at the table, gentlemen. We have business to take care of."

Turning, Gus drew up the venetian blind and forced open the heavily painted window sash. He saw that Chief Anderson had left the door open on purpose, to create enough of a draft to get the heavy smoke out of the room. Walking to the green metal table, he sat at her right elbow.

Cam forced herself not to appear nervous. She told herself to slow down, to take her time. Never mind that she had jet lag, or that she hadn't slept in the last twenty-four hours because she was so anxious about this assignment. Never mind that two of the pilots obviously resented her and were barely giving her the respect the situation demanded. Opening her briefcase, she set several folders and a notepad on the table.

She noticed that Chief Morales took a pad from the right pocket of his flight suit and pulled out a pen from his left breast pocket. The other two pilots sat back, arms crossed, watching her with obvious distaste. Cam swallowed hard. Her throat felt dry, as if it was going to close up. She had to continue this charade and make them think she was in charge.

Taking a pen from her own flight suit pocket, Cam opened the top file. "First order of business is to ask each of you about your flight experience," she told them.

"You've got our personnel jacket," Luis drawled, his voice condescending. "Haven't you read it?"

Antonio snickered.

Cam glared at them. "Lieutenant Dominguez, tell me the extent of your flight experience with helicopters."

Shrugging nonchalantly, he said in a bored tone, "I joined the Mexican Air Force because it is a tradition in my family. I went through flight school and was assigned to helicopters."

"How many hours have you flown?"

"Two hundred."

Cam turned to the other pilot. "And you, mister?"

Chuckling, Zaragoza said, "Only two hundred hours, Luis?" He shook his head mockingly.

"Forget him," Cam ordered tightly. "I'm interested in your hours, mister."

"Four hundred." Antonio nearly spat the words.

"And how did you earn them?" Cam asked, jotting down the information on her yellow legal pad.

"I started flying helos when I was seventeen years old."

"And why did you join the Mexican Air Force?"

Glowering at her, Antonio said, "Not that it's any of your business, *señorita* or *señora,* but I *like* to fly."

"Mister, you will address me as either Chief Anderson or ma'am. Got it?"

"Yes."

"Yes, what?"

Antonio's jaw clenched. He held Cam's narrowed gaze.

"If you can't say it, mister, get out of this room and don't bother coming back."

His eyes flared with surprise. "You cannot threaten me—"

Cam leaned forward, her elbows on the table. "It's not a threat, mister. It's a *promise*. Now, you make up your mind here and now. Either go by strict military protocol from this moment forward or get up and get out of here. *Comprende?*"

Anger surged through Luis. How dare this slut of a woman make such a threat to him? "This—this is an insult! Do you know who I am?"

Cam gave him an icy smile. "Yeah, a pilot in a helluva lotta trouble with me and his superiors if he doesn't square away right now."

Silence fell in the room. Luis slanted a glance toward Gus, who was sitting there relaxed, hands on the table. He had a poker face, but Luis could see the laughter in his cinnamon-colored eyes. He knew Morales was laughing at him. That stung even more. Nostrils flaring, he jerked his gaze back to the woman who sat across from him.

"Your call," Cam told him quietly. "Do it right or get the hell out of my sight, Mr. Dominguez. I don't think your father will be very proud to learn that you can't carry out simple military protocol, do you?"

Cam's heart was thundering in her chest. She knew this was high-stakes poker. And she knew she held the cards to Luis's career. If, indeed, he was in the Mexican Air Force to fulfill a family obligation, the last thing he would want was a dark blot on the family record by being thrown out of the U.S. Army's Apache program—by a woman, no less. That would be an insult he would never live down, and she knew it. Cam was prepared to do just that, however. She'd get rid of any pilot who didn't want to play by strict military rules.

Grinding his teeth, Luis looked for help from his friend, Antonio. The unhappy grimace on his friend's face, the anger banked in his dark eyes, indicated he felt similarly. Yet he obviously didn't want to be kicked out of the program, either.

"You do not have that authority over me!" Luis snarled.

Cam reached down into her briefcase, located another file and opened it before her. Lifting out some papers, she turned them around so that Luis could read the top.

"I'm sure you recognize this, Mr. Dominguez. It's a set of orders. All I have to do to reassign you is fill in this blank—" she pointed to the page "—and sign my name down here, at the bottom. Now, I'll be more than happy to do that for you. There's a lot of good pilots who didn't get this mission, and who want it a lot more than you do, apparently. So which is it? You want me to fill you out a new set of orders, sending you back to your superior? Or do you want to stay with us? Your call, mister. Just make it in a hurry, because I don't have time to play games here."

"You cannot do this!" Luis shouted, balling his hands into fists beneath the table.

"Try me. I'd love to sign you off, mister. I don't need sulky little boys on my team. I need mature men who are ready to be responsible, who are hungry to fly and who want to go after the real bad guys. You want to target someone in your gun sights, you aim at them, not me. Is that understood?"

Wiping his wrinkled brow, Luis cast a desperate glance toward Antonio. His friend stared straight ahead and refused to look at him. Jerking a look at Morales, Luis saw the same hint of laughter in the warrant's eyes. He thought this was funny! Angrily, Luis swung his gaze back to the C.O.

"I'm staying."

"No, mister, you will say 'Chief Anderson, I'd like to stay with the team. Please?'"

Breathing hard, Luis repeated the words through gritted teeth. He watched with relief as Anderson put the order back in the file and the file back in the briefcase.

"Very good, Mr. Dominguez. Thank you for the information on your flight background."

Cam turned to the last pilot. Her heart speeded up, but not out of fear. It was something else—some other feeling that emerged so quickly under the tense circumstances that Cam couldn't name it. As she looked into his warm, cinnamon-colored eyes and saw the slightest hint of a smile on his full, well-shaped mouth, she struggled to keep her voice low and firm. "Chief Morales?"

"Ma'am, I was born in a helicopter."

She looked at him and blinked once. "Excuse me?"

Gus grinned and opened his hands. "My mother

was in labor with me. She's Yaqui Indian, from northern Mexico. She was visiting her family when she went into labor with me. My father, who is a U.S. Army helicopter pilot, had flown her to the desolate area where her parents lived, and flew her out again when her water broke. He was hoping to get to Nogales, and then across the border into Texas, to get her to the hospital on time."

Cam smiled. "Don't tell me! You were actually born *in* the helo?"

He liked her smile. There wasn't anything not to like about their new C.O., Gus decided. That pale sprinkling of freckles across her broad cheekbones, the way her hair glinted with red-gold highlights beneath the washed-out fluorescent light above them… Chief Anderson suddenly looked a lot less threatening than she had earlier.

"Yes, ma'am. By the time my father landed the helo on the hospital roof, she'd given birth to me." Gus's smile widened. "The attendants who came out were kinda surprised."

"That's a great story, Chief Morales. So, did the helicopter ride stay in your blood?" Cam liked the way his eyes crinkled and dimples flashed as he smiled fully.

"Yes, ma'am, it did. My father flew civilian helicopters for the Civil Air Patrol in his free time. I got my helo license when I was thirteen years old, when my legs were long enough to reach the pedals."

"I see," Cam said, trying not to sound impressed. But she was. The natural warmth and openness of Morales compared to the other two pilots was like night and day. Cam realized instantly that he didn't have a problem with his C.O. being a woman, as the other two did. Jotting down the info, she asked lightly, "And I suppose you have over a thousand hours built up in helos?"

"Yes, ma'am. I got fifteen hundred in civilian types. When I joined the army air program, I acquired six hundred more hours."

"And in the Apache?"

He shrugged. "Not enough."

Cam grinned. "Don't worry, you're going to be getting plenty of hours shortly. We'll make up for it."

"Sounds good to me."

"Hours in the Apache?"

"A hundred and fifty."

Cam knew that the school gave each student seventy hours of flight time. She frowned and looked at Morales's personnel jacket. "Where did you get eighty more?"

"Oh…" Gus opened his hands and had the good grace to flush beneath her sharp gaze. "Well, I volunteered for a special class on drug interdiction tactics *before* I went through Apache school."

Frowning, Cam studied him. "How is that possible, Chief?"

Slightly embarrassed, Gus said, "My father's influence, if you want the truth, ma'am. He's head of an Apache squadron. He wanted me to learn the drill. At the time, I was flying another type of helo. Within his squadron, he had set up a unique program of flight interdiction tactics, so he wrote orders for me to attend it."

"I see family nepotism at work," Cam murmured. "Well…that's good."

"Yes, ma'am. I loved it."

"And that's what got you into Apache school, officially?" Cam knew there were hundreds of applicants for each seat in the training program, and it was the most highly prized aviation school in the army. Morales had the good grace to look humble when he owned up to the nepotism that had gotten him that far.

"I got in because I passed all the tests and qualifications," he told her seriously. "Not because of my father."

"I understand, Chief." Cam brightened and sat back. She looked at all three pilots. "We're officially a squadron, according to the U.S. Army, as well as a black ops branch of the Mexican Air Force. We're Black Jaguar Squadron 2, a spinoff, as it were, of my squadron down in Peru." Cam pulled three patches from her briefcase and carefully laid them out on the table.

"This is our squadron patch, gentlemen. As you can see, it is square, with a red and blue border around it. In the center is a black jaguar with gold eyes on a white background, and our squadron name is embroidered at the bottom in gold." Cam pointed to the patches. "You're going to earn them the hard way— through a lot of work and elbow grease, consistent one hundred and ten percent effort on your part. I have it in my power as C.O. to release you from the obligation to learn drug flight interdiction at any time, if you fail to jump over the bar I hold up for you. Where I come from, you earn every hour you spend in the seat of an Apache. It's not a given that you deserve to sit there."

Gus saw Anderson's expression grow even more serious as she perused the three of them, her hands folded on the table. On the right shoulder of her uniform he saw the identical patch, on the other shoulder an American flag.

"If you thought Apache school was tough, just wait. This is where we separate the women from the girls…" Cam smiled slightly "…or in this case, the men from the boys. If you've got what it takes, at the end of an eight-week period you'll be awarded this patch. If not, I'll be calling you in, writing you up a new set of orders and you're out of here. Do you understand?"

"Yes ma'am," the men murmured in a subdued chorus.

"Good," Cam said, relief flowing through her. She gathered up the patches and placed them back in her briefcase. "Now, I need an X.O.—executive officer." She looked at Morales. "You're it, Chief Morales."

"Me?" Gus hooked a thumb toward his chest, surprised. He saw a hint of approval in Chief Anderson's green eyes.

"Why not you? You've got more hours in helos. You've had advanced drug flight interdiction training. From this moment on, you're my X.O., which means you get a lot more duty and a lot less free time to party in Tijuana. Are you up for it, Chief Morales?"

Straightening in his chair, Gus took a deep breath. If he carried out his duties well, he just might go from a CWO2 to another pay grade. He could barely conceal his excitement. "Yes, ma'am, I'll take it. Thank you. I hope I won't let you down."

Cam smiled thinly. "The only way you fail, Chief,

is by not trying.'' She looked at the other two pilots, whose sulky expressions indicated their current mood.

''Okay, let's roll,'' she told them. ''Get on your feet, gentlemen, and let's go out and meet our ladies.''

Chapter 4

Gus could hardly wait to get his turn in the Apache with Chief Anderson. The rest of the day was spent studying special manuals of flight interdiction operations back in their tiny H.Q. office while she took each of them for an introductory flight. Gus was still champing at the bit when he saw Luis Dominguez come back from his hour-long stint. The Mexican was looking disgusted. His brow was beaded with sweat and the underarms of his flight uniform were dark with perspiration. Chief Anderson escorted him to the office and ordered Zaragoza to come with her next.

The moment Dominguez was alone with Gus, he started bitching. "That woman is loco! Crazy!"

"Why?" Gus asked, placing his hand across his manual to keep his place. Luis's face was dark with frustration. He started to reach for the pack of cigarettes he kept in the left thigh pocket of his flight suit

and then thought better of it, remembering the orders
that this area was now off-limits to smoking. Cursing,
he glared around the simple but clean facility.

"She put me through a flight test of maneuvers I've
never done before!" he fumed, crossing his arms and
glaring down at his unopened flight manual.

"Isn't that what the introductory flight's about? To
find out what areas we're weak or strong in?" Gus
asked Luis mildly.

"Bah! The witch had me trying to do things I
wasn't taught in school. I failed miserably. She sat in
the back seat with that clipboard across her knees,
rating me on every damn movement I made in the
Apache."

"Did she say you failed?"

Luis blew out a long breath. "She let me know
every time I did something wrong! I heard her voice
in my helmet every minute of that damned flight!"

Gus shrugged. "School doesn't fully prepare us for
what we have to do out here, Luis. No matter what
squadron we got sent to, we'd have a lot to learn. It's
called advance training, amigo."

"Oh," Luis sneered, lifting his upper lip, his ca-
nine teeth showing, "and I suppose you're looking
forward to getting graded on every flight maneuver
out there?"

"It's inevitable. It's part of our learning curve.
How can Chief Anderson develop a proper training
program for us if she's not familiar with our abilities
and skills?"

Getting up, Luis shoved the chair away in disgust.
Pacing the room, he growled, "I can hardly wait until
she flies with all three of us. It will be like the Spanish

Inquisition. She'll peel off our hides, one at a time. It's shaming. It's cruel. At least the inspector pilots back at Fort Rucker did it on a one-to-one basis. She'll enjoy shaming us.''

Grinning, Gus said, ''Luis, you never had this reaction to any of your instructors at Fort Rucker.''

''None of them were women, that's why!'' Standing, he glared out the window and tapped his boot on the floor.

Gus smiled to himself. He knew Chief Anderson was going to put him through his paces and then some. However, he wasn't worried, because he felt intuitively that she would be fair.

''This wasn't a flight test to see if you get to stay or not,'' Gus reminded him. ''If you screwed up out there, look at it this way—you have only one way to go. Up.''

''Bah! I need a smoke.'' With a snort, Luis headed out the door and down the hall to the back door.

Sitting there, Gus closed his eyes and pictured Anderson in his mind. She was tall and womanly, curved deliciously in all the right places even though she wore that drab and loose-fitting flight uniform. He liked her face, liked the sprinkling of freckles that made her look younger than she probably was. Her face was oval, with huge green eyes that he could easily read, although Gus wasn't sure she realized how much her emotions were revealed in them. Oh, Anderson tried to keep a poker face, but Gus felt he had an edge because he could see her feelings clearly in those evergreen eyes of hers.

He liked the fact that although she worked in a man's world, she kept her reddish-colored hair long, wearing it parted in the middle. He liked the way it curled slightly around her attractive face. He longed to ask her personal questions. Maybe he'd get the chance on the flight, but he didn't think so. She was all-business.

Gently closing the manual, after marking his place with a piece of paper, Gus got to his feet. Glancing at his watch, he realized it would be another forty minutes before Chief Anderson came back and asked him to sit in that cockpit and fly the Apache. A thrill raced through him. He loved flying that helicopter. And he sensed that Anderson was one helluva pilot at the controls of that combat machine. Gus could barely rein in his eagerness to learn the finer techniques of flying from her.

After pouring himself another cup of coffee, he stood at the window and pondered another reaction he was having to Anderson. She was a woman. Not just any woman, but a very unique one in the highly skilled role of combat helicopter pilot. That excited him. Enthralled him. Made him very curious about her. Who was she really? Where had she been born? What had happened to her as she was growing up to push her into this line of work? Was flying a passion with her or just a job?

So many questions and no answers. At least, not yet, he thought, grinning a little as he lifted the cup to his lips.

As he stood there eyeing the small, sun-baked military airfield and the many red roofs in the distance that showed where the sprawling city of Tijuana began, Gus felt a twinge in his heart. Frowning, he wondered where it had come from. Unsure, he turned and

went back to his manual. The more he read, the more
he would be prepared for what Chief Anderson would
put him through. He didn't want to fail her. He
wanted to at least scrape by with a shred of her respect for him intact. After all, she'd chosen him as
X.O., and he didn't want to start off by having her
questioning her choice.

Cam's heart wouldn't settle down as Chief Morales
flawlessly took the Apache off the ground and rose
to an altitude of five thousand feet, heading in the
direction of San Diego.

The shaking and shuddering of the Apache always
soothed her fractiousness when she felt uptight or nervous. Now, as she sat in the piggyback seat above
and behind the pilot's cockpit, with the late afternoon
sun shining through the Plexiglas and the cooling air-
conditioning sweeping around her, Cam smiled for
the first time. She settled the clipboard on her lap, the
pen in her gloved hand shaking with the vibration of
the aircraft.

"Memorize this route, Chief," she told him over
the cabin intercom, moving the mike a little closer to
her lips. Pulling down the dark green visor that
shielded the upper half of her face from the invasive
sunlight, Cam kept her attention on the two HUDS—
heads-up displays—in front of her.

"The U.S. and Mexico have authorized us to use
one specific air corridor along the border for takeoffs
and landings during our training phase. Because the
president of Mexico doesn't want the civilian population to get overly concerned about military gunships
in the vicinity, we have to fly in restricted airspace."

"I understand, Ms. Anderson," he replied.

"It was in your new flight manual."

"Yes, ma'am, it was, and I'd already read that part of it."

Cam chuckled. "You're probably the only one who's cracked the manual."

Gus grinned. He liked the feel of the Apache around him. She was a deadly machine—board ugly, but dangerous and efficient. His right hand on the cyclic between his legs, his left hand around the collective, he said, "I'll bet they're both looking at it in detail now."

How badly Cam wanted to break down the all-business facade with Morales. She liked his easygoing nature. Earlier, when he'd walked around the gunship as part of the ground check, she'd seen his eye for detail. He missed nothing. How friendly a C.O. could be with her X.O. was something Cam hadn't a clue about. Was an executive officer like a best friend? Someone she could confide in? Or should she trust her X.O. only up to a certain point and try to keep an emotional distance from him? Cam wished she could talk to Maya about this. And she would, tonight, after she went to her barracks room. In the meantime, she would simply enjoy Gus's warm, low laugh, which sent tingles through her for no explainable reason.

"Once you hit the San Diego vector at Imperial Beach, make a ninety degree left turn and head out to sea for fifteen miles, Chief Morales."

Below her, Cam saw the sagebrush-covered hills of Mexico disappear as they moved into U.S. airspace. She pressed a button in the cockpit, which sent out an automatic signal to the radar scanners that swept the border area, showing who they were. Cam had no wish to be intercepted as a possible unfriendly aircraft.

Below them the dry hills were covered with twelve-lane freeways and housing estates. San Diego was a beautiful large city on the Pacific Coast. Ahead she could see the graceful sweep of the Coronado Bridge, connecting the island of the same name, with its naval air station, to the city.

Morales, so far, had a light, silken touch with the Apache. When he made the requested turn out toward the deep blue, sparkling ocean, Cam smiled.

"Your hours are showing, Chief," she murmured, marking down a grade on her sheet regarding his flight skills.

"Oh?" Gus watched the light green of the ocean turn to a marine blue, indicating deeper water, as they flew quickly away from the coast. The western sun was shining straight into his eyes and he was glad for his visor.

"You have a nice touch with her."

"I love this woman."

Chuckling, Cam said, "You see the Apache as a 'she'?"

"Always did. Always will."

Luis and Antonio didn't. To them, it was merely a machine to be wrestled around in the air. "That's good," she stated.

"Every helicopter has its own personality. I'm sure you've noticed that?"

Pleased that he'd speak with her as an equal, Cam

said, "Oh, yes. We have names for each of our ladies down at the squadron."

"Any hangar queens?" These were helicopters that broke down frequently and spent more time in the hangar than flying on missions.

Laughing, Cam said, "No. The Apache has a pretty low breakdown record. No hangar queens, thank goodness. The way we push them, they've stood up when they shouldn't have over the years even in high humidity. An Apache's a tough machine."

"I'd like to know more about your squadron, any time you have a free moment to fill me in."

Hearing the excitement in his voice, Cam said dryly, "Chief, it's a black ops, so I can't say much about it."

"That's what I thought. Well, you can't blame me for asking, can you?"

"No. Nice try. Okay, once you hit the five-mile mark, I want you to turn ninety degrees south."

"Yes, ma'am." On the mark, he brought the Apache over in a quick, banking turn. From this elevation, he could still see the rim of land to his left and the mighty Pacific spreading out to the south and west.

"Good. You're going to fly southward exactly twenty miles. We're going to parallel the Baja Peninsula, as you well know. At the twenty-mile mark, you will execute another ninety degree left turn, moving due east. That will take us into our authorized military flight test area."

"That's all mountains and hills, with very little population," Gus said.

"That's right, Chief. Our playground for the next eight weeks."

"I used to hike in those mountains," Gus said.

"Really?" Cam was hungry to know something about Morales on a personal level. "How old were you?"

"I told you my mom is Yaqui Indian?"

"Right, you did." With his golden skin and the hint of a tilt at the corners of his large eyes, Morales reminded her of a lean, golden jaguar. There was a strength to him as well—quiet, powerful and yet steady. Cam could feel it. There was something so solid and grounded about him that it made her want to trust him. The man was terribly good-looking, in her opinion. One moment he'd appear serious and mature, and the next he'd give her that unexpected, little-boy grin of delight. She liked him more than she should, Cam realized.

"My father was an attaché to the U.S. Ambassador to Mexico when I was a kid, and he used to take me over here to go hiking. My dad is a great outdoorsman to this day."

"A hunter?"

"No, a hiker."

"Did your mom go along?"

"No. My dad has a great love of the land, and he would show me animal tracks and interesting plants. We'd take a camera along and shoot the birds and animals we saw. I have scrapbooks at home filled with pictures we took."

"Better to shoot them with a camera than a gun," Cam said.

"Right on."

"And yet you're an Apache pilot. A combat pilot who will have to pull the trigger someday, and possibly kill someone. How does that set with you, Chief Morales?"

Making the turn at the twenty-mile mark, Gus pushed the Apache toward the brown-and-green looming mountains in the distance. "I don't know. All my targets have been wooden, with no human involvement."

It was a good answer.

Cam got down to business. "All right, Chief, I'm going to give you a series of flight maneuvers. When I give the orders, I want them executed immediately. Understand?"

"Yes, ma'am." Gus felt his heart speed up a little. Below, the ocean was an aquamarine color, indicating it was becoming shallow. Up ahead rose mountains that were anywhere from two to six thousand feet in height. The bumpy foothills in front of them were lined with green valleys filled with brush and short trees; the sloping sides were dotted with sagebrush and cactus. Beyond them the tops of the mountains were bare and brown.

Gus tightened his hands around the controls as he anticipated the series of flight commands Chief Anderson would put him through.

"Climb to twenty thousand."

Instantly, Gus followed her orders. The engines howled. The Apache strained. Nose up, the helicopter clawed for the blue sky, which was dotted with white cottony clouds. The gravity pushed Gus back in the pilot's seat. It was always a good feeling to him. This was what he loved best—flying this powerful, responsive machine.

The moment he hit the targeted altitude, he heard Anderson snap, "I want an inside loop."

Gus was surprised, but didn't hesitate. Immediately he sent the aircraft nose down in a sharp descent toward the green-and-brown earth. The Apache was the only helicopter in the world that could do an inside loop. Because gravity would drain the fuel from the lines on other machines, none but the Apache could attempt this maneuver. Boeing engineers had figured out how to keep the fuel pumping to an Apache's engines to keep it from dropping out of the sky.

Cam was pinned back in her seat as gravity built during the loop maneuver. She felt the sureness and confidence in Morales's handling of the Apache as he executed the required moves. They had eaten up ten thousand feet of airspace in the process, and now, as he brought the shrieking Apache into the lower part of the loop, gravity tried to pull them to the earth.

Cam had had to take the controls from the two other pilots at this point because they were awkward and lacked the confidence to get the screaming helicopter up and out of the dive. Morales, she knew, would finish the loop without her intervention.

As Gus brought the Apache back to its original altitude, he felt a thrill of joy arc through him, and he laughed. It was a sound of triumph. When he heard Chief Anderson laugh with him, his heart opened with an incredible sense of happiness. She understood his joy. Knew how he loved riding this fearless machine, which could do nearly anything that was asked of it.

"That's incredible!" he said, emotion in his voice.

"Vertical dive to ten thousand."

"Yes, ma'am!" And he plunged the Apache straight downward, the rotors thumping hard and sending battering waves of vibration through his body.

Pleasure surged through Cam as, for the next twenty minutes, she put Morales through his paces. He was nearly flawless in his command of the Apache. It was a relief to her. At least one of the three pilots on her team had the goods to do interdiction work. Concerned about the other two, Cam wasn't sure what to do. Putting that worry aside, she ordered Morales back out to sea to follow their designated corridor back to the air base.

Over the Pacific, Gus began to relax. He knew he'd done well on the flight test. "Are you sorry yet that you asked me to be your X.O.?"

Cam lifted her head and stared down out of her cockpit. Below, she could see the green helmet Morales wore, but not his face. "Not at all."

"Then," he suggested, "when we're alone, could we be on a more friendly footing with one another? Could you call me Gus?"

Cam smiled slightly. "So long as the other pilots don't overhear us, that's fine. You can call me Cam."

"Cam? Now, that's an interesting name."

"Short for Camelia. My mother had three daughters, and she named us after her favorite flowers—camelias, iris and dahlias."

"Very nice," Gus murmured. "I'm an only child—an army brat. My mother had me and said that's it. One kid born in a helo and no more dramatics." He chuckled indulgently. Below, the dark blue of the Pacific blazed with gold highlights as the sun sank closer to the western horizon.

"So, you were a handful, eh?"

Shrugging, Gus swept his gaze from the instruments to the ocean below, then to the sky above. It was a habit and a necessary part of flying. "I was a good kid."

"You seem like you would have been."

"Oh?" He was very curious about how Cam saw him.

Laughing a little, she said, "You strike me as someone who is very serious about work, but also knows how to play and be a big kid at times, too."

"Very perceptive," he murmured. "But that's why you're the C.O. You have this radar vision to see straight through your personnel and know what and who they are."

"Oh, don't give me that kind of credit," Cam protested, frowning. "This is my first time at it. I'm learning as I go. The hunt and peck method, with a lot of mistakes along the way."

"I'd say you're doing real good so far."

Mouth flexing, Cam looked up, enjoying the view of the sparkling ocean beneath them. With Gus, she could relax. He made it easy for her to banter with him. "Well," she muttered, "I'm not so sure of that. At least not yet."

"I'd say you've done a credible job of handling those two jay birds."

Smiling, Cam said, "Thanks."

"They threw the kitchen sink at you. I was shocked. I watched you deal with their insubordination and turn it against them. I know a lot of C.O.'s who would have strung them up on court-martial charges. You did it differently than a man would, but I think your way may give them a chance to grow instead of being canned. You were patient and firm with them. You let them know what their choices were, and then left them to hang themselves if that's what they wanted to do. I found your method very instructive.''

Savoring his praise, Cam felt more relief flow through her. Folding her gloved hands on the board in her lap, she muttered, ''I wasn't expecting that kind of reception, to tell you the truth.''

''Yeah,'' Gus said. ''I wasn't, either. Those two do a lot of bluffing, but this time they were serious.'' He smiled and sheepishly admitted, ''I wanted to speak up and defend you.''

''I'm glad you didn't. It would have eroded my authority.''

Gus chuckled. ''I still have some old officer-and-gentleman habits ingrained in me from my dad. Women are still goddesses to be worshipped on a pedestal, not hung out to dry.''

Unable to help herself, Cam laughed with him. ''You're good for my soul, Gus. Thanks for being here.''

''Believe me, it's my pleasure.''

The sincerity in his baritone voice moved through Cam like a lover's caress. She sat there assimilating the sensation. She'd heard the huskiness, the emotion, behind his words. Knowing that Gus meant them, Cam felt a little more confident in how she'd handled the two rebellious pilots.

''What, exactly, am I to do to help you as X.O.?''

Gus asked. He saw they had five miles to go before he initiated the turn to fly over San Diego. He wished he could slow time down, but knew he couldn't. The only thing missing in this private and personal conversation was being able to see Cam's facial expressions, her reactions to what he said. Some of it he could hear in her soft, low voice.

"Not protect me when I'm toe-to-toe with either of those pilots in future, that's for sure."

He heard the derisive tone in her voice. Frowning, Gus murmured, "They shouldn't have gone after you like that. They did it because they don't respect women in general, not just you."

"They're not used to working around military women," Cam agreed quietly.

"Part of it is the Mexican culture," Gus said.

"I know. I was warned of it before I took this mission."

Brightening, Gus made the turn. San Diego spread out for miles along the coastline, and the windows of the tall skyscrapers in the downtown area glimmered golden, reflecting the setting sun. "Well," he drawled "at least one of your team isn't prejudiced against women."

"You. I think it's because you're part Indian. My C.O. comes from Indian and Brazilian heritage, and she's from a matriarchal culture like yourself. That's probably why."

Nodding, Gus paid strict attention to flight protocol at this point. "My mother drilled into me at an early age that women are just as strong, smart and capable as men. She was right." He really didn't want this flight to end, because he was enjoying talking to Cam so much. Making the next turn, they began heading over the border toward Tijuana.

Moistening her lips, which were dry due to the desert environment, Cam gazed down at the landscape. Tijuana was a major border city, a city of haves and have-nots. The poor lived up on the hillsides, sometimes in shacks made of cardboard, with pieces of corrugated tin for roofs. It was a heart-wrenching sight to her. No one should live in that kind of poverty.

As Gus brought the Apache in for a perfect three-wheel landing, Cam felt sad. He had been the only positive part of her day. She gritted her teeth, girding herself for her next duty, which was to talk individually to each pilot about what she saw as his weaknesses and strengths. The task was not going to be fun at all.

Cam missed the camaraderie of her sisters, as well as her fellow pilots at the BJS base in Peru. Akiva had been right; when one assumed a leadership role, the fun of being a pilot went out the window—pronto. Having no one to talk to on a personal level weighed heavily on Cam.

She gazed out the windshield as the rotors stopped turning. Below, a U.S. Army crew tethered the rotors and the chief of the ground crew gave the signal that it was safe to open their individual cockpit covers. Until Mexican Army crews could be trained to take over these jobs, the U.S. Army would supply ground crews to Mexico.

Pushing up the canopy, Cam unharnessed herself, trying to tuck all her fears away. Somehow she had to look confident and authoritative, as if she knew what she was doing when she talked to Antonio and Luis. It wasn't going to be pleasant.

On the ground, she saw Gus take off his helmet. He quickly ran his long fingers through his short, thick black hair, taming it back into place. When she looked at him, he grinned at her like an excited little boy. In that moment, all her consternation dissolved beneath the warmth and joy in his eyes as he held her gaze. Taking off her own helmet, Cam set it on the fuselage of the Apache as the ground crew rapidly worked around them. She had her hair in a ponytail, and reaching up, she loosened it so that it flowed down around her face and shoulders once again.

Unexpected hunger sizzled through Gus as Cam's hair flowed like a chestnut cape around her proud shoulders. The sunlight caressed her as she picked up her helmet and tucked it beneath her left elbow, then picked up her clipboard. The breeze lifted some strands, highlighting the gold-red tones. She was incredibly beautiful to him in that moment. The world seemed to stop turning for Gus as Cam looked up at him from only a few feet away. The voices of the ground crew, the calls of the seagulls wheeling above them, the noise of a diesel fuel truck coming toward them, all dissolved. He was aware only of her. That oval face dotted with girlish freckles, those thoughtful but worried green eyes of hers and her very soft, parted lips all conspired against him.

As their gazes locked and held for an instant, Gus felt the armor he'd placed around his heart crack. He literally felt and heard it, and the sensation was startling. Frightening. Euphoric. He stood there staring at her, and really looked at Cam for the first time, man to woman.

Swallowing hard, he forced himself to tear his gaze from hers a second later. But not before he saw her cheeks turn a distinct rose color. Had he seen her eyes change? Had they really become a velvet green with flecks of sunlight in them as she'd stared back at him? Trying to shake off the sensation, because it wasn't appropriate under the circumstances, Gus turned away. But he remembered her eyes. They were like dark, placid green pools he'd seen in the jungles of the Yucatan peninsula that he'd visited with his parents as they taught him about his ancient Mayan heritage. If she met her, his mother would whisper that Cam had "jaguar eyes." Eyes that now held Gus frozen, a captive—but what an eager one he was! To his consternation and shock, he realized that he could have fallen helplessly into Cam's gaze, a willing prisoner.

Turning, he fell into step with her as they headed back to the barracks. Cam kept a casual distance between them, and glancing at her out of the corner of his eye, Gus wondered if she'd felt anything toward him in that crazy moment out of time. Her cheeks were still a high pink color, and she was looking down at the ground, her brows drawn downward. Realizing abruptly that she probably hadn't, Gus found himself in an unexpected quandary.

He liked Cam. Liked everything about her, probably more than he should, given their professional relationship. Wiping his mouth with the back of his hand, he took off his flight gloves and jammed them into the left pocket of his flight suit. Within moments they would be at the two-story barracks, climbing the outside wooden stairs to the second floor, where their H.Q. was located. Time. He needed some quiet time to think about what had just occurred. Tonight, when he went to his assigned cubical on the first floor, and the lights were out, he'd feel his way through it all. Maybe then he'd get some answers.

Chapter 5

Exhausted, Cam walked down to her small room on the first floor of the barracks—her "home" until she could find an apartment near the base. Darkness had fallen. After spending so much energy talking individually to the two arrogant Mexican pilots, she was emotionally whipped. Gus had been a dream in comparison. He'd hung on every word of her critique of his flight performance, asked good questions on how to become better the next time around. Gus was her only bright spot in the whole day.

Heart heavy, Cam realized she wasn't even hungry. It was 1900 and she knew she should eat, but she was too upset. Being a leader was harder than she'd ever envisioned. Gaining a new respect for her own C.O., Major Stevenson, Cam unlocked the door to her room. Stepping in, she turned on the overhead light. Earlier in the day, when she'd arrived at the base via commercial airline, she'd thrown her two pieces of luggage into the room, shed her civilian clothes and quickly donned the dark green flight suit worn by U.S. Army aviators.

Looking around as she quietly closed the door, Cam decided that even though this was a spare room, it was posh in comparison to her digs at the cave in Peru where the squadron was based. Here she had a double bed, a wooden dresser with a mirror, and two large metal lockers to store her few clothes in. A television, DVD player and radio were all unexpected bonuses to her. At BJS, no one had these things, though one building on the other side of the mountain—the mining operation that was a front for their black ops—had a satellite dish where off-duty personnel could go watch television and find out what was happening in the rest of the world. It was a treat to have time to do that.

Cam's new room had a small desk and a phone, and she'd brought her Mac titanium G4 laptop, which she'd use to communicate with her colleagues. Next to it she placed the very expensive iridium satellite phone.

Cam reached for the Velcro closing at the top of her flight suit and tugged it open. Pulling out the white silk scarf she always wore around her neck in order to stop the uniform from chafing her skin as she scanned the skies, Cam sat down. She needed someone to talk to. Someone whose advice could help her get through this messy situation. Picking up the satellite phone, she dialed a number.

"Stevenson here."

"Maya? This is Cam. I hope it's not too late?"

Chuckling, Maya said, "I figured I'd hear from you. And late? When I'm known to stay up half the night and then crash for a few hours on the bunk in my office? I don't think so."

"It's great to hear a friendly voice," Cam said, meaning it. She gripped the phone anxiously.

"So, you hit a brick wall with your pilots?"

Sighing, she nodded. "Yeah, two out of the three are challenges. Only one, Chief Gus Morales, is the material we're looking for."

"So, give me the down and dirty on all of them. Let's talk."

Relieved, Cam quickly related the day's events. Her heart was beating hard in her chest because she didn't want to disappoint Maya. She didn't want her to think she wasn't up to the job before her. Right now, Cam felt like a loser.

"Let me do some more background snooping on Dominguez and Zaragoza, okay? If they're that bad, why the hell did the army allow them to pass? That's my first question. Secondly, I know that the Mexican military have been putting only two students per rotation through Apache school. Why should these two get it, instead of guys who really want the training?"

Rubbing her aching head, Cam muttered, "I don't know. There's nothing in their personnel jackets to indicate why."

Chuckling darkly, Maya said, "Personnel jackets are sanitized versions of reality, and tell you little. Don't worry, I'll get to Morgan and have him do some looking into the *real* records at the flight school at Fort Rucker, to find out what you need to know."

"I feel inept, Maya."

Laughing, she said, "Welcome to the real world of being a leader. Crappy, isn't it?"

"No kidding. I sure have a new respect for you...for what you must go through every day down there, while all we do is climb into the cockpit and fly."

"Well, Cam, you pilots put your lives on the line. I don't. I fly a desk most of the time. I take other slings and arrows—glares, silent name-calling and outbursts of anger from time to time with my people, but that's not often. And you're in another league on this. With an all-woman squadron down here, we have a natural tendency toward teamwork and helping one another. Whereas with men, at least most macho ones, there's nothing but rivalry. Some guys just don't like to work together. They like to show off—strut their stuff and show you what they know as an individual, not a team member."

Laughing softly, Cam nodded. "Well, the one bright spot, like I said, is Gus Morales. He's a dream, really."

"Yeah?"

Cam filled her in on the Mexican-American pilot.

"He was a good choice as X.O.," Maya affirmed.

"Maya, I'm going to ask a stupid question."

"No question is stupid, Cam. Only the one that goes unasked. What is it?"

Relieved that Maya didn't mind holding her hand as she learned how to become a leader, Cam felt the courage to go on. She shifted in the chair and crossed her legs.

"I see the closeness and confidence you have with Dallas Klein, your X.O.—the confidence you have in her. I was wondering…well, do I want to create that same situation with Gus?''

Chuckling, Maya said, ''X.O.'s are people, Cam. Sometimes you get lucky, like I did with Lieutenant Klein, who became an immediate friend. She's someone I can blow off steam to, cry in front of, talk and laugh with. And whatever I say to her stays with her. She knows how to keep a confidence. She's not a gossiper. As a leader, you can't cry in front of your people. You have to look confident, strong and sure of yourself even if your gut feels like jelly and you're questioning yourself every step of the way. The right X.O. can give you a safe harbor to vent your anger and frustration, share your humor over dumb things, mistakes, talk about your personnel, and in general, help you run the command. You want an X.O. who is perceptive, who can give you feedback and who isn't afraid of you just because you're the boss. You don't want a boot licker.''

''Gus isn't that.''

''Good. Is he reliable, you think?''

''In my gut, he's like Dallas, I feel.''

''Trustworthy?''

''Yes, but I haven't had time to really verify that. It's just an instinct thing.''

''Well,'' Maya drawled, humor in her husky tone, ''you know how much we work on gut instinct around here. And you know how accurate it is. Often, it saves our lives when a Black Shark is lurking around and our Apache is unable to pick up its identification signal. The only thing keeping us from getting blasted out of the sky sometimes is our intuition.

If Morales feels right to you, feels like he's trustworthy, I'm sure he is, whether he's proved it yet or not."

"You're right," Cam murmured. "You'd like him, Maya. He's enthusiastic, he's smart and he catches on fast."

"Well, at least one of the three is a winner, Cam. What you have to do as a leader is figure out how to bring these other two dudes not only into line, but also up to scratch with their air skills."

"I'm going to work out a mission plan when I get off the phone with you. I'd like to discuss it with you tomorrow night, if that's okay with you?"

"Sure."

"You don't mind?"

"Heck no! I'd be worried if you weren't calling me, Cam. Good leaders aren't born, they're made one grueling day at a time."

"Gosh, that's true," Cam whispered, wrinkling her brow. "I've got to learn not to get emotionally involved when dealing with those two pilots."

"That's right. They'll teach you what I call the Zen-like art of detachment," Maya chuckled. "You've got to change your attitude, Cam. Down here at BJS, everyone likes everyone else. We all get along. We're one big team. We're like a bunch of sisters out on this wild and crazy adventure together. From what you've said, Zaragoza and Dominguez want to set you up to fail, to embarrass you, to show your faults instead of reflecting on their own skills and weaknesses. It's a game, and you've got to learn the game in a hurry and turn it back on them."

"I have to be tough in ways I never wanted to be,

Maya. The only way I got through today was to act like our Inspector Pilots back at Fort Rucker.''

"Yeah—lean, mean mother machines,'' she said derisively.

"And *mother* wasn't used as a nice word, either,'' Cam said, smiling a little.

"Right on. So be a mean mother. Don't give an inch. And don't let them know they've taken a pound of flesh out of you. Keep them off balance. That means you have to be thinking way ahead of them. You have to know them so well, their individual personalities, that you know what their action or reaction is going to be before they initiate a response.''

"I think I need four years of psychology, Maya, to do that.''

Laughing, Maya said, "Nah, real life will teach you in about three months' time.''

"I'm supposed to turn these pilots into interdiction specialists in two months,'' Cam said, anxiety tingeing her tone. "And I don't know if I can do it or not.''

"Listen, just set up your mission plan, then get back to me tomorrow night and we'll talk. Give these two a week with that plan and see what happens. If they don't improve, if they continue to fight your authority, then other, more drastic measures will need to be invoked.''

"Okay,'' Cam said, wondering if Maya might yank her out of the C.O. spot as one "drastic measure to be invoked,'' and put someone else who was better and tougher in the slot instead. That was all she could see happening, but she didn't say that. Worried that Maya would think her a poor leader if she couldn't turn these two pilots around, Cam compressed her lips and withheld her worst fears from her.

"Get some sleep, Cam. And remember to eat, okay? Food is fuel. It keeps you sharp."

Smiling wryly, she said, "Okay, mother hen, I will."

"G'night, Tree Trimmer. Hang in there…"

Clicking off the button on the iridium phone, Cam set it gently back on the wooden desk. Her stomach growled, but she still wasn't hungry. Looking around, she felt as if the cubicle was closing in on her.

"Get moving, Anderson," she told herself grimly, and stood up. She planned to take a quick shower to wash off the smelly sweat of fear she'd garnered today, and change into civilian clothes. Heading down to the end of the hall, where some vending machines were located, she'd grab a quick snack and take it outside. Cam loved the outdoors and missed it acutely. Maybe munching on potato chips under the stars would help her.

There was a quarter moon shining brightly in the night sky as Cam stepped out of the barracks and away from the floodlights surrounding it. Every window in the barracks was lit up as well as the inhabitants, both enlisted soldiers and officers relaxed after a long day's work. It was a noisy place, Cam realized, at this time of night. Lights would be doused at 2100 hours, and then things would quiet down. Until then the place was a cacophony of sound that had bled through her door as she jotted her mission ideas down on paper. She was glad to be outside now, dressed like a civilian in her jeans, pink tank top and a light denim jacket with flowers embroidered on it. In her hand, she had a small package of potato chips.

Though the barracks were surrounded by asphalt, earlier in the day Cam had spotted what appeared to be a picnic area with tables, benches and several barbecue grills under a grove of trees about a quarter mile to the west. She felt lighter with every step as she headed there now, into the darkness. In the distance, she could see the dark shapes of the trees silhouetted against the moonlit sky.

Cam released a long, painful sigh as the night embraced her. Oh, to be hidden again! Out of the glaring spotlight of real life, with all those responsibilities bearing down on her. As she stepped off the edge of the asphalt and onto the sandy earth, her ears picked up the faint sound of guitar music.

Stopping to listen, Cam realized the sound was coming from the grove. Hesitating, she wondered who was there. Was it one of the pilots? The last thing she wanted to do right now was come face-to-face with Zaragoza or Dominguez.

Standing there uncertainly, Cam felt her heart give a tug. Then her gut told her to move on to the grove. Curious, she followed the sound. The guitar music was soft and unobtrusive, sounding friendly and welcoming in the dark. It was such an unusual sound to hear on a military base. Music and military. They both started with an *M*, but that was all they had in common, Cam decided, a crazy smile coming to her lips.

As she approached the trees, she halted. Her night vision was excellent, and with the quarter moon's luminescence, she could make out several wooden picnic tables with benches scattered around the large grove. At a central one, a dark figure was sitting on the table, his feet resting on the seat as he hunched over his guitar.

Her heart jumped as she recognized the man's profile. It was Gus Morales! Standing quietly, Cam felt tension begin to bleed out of her as she allowed the soft, haunting strains of the music to envelop and heal her. He played wonderfully, and she was once again surprised by his talents. Not only was he an excellent pilot who had a natural feel for the Apache, but those same long, lean fingers could stroke a guitar and make it sing beautifully as well.

Something pushed her to move toward him as he ended the song, and her pulse bounded unsteadily as she did. She saw him lift his head and gaze through the darkness at her. Cam was feeling euphoric. Hopeful. He was a friend, not an enemy, she reasoned. That had to be why she felt so at ease around him. Gus had been like a safe harbor during the hurricane that had swept around her all day.

"Hi, Cam. Come and join me?" Gus said, lifting his hand and gesturing for her to come and sit at the table with him.

Smiling hesitantly, she halted in front of him. "That was beautiful, whatever you were playing." She met his gleaming eyes, which were dappled with moonlight. Her entire body responded boldly to his look. The feeling made her happier than she'd been in a long time, but at the same time she was scared to death.

"Thanks. That was a healing song from my mother's people," Gus murmured, as he studied her in the darkness. He liked what he saw. The pale tank top she wore outlined her upper body to perfection beneath her denim jacket. Her jeans were loose, and yet, as he quickly perused her figure, he decided she was beautifully built for her five-foot-nine-inch frame. She was medium boned, and probably weighed around a hundred and fifty pounds. Gus liked women who had some meat on their bones, not the skinny sticks whose pictures were plastered on magazine covers.

Gazing up into her eyes, he saw her shyness. "Have you eaten yet?"

Cam lifted the unopened bag of potato chips. "Dinner."

"Ah, I see." Gus pointed to a box on the picnic table. "I went into town earlier, to a great little Mexican restaurant, and bought some chicken enchiladas. There's more than enough for both of us. Would you like a couple?"

She felt his gaze scan her, as if he could read her feelings and her mind. "How did you know I hadn't eaten anything?"

Chuckling, Gus quietly strummed the guitar, gazing down at it. "The whiplashing you took today would wreck my appetite as well. Come on, sit down. Share my enchiladas with me." He lifted his head and grinned, his teeth pale against his shadowed face. "You could probably stand a little quiet company with someone who isn't interested in disemboweling you because you're a woman."

At first unsettled by his perception, Cam wavered. And then she recalled Maya's sage words of advice and moved to the table, sitting down near the white box of food. "How did you know?" she asked, putting her feet on the rough-hewn seat.

"Know what?"

"That I was tied in knots? Was I that transparent today?"

Gus put the guitar aside and picked up the box. "Want the truth?" he asked, opening the container and handing her one of the wrapped enchiladas. Their fingers touched briefly, and he saw her eyes go soft once again at the contact. "No, you weren't." He opened the crinkly paper and placed his own fragrant enchilada on his lap. Watching out of the corner of his eye, he saw Cam delicately unwrap hers and carefully pick it up. She was so graceful. Her fingers were long and artistic looking. Pilot's hands.

"Speaking as your X.O.—" Gus gave her a humorous side glance as he bit into the enchilada "—I thought you carried the day well."

Munching on the delicious chicken dish, which had been well spiced, yet wasn't hot enough to numb her mouth, Cam nodded. Just sitting quietly with Gus was healing her. She didn't know why, but right now, Cam needed that safe haven he was automatically providing.

Gus handed her a white paper napkin from the box. "You've got sauce on the right corner of your mouth...." He fought the urge to lean over and wipe it off himself. He hadn't realized how beautiful Cam's mouth really was until now. Now that she was relaxed, he discovered that her mouth was really full and marvelously shaped—for kissing. For loving. Those thoughts hit him hard, and he felt his stomach clench for just a moment.

In the moonlight, her thick, slightly curled hair looked like a cloak about her graceful neck and proud shoulders. Gus squelched the urge to run his fingers in exploration through those strands, which gleamed in the watery moonlight. Her looks invited touching. That was disconcerting.

Cam took the napkin from him and quickly wiped away the offending sauce. She saw his mouth twist in a slight smile. The shadows emphasized the strength of Gus's face, from his broad, unlined forehead and large, alert eyes, to the high cheekbones and hawklike nose he'd inherited from his Indian ancestors. And then there was his strong, full mouth... She felt incredibly drawn to Gus. Still, she checked her emotional response, quickly stuffing it back inside her.

"I'm glad you picked me as your X.O.," Gus confided as he continued to enjoy his enchilada.

"Why? It's a tough job with little thanks." Cam wiped her mouth after the next bite. The food tasted good. More than good. She suddenly discovered she was famished.

"You know my dad runs an Apache squadron?"

"Yes, that's what you said earlier."

"He's over in Afghanistan right now on a covert ops."

Hearing the concern in his voice, Cam said, "You wish you were with him?"

"Yeah, I do, but the army isn't going to put a son and father together in the same squadron."

"No, they won't."

"Besides, I don't have the degree of training I need

to do that kind of work. I'm still a baby learning the building blocks." Gus chuckled indulgently.

"I like your attitude," Cam said sincerely. She caught and held his glance and gave him a slight, one-cornered smile. "You'll do well in the future with it."

"I don't like the other choice," he stated, then chuckled sardonically. "The attitude Luis and Antonio wear like a bad friend isn't my style."

Cam groaned. She hesitated before taking another bite.

Gus saw her face turn dark with worry. "Sorry," he murmured, "let's talk about happier, more positive things." Instantly, he saw her expression change from consternation and pain to one of hope. How readable Cam was! But then, Gus realized that she was allowing him to see her emotional side right now, and not that C.O.'s poker face she'd put on earlier today.

"I was sayin' that my dad runs an Apache squadron. When I was in my late teens, I remember him getting his first assignment as X.O. for a helo squad. He was always the type of father who would sit down with you and tell you the good and bad, the ins and outs of his day. I used to sit with him at the dinner table, over dessert my mom had made, and he'd share with us all this stuff that went on in the squadron." Gus gave her a measured look. "I learned what being an X.O. meant, through his eyes and experience, and that's what I wanted to share with you. I think I can be a good assistant to you, Cam. At least, I'll try."

Heat moved into her cheeks as his husky voice reached her, an invisible, supporting caress. "It's good to hear that. You probably have a lot more education on being an X.O. than I do on being a C.O., if you want the truth.''

Gus heard the pain, the self-doubt in her voice. ''You were a pilot in the BJS before you came here, right?''

''Yes. *Just* a pilot. I didn't have any management training for leadership stuff like this....'' She waved her hand toward the brightly lit barracks in the distance.

''You got thrown to the wolves then,'' Gus murmured in concern. ''I don't know that I could do half as good a job as you did on your first day as C.O. You held your own against two men who were really challenging your authority.'' He gave her a slight nod. ''You handled them well. I would have decked them.''

Words of praise were exactly what Cam needed. ''Coming from you, that's music to my ears. Thanks.''

Gus wiped his hands then his mouth, and stuffed the used napkin back into the empty food carton. ''Speaking of music...'' He grinned at her as he picked up his guitar and settled it like a lover against his body, strumming the strings quietly. Gradually, the music began to ease the worry he saw in Cam's darkened eyes.

Sighing, Cam finished her enchilada and tidied up. Then she folded her arms and sat there, allowing the melodic notes to wash her clean of all her angst. Closing her eyes, she absorbed the heat and energy of Gus, sitting so close to her. His quiet demeanor, his insight, seemed like a huge gift to Cam, for she desperately needed what he offered as a man and as a friend. For the next ten minutes Gus played, and she allowed herself to become lost in the sounds as his fingers stroked the strings and brought them to life.

When he finally stopped playing, Gus turned and looked at Cam. She was sitting there with her elbows on her knees, her profile sharp and clean, outlined in moonlight. Her mouth, once grim, was now parted and relaxed. The wrinkles in her brow were gone. Her eyes were closed, and he noticed how thick and long her lashes were against her freckled cheeks.

In that moment, Gus had the powerful urge to put his guitar down, place his arms around Cam and draw her close, in an embrace that would protect her. Soothe her. Let her know that someone respected her, supported her and liked her. Frowning, Gus looked away. He couldn't ''like'' Cam. Telling himself that over and over again, Gus resolved to keep her at arm's length. She was so soft, so womanly, a powerful package in combination with her pilot's confidence and courage. But then women who lived on the ragged edge of life and death always drew his interest.

Giving himself an internal shake, Gus sternly warned himself that he'd already lost the woman he loved because of her dangerous career. He couldn't stand to do that again; his heart simply couldn't take that kind of blow. No, somehow, he had to stop his blind, stupid heart from longing for Cam. It had to be all-business between them. Only business.

Chapter 6

It wasn't working, Cam thought as she sat, hand pressed against her head, elbows resting on her desk, with the flight scores she was studying blurring in front of her eyes. For a week she'd been running a flight training program to bring Luis and Antonio into line. The statistics spoke for themselves: Gus had made a seventy percent improvement, while the other two pilots, who were purposely dragging their feet, had gained only ten and twenty percent, respectively.

It was nearly midnight, but lifting her head, Cam picked up the iridium phone, which she kept on the desk. Her heart was heavy and she felt like an utter failure. Sensing Maya would still be up even at this late hour, she punched in her number.

"Stevenson here."

"Maya, it's Cam. Am I calling too late?"

"Oh…no, that's fine. You sound down. I've been

checking in on you all week and haven't been feeling
very good about it. You okay? What's goin' on?''

Tears flooded Cam's eyes. Just the way Maya
spoke, in that warm, concerned tone, broke through
her reserve. That was one of the many things Cam
loved about her superior. Maya was tough, but fair.
She was a steady guiding hand that Cam could always
count on. The fact that Maya had been ''checking on
her'' was part of the mystery surrounding this legendary woman. Cam knew what most of her colleagues knew of their illustrious leader: that she was
a member of the fabled Jaguar Clan, a secret organization steeped in mystical tradition. Many times in
the past, Cam could swear Maya had read her mind,
because she'd speak about what Cam was thinking
before Cam had uttered a word.

Tonight, Cam was glad that Maya had that ESP or
whatever it was. Sitting back in the chair, she blinked
rapidly to clear her eyes of tears. ''Maya, I'm feeling
like a failure, but before you say anything, let me also
say I have a fall-back plan that I created in case this
first plan didn't work.''

''Good!'' Maya exclaimed warmly. ''A leader always has plan B in case plan A goes to hell in a hand-
basket.'' She chuckled. ''So, I've got a fresh cup of
coffee in front of me and I'm sitting here at my desk,
which is miraculously cleared of all paper, and I'm
all-ears. What's goin' down?''

Laughing a little, her voice strained, Cam looked
at her own desk. It was a mess, piled high with work.
Some of it was done, much of it not. ''I'll cut to the
chase.'' She knew Maya wanted the bottom line. As
a C.O., she didn't have time for preambles. ''My orig-

inal plan, which was to fly with each of the pilots two hours a day, and put them through advanced flight training, hasn't worked. It worked with one of the three pilots.''

''Morales, right?''

''Yes.''

''Good. At least you have one who's handling his end of the deal. The other two dogging it?''

Cam hated to admit it. ''Yes.''

''Okay, you're outnumbered, so what do you do?''

Cam knew Maya wasn't going to give her any easy answers. The way she taught was by asking people hard questions, and letting them search their own experience and intelligence and come up with a fix.

''You aren't going to like it. And neither will Morgan.''

''Plan B, right?''

''That's a roger.''

''I'm listenin'.''

Taking in a deep breath, Cam launched into her other idea. ''I need a third Apache. And I need two women from the squadron, specifically Wild Woman and Snake. I can't divide my time among three pilots, especially when two of them are playing around and not getting serious about their commitment to this mission. I need enough Apaches to set up a game plan, so that I've got an IP—inspector pilot—with each of the students. That way, it forces the two Mexican pilots to put up or shut up. I'd like to be able to tell Dominguez and Zaragoza that if they don't start crunching the percentages and improving, they'll be washed out and two new pilots will replace them.''

Cam frowned and went on. ''Gus Morales is wonderful, Maya. He's learning, he's hungry and he's committed. But the other two hate me because I'm a woman telling them what to do.''

"And they're acting like petulant teenagers rebelling just because you are a woman.''

"You got it.''

"That's your plan?''

She gave a sharp, sad laugh. "Yeah. I know it's not a good one. I know that asking you to send two of your top pilots on TDY—temporary duty—up here, leaves you shorthanded. You run on the lean side with pilots at the best of times, I know. I've been beating my brains trying to come up with another solution, Maya. But I haven't found one. There's no one I can pull from Fort Rucker to stand in their stead. I need pilots with interdiction experience to pull this plan off.''

"Tell me more about what would happen if you got that third Apache and two of my pilots.''

Heartened, Cam launched into her plans for the next five weeks of training based upon having an extra bird and two IPs to help her bring it about. At the end of her explanation, she fell silent and waited for Maya's reaction. The phone was quiet for a long time. Cam began to sweat in earnest.

"Of course, the other option here,'' she added quietly, "is to pull me as C.O. and get someone else up here that you feel is better qualified, or who can force these two pilots to perform up to expectations. It could be me, Maya. A personality conflict. I've pulled every rabbit I know out of my hat, and nothing is working. Right now, as it stands, I'll never make that projected deadline to get these three pilots up to interdiction duty standards.''

''A good leader assesses all possibilities,'' Maya told her gently. ''And yes, you have to look at yourself. You have to ask yourself what part do I play in this problem? How can I change myself? Is it my attitude hurting the people that work under me? You've asked those questions.''

''Yeah,'' Cam said bitterly, ''I have, and I see I come up wanting, but I don't know how to fix it.''

''Sometimes a leader has to accept that there are going to be personality conflicts. The key is to try to dissolve them, to try to move on and motivate that individual, anyway. And sometimes,'' Maya said, ''there's nothin' you can do. That person or group of people are gonna hate you just because.''

''The core of this problem is gender prejudice.''

''Right. And you can't change your gender, can you?''

Chuckling, Cam shook her head. ''No, and I wouldn't want to, either.''

''Okay, so you've assessed yourself and come up with the root of the problem. And it's not something you can fix. So, that leaves you out of the equation. You don't have to change. You don't have to quit your command.''

Relief spread through Cam. ''When I talk to you, Maya, everything seems so simple and clear.''

Laughing, Maya said, ''With experience, leading gets easier, not harder. Okay, as to your two boys? I called Morgan a day after we first talked a week ago, and here's the scoop on them. They had the lowest grades in their class in Apache school. Morgan made some phone calls to Fort Rucker and talked to one IP there who admitted privately to him, off the record, that he was pressured into giving Dominguez a passing grade simply because this was a political hot potato.''

"Political?"

"Yeah," Maya growled. "Dominguez is the son of old money in Mexico. His father is allied closely with the president of Mexico, and is looking to run for mayor of Mexico City in two years. Pressure was put on the IP because the father doesn't want his record besmirched by a son who is a playboy and isn't really serious about much of anything. I had Morgan check into Dominguez's past, and this guy behaves like a fourteen-year-old most of the time. He's consistently shown a lack of responsibility and maturity no matter where he's gone."

"And Zaragoza?"

"New money, father is very rich and has spoiled Antonio completely. He floats through life with the same attitudes as his wealthy friend."

"They're a pair," Cam said unhappily.

"Right, so here's the bottom line. You're stuck with them, and so is the army and the Mexican Air Force. They're screw-ups, to put it bluntly, and no one wants to handle them because they have power, money and political influence behind them. These two good ole boys know it, too, so that's why they're not getting serious with you."

"And I can't get rid of them?" Cam's voice rose in consternation. It would be hell on earth to keep these two in her command.

"Listen, you get some bad apples in every squadron, almost always. When it comes down to biting the bullet, you have to find something that will force these two pilots to *want* to do what you demand of them."

"But," Cam said helplessly, opening her hand in frustration, "if they can skate through Apache school, get their grades changed, and they still don't care, what can I do to *make* them care?"

Maya chuckled. "What do they value, Cam?"

She snorted. "Oh, they can hardly wait to get out of here at night. They hit the party spots in Tijuana, dance and drink and woo the *señoritas* until dawn. When I see them the next morning at muster, they're hungover, their eyes are bloodshot and they look like death itself because of lack of sleep."

"Okay, so you order them to stay on the base. They don't get any liberty unless they produce. And they must produce up to the bar—standards you've set— with a minimum passing percentage."

Nodding, Cam said, "Okay…" She could imagine how angry they'd be over her ordering them to stay on base twenty-four hours a day. "What else?"

"Well, what else do they value?"

"Dancing, drinking, smoking their cigarettes…"

"Enforce a non-smoking rule. No smoking until off base." She chuckled darkly. "You and I both know that smokers have to satisfy their addiction. If you cut them off, they're really going to scream. But let them."

"None of this will work unless they think they can be held to it," Cam protested.

"What are you prepared to do if you find them smoking on base?"

Shrugging, Cam said, "I don't know...."

"Have them wash the Apaches—inside and out. Or have them run five miles with fifty pound packs on their back. Put Morales out there to make sure they do it. He's your X.O. He gets to do the dirty work."

"And what about banning them from partying?"

"Well," Maya said, "if they are stupid enough to go off base when you've ordered them to stay, then that's a major offense, and they can be thrown out of the military. It's called going AWOL. I don't feel they're willing to test the combined might of the U.S. Army and the Mexican Air Force on that one. And if they do, then you have them dead to rights and you can, at that point, get rid of them."

"I see...."

"Yeah, always think about what someone isn't willing to give up. That is where you work with them, Cam. That's the ground you plow."

"Okay...I can do that."

"As to the other thing," Maya said, murmuring more to herself than to Cam. "I'll contact Morgan and see about gettin' you a third Apache. Your plan makes a lot of sense."

"But you can't really afford to lose Snake and Wild Woman...." Cam said worriedly. There were no extra pilots to pick up the slack at Maya's squadron if the two left, even for six weeks.

"There you go, mother hen," Maya teased. "The problem is getting the army to let loose of one of their Apache Longbows for six weeks. I can get the women you want up there, no problem."

"But—"

"Look at it this way," Maya told her. "Dane and

I will step in and make up the difference while they are gone, so it won't be a problem.''

Disheartened, Cam sat there in silence. That meant Maya and her husband, Dane, would not only be handling their immense responsibilities at the squadron, they'd take on twenty-four-hour flight duty as well. That was an awful strain and Cam knew it.

"I thought you'd say that."

"That's the way the cookie crumbles, Cam. Sometimes you bite the bullet and just do it. No one said life was always easy, did they?"

"No," Cam grumped, "just damned unfair."

"The way I see it, your two rich boys need a boot in the butt. You've selected two of the best pilots to ensure they're going to be living in hell from now on, once they get up there and start working with them."

"Yeah," Cam laughed, "Snake and Wild Woman won't take any crap from either one of them."

"That's right, they'll be in their faces. And what you need to do is stand out of the way. So does your X.O. You let the ladies handle their immature charges. You back them and support them and keep the two Mexican pilots on a real short leash. No liberty unless they produce. No smoking unless on liberty. These two boys are gonna find out in a helluva hurry that playtime is over and it's nose to the grindstone time instead."

"I'm feeling better, Maya…thanks so much! I know what kind of effort you're putting into this to help me."

"Listen, that's what this is all about—teamwork and support. You have a mission to complete. You're going to need help we didn't think of at first, because of the players you're stuck with and can't get rid of. So, in essence, we're callin' in the calvary—Snake, Wild Woman and a third Apache. I'll get it done for you, so don't worry. You need to tell your X.O. what's going to happen, though. He needs to know and then support you a hundred percent when the crap hits the fan.''

''I know Gus will,'' Cam said. ''He's supported me from the beginning.''

Maya laughed lightly. ''Do you realize that every time you mention that dude's name, your voice goes soft and mushy, Anderson? You like him or what?''

Shocked, Cam sat up straight. Her heart pounded briefly as she considered her C.O.'s words. ''What? Er…no. Why…no, of course not. I mean, he's a likable guy, Maya. Real easygoing compared to the other two jerks. But like him?''

''Whoa!'' Maya chortled. ''Rein in your horse, lady, I was just wonderin' out loud, was all. Your energy changes when you talk about him. Your voice changes.''

''Well,'' Cam sputtered, ''probably because he's my only safe port in this storm!''

''I see. Okay, gimme a couple of days to put plan B in motion for you. I'll give you a call at midnight, your time, in forty-eight hours.''

''Thanks, Maya…as usual, you're magical, the way you pull rabbits out of hats to save my butt.''

''Your butt's worth protectin', Cam. Relax. You're doin' things right and to the best of your abilities. No one can ask more of you. Now, I'd be hunting down my X.O. and lettin' him know ASAP about plan B. I actually feel sorry for Zaragoza and Dominguez. You need to decide which one gets assigned to Snake and which to Wild Woman.'' She chuckled darkly. ''I wish I could be there to see their faces when my women pilots get into *their* faces. It oughta be a Kodak moment.''

Laughter spilled from Cam's lips. She loved the black humor that was so much a part of BJS. ''Maya, if I didn't know any better, I'd say you were going to enjoy this.''

''Damn straight. I don't put up with crap like that from a green pilot, man or woman. They're in the military and they're damn well gonna respond accordingly or else.''

Relief flooded Cam and she rested her elbow on her knee, the phone in her hand. ''Maya, thanks. I don't know what I'd do without you.''

''Same here, Cam. We miss you down here. Our mother hen is gone. The women miss your nurturing, the chicken soup, the chocolate chip cookies you bake for them when they have pilot duty.'' She chuckled. ''Get some sleep, Tree Trimmer. Tomorrow's another day. A better one, I promise.''

Gus sat with Cam in the darkness of the grove on the picnic table that had become their ritual meeting place. He had his guitar in hand, his arm resting over it as he listened to plan B. Overhead, the stars were bright in the blackness of the night.

He liked Cam's husky, soft voice. He liked the way she used her hands to gesture as she spoke. Did she realize how beautiful her hands were? ''Flight hands'' was what they called them in the military. Good pilots had a certain look in their eyes, and hands that were long, graceful and lean—all hallmarks of a good flyer. She was certainly that—and more—but Gus refused to go there no matter what the cost to him personally.

He liked to bring dessert out to the grove and share it with Cam during their nightly chats. It was the only time she seemed to have free to discuss his X.O. duties. If Cam wasn't flying six hours a day and trying to bring the two Mexican pilots up to par in flight skills, she was at her office plowing through a mountain of paperwork. Some of it Gus had been able to talk her out of, and do himself. Little by little, they were learning what a C.O. and X.O. did to help one another and balance the workload.

Looking down at the opened box of chocolate chip cookies he'd bought in town Gus saw that half of them were gone. He looked up at Cam, sitting two feet away from him on the table, waving a fifth cookie in her hand as she talked. Smiling to himself, he felt his heart growing warm as he studied her profile.

"So, that's what is gonna happen," she told Gus, turning and looking at him. She watched as he picked up another cookie and bit into it. "What do you think?"

Raising one eyebrow, he murmured, "I'd invoke the loss of privileges after the third Apache and the two IPs arrive. I wouldn't try it now."

Nodding, Cam said, "Okay."

"That way, you're hitting those two with maximum firepower all at once. What you're trying to do is jolt them out of the cozy little world they've established here under your command. When you have three IPs around, they're less likely to buck you, I think. It's a matter of numbers. It's a matter of overwhelming them with equal or greater firepower.'' He grinned.

"That sounds right," Cam murmured. "Good advice.''

Heart thudding as Gus gave her that wicked little-boy smile, Cam eagerly drank in the look in his darkened eyes. Oh, how she looked forward to these nightly talks. Of course, Cam said it was business—serious business—and he'd agreed. However, tonight of all nights, Gus had brought her her favorite cookies. She'd casually mentioned it a week ago, when their talk had strayed into the personal realm, and he'd asked her what her favorite dessert was.

Finishing the cookie, Gus wiped his hand on his jeans and then stroked a few chords on the guitar. The music filled the grove and he saw Cam's face relax. When the little things he did for her made her happy, his heart soared. He knew the pressures Cam was under. Yet she had a quiet strength, a steely quality that wasn't revealed outwardly. Cam had a kind-looking face, but she was tough when she had to be. Maybe there was a difference in how a woman commanded, Gus mused. It was an interesting fishbowl experiment, as far as he was concerned. He knew a man could sometimes be aggressive and in-your-face as a C.O. But Cam's quiet firmness worked for him. Not on his two cohorts, however.

Strumming the guitar more loudly, Gus played another melody. Cam smiled and his heart melted. Her eyes grew dreamy, as she sat with her arms wrapped around herself, elbows on her thighs. Smiling back, Gus lost himself in the tune.

For ten minutes he played, and Cam was able to

surrender to the gentle, healing melodies that Gus coaxed from his old, beat-up guitar. For the first time today, Cam utterly relaxed. It was him, she decided— Gus was quiet, yet so perceptive of her needs. It was as if he could read her mind and see inside her heart. Cam had never met a man who had that ability or effect on her.

When he ended the tune, she turned to him. "That was beautiful. What was it?"

"It's a lullaby of the Yaqui people," he murmured, his fingers brushing the guitar lovingly. "My mother used to sing it to me. I grew up listening to it."

"It's lovely. I'm glad you bring your guitar out here when we meet."

"Yeah?" Gus grinned a little. Her eyes lightened.

"Yeah. It makes a good ending to a tough day." And Cam frowned.

"Well," he murmured, "your bad days are comin' to an end. Your C.O. said the Apache will be here tomorrow and so will the two IPs. Then those bad days will land on Zaragoza and Dominguez." Chuckling, Gus added, "And it couldn't happen to two nicer dudes, in my opinion."

Heartened, Cam gave him a weak smile. "I'm glad your dad taught you about the life of an X.O. I'm almost jealous. I wish I had better skills, more education in management."

Reaching out unthinkingly, Gus slid his hand over her slumped shoulder. His fingers grazed her denim jacket and he felt the strength of her beneath the rough material. The look in her soulful eyes at his unexpected touch affected him deeply. For a moment, just a brief moment, Cam had leaned into his hand, as if starved for a human touch. A little care. It was then that Gus realized—too late—that his gesture was personal and intimate. Certainly not military.

Unhappy with himself, Gus pulled his hand away and muttered, "You're making the best of a bad situation, Cam. I think you're doing a good job."

Skin tingling where Gus had briefly and unexpectedly touched her, Cam stared at his profile. His mouth was set in an unhappy line; his dark brows were knitted. She had never expected him to touch her—ever. But he had. And that instant had been a wonderful, healing gift. His hand had slid across her shoulder in such a gentle, caressing gesture that Cam had automatically, without thinking, leaned closer, starved for his touch. Really starved for him to embrace her and hold her.

The whole brief moment was so shocking to Cam that she straightened up, her hands clenched on her thighs. Somewhere in her colliding thoughts, she realized a huge part of her had wanted desperately to walk into his arms and be held. Gus gave her that—a sense of safety and protection in a world where she felt continually exposed and vulnerable, especially in the presence of the other two pilots. With Gus around, Cam relaxed. She felt safe with him. They always laughed and joked in the cockpit, even though they were in training. It was fun. Being alone with *him* was something she looked forward to daily.

Swallowing hard, Cam whispered, "I think we'd better go. I gotta get up early tomorrow…." And she slid off the table and dusted off the rear of her jeans. Cam saw the sober look on Gus's face. He seemed unhappy about his action toward her. She tried not to take it personally, but she did anyway.

Her heart cried out in protest as they began the trek back to the barracks. Cam made sure there was plenty of space between her and Gus as they walked so there'd be no possibility of their hands brushing.

Floundering around for a safe topic, because she felt so awkward and unsure of herself, Cam said, "You must have a wonderful woman waiting for you stateside, right?"

Moving the guitar strap to his left shoulder so that the instrument was between them, Gus felt his heart contract. He slowed for a moment, then resumed his usual stride. "No," he said, more abruptly than he'd meant to. "There's no one." He looked over at her, his face in shadows. "What about you? You said the BJS is primarily all women, with a few support men. Is there someone special down there waiting for you to come back?"

Cam shook her head. "No..." She chewed on her lip. "I...I don't have a good track record with men. I swore off them for a while because of it. The last three years have been wonderful in some ways without men in my life."

"Yeah, relationships are hard," Gus muttered. Then why did his heart soar when he heard Cam admit she had no man in her life?

"And right now," Cam added, her voice growing strong with conviction, "I'm more focused on my career than a personal life."

"Makes two of us," Gus said fervently, meaning it. Or did he?

Chapter 7

Gus knew things were going to explode the moment the two BJS women pilots confidently sauntered into their small classroom the next morning. Gus and the two pilots were sitting at their respective desks, facing a green chalkboard, where Cam stood, briefing them on the day's flight mission. Only he had been taking serious notes on the upcoming maneuvers. Luis and Antonio, upon hearing the door open behind them, turned. Gus, who was sitting on one side of the room, his desk positioned so he could see them all, lifted his head.

The two women pilots who walked in were in typical U.S. Army flight uniforms. What wasn't typical was the blond woman; she had a red streak dyed in her hair. The other one, taller and leaner, followed her in like a cat on a prowl for its quarry. Shifting his gaze, Gus saw Cam smile slightly at them in welcome. By the gleam in her eyes Gus knew she was glad to see her sisters from her old base in Peru.

"Come in," Cam invited them, "and stand up here. Let me make the introductions."

Gus saw the mischievous glint in both pilots' eyes as they walked toward the front of the room. They each wore the patch of the Black Jaguar Squadron on their left shoulder and an American flag on the right. The black leather patch above their left breast pocket had their pilot handle or nickname, their real name and their rank.

As Wild Woman, the shorter of the two, started to walk past Zaragoza, he gave a low wolf whistle of appreciation.

Instantly, she turned around. The expression on her face changed from one of innocence to a snarling grimace. She grabbed the collar of Antonio's flight suit, pinned him against the chair and put her face an inch from his own, their noses nearly touching.

"What do you think you are doing, mister?" she snarled. "Whistling for your dog? Funny, I don't see any dogs in here. I see a stupid jerk, though. Right in front of me. Now, you wanna do that again?" Her lips curled back from her clenched teeth.

Zaragoza croaked. He jerked his hands into the air, not daring to touch the hissing woman pilot.

Gus squelched his laughter. Antonio was sliding down in his seat, trying to escape the gringo woman's unexpected response. *Serves him right.*

"Well?" Wild Woman barked. "You got a dog in this room, mister?"

"Uh…no. No, *señorita*—"

"What?" Wild Woman practically roared into his

face, her hand tightening on his collar and jerking it savagely. "I don't see any *señoritas* in this room, either. What's the appropriate military response, mister?"

Antonio choked and coughed, his eyes growing huge. Waving his hands spastically in surrender, he tried to move, but was pinned. "I, uh…*Sí*, ma'am."

Releasing him and giving him a look of utter disgust, Wild Woman growled, "That's better, mister. You do any more whistling and I'll rip your lips off your face. *Comprende?*"

Shocked, Zaragoza tried to sit up and straighten his flight suit. "Uh…yes, *sí*, ma'am, *sí*…" he mumbled, highly embarrassed.

Luis, who sat beside his friend watching the whole thing with widened eyes stayed very still. Gus thought he might be in shock. The two women pilots continued their nonchalant walk to the front of the room as if nothing had happened.

They came to attention, saluted Cam and did everything militarily correct, under the circumstances. Gus silently applauded them. Nothing like showing the "boys" in the room what was expected of them. Cam returned the salute.

"About-face," she ordered the two women pilots, "and stand at parade rest."

Instantly, the two concurred, performing the move crisply, in unison. They stood in front of the room, to Cam's right, hands behind their backs, their booted feet slightly apart, chins high and shoulders thrown back with pride. Gus thought they were magnificent looking. He saw rock-solid confidence in every inch of their unsmiling faces, especially in their eyes, which reminded him of alert eagles, poised and ready to strike. The caliber of these women blew him away. Gus understood from talking with Cam earlier that they all had three years of wartime combat flying under their belt. Whoever had trained them had done so to a blade's fine edge. They looked intimidating. Dangerous. Moving his gaze to the two male pilots, he slid his hand across his mouth to hide his burgeoning smile.

Zaragoza was completely shaken. He'd thought he'd get away with a wolf whistle. The last thing he'd expected was for the blonde to turn and confront him on his undesired male behavior. Now he sat stiffly at his desk, hands fluttering nervously around his collar, constantly readjusting it. His skin, normally a golden-tan, was rosy and flushed.

Luis Dominguez wasn't smiling. He was scowling, and Gus could see him measuring up the two pilots who had just come in. Though Gus wasn't sure about what Luis was thinking, he wasn't about to whistle, that was for certain.

Cam smiled benignly at the three male pilots. "Gentlemen, I want to introduce the rest of our squadron." Lifting her hand toward the woman nearest to her, she said, "Chief Warrant Officer 2 Jessica Merrill. We call her Wild Woman." Cam kept her face serious as she nailed the still-shaken Antonio with a look that spoke volumes. He'd just had a taste of her wild, unpredictable side.

"And to her right is Chief Warrant Officer 2 Vickey Mabrey. Her handle is Snake." Cam went on to quietly introduce the three student pilots. Then she went to her lectern and picked up a set of papers.

Holding them out to Gus, her X.O., who stood up and approached her, she said, "Mr. Morales, please pass out this new set of orders to everyone?"

Gus nodded. "Yes, ma'am." And he turned and handed a set each to Luis and Antonio. Returning to his seat, he sat down with his own copy in hand. He knew what they contained, because he'd typed them up earlier that morning.

Cam passed sets to Wild Woman and Snake. "All right, let's go over them together, because these orders are in force as of right now."

Gus watched covertly as Cam read the pages in a low, authoritative tone. He saw first shock, and then rage in Luis's and Antonio's eyes as they found out they were ordered to stay on base—permanently—until their flight scores improved to eighty percent. Right now, their marks hovered in the thirty to forty percentile range. When Cam told them they couldn't smoke until they were off base, their mouths dropped open.

"But...but—" Luis stammered, starting to get out of his chair.

"Sit down, mister," Snake snarled at him. "Where I come from, you sit and raise your hand. Do it."

Stunned by the tall, dark-haired pilot's order, Luis sat. Immediately. Shock was clearly written on his face. It took him a moment, but he hesitantly raised his hand.

"Mr. Dominguez?" Cam said. "You had a question?"

"Uh...*sí,* ma'am."

"And what might that be?" Cam kept any satisfaction out of her tone. She silently thanked her sister pilots for their aggressive, intimidating stance. Though Cam hadn't known exactly what to expect from them, Wild Woman's and Snake's behavior seemed appropriate under the circumstances. Never had Cam been so glad to see them as now. Already, just having them here was tilting the balance in the room to her favor. Now there were three women pilots, all skilled, and two petulant male students who clearly realized things were changing.

Luis wiped his sweaty brow. "Ma'am, no smoking?"

"Oh, of course, Mr. Dominguez, you can smoke. Once your flight marks hit eighty percent, you can smoke in your room or outside the barracks."

Gulping, he cast a wild look of appeal in Gus's direction.

Gus shrugged eloquently, his body language clear: he couldn't get the orders changed.

"But—but—"

"No buts, Mr. Dominguez," Cam said smoothly. "You perform in the cockpit, you get to smoke. If you choose not to try and become more skilled in flight interdiction, then I guess you've chosen to stop smoking for the time you are with this mission." She smiled faintly. "Of course, you can choose to leave this mission at any time." She picked up a set of papers from her lectern. "The necessary forms are right here. All you have to do is ask for a transfer and I'll be happy to give it to you. All any of you need to do is ask." Cam couldn't help it; she gloated. A good leader probably didn't do that, but she couldn't stop herself right now.

Cam knew that neither pilot would take that option.

It would shame them to their families, and being first-born sons, much was expected of them. They were supposed to excel, not run away from something. No, she knew they'd tough it out, but down deep inside her she prayed they'd jump at the chance to leave.

Both pilots stared at her as if she were Cerberus, the three-headed dog from Greek mythology who protected the gates to hell.

"No takers?" Cam asked them sweetly, raising an eyebrow. "No?" She put the orders down on the lectern. "Very well. Then this means, gentlemen, that I need to assign you an IP for the duration of this mission."

"Ms. Merrill?"

"Yes, ma'am?"

"I'd like you to teach Mr. Zaragoza the finer points of interdiction in the cockpit of the Apache."

Wild Woman smiled, gazed at Antonio, who had another shocked look on his face, and said with great pleasure, "Yes, ma'am!"

"Excellent," Cam murmured. "And Ms. Mabrey?"

"Yes, ma'am?"

"You're to take Mr. Dominguez under your wing and teach him the more refined aspects of interdiction in the air."

Snake didn't smile. She rarely did. Giving Dominguez a glare that spoke volumes, she saw the Mexican pilot, whose ego was larger than the Empire State Building, begin to deflate. "My pleasure, ma'am. We'll make it happen." Her mouth twisted into a smirk. "Or else…"

"Excellent," Cam murmured, pleased. She saw

Dominguez go white as a proverbial sheet. And she saw the rage in his eyes, but he had the good sense to keep his mouth shut. With Wild Woman physically intimidating Antonio, she knew Luis didn't want Snake descending upon him. And she knew Vickey was fully capable of doing it, too. These women didn't put up with gender prejudice one iota, especially in the military world.

Luis raised his hand.

"Yes, Mr. Dominguez?"

"Er...ma'am...how is it we cannot leave the base? We have left every night so far."

Cam opened her hands and gave him a stern look. "You've made choices that aren't appropriate for good military training, so something had to be done about it, Mr. Dominguez. When you demonstrate to me, on a daily basis, that your flight training can maintain an eighty percent, then you will be authorized liberty for that night. Your curfew is 2200."

"Twenty-two hundred hours?" Luis yelped.

"Mister," Snake hissed, "you want me to come over there and rearrange that mouth of yours? Your response to our commanding officer is 'ma'am.' Got it?"

Gulping, Luis nodded jerkily. His gaze was pinned on Snake, who had taken one step toward him, her entire body suddenly tense, her hands tightened into fists at her side. The look on her face made it clear she shouldn't be messed with. Luis had no desire to have this woman, who was at least six foot tall, come over and do something to him similar to what Antonio had just experienced.

"*Sí,* ma'am. Yes, ma'am."

Snake gave him a narrow-eyed look. "That's better, mister." And she snapped crisply back into parade-rest position.

Luis sent Cam a desperate glance. "Ma'am, you cannot do this to me. To us!"

"Of course I can, Mr. Dominguez. It's my responsibility to see that you three pilots meet our expectations. If you do, you get rewards. If you don't..." Cam shrugged eloquently and opened her hands "...well, then it's your choice, and your own fault. These women are IPs in the Apache Longbow. They've got three years of daily combat experience in South America chasing down bad guys who are trying to haul cocaine out of the country where they're stationed. I assure you that if you set your minds and hearts to learning from them, in five weeks time you will become excellent at interdiction."

Disheartened, Luis sank back into his seat.

"Mr. Morales, please hand out today's mission folder to everyone? Chiefs? If you'll have a seat." And Cam motioned for her sister pilots to sit down at the desks at the rear of the room. Both of them came to attention and then quickly took their seats.

While Gus distributed the mission plan, the room practically vibrated with tension. Luis and Antonio were clearly in shock over everything that had just transpired. Gus was glad for more reasons than one that Cam was going to be his IP. As he handed out the mission flight plan and training techniques to be flown, he tried not to admit to the secret personal pleasure he felt at being in her company. The emotional wounds of his past ate at him hourly when he was around Cam now, and it was getting to him.

* * *

"Very good, Gus!" Cam said over the intercom of
the Apache he was flying. As they flew over the
mountainous training area at four thousand feet, she
wrote down his final grade for today's flight on the
clipboard on her lap: a ninety percent. Sitting in the
upper cockpit, she glanced down proudly at his helmeted head and saw his hand resting confidently on
the collective between his legs.

"You get to go on liberty tonight," she said, laughing.

"That's great to hear," he said, joining her laughter. Although he'd been focused on his own training,
he wondered how the other two pilots were faring.
Not well, most likely, but they weren't in radio contact. At least he wasn't. He was sure Cam was, as
C.O. From time to time this afternoon he'd seen the
other two Apaches in the distance over the mountains,
but that was all.

"Well," Gus said, turning the Apache back to the
usual restricted flight corridor that would take them
fifteen miles out over the Pacific Ocean, "if I get
liberty tonight, do you want to meet me in the grove
around 2100?" His heart beat a little harder in his
chest. God help him, but he really enjoyed spending
time with Cam. Her soft, low voice was always nurturing to him. Even when he made mistakes and she
corrected him, she did it gently. She was such a di-
chotomy. Gus knew that, in the air, she could be an
aggressive combat pilot, and yet with him that ag-
gression was never apparent, just the nurturing
teacher who shared her delight with him when he per-
formed flawlessly.

"Sure," she answered promptly.

Feeling relief, Gus smiled as he urged the Apache to the required five-thousand-foot altitude. Below, the Pacific was a smooth, dark blue color, with rolling waves sparkling in the setting sun. "Business, of course," he assured her. "I think we've got a lot to talk about tonight, C.O. to X.O."

Cam finished her remarks on his flight test for the day and slipped the pen back into the pocket on her left sleeve. "Of course," she murmured, "all business." Sliding the clipboard into a pocket on the left side of her seat, she sighed.

"I'm going to have a meeting with Snake and Wild Woman at 1800." She glanced at her watch; that was an hour from now. The mission they'd flown today was four grueling hours of nonstop training. Cam knew the two Mexican pilots were probably feeling like limp dishrags at this point. Or they should be if they cared. Only time would tell, after they landed and she got together with her sister pilots to be briefed on their flights.

"Okay. You want me to sit in?"

"Absolutely."

"And then chow?"

Chuckling, Cam said, "You're never far away from that chow hall, are you?"

Gus grinned and studied his HUDs carefully for other aircraft, authorized or not. "I'm a chow hound, for sure. Guilty as charged. Are you going to go eat there tonight after the briefing?"

"Yeah," Cam said, relaxing in her seat and enjoying the ride, "I probably will."

Gus couldn't help but get excited. Cam was like an

addiction to him emotionally. He went to bed dreaming about her. When he woke up in the morning, he'd hurry through his routine to get to the chow hall because he knew she always ate breakfast. From then on, he was with her most of the day. Usually, Cam didn't eat at the chow hall at night. Understanding that she was stressed out about Luis and Antonio, Gus ate alone. Now that the new IPs were here, she was going to be able to relax and enjoy an evening meal. That made him happy.

"Maybe you want some personal time with your friends at the chow hall, though?"

Cam was finding Gus very astute about relationships. It was one more plus in his column. "Yes…I'd like that. At least tonight, Gus. Can I meet you at the grove later?"

"Sure, no problem. I imagine you'll have a lot to catch up on with them."

"Yes," Cam murmured, "I do."

"You really miss your squadron, don't you?"

"Is it that obvious?"

Chuckling, Gus said, "Maybe just to me, because I've been around you a lot more than the other two."

"They're like a second family," Cam explained, flexing her gloved hands. The sunlight was strong and bright in the cockpit. She was glad for the constant air-conditioning that kept the space cool.

"Judging from the looks in their eyes, they were glad to see you, too."

Cam smiled wistfully. "Down at BJS, I'm the squadron mother hen. I take care of them when they're sick. I make chicken soup and bring it to the barracks for them."

"You're a good listener," Gus murmured. "I like talking with you. Sharing. I always feel like you're there for me, a hundred percent. You aren't just there in body, but in heart, mind and spirit, too."

Warmth flooded her face, and Cam knew she was blushing. "Snake calls me Big Mama in the Sky."

Gus grinned. "Nice. Yeah, that fits you, Cam. Anyone with an ounce of intelligence can see you care. You nurture others, you don't take a pound of flesh out of them."

"Well," Cam answered dryly, "that depends upon the person I'm dealing with. You *want* to learn flight tactics. Luis and Antonio didn't, so I don't think Snake or Wild Woman are going to be very nurturing or pleasant to them."

Gus laughed heartily. "No, I don't think there's any mothering coming their way right now. Just hell on earth. But they've sown the seeds, so now they'll reap the harvest."

"Yep, where we come from, we call it rubber band karma. You put it out there, and that's what's gonna come snapping back at you in an instant."

"Well, I'm grateful to you for passing on what you know to me. I've learned more from you this week alone than I did in the ten weeks of Apache flight school. You're hard, demanding, but you teach like no one I've ever encountered."

"Are you bucking for a hundred percent on your grade?" Cam teased, privately pleased at his praise. It was nice to get some feedback.

Chuckling indulgently, Gus swung the Apache toward San Diego and followed the invisible flight corridor over the sprawling city. "No, ma'am, I'm not.

It's just that I feel you need to know how good you are at what you do. If you ever questioned volunteering for this assignment, you should stop that.''

''With the other IPs and a third Apache, I think we can get this mission accomplished,'' Cam said. She saw the graceful arc of the Coronado Bridge on her left. Rush hour was upon them, and there were thousands of cars moving slowly across the bridge, bumper to bumper. She was glad to be in the Apache, above it all.

''Well, let's see how Luis and Antonio took to their lessons today,'' she murmured in a droll tone.

''Yeah,'' Gus said merrily. ''I can hardly wait for the briefing.''

The truth be known, he was really looking forward to meeting Cam tonight, as he always did, in that darkened grove. It was their quiet time together, something Gus hungered for and counted on. Did she? As he made a right turn for the downwind leg of their flight corridor, over the Mexican border once more, Gus wondered if Cam liked him at all. In his heart, he wanted her to. In his mind, when he remembered his tragic past, he knew he shouldn't dare dream of loving Cam.

Chapter 8

"Who the hell gave these two dudes pilot licenses?" Snake growled as she dropped her report on the green metal table in front of Cam in the briefing room.

Gus sat with Cam behind the table. The room was barely big enough for a dozen people. Snake was visibly agitated, her green eyes angry slits as she came and sat down opposite him.

"Yeah," Wild Woman muttered as she shut the door and handed Cam her report on Dominguez. "Snake and I are in agreement—the only thing they should have licenses to drive are tricycles. That or go to Disneyland. Take your pick."

Squelching a laugh, because he knew it wasn't appropriate, Gus said nothing as Wild Woman pulled out a metal chair and sat down. Blowing out a sigh of obvious exasperation, she ran her fingers through her blond hair, which was flattened from wearing her flight helmet.

"Hold on...." Cam murmured, quickly paging through the grades on each mission priority that the pilots had had to fly that day.

"I need a drink," Snake said, looking around. "A double." To her dismay, she saw there wasn't even coffee available.

Chuckling, Wild Woman put her hand on Vickey's shoulder and patted it. "Don't let those two macho egos drive you to alcohol. They aren't worth it, believe me."

"Ain't that the truth?" Vickey said, scowling darkly.

"Here," Cam said to Gus, and handed him Zaragoza's graded report, "read this."

Nodding, Gus took the flight report. He was familiar with this type of report because during school he'd been graded every single day on every single flight. After he'd landed, the IP would go over what he'd done right and wrong, and give him a final grade. Gus hated the schooling and he hated the grading. He always walked away from the cockpit with sweat staining the underarms of his flight suit. It was a tense time, and he had a lot of sympathy for Antonio and Luis. But then, he reminded himself, they had chosen to do things their way and not the army's way. They had literally skated through Apache school because they were foreign nationals, and no one wanted to flunk them out even if they deserved to fail. Such was politics, he guessed.

His gaze fell to the bottom line of the evaluation: twenty-five percent. Quirking his mouth, Gus set the report aside and glanced over at Wild Woman, who was sitting back, her arms crossed, legs spread out beneath the table, studying him.

"Stunning figures, aren't they?" she said.

"Very," Gus agreed. He saw Wild Woman assessing him, not sure at this point if he was friend or foe. He wondered if it was because he was male. Gus wasn't sure. He knew these women were a tight group, and he felt like an outsider right now.

"The other one," Cam said dryly, and handed him Luis Dominguez's report.

Gus quickly paged through it. Cam waited, her hands folded, while he skimmed it. Dropping to the bottom line, he saw that Snake had given him eighteen percent as a final grade.

"Well," he said, putting the second report down, "they didn't do very well."

"That is an understatement," Snake muttered defiantly. She shook her head.

Cam nodded and pursed her lips. She remembered her training at their secret base in Peru, and how Maya would bring all the pilots together afterward to talk about their flight. A part of her wanted to bring Antonio and Luis in, but right now her gut said not to. Unfolding her hands, she looked at her sister pilots.

"Give us the scoop. Wild Woman? Tell us what went wrong up there with Zaragoza."

Rolling her eyes, Wild Woman sat up. "He peed his pants."

Gus looked at her. "Excuse me?"

"I pulled a twin engine failure on him at five thousand feet, and he freaked out. He couldn't remember how to set the Apache up for anything. In flight school, we always got single and double engine failure tests. Everyone has to know how to set the bird up so it can make an emergency landing without power. This is preliminary, basic training, so I followed your protocols, Cam. He blanked out. I was the one who had to do the recovery." She shook her head. "On the ground, when he left the Apache, the seat of his pants were dark and wet. I figured out the rest."

Cam gave Gus a glance that spoke volumes. On their first day together, she'd tested him on single and double engine failure, and he'd done everything right and recovered without stress.

Gus gave her an unhappy look. "Is there more to this, Gus?" she asked him.

"Yeah, there is." He looked across the table at the two scowling women. "I went through Apache school with them."

"Oh," Snake muttered, "so you know these dudes intimately."

"Unfortunately, I do. In school, they didn't haul their weight. They thought it was playtime, not serious work. They kept passing the flight tests and I couldn't figure out why at the time."

"And," Cam told them grimly, "we found out from Maya that there were serious politics being played to get these two boys through the school no matter how badly they flew. There are indications that IPs signed off their flights with a passing grade when they shouldn't have."

Groaning, Snake got to her feet. She scratched her head and paced the length of the room, then stopped.

"Okay, so what I'm gathering is we've got two so-called 'pilots' who really aren't anywhere near up to grade. They skated by because of the smoke and mirrors, right?"

"Right," Cam agreed quietly. She saw Wild Woman's blue eyes widen.

"Then how the hell do they expect *you* to have this drug interdiction mission up and running in four weeks?" Her voice was high and off-key with anger.

"Bingo," Cam agreed. "That's why I called you two in. I needed help."

"Help?" Snake asked, frustrated. "How about kicking these two jerks out of the cockpit and going back to the school and getting two people who *did* pass?" She pointed to Gus. "He passed. And he's doing a good job, according to you. So why not find two more Mexican pilots who are hungry, who are damn good pilots, and trade them off for these two playboys?"

"It's not that easy," Gus told her.

Snake glared at him. "I'll tell you something, Chief. Our C.O. down at the base would kick these two guys out in the blink of an eye. She wouldn't stand for this kind of ineptness in the cockpit. They'll get someone killed up there real fast, and it isn't gonna be me in the back seat getting it because they're sloughing off and don't know what the hell they're doing. No. Not on my watch."

"I agree," Gus said. "But Cam's been saddled with them. This mission is more than just what it seems on the surface. It's political, too."

"Yes," Cam agreed, growing grim and giving Vickey a sober look. The pilot sat down.

"I'm caught between a rock and a hard place," Cam told Jessica and Vickey. "The only way I can get rid of them is to force them into signing those papers that say they agree to be reassigned elsewhere."

"And if you know anything about Hispanic men," Gus added, giving Cam a glance, "they have machismo and ego to burn. My personal opinion is that now that Cam and you have put them up against the wall, they'll try to come around because they won't opt for the second choice."

"Which is to look bad, look like the failures they are," Snake muttered, rolling her eyes. "Dude, this sucks."

Cam sat back in the chair, her hands on her thighs. "Yeah, it does. I didn't realize what I was stepping into."

"Dominguez threw up in his cockpit," Snake said. "I made him stay out there and clean it up himself. I wasn't about to let the ground crew clean up after he barfed."

"Good!" Cam exclaimed. "What maneuver did it?"

"Inside loop," Snake growled. "He couldn't do it. I had to take the controls and get the bird out of it. He was barfing all over the place and complaining he has a 'delicate stomach.'"

Jessica laughed and looked at her friend. "You gotta be kidding me!"

Snake gave her a dirty look. "I'm glad our cockpits are separate. I'd hate to have had to smell that awful odor for three hours."

Cam wrinkled her nose. "You mean you didn't land right away?"

All the women chuckled. Everyone who flew experienced nausea and at times threw up. But they kept on flying.

"No," Snake said, "because the dumb idiot forgot to put his barf bag in the thigh pocket of his flight suit. If he'd had it with him, he coulda used it and things wouldn't have ended up so bad. So—" she grinned wolfishly "—he suffered the consequences of not making sure he had the appropriate gear during preflight. Oh, well..."

"I'll bet next time he will," Gus said.

"That's my bet, too," Snake agreed, her mouth pulling into a sour smile. "You only forget once in our business."

"Well," Cam said, "that's the least of our problems, as I see it."

"Yeah," Wild Woman griped, "how do you get these two dudes to qualify for legit flight status? They can't possibly learn interdiction at this point. Isn't there something you can do, Cam? Can't you *force* the Mexican government to give us two *qualified* pilots?"

Shaking her head, she murmured, "No, I can't."

"Okay," Snake said, "then we'll force these dudes to quit by making them work so hard they'll want to leave here screamin'."

"That's the plan," Cam said. "I have no other options. That's what I saw before you came." She gave Gus a slight smile. "If we had two more pilots like Chief Morales, we'd be on easy street, but that's not what we got handed."

"Okay," Wild Woman said, rising and giving Snake an evil look as she stretched her hand toward Gus. "You got our flight mission for tomorrow?"

"Yes," Gus said, and handed it to them.

"Good. C'mon, Snake, let's go into TJ, have some tequila and lime straight up, plot, plan and figure out how to chase these two tricycle pilots outta here so we can get two good replacements on this mission."

Gus saw Cam smile as the two women left. There was relief in her wide, beautiful eyes. She deserved to have help, under the circumstances. When the door shut and the room grew quiet, he slowly rose to his feet.

"Want to have chow with me?"

Looking up, Cam smiled. His face was strong and chiseled. There was nothing not to like about Gus. "Yeah, I'd like that, X.O."

Grinning, Gus said, "I kinda like this new position. I'm privy to all the dirt that's goin' around in the squadron."

Laughing, Cam stood and gathered up the reports. She would transmit them to Maya and Morgan later as proof that the two playboy pilots were as bad as she had originally described them. Over time, she hoped the mounting evidence in each day's flight would, perhaps, force Morgan Trayhern to do something about it.

"Yeah, well, I'd rather *not* have dirt to sweep under the rug of our squadron, if the truth be known."

Opening the door, Gus smiled down at her as she hefted the dark brown briefcase in her left hand. "I know. There's nothing like a well-oiled, well-run squadron. My dad has that touch. He's a great manager of people."

"I'm learning how to be," Cam said goodnaturedly as she stepped out into the hall. A number of crews were coming in for the night, making the place noisy. Looking up and down the corridor, she saw nothing of Zaragoza and Dominguez. They were probably in their rooms on the first floor, nursing their wounded egos after today's humiliating flights.

Heart lifting with joy, she walked with Gus at her side. This was the first time she'd be with him at the chow hall. It was something Cam was looking forward to. "Does this mean we won't have our nightly meeting out in the grove?" she asked, because she really looked forward to that quiet, uninterrupted time with him.

"Heck, no. That's still on the table, if you want it to be?" Gus searched her wide, forest-green eyes, which shone with gold flecks in their depths. Cam was happy, he realized. And that made him feel good.

"Great," Cam sighed. "It's a special time and I look forward to it, Gus."

The strumming of the guitar made Cam want to melt into Gus's arms. It was nearly midnight, and the stars shone brightly, like glittering pinpoints overhead among the black branches of the trees. Tonight Gus had brought her fresh baked cookies once again. She'd learned that he'd found a Mexican woman not far from the base who could bake them so long as he supplied the ingredients. Somehow—Cam didn't know when—Gus had made a trip across the border to San Diego, to go to a grocery store and buy the items needed. His thoughtfulness was never ending, in her opinion. The bag of chocolate chip cookies sat between them. She sat on the rough picnic table, her feet on the bench below.

As he finished one of his many songs, Cam smiled over at him. "I really love your music."

"Thank my mother. Maybe mothers humming lullabies to their children from birth on put songs like these in musicians' memory." Gus gazed back at Cam, absorbing her soft, dreamy smile. Tonight her hair was newly washed and hung in chestnut folds around her face and shoulders. She wore a pale green tank top, her denim jacket and a pair of dark green cotton slacks. In his eyes, she looked like a lovely young woman, certainly not an Apache gunship pilot.

"I think you got the best of both worlds growing up," she murmured.

Running his fingers across the smooth surface of his guitar, Gus nodded. "Tell me about your growing up years, Cam. You said your mother named you and your two sisters after flowers?"

Munching on a cookie, she said, "Yes. I'm the oldest. Iris is twenty-four and Dahlia, whom we call Dal, is twenty."

"And are they in the military?"

She shook her head and wiped her fingers on her slacks. "No. Just me."

"So how did you get interested then, in the army? And flying combat helicopters?"

"My dad, who runs an automotive shop, was a helicopter mechanic when he was young and in the army. I guess he passed it on to me." She gave Gus a humorous look. "When I was little, my dad used to let me come to the garage, and he'd show me how car engines worked. By the time I was ten, I was changing oil and spark plugs and adjusting carburetors.''

''That's where you got your interest in mechanics,'' Gus said with a nod. In the moonlight, her profile was clean and soft. ''So, where did you get the passion, the assertiveness a combat pilot needs, I wonder?''

''My dad was a super athlete, Gus. He's a quiet kind of guy and you'd never realize he had the heart of a lion inside him. He's intense and focused when he works on a car engine. In high school, he was track champion, and went on to the nationals. He could have gone on to the Olympics, but he suffered a knee injury that took him out of competition.''

Nodding, Gus said, ''But like his daughter, he never quit.''

''No…my dad's not a quitter. Ever.''

''And your mother? What do you have of her in you?'' Gus saw her lips curve softly.

''Oh….my mom.'' Cam's voice dropped as she spoke. ''Well, she's a schoolteacher in a middle school. She's a biologist. Actually, a microbiologist. That's what her degree is in. She loves to teach kids about nature, about the life that surrounds them.''

''So that's why you all were named after flowers. I see.'' Gus grinned as Cam smiled at him. How close they were. And how much he wanted to touch those full lips. An ache grew in him, keen and sharp. Would Cam let him kiss her? Gus wasn't sure. But he wanted to, despite the loss he'd endured that had nearly destroyed him.

"Yes, she used to tease us fondly and call us her 'blooming idiots.' She meant it lovingly, because she really supported us in doing whatever our heart, our passion, led us to do."

"And you wanted to reach for the sky?"

"Yes," Cam murmured, taking another cookie. "I love flying. No one else in our family flies now, but my parents think I got the bird blood from my grandfather on my father's side. He was a pilot during the Korean War. He flew P-51 Mustangs, and he was an ace."

"Impressive."

"What about you? What moved you to fly? Your dad?"

"Yes." Gus strummed the guitar gently, the sounds vibrating softly around them. "I admired him. I still do. He's been my best teacher. My role model. I want him to be proud of me."

"I don't know how he couldn't be," Cam said sincerely. She liked the slight smile that curved Gus's mouth. A bolt of heat went through her as she studied those lips. She wanted to taste that mouth of his with her own. Would Gus be as strong and cherishing as she suspected? Sharing something more with Gus was too much to expect, Cam tried to tell herself, especially with her bad past history with men. She knew her idealistic side, the dreamer, wanted someone exactly like him, but that in reality dreams like hers never came true.

"My dad said I was like an eagle," he chuckled. "My mother, who as I told you is Yaqui Indian, said I had the earth in my blood. The blood of the Jaguar."

"Jaguar? That's really something. I wonder if

you're a member of the Jaguar clan in South America like Maya is?''

"My mother never mentioned that. She said I had a jaguar spirit guide but I've never seen it."

"Looks like the eagle won out?"

Shrugging, he said, "I guess so…."

"You don't sound so sure."

Gus strummed the guitar again. He liked the vibration of the wood against his body, and the sound of the chords. "Maybe I'm both. I'm not sure of that yet. I thought I was, but…well, life changes you sometimes."

She heard pain in his voice and saw his hooded eyes darken. "Something bad happened." It was a statement. Cam knew what she'd sensed was true because she felt an enormous sadness cloaking Gus.

Looking over, his hand stilling the strings of the guitar, he searched Cam's luminescent eyes, which radiated concern for him. His heart almost burst with a shaft of pain. Without thinking, he spilled his trauma to her.

"I fell in love with a woman three years ago," he began quietly. "Sandy Grove was an aerobatic pilot of international caliber. In some ways, she was like you, Cam. She had that quiet confidence, that gutsiness that didn't always show until she was in her plane, doing the tricks. She was superconfident, a good person who lived life with a passion, right at the edge." Frowning, Gus looked down at his boots. "I fell in love with her. She was an incredibly heart-centered person, so full of life. Unafraid to grab it and go for it."

Cam frowned as she heard the sadness in his tone.

Gus straightened up and looked at her. "Sandy died two years ago in a flight accident. She was creating a new maneuver for an air show over in France when the wing of her plane tore off...."

"I'm so sorry," Cam whispered, and without thinking, she reached out and gripped his left arm for a moment. "So sorry. I can tell you loved her with your heart and soul."

Mouth quirking, Gus said, "Yeah, loving a woman in a dangerous profession isn't a wise idea." He felt her hand, the firmness of it, the gentleness of her touch on his arm, and his flesh tingled wildly. Seeing the tears in Cam's eyes, he felt like crying himself. In that moment, he wanted to pull her close and bury himself in her warm, comforting arms. But he couldn't. He didn't dare. As beautiful, caring, brave and wonderful as Cam was to him, Gus was too scared to reach out to her.

His words sank deeply into Cam's pounding heart. Gus had loved a woman in a dangerous profession.... Searching his shadowed face, caught in the mire of grief and longing she saw in his eyes, Cam sat there, confused. She couldn't understand the look of longing in his eyes as he held her gaze. Was that desire emanating toward her? Releasing his arm and shaking herself internally, Cam fiercely told herself no, that was impossible. His grief-stricken statement about never loving another woman in a dangerous job included her, no doubt. For she was an Apache gunship combat pilot. Her life could be snuffed out at any minute, Cam knew. And so did Gus.

She sat there, feeling a sharp pang of anguish in her heart.

Chapter 9

Cam was in her office at 0530 the next morning, working on the mountains of paperwork she had to process. Now she understood what Maya and her X.O. Dallas Klein, went through. No wonder they looked forward to getting away from their offices! Giving the piles of paper a glum look, including her Out basket, stuffed full of things that Gus would have to handle, Cam stopped working for a moment.

Gus's words came back to haunt her—again. He wouldn't or couldn't fall in love with another woman who was in a dangerous profession. That meant her. Frowning, Cam tightened her fingers around her pen. So why was she so bummed out about it? Gus had never said he loved her. Maybe because she was so lonely for male companionship, she had misinterpreted his looks and all too brief touches as meaning more than they really did. Cam had committed that crime before, in other relationships, and had gotten badly burned. Why, when she knew better, was she allowing herself to get emotionally involved with Gus, then? She sat back and digested all these revelations.

She hadn't slept well last night. The mission was weighing heavily on her. Cam was unsure what kind of knee-jerk reactions the two Mexican pilots would have to being firmly boundaried and forced to work. She wondered if it would really turn them around. Her personal life was an unexpected part of this mishmash as well. That was disconcerting. Never in a hundred years had Cam even *thought* of the possibility of being drawn to another man.

There was a knock on her door. Who could that be? Cam looked at her watch. No one was due for another twenty minutes.

"Enter," she said in a loud, firm voice.

Snake stuck her head around the opened door. "Got a sec, Cam?"

"Hi, Snake. Sure," she said, gesturing for her to come in. "Yeah, always. Just shut the door. I don't want any pilots eavesdropping as we chat." She grinned widely.

Snake laughed and quietly shut the door behind her. She was dressed in her one-piece olive green flight suit, her helmet tucked beneath her left arm.

"Gettin' to see you without the students around is proving to be a major chore," Snake said, setting the helmet on the edge of Cam's desk.

"Yeah, no kidding. I miss our easy talks in the chow hall back at the cave."

"Or in the hall. Or in the cockpit," Snake griped

good-naturedly. She took her shoulder-length, straight brown hair and expertly wrapped it up into a chignon at the base of her neck as she usually did before she put on her helmet, to keep her hair from getting in the way.

"I know," Cam sighed. She sat back in the chair and smiled up at her friend. "How are you doing in this mess? I haven't really gotten to talk with you one-on-one since you arrived."

Hitching a hip on the edge of Cam's desk, Vickey nodded and pursed her full lips. "I know. I was talkin' to Wild Woman last night." Her mouth curved in a feral smile. "We went carousin' around TJ last night in that rental car we got at the civilian airport where we landed. Some dude told us Club Flamingo was a good place to drink and dance."

"Was it?" Cam asked, smiling more widely. She was glad to see that they could cut loose and enjoy themselves despite the stresses they were under here.

"You'd better believe it." Vickey waved her right hand as if she'd touched something that burned her. "I gotta tell you, doin' the tango with these Latino dudes who know what they're doin' is awesome!" She laughed heartily.

Joining her laughter, Cam said, "Kinda nice to have guys around, isn't it?"

"Well," Snake growled, "*Some* guys. Not those two nose-outta-joint student pilots we have to play kindergarten in the sky with. But yeah, the guys we hooked up with last night were terrific." Vickey rubbed her hands together in anticipation. "We're gonna meet them there tonight for some more rousin' rounds of dancing."

"No hangover?" Cam inquired politely. She saw Snake's smile grow.

"Ah, maybe a touch. You know, we don't do much drinkin' and dancin' back at BJS. It's not the same. Here…" Vickey waved her arm "…you got a real city, close to the good ole U.S. of A., and it's like being back home, almost."

Hearing the homesickness in Vickey's tone, Cam lost her smile. "Yeah, it's been a long time since any of us have seen home."

Becoming more serious, Vickey tilted her head and gave Cam an intense look. "Maya is now giving us thirty days a year starting this year. That's as good as it gets."

"I know. I'm not blaming anyone," Cam murmured. "But we've been putting in three unrelenting, drug-busting years down there and it's getting old for all of us."

"Maya included," Vickey agreed. "I think we're all pining for 'home' one way or another."

Nodding, Cam said, "I don't know how Maya is going to overcome that. We can't stay down there forever, flying combat without a change of tour. I know the army's pressuring her right now to get more male pilots rotated down there to give us relief."

"Yeah," Vickey chortled, "and I heard that Maya's telling them to get her more *women* Apache pilots down there, instead."

Cam chuckled. "Good for her. Women work well together."

"Yeah, we do," she agreed. Moving her long, graceful hand down the right thigh of her uniform to smooth out the wrinkles, Vickey continued, "I dropped by to see how *you* were doin'. Wild Woman and I can see you're in over your head with this rotten situation. Talk about bein' handed crap.'' She shook her head, scowling.

"A bag of worms, for sure," Cam agreed. She laced her fingers across her stomach and leaned back in the chair. "But it's not all bad, Vic. I have Gus, and he's been a great help and support."

"Ah, Gus…" She gave Cam an evil grin.

"What's *that* look for?"

"Don't you know? Geez, Cam, both of us saw it the moment we walked into your briefing."

Frowning, Cam muttered, "Saw *what?*"

Snake rolled her eyes. "Are you blind, deaf and dumb, girl? Or just pretending with me?"

"I don't know what you're talking about. Wanna spell it out to this dummy?" Cam said with a laugh. Her friend's face glowed with humor, and Cam liked the dancing, elfin expression in Vickey's dark green eyes. Usually Snake was very quiet and said little to anyone. She was a Scorpio, and fit that zodiac profile well, in Cam's opinion. Normally, she was a highly private person, an introvert, and never said what was on her mind unless someone pried it out of her. Today she seemed just the opposite. It must have been the tango and tequila last night, Cam surmised, with an inward smile.

"You really don't see it, do you?"

"I must not. Wanna come clean and tell me what you two divas see that I don't?"

Grinning, Vickey leaned across the desk and in a hushed, dramatic voice whispered, "Gus Morales. That's who, dummy!"

Blinking, Cam said, "Gus? What about him?"

Sitting up, Vickey shook her head. "You really deserve the name Tree Trimmer, Cam. You got sawdust for brains on this one. And generally you're sharp as the razor edge of a sword."

Seeing the smirk on her friend's face, Cam sat up. When Snake wriggled her eyebrows, which was something she did when she was up to no good, Cam got it. "Oh!"

"Yeah, no kidding. Oh. Now you see where we're going with this little collective observation of ours."

Heat swept up Cam's neck and into her cheeks, and she avoided Vickey's prying look.

"Now you're blushin', Tree Trimmer. That confirms what we thought."

"You two," Cam managed to choke out in defense, "have nothing better to do than—"

Holding up her hands, Vickey slid off the corner of the desk and grinned hugely, flashing her even white teeth.

"Whoa, girl, whoa! I'm just tellin' you what Wild Woman and I see goin' on. Gus *likes you.* Don't you know that? We thought you did, but I can see you don't. The guy has *eyes* for you, Cam. He's like a puppy mooning over you every time he thinks no one's noticing." Snake gave an evil laugh. "But we don't miss a thing, Wild Woman and I. These dudes don't realize how sharp and alert we really are. Combat-honed alertness makes us look at every teeny, tiny detail."

Groaning, Cam sat back and covered her eyes with her hand while Vickey chortled delightedly.

"You like him, Cam?"

Hearing the serious tone in Vickey's voice once more, Cam removed her hand from her eyes and looked across the desk at her friend. She had her helmet beneath her left arm once again and was standing there expectantly, a warm look on her face. Vickey could be a merciless tease at times, which was typical of her Scorpio nature, but in the end, Cam knew, she cared deeply for the friendship that had built between them over the years down at BJS.

"Where do I begin on this one?" Cam muttered, more to herself than to Snake.

"So there *is* something? Wild Woman thought so. I said no, that you're too busy runnin' this squadron to have a personal life right now. Looks like I was wrong and I owe her a hot fudge sundae. That was our bet, and that's why I came to see you before the fireworks began again today—to see if Wild Woman was right. Damn, I shouldn't bet with her. I always lose."

"You owe her the hot fudge sundae, Snake," Cam said unhappily.

"Why so glum? The dude has got some things goin' for him." She grinned suddenly and then looked at her watch. It was time to go. "Hey, you have our seal of approval on him, if you're interested. We think he's a cool dude. Gotta rock 'n roll. See you later...."

Waving her hand, Cam regretted that they'd run out of this precious, private time with one another. "It's a long story, Snake. Yeah, later..."

Snake hesitated at the open door and turned back. "Well, when you want a night outta this evolving nightmare, come and tango with us and these hot Latino dudes over at Club Flamingo. Maybe then we can talk more?''

Right now, Cam didn't feel like partying. She was beginning to understand in earnest the difference between being a pilot and being a C.O. "No, dancing isn't my thing. But you two go ahead and enjoy yourselves. You certainly deserve a diversion from Luis and Antonio, that's for sure."

Snorting, Vickey said, "Ain't *that* the truth! I've never seen such sniveling, immature Apache pilots in my life. The army ought to be ashamed for even passing Dominguez. I guess Wild Woman is about ready to pitch her student out through the front cockpit Plexiglas." The front Plexiglas on an Apache was hardened to the point where it could take a direct hit from a twenty millimeter cannon and not crack.

Cam nodded. "Stay on 'em. Don't give them any breathing room at all," she growled. "They're either gonna shape up or ship out."

"Ha! I hope it's the latter," Snake crowed. "We're doin' our best to crowd these two ego-bustin' rich boys and break 'em down so we can cobble them back together and make real pilots out of 'em. But I don't know that they're gonna break, Cam."

"I don't, either, Vic. Just stay on them. Keep up the pressure."

"Well," Snake said with satisfaction, "last night Dominguez was nearly in tears, his hands shaking because he hadn't gotten to smoke at all. He's going into real nicotine deprivation today, I'm sure, and he's gonna be a grouchy bear in the cockpit because of it. He probably spent half his night trying to buy cigs

off the people here in the barracks after you had Gus
go confiscate his stash in his quarters.''

"Well, if any of us catch him smoking, he knows
he's out of here—permanently.''

"Yeah, he knows that. But he's a sneaky bastard.
My gut tells me he'll manipulate others, pay lots of
pesos to some poor enlisted guy to provide 'em.''

"If he does that, then it's one more mark against
him. He has no morals and doesn't respect the military system.''

"Like we didn't know that already. Hey, I gotta
turn and burn. Have to walk my prize student around
the lady out there.''

Nodding, Cam lifted her hand. "Yeah, okay. Five
hours of flight ought to reduce these two to puddles
by this afternoon.''

Chuckling, Vickey said, "I sure hope so. Have
those transfer orders ready to be signed when we get
back.''

After Snake left, Cam felt lonely. How much she
missed the chatter between herself and her sister pilots! Talking with Gus was always a high, but after
last night's admission from him, Cam felt as if ice
water had been thrown on her. Telling herself that
honesty was always the best policy, she decided to
tuck away her feelings and work with Gus on a less
personal level because that's what he wanted. Besides, Cam told herself sternly, her experience in male
relationships was less than stellar. So why would she
want to put herself through that kind of horrendous
pain and humiliation again? She didn't. Not ever.

Sighing, Cam grabbed another report and began to
fill it out. Gus was due to drop by in thirty minutes,

and they'd begin their mission flight for today. Just thinking about it made her inexplicably happy.

"Well done, Gus," Cam said into the mike positioned near her lips. She scribbled intently on the clipboard resting on her thighs. The shaking and shuddering of the Apache surrounded her like a lover's caress. It also played hell on her ability to write legibly.

"Thanks," he called out. "Want me to head back to base now?"

"Yeah," Cam murmured, finishing up the totals on each of his flight demand columns for the day. Sunlight poured into the cockpit, making her squint. It was 1300—1:00 p.m.—and they'd just put in five grueling hours of maneuvers over their stay-and-play area in the mountains south of Tijuana. From time to time Cam had eavesdropped on Wild Woman's and Snake's communications with their students. Things weren't going well at all, it seemed. But to give the two male pilots credit, they were trying today, so that was a hopeful sign. Emotionally, Cam had to gird herself for facing Luis and Antonio when they got back to the base. Things were coming to a head and she knew it. Would they stay or leave? Did they have the strength to gut it out? She wasn't sure.

Gus looked around, as he'd been trained to, from left to right, and then down to the two HUDs on the instrument panel in front of him. Feeling euphoric, he knew he'd excelled at the demanding flight tests, and he grinned.

"Has anyone ever told you how good a teacher you are? I think you missed your calling. They should have had the smarts to pull you back to Fort Rucker, to be an IP and teach students the ropes there.''

With a laugh, Cam said, ''The only thing they ever wanted to do with the first all-woman Apache Training class was get them through and out of there, Gus. Out of sight, out of mind was the army's motto.''

''But you've shown them that they were wrong about women pilots in a combat gunship,'' he argued.

''Yeah, that was three, nearly four years ago now,'' Cam murmured. How she looked forward to talking with Gus personally. It was one of the few rewards of her day.

''Your stats speak for themselves,'' Gus said. ''I was talking with Wild Woman and Snake yesterday and they told me a lot about BJS. I'm really impressed. Major Stevenson is way ahead of her time, a real visionary.''

''And the army doesn't like visionaries, believe me,'' Cam growled. ''She was a woman with an idea. A good one. If her father, an army general, hadn't been there to make sure it got instituted, Maya's dream of BJS would have gone unnoticed.''

''Sometimes,'' Gus said as he eased the Apache into a banking turn toward the blue of the Pacific, ''it's not what you know, but who you know.''

''Unfortunately. That's one of my many gripes with the army. Creativity and ingenuity aren't always welcomed with open arms. If you don't happen to be male, or of the proper rank, and have no political strings to pull, you aren't going to be listened to.''

''You'll be ignored,'' Gus agreed. The ocean glittered beneath them, with sunlight dappling its rough surface. White, cottony clouds surrounded them. A front was coming through today, and the winds were a lot stronger from the west. The turbulence had been rougher than normal, and it had taken all of Gus's skills to do as well as he had on the flight tests. When the weather worked against a pilot, it was harder to fly at specific altitudes and aim electronic "missiles" at stationary targets on the ground and accurately hit them. But he had. Gus felt proud of his abilities. He liked showing Cam that he had the right stuff to be an Apache pilot like her. Any pilot who had seen combat was usually set upon a pedestal and worshipped by the others. For a pilot, experience counted for everything. Gus held all three women pilots in high esteem. They had not only gutted it out for three years in combat mode, they had survived. And there was a lot he could learn from them, he knew.

As the Apache bounced and bobbled, hitting an invisible air pocket at five thousand feet, Gus steadied the machine with his feet and hands. The Baja coast grew small behind them as he flew the required five miles out to sea.

"Hey, on a personal topic, how would you like to leave this coming Saturday night open for something special?" His heart beat a little harder in his chest as he asked the question. He was afraid Cam would say no. Hand tightening momentarily around the cyclic, Gus held his breath as he waited for her response.

Lifting her head from her work, Cam said, "What?"

"Saturday. You know, that's two days away? I thought...well, we always meet every night in the grove, on the picnic table for an hour or two. I thought that I'd like to take you someplace else."

Cam felt a frisson of fear. And then joy. She tried to ignore both feelings. "Not a date." Remembering Gus's words, she wanted to be clear about this request and have no illusions about it. Still, she wished it *would* be a date.

"Er…why, no. Business. Just like always," he mumbled. "You know how we sit on the picnic table and talk over the day's events? C.O. to X.O.?"

"Yeah…" Cam's hand stilled over the clipboard, her pen poised. His stubbornness made her feel sad. Still, it was a chance to be with Gus, and Cam wasn't going to cut him out of her life. Somehow she was going to have to learn how to turn desire for him into friendship. That was a tall order and something she'd never attempted before.

A trickle of sweat ran down Gus's left temple. He had the wild urge to push it away. Setting the collective, he did just that, shoving his index finger up beneath the dark green visor that protected his eyes from the harsh sunlight. He tried to gage Cam's tone of voice because he wasn't sure she was happy with the idea.

"I know a sweet little spot in Puerto Nuevo. In fact, I can point it out to you on the way home today. One of the bays where Mexican trawlers come in and sell their goods, Puerto Nuevo is known for its lobster. I know a great restaurant there, Café Flor, which has the best seafood in town. It's small but it's clean. I'd like to buy you dinner."

Cam loved lobster. In fact, after being at BJS for so long, she'd almost forgotten how much she loved seafood. It was rare to get anything but local trout from the Urubamba River in their chow hall.

With a slight grin, she asked, "How did you know I love seafood?"

Gus heard the joy in her tone. It made him suddenly feel lighter. Happier. "Just a hunch. Besides," he replied, "as X.O., I need to take care of my C.O. You need a break. I heard from Wild Woman and Snake that they're having a high old time at Club Flamingo in TJ. They, at least, are getting away from this heavy energy and drama Luis and Antonio stir up. I think you should, too."

"I see. A little R and R—rest and relaxation?"

"Sure," Gus coaxed enthusiastically. "I have my car. I drove it down here from Fort Rucker, so we got wheels. Interested?"

Was she? Cam pursed her lips and stared at his helmeted head below her. The thumping of the blades soothed some of her fear.

"Just business. Right?"

"I promise," Gus told her fervently. "Just pretend we're in the grove, that it's dark and we're on our picnic table, and I'm strumming on my guitar from time to time as we talk over the day's events. Okay?"

Thrilled and yet wary, Cam said, "Okay…"

"Great! I can hardly wait. You'll love Puerto Nuevo. You'll love the lobster."

There was that word *love,* Cam thought darkly. Placing her gloved hands over the clipboard, she looked out the cockpit window, unsure of how to feel. Still, as she sat there mulling it over in her heart, a thread of happiness wound through her. Suddenly she felt like a teenage girl who had just been asked to the prom by the boy she had a wild crush on.

Chapter 10

"**M**aybe this isn't a business comment," Gus told Cam in a low, intimate tone as they sat at the white-linen-draped table at Café Flor, "but you look beautiful."

Cam looked down at the pale lavender tank top she wore with a ballerina-length, silk skirt of the same color. Around her shoulders was a silk shawl in a deep plum. She touched the amethyst pendant at her throat and smiled. "Thanks...."

"It's a far cry from seeing you in that shapeless flight suit," he mused as he picked up his glass filled with a pale chardonay wine. In the background, several men played guitars in one corner of the busy restaurant. "Here's to R and R, Ms. Anderson."

Cam lifted her glass and gave Gus a shy smile. "We clean up pretty good, don't we?" she murmured, gently touching her glass to his. Gus looked devastatingly handsome in his navy blue blazer with brass buttons, white silk shirt, paisley tie and tan slacks. He'd shaved earlier, and Cam realized the pains he'd taken getting ready for tonight. His black hair gleamed beneath the low lights overhead.

Cam tried to stay detached, to keep her heart at bay. It had been too easy to be lulled by Gus's quiet voice as he chatted about the day's events on the drive down to Puerto Nuevo. She'd bitten her lower lip many times during that forty-five minute drive in his red sports car, to stop herself from asking him personal questions instead of staying on track with business only.

"Here's to R and R," she agreed throatily, and took a sip of the white wine.

A Mexican waiter, dressed in a long white apron, black slacks and a starched long-sleeved shirt with a black bow tie, came over and handed them menus with an elegant flourish.

Cam thanked him in Spanish and so did Gus. The man beamed with pleasure. When Cam had entered the second-floor restaurant, with its huge windows facing the Pacific, she'd noticed most of the patrons were from the States. Most spoke English only. The gleam in their waiter's eyes told her he was grateful that they spoke his language. It was a way of honoring where they were, Cam felt.

"Well," she told Gus wryly, glancing over the tall menu, "I really don't think I have to look at this thing. I want lobster with all the trimmings."

Chuckling, he nodded and put the menu aside. "We do lobster down here a little differently than the folks in New England," he cautioned. "It comes with soft corn tortillas on the side, rice and hearty black beans.'' He smiled. ''Plus a knockout salsa you can dip your lobster into.''

''No drawn butter?''

''Sure, if you want. Aren't you adventurous, though?'' he teased, watching her eyes grow warm with humor. ''Ever had lobster tail dipped in a dynamite salsa that makes you want to smack your lips because it tastes like heaven itself?'' Placing his elbows on the table, he clasped his hands together and rested his chin on them as he studied Cam's softly glowing face. The lighting was perfect, he decided. Her thick chestnut hair was in a French braid, with strands loose across her brow. It made her look very different—younger, perhaps. Her usual C.O. mask was gone. The change in her was breathtaking and Gus hadn't realized until just now what a chameleon Cam could be.

''Oh, I'm adventurous, all right,'' Cam said, her lips lifting wryly as she placed her menu on top of his.

''So that's what drew you to fly a combat aircraft?'' Gus wondered out loud. He hoped she thought that was a business topic. When her brows lifted and she laughed, his heart expanded.

''Yes. Underneath this—'' she pointed to herself and the outfit she was wearing ''—I'm competitive and have a deep patriotic streak in me. My parents raised us to know that we have freedom today because of the people who gave their lives, their time in the military, to make it so. I see this as paying my country back for the privilege of living in it.''

''Never mind that you've spent nearly four years

out of it," he said, unclasping his hands and sipping his wine.

Shrugging, Cam said, "What is duty? Where do we rank what's important to us, Gus? How do we pay our share of dues for what we have?" She gazed through the windows at the cobblestone street below, saw how each stone had been lovingly laid by hand to create the roadway along the sea. The village was poor but bustling. The people who lived in Puerto Nuevo relied heavily on their American neighbors to come down, eat and put money into their coffers. Not that anyone was rich here.

"When I look out there," Cam told him in a hushed tone, "and see little kids five or six years old barefoot, their noses running, their hair needing to be combed, or adults wearing worn, tattered clothes, I know how lucky we are. It breaks my heart that we can't bring all countries up to our standards." She looked over at him. "And in Peru, it's the same thing. I don't take what we have in the U.S.A. as a given. We have to earn it and keep earning it."

Nodding, Gus said, "I understand."

"You would. You said you visited your mother's people in Mexico as a child?"

"As often as I could," Gus said. "My father was being shipped around the world as an army pilot. I grew up mostly in the Far East and Europe, because of his assignments. My mother, bless her, was a real trooper. She taught herself German. And then, when we went to Japan, she learned Japanese. She has an amazing ear for languages and she likes learning how to fit into different societies."

"It shows in you," Cam said, giving Gus a slight

smile. She warmed at the look in his darkened eyes, which smoldered with an undefined emotion. Cam tried to resist that look, but Gus was too close, too appealing, and she felt irresistibly drawn to him.

"Thank you. I think the best thing that happened to me as a kid was having the opportunity to kick around the world and learn about other cultures. I never regretted that."

"And what did you think of your mother's people when you went down there and saw where she'd grown up? How did it compare to those other cultures?"

Gus sat back and gave her a lazy smile. "I like your perceptiveness, Cam. You ask the right questions."

Picking up her wineglass, she murmured, "We are what we are today because of where we came from. Our roots. I'm curious how the Indian side of you integrates with the American side."

Grinning, Gus sipped his wine and then set the glass back on the linen tablecloth. "My mother lives in a magical world. My father lives in a black-and-white, hard-core-reality world."

Tilting her head, Cam said, "Interesting. So now you've really got my curiosity going. How do you mate magic with reality?"

"My mother has often told me that I live with one foot in her people's world of magic and transformation, and the other foot in my father's world of fact. I grew up listening to stories of her people that have been passed down through generations. And my dad, when he could, would read to me at night. I grew up with stories of endless possibilities. I think that gave me the ability to see the world a little differently, or at least more broadly, than other people do.''

Cam was caught in a spell by his deep, quiet voice, mesmerized by Gus's ability to convey his thoughts. Understanding clearly that that was a gift of his— verbal communication—she simply absorbed his words into her heart and listened.

''Give me an example?''

Opening his hand, Gus said, ''Okay. This game with Luis and Antonio. I see them on several levels at once. In one way, I see them as struggling through life because of the choices they've made along the way. On another level, a more symbolic one, which is how my mother sees the world and how she taught me to see it, they are men wrestling with authority. They are learning about authority. The question is,'' Gus murmured, ''what will they do with the lesson?''

''So, you see life as lessons?''

''I see people as teachers coming into our life, to show us something. We're to learn from them.''

''That's your mother's contribution?''

''Yes, and it's a good one.''

''And that's why you didn't have a knee-jerk re- action to having a woman commander?''

''Yes.'' Gus smiled slightly. ''By seeing you as my teacher, I left open all possibilities. I didn't try to catalog you, define you or put you into some conve- nient, labeled box as Luis and Antonio tried to do.''

Nodding, Cam murmured, ''I like that idea. That people are our teachers.''

''That's not to say all teachers are going to give us happy experiences,'' he noted with a grin. ''Pain makes us learn, too, unfortunately.''

"But," Cam said, sipping her wine, "if you go into the situation with an attitude that you're going to be taught something, then you can decide whether to learn it right away or repeat it again and again until you do get it. Am I on the right track?"

"Bingo," Gus exclaimed. "You're fast on the uptake."

"In our business you'd better be or you're dead."

Laughing softly, Gus nodded. "No doubt about it." How beautiful Cam looked in that moment, sitting there in her feminine dress, her face glowing with interest and that strength and confidence shining in her eyes. Only a person who had powerful experiences and lived to tell about them had that look.

"Was it hard on you, going through Apache training with Luis and Antonio?" Cam asked.

"Not really. Oh, we were the only three Latinos in the class, so we got judged, right or wrong, by that label." Grimacing, Gus said, "But they pretended I didn't exist, and that was fine with me. When they started sloughing off and not working to get passing grades, I really wanted to be separated from them in every way. I didn't want the rest of the class or the IPs to think all Hispanics were lazy like they were."

"And so you worked twice as hard to show everyone that wasn't so?"

"Yes."

"I saw your flight scores from school," Cam said, "when I was going over your personnel jacket. You graduated at the top of your class, with a ninety-five percentile. That's pretty impressive."

"I worked my butt off to prove that we weren't all like the two spoiled rich boys," he muttered defiantly.

"I'm sure you succeeded," Cam said. "I graduated with a seventy-eight. Of course, the head instructor was completely against our all-women class, and downgraded all of us. I passed. That's all I cared about."

"More prejudice," Gus murmured, shaking his head.

"Yeah," Cam sighed, "it's everywhere. You're fighting for people to respect Hispanics and their abilities, and I'm fighting a gender war." She gave him a twisted smile. "Two peas in the same pod?"

"I kinda like being in the same pod with you," Gus said, looking into her eyes. Noticing that the band was playing a soft, slow tune, he said, "Want to dance?" and he rose and held out his hand.

Seeing the startled look on Cam's face, Gus knew this wasn't in the playbook they'd agreed to. Asking Cam to dance was not "business." But he couldn't help himself. She was beautiful, radiant, desirable, and that smile of hers was driving him crazy. How many nights had he lain awake wondering what it would be like to have Cam in his arms? How she would feel?

Holding her startled gaze, Gus gave her his best boyish smile. "All women know how to dance," he challenged.

Grinning broadly, Cam said, "Oh? Is that another one of those stereotypical labels?"

"Yeah, I guess it is." He kept his hand stretched toward her.

Cam lifted her chin and gazed up at him, and he could see that she was in a quandary. Was it because she really didn't like him as much as he did her? That was a crushing thought, and Gus pushed it away. A feeling that she did want to know him better warred with his other sense about Cam. She seemed, at times, to seesaw back and forth with him, as if she wondered how much intimacy was the right amount. Maybe she was unsure because she was still learning how to be a C.O. Still, his heart told him that no, she wanted him just as much as he wanted her.

Gulping, Cam saw that Gus wasn't going to take no for an answer. Several other couples had moved out on the polished wood floor. "Okay...but I haven't danced in a long time..." she murmured.

Moving around the table, Gus pulled out her chair, then removed the shawl from her proud shoulders and draped it over the back. The small, teardrop-shaped amethyst pendant at the hollow of her throat gleamed in the low light as she turned toward him.

"I promise not to step on your feet," he assured her, taking her by the hand and leading her onto the floor.

His hand was strong and warm. Cam tried to ignore the quiet strength he emanated as he turned and drew her confidently into his arms. She was tense, expecting him to grab her and press her against him. He didn't. Looking down at her, Gus held her at a comfortable distance, one hand placed lightly at the small of her back, the other grasping her hand.

Moving with Gus was like moonlight slipping over the surface of the dark, calm Pacific, Cam discovered. She looked up into his hooded eyes and drowned in them. She felt lost and yet secure. Scared, but happy. Wanting to run and wanting to stay. So many feelings coursed through her as they moved fluidly to the slow guitar music. Inhaling his male scent, Cam enjoyed his closeness.

"Not bad for someone who hasn't been on a dance floor for a long time," he teased, leaning down near her ear and whispering the words.

His moist, warm breath brushed her cheek, and Cam closed her eyes. Gus's voice vibrated through her, embracing her with its husky, intimate tone. Heart expanding euphorically, Cam felt her defenses crumbling quickly as she swayed in his strong, guiding arms.

"You make it easy for me to look like I know what I'm doing," she said as she opened her eyes. He was smiling down at her and warmth sheeted through her. Feeling him squeeze her hand briefly, she squeezed his back. It was a bold move. The look in his eyes grew smoky, and Cam knew he desired her. The thought was enticing. Scary.

Seeing the momentary panic in her green gaze, Gus decided to give Cam the distance she needed. "Well," he said lightly, straightening up again, "you do the same for me up in the air. You teach me some pretty complex flight maneuvers and make it easy for me to learn from you."

"Maybe we're both good teachers to one another?" Cam's heart wouldn't settle down. The desire she'd seen for an instant in Gus's eyes was gone, and her panic was abating to a degree. Still, he was so incredibly masculine that she found herself wanting to lean up and kiss that cockeyed smile she'd come to love so much. At the craziest moments, Gus would give her that rakish smile and her heart would melt, and all the tension she was feeling would flow out of her. He was part little boy and part man. She'd never encountered anyone like him in her life.

"Certainly."

"That just goes to prove your mother's world view."

"Yes, it does. But you're a teacher I like, and I want you to teach me everything you know, Cam."

Hearing the sincerity in his voice as Gus brought her around in a circle, she closed her eyes again. Oh, if only that were true! All the mistakes she'd made in the past with men were still haunting her. What had they taught her? Bitterly, Cam opened her eyes and stared past Gus's broad shoulder. They had taught her that she consistently made bad choices. That she wasn't seeing the men or herself properly. Turning her head, Cam looked wonderingly up at Gus. He looked down and held her gaze.

"I see so much in your eyes, Cam. What are you thinking so hard about? I can practically feel it."

How easy it was to talk to Gus. For the first time in her life, Cam found that revealing her inner self to a man could be painless. "I was thinking about my past. My mistakes. My poor judgment."

"Oh?" he murmured, keeping his voice light as he moved her smoothly across the floor.

Compressing her lips, Cam said, "I've never talked about this to anyone. I'm really ashamed, Gus...."

Squeezing her hand gently, he said, "I can't ever conceive of you doing something you'd be ashamed of." Yet he could see the war in her eyes, the way her brow wrinkled. Wanting to hold her, caress her and take away that pain he saw in Cam's eyes was nearly his undoing. Still, he continued to lead her across the dance floor in rhythm with the guitar music. Right now, he could see that she wanted to entrust him with some awful secret that she was grieving over. Was this C.O. to X.O., woman to man? Unsure, he cocked his head and leaned close to her ear to say, "I'm here. I'll listen...."

"This is going to sound silly," Cam told him.

"Nothing you say will ever be silly."

Cam stared at his Adam's apple. Finding the courage, she whispered, "You talk about people being your teachers, Gus. I've been thinking a lot about that, seeing everything from that more macrocosmic perspective. I've been thinking about people who have come in and out of my life. What did they teach me? What did I learn?" Cam frowned. "Or did I? Sometimes I wonder if I even knew *what* I was being taught. I look at some situations, especially with guys..." She shrugged painfully.

Gus held his breath. Cam was obviously revealing something that was incredibly painful to her. Nearly losing the beat of the music, he forced himself to concentrate, worried that she'd stop.

"Well," Cam muttered defiantly, "I just wonder what the heck my three very bad wrecks of relationships taught me. Three men. I crashed and burned with every one of them."

Gently, Gus squeezed her hand. "Why do you blame yourself and not them?"

It was a fair question, and Cam had no logical answer. Feeling the warm strength of his hand as he squeezed hers reassuringly, she shrugged. "I don't know, Gus.... I guess I have a lot more thinking to do about it all...."

"Relationships are a two-way street," he agreed. "I found that out growing up and watching my parents in their marriage. It isn't easy. It's painful sometimes, and what I realized more than anything was that there had to be respect between the two people involved. If there wasn't, the relationship gets railroaded and becomes a power play for one individual, disempowerment for the other. The marriage becomes a war game, with winners and losers. In a good relationship, people look at one another like team members. What do they bring to the collective table? What are their innate strengths? Their weaknesses?" Gus gazed down at Cam's troubled expression. "In a good partnership, the people are a team, and the team operates from their strengths, not their weaknesses."

Wrinkling her nose, Cam muttered, "I fall into the first category. The relationship wars."

"I think we all do," Gus said, listening to the music begin to fade away at the end of a song. He slowed his steps until they stood in one another's arms on the dance floor. "The trick is learning that that's a painful way to live and getting out of it. And then, hopefully, learning from the mistake. Try not to draw the same teacher, the same lesson again. Grow. Reach out. Start over, but take what you've learned and put it into play in the new relationship."

Cam didn't want to leave Gus's arms. But the music had ended and the other couples were heading back to their tables, so she reluctantly stepped out of his embrace. Inwardly, Cam wanted to move closer to Gus, to stay in the circle of his arms and be held by him. Seeing the smoldering look in his eyes as he watched her, Cam felt her mouth go dry. The expression on his face was clearly readable. He wanted her. In all ways.

Swallowing hard, Cam whispered unsteadily, "The music's stopped...."

"The music we make here—" Gus released her and pressed his hand to his heart "—with one another, Cam, makes me happy. It's ongoing...."

With a jerky nod, Cam gazed up at him. How courageous Gus was compared to her. She felt like an emotional coward of the worst sort. "I—I wish I had that kind of courage, Gus," she said, then turned and walked quickly back to the table. Suddenly she was more scared than she'd ever been. Even staring down a Black Shark combat helicopter paled in comparison. Cam wanted to run. Anywhere. Now.

Chapter 11

"Four weeks," Wild Woman said to Cam as they walked across the revetment area after landing the Apaches. They'd been on a grueling, five-hour final test with the student pilots.

"An unending nightmare," Cam agreed as she walked with Jessica. Taking off her helmet, she ran her fingers through her damp, flattened hair. She cut a smile toward her friend, who was taking her own helmet off. "But it looks like we've made the grade with all of them."

Chuckling, Wild Woman nodded. "Yeah, Luis and Antonio took the challenge. I didn't think they would, but those rich boys dug deep and bailed their collective butts out of the hole they'd dug for themselves."

"Yes," Cam said, relieved, "they have."

"Did Antonio pass?"

"Yeah, barely. I'm givin' him a seventy-five per-

cent, the lowest mark you can have and still pass,"
she told her wryly. "He tried his best, though his
nerves got to him. He's flown better before, so I'm
giving him a passing grade."

The sun was warm as they walked toward the barracks, across from the revetment area where the aircraft were parked. Cam sighed. The fresh, warm air
felt good on her face.

"How about Gus? I'm sure he passed?"

"Yeah. I'm giving him a ninety percent."

"That dude is good. I'm glad we switched the students around every three days. I really looked forward
to flying with him. He's incredible. He's got great
flight hands."

Cam's heart thumped in her chest. "Yes...yes, he
does." Ever since that night on the dance floor, she'd
retreated from Gus—out of fear. And to his credit,
he'd backed off, too. They kept everything strictly
business between them now. Cam missed the warmth
that she'd always seen in his eyes when they were
alone together. Well, she had no one to blame but
herself. She'd been in a constant state of grief since
that night on the dance floor. Her fear overcame her
desire to open up and get to know him better.

Opening the door to the barracks, Wild Woman
gestured for Cam to enter. "Well? What now? Are
you going to call Morgan and tell him these three are
ready for real-time drug interdiction?"

Nodding, Cam led the way up the stairs to the second floor. "Yeah, I will."

"Where does that leave us? Do we get to go back
to BJS?"

Sadness moved through Cam as she unlocked the

door to her office. "Yes. I'm gonna miss you and Snake. You're the reason these guys are ready to do their job." Pushing the door open, she walked in and hung her helmet on a peg. Divesting herself of her chicken plate—the mandatory bullet-proof protective jacket they always wore while flying—she hung it next to the helmet on a wall hook.

"This has been a great diversion," Jessica said, sitting down, her helmet in her lap. She smiled at Cam, who sat down behind her desk. "Snake and I sure are gonna miss those weekends over at Club Flamingo. We had fun dancing every night with those great Latino guys. You won't find those kind of men down in Agua Caliente," she said with a scowl.

Chuckling, Cam shook her head. Agua Caliente was the closest town to the BJS base in Peru. It sat at the foot of Machu Picchu, one of the largest and most sacred temple sites of the whole Inca empire. "No, not there. But hey, you girls always found guys to dance with in Cuzco." Of course, it was a forty-five minute helicopter ride from their base to the city, situated at eleven thousand feet in the heart of the Andes Mountains.

"Yeah," Jessica pouted, sliding down in the chair and spreading her booted feet out before her.

Snake entered the room, her helmet beneath her left arm, her clipboard in her hand. "Hi, girls. Mind if I join this party?"

Cam smiled. "Not at all," she said, gesturing for Vickey to come in. "We got business to attend to, anyway."

Shutting the door, Snake took the second chair in

front of Cam's desk and sat down. She grinned at Wild Woman. "Well, did Antonio ante up?"

Laughing, Wild Woman said, "Yeah, the dude passed. How about your boy?"

Snake grinned and handed Cam her final report. "I'm passing Luis with a seventy-five percent. He froze in the clutch, but he's flown better than that in earlier sessions. He's got the heart, just not the nerves yet."

They all smiled at one another.

Cam looked at the reports on the men's flights. "Well," she murmured, going through each page of the official flight forms, "looks like they've carried the load."

"Yeah," Snake chuckled, setting her helmet down beside the chair. "I'll give 'em that. They decided to stop sulking and pouting like a couple of schoolboys and took the bit in their teeth and ran with it."

"They didn't have a choice," Wild Woman snorted. "They feared being embarrassed and shamed before their fathers more than anything else. It was a good hammer to hold over their heads so they'd haul ass and produce like they were supposed to."

"They've come a long way in four weeks," Cam agreed, dropping the reports back on the desk. She folded her hands over them and gave her cohorts a sad smile. "And I have you two to thank for that."

"Hold on," Snake said, lifting her long, thin hand. "If it weren't for the planning you did, they wouldn't be anywhere. So give yourself credit in this dance, too, Cam."

"Oh, I do, but I'm the C.O., Snake. I'm expected

to come up with bubble gum and wire to fix a problem.'' She grinned, though her heart was heavy.

Wild Woman looked over at Snake. ''So, now that our boys have passed through the collective fires of female hell, you know where that leaves us, don't you?''

With a sigh, Snake sat back and ruffled her brown hair with her fingers. ''Yeah, home to BJS. Damn, I'm gonna miss all our dancing, Cam. This has been a lot of fun. A great break.''

''I know,'' Cam whispered, blinking back tears. Opening her hands, she said, ''I'm gonna miss you two.''

''Yeah, you're stuck here with the three of them,'' Wild Woman said. ''Gus is easy to be around, but I think you're going to have to keep riding roughshod over Luis and Antonio. I'll bet they try to slough off now, with us gone. They won't have one of us always watching them in the cockpit.''

''We'll be going down to two Apaches,'' Cam said. ''I'll be doing a lot of flying to make sure they stay in line.''

Rubbing her hands, Wild Woman said, ''Yeah, we get to fly this third bird all the way back to BJS. I'm lookin' forward to it!''

Snake gave her a dark look. ''You would, you crazy woman. Who wants to sit with their butt in that cockpit for twenty-some hours?''

Snickering, Jessica said, ''Well, hey, it gives us a chance to practice our in-air refueling. We need to have that on our record every year. I'm lookin' forward to seein' that C-130 herky jerky coming out of the blue and trailin' a fuel line from its wing. We'll each get a chance to do it. I'm kinda excited.''

''You get excited over the weirdest stuff,'' Snake growled, rolling her eyes.

Cam didn't relish the idea of a long flight for her friends, either. Still, it meant that Maya would have one more Apache to add to her squadron, and that was good. Cam was sure Maya was looking forward to having her pilots back, too.

''So, you gonna hand out the BJS2 squadron patches to them in a little while?'' Wild Woman asked.

''Yeah, I will. They've earned them.''

''They've got to *keep* earning them,'' Vickey said darkly. ''I know Gus will. I'd love to have that guy with us down at BJS. He's hell on wheels up in the air. He's all combat mode. But Luis and Antonio? Nah.''

''You're prejudiced,'' Cam teased her lightly. Her heart squeezed when Gus's name was mentioned. How much she missed their private, searching conversations. ''Well,'' she sighed, opening a drawer and handing them two sets of orders, ''here are your passports back to BJS. You'll take off at 0500 tomorrow morning.''

Grinning wickedly, Vickey looked at Wild Woman. ''Great! Wanna kick up your frisky heels tonight, girlfriend? Club Flamingo? One last hot rumba? A tangle of tangos? You up for it?''

Laughing, Wild Woman said, ''In a heartbeat, Snake. Let's go get outta these army duds and into some hot mama movin' dresses with lotsa fringe on 'em!''

"Have fun," Cam told them as they stood.

"Why don't you come with us?" Snake invited as she opened the door.

Shaking her head, Cam said, "No...I'd cry all the time because I'm going to miss you so much. I would just rain on your party."

Nodding, Jessica smiled. "Well, we'll see you before we leave tomorrow morning?"

"That's a promise," Cam said. She had duties to perform now.

She saw Luis and Antonio standing tensely outside the door. Their faces belied their stress and worry as to whether or not they'd passed the final flight test. "Ask Mr. Dominguez to come in, will you, Snake?"

"Sure," she called, lifting her hand. "See you mañana...."

Gus was the last man to be called into Cam's office. Her heart picked up in beat as he quietly entered, still in his flight suit. How handsome he looked. Her gaze centered on his mouth. Gus had a beautifully formed mouth, and Cam had stopped counting the times she'd wondered what it would be like to kiss him and to feel those lips against her own. As he shut the door and turned around, Cam forced a smile she didn't feel.

"Congratulations, Gus, you've passed." She stood up and held the BJS2 patch across the desk.

Grinning, he took the patch, their fingertips briefly touching. In his heart, Gus felt an incredible sadness. Ever since the night he'd taken her out and spoken those words on the dance floor, Cam had retreated from him. He was so sorry those words had flown from his mouth.

"Thanks, Cam," he said.

"You're welcome. Sit down." Her heart beat even harder as he slowly sat down in front of the desk. Just the way he reverently touched the patch made her yearn for him to touch her in the same way.

Gus smiled gently. "Looks like I know what I'll be doing tonight—sewing this on my flight suit."

Chuckling, Cam nodded.

"Luis and Antonio looked relieved."

"Yeah, they passed. Barely. But they've got good training under them, so I feel confident in the next step—actual night interdiction."

Nodding, Gus looked down at the patch. Running his fingertips across it, he said, "So, where does this leave you? I know you were brought here to whip us into shape, to give us form and substance." Grief ate at him. Looking up, he held her dark green gaze. Was Cam leaving, too? Gus had never heard her say one way or another. After his faux pas at the restaurant, he wondered obliquely if she had put in for a transfer, to get away from him as soon as he graduated from training.

"Me?" Cam asked, surprised. She shut the desk drawer that held the flight tests. "I'm going to continue to command this little squadron of ours. Why?"

Glancing up, she saw his cinnamon-colored eyes lighten with obvious joy, and the look caught her completely off guard. It was then that she realized Gus still liked her.

The thought was euphoric. He was still going to be her X.O. She was still going to have to work with him, closely—on a daily basis now, but on an equal footing.

"Oh…" Gus shrugged and gave her a boyish grin, "I just thought that…well, it doesn't matter. That's great news."

"Is it?"

Feeling her gaze dig into him, Gus smiled boldly. "Yeah, I'm glad you're staying." Hooking his thumb across his shoulder toward the door, he said, "Now, I can't speak for Luis and Antonio, but I'm glad you're still running our ship, Captain."

Warmth sheeted through Cam and she felt suddenly vulnerable and nervous. "It's been hard," she muttered, avoiding his warm perusal by nervously moving a number of papers on her desk.

"But worth it," Gus insisted. Seeing her nervousness, he tightened his lips. "You're a great leader and teacher, Cam. I hope you know that. Look how far I've come. I learned more from you and the other women in the past six weeks than I did at flight school. Your experience, your generosity and the way you taught us was a gift."

Cam's fingers froze over the papers as Gus spoke in a low, emotional tone. Within her, she felt the armor plating around her heart give way beneath his fervent sincerity. How many men had the guts to come clean and be honest with her? Gus had shown, nonstop, that he was someone she could always rely on. He'd never lied to her, as men in her past had done. He'd always been straight with her, and he could admit he'd made a mistake.

Chewing on her lower lip, Cam looked across the desk at him. His face was open and readable, as it always was when they were alone. The care radiating from his eyes was undeniable. "Thanks for your words, Gus. They mean a lot to me. And I'll pass them on to Snake and Wild Woman, too.''

Opening his hands, he took a huge risk. "Listen, Cam…" His voice dropped to a whisper. "I know you've been dancing on the edge of a sword around here since you arrived—learning how to be a C.O. and balancing it against army regs. And dealing with me as your X.O., I know, hasn't been a lot of fun. It's been trying on you.'' Gus saw her eyes narrow as she sat there, weighing his words. "Well, what I mean is, maybe you want someone else as your executive officer now?''

"What?" Stunned, Cam sat up, blinking.

Gus shrugged. "I'm gonna come clean with you, Cam. That night at the restaurant, well, I crossed some lines with you that I shouldn't have, militarily. But it happened. In my heart, I'm not sorry I said what I did, but I know it adversely affected you—and our relationship. I just want to give you the out to get another X.O., is all. I don't like the tension that's always hovered between us since then. It's got to be a special hell on you because you see me so often, working together as we do.''

Sitting back, Cam wiped her mouth with the back of her hand. He was giving her a sad look, one that nearly broke her heart. Gripping the arms of her chair, she closed her eyes for a moment, then stared at Gus, who sat forward in his chair, his hands—those wonderful hands that had held her so gently while they danced—resting on his long, hard thighs.

"Gus, you have a way of forcing me to come clean, too,'' Cam muttered with a frown. "The least I can do is be honest with you.'' Looking up at the ceiling, she continued, "I've had three relationships with men. I have a flaw somewhere in me, and damned if I know why, but I draw the same kind of guy every time. A guy who wants to manipulate me into bed, lie to me, and take what he wants and then just walk away as if he has no responsibility toward me."

Gus sat very still. His heart ached—for Cam. He saw the pain in her eyes as she admitted her past to him. "That must have been terrible for you, because you're not that kind of person." Right now, he wanted to beat the hell out of all of those men, for he could see the damage they'd done to Cam. And how it was keeping her from trusting him. Rage flickered in him. Life was so unfair.

Taking a deep, ragged breath, Cam got up. She crossed her arms and began to pace behind her desk. The venetian blinds were open, allowing horizontal bars of light into the room. They reminded her of prison bars. Looking out at the revetment area, where a crew worked on the Apaches, she hung her head.

"I've been running, Gus," she admitted quietly. Turning, she looked over at him, tension swirling around the room. "Running from you, even though you aren't like them. I'm scared."

Swallowing hard, Gus wanted to get up, walk over and take Cam into his arms. That's what she needed, judging from the stricken look on her face. His heart, however, cautioned him. She would rebuff him, he knew. "I understand now," he told her. "And, for what it's worth, Cam—" he opened his hands in supplication "—I'm sorry. As a man, I'll apologize for their selfish behavior toward you. You didn't deserve to have that happen to you. You're a good, kind person who's honest and likes to treat the world that way.'' He gave her a twisted smile. ''But not everyone in life is going to play by your rules, with your idealism.''

''Yeah,'' she whispered, ''I know that—now. One of life's little chucks under the chin—to tell you that not all people have your best interests at heart in a relationship.''

''People play games, Cam. You're not a game player—you play for keeps. You bring your honesty, your hard-work ethic, your high moral values and standards to the table with everyone you deal with.''

Amazed that Gus could see all that in her, Cam felt her heart lift a little. She felt some of the grief dissolve beneath his probing cinnamon gaze. When he stood up, her pulse bounded. He held her gaze as he slowly walked around the desk and stopped within a few feet of her.

''You don't have to apologize for those jerks,'' she muttered. Cam stood there, tense and tall, her arms wrapped around herself defensively. Gus wasn't stupid. He could read body language pretty well and he knew that she was feeling very prickly right now, even toward him—because he was a man. It had been men who had so deeply wounded Cam to the point where she no longer trusted any of them.

''Are you comfortable with me being your X.O. and knowing that I care for you on a personal level, too? That on some days, I might slip and be intimate with you? I'll try my darnedest to always be businesslike, Cam. You have my promise...but I'm human, too. I might slip. I won't do it on purpose. I won't manipulate you like those other men did, but

I'm an ordinary guy. Like on the dance floor that night—those words just came out of my mouth, straight from my heart, and I didn't even realize it until it was too late.''

Gus pursed his lips and held her dark, shadowed gaze. Seeing tears glimmer dangerously in her eyes tore at him. The desire to take two steps toward Cam, hold open his arms and ask her to come into them nearly undid him. It was so tough not to speak what was in his heart.

Choking back the tears that came out of nowhere, Cam slowly unlocked her arms and let them fall to her sides. How badly she wanted to move into Gus's arms. Cam knew from the searching look on his face that he'd hold her. And she'd be safe. And loved. Stunned by that realization, Cam stood there in shock, staring dumbly at him. Words jammed in her throat and she couldn't speak for a long moment.

''There isn't a day that goes by here, Gus, that I don't look forward to seeing you,'' she finally murmured brokenly. ''And it scares the hell outta me admitting it to you.''

''Because you think I'll use it against you? That I'll try and get you in bed and then walk away, like they did, right?''

''Stupid, isn't it? But yeah…''

''Listen to me, Cam.'' Gus took a huge risk and reached out, sliding his hand against her jaw and cupping her flushed cheek. He saw the tears trail silently down her face. Groaning softly, he rasped, ''I won't *ever* do that to you. First, I need to earn your trust. Without trust, we have nothing. We can go nowhere.'' Her flesh was warm and firm beneath the

palm of his hand. When Cam closed her eyes and
nuzzled her cheek into his hand, Gus held his breath.
Elation soared through him. Cam's action shouted
volumes. She could have slapped him. She could have
jerked away. She could have gotten angry and told
him to back off, but none of that had happened. Instead, she was trusting him enough to allow this intimate moment with her. The tears, however, were
unstringing him.

"Just…let me hold you, Cam? I'll just hold you
for a moment. I think you need to be held. I can do
that for you. No manipulation. Just two humans being
here for one another?"

A sob jammed in her throat. Gus's face blurred as
she willed herself to look up at him. His hand was
warm and stabilizing. Cam ached to ask so much
more of Gus, but her fear overrode that. Two feet of
space—that's all that was separating them. That's all
she had to walk. Gus was offering her a safe haven
against her pain. Her past. Getting up the courage,
Cam tried to smile through her silent tears.

Without a word, she stepped forward.

Groaning softly, Gus placed his arms around her
tense shoulders. "Come here, Cam…." he whispered
harshly against her ear. Her chestnut hair tickled his
nose and cheek. Wrapping his arms around her, he
drew her gently against him. Closing his eyes, Gus
realized a fragile truce was being built between them,
and that Cam was giving him a gift. As she shyly,
hesitantly slid her arms around his shoulders and laid
her head against his chest, Gus sighed raggedly. Little
by little, Cam relaxed against him. Feeling her torn

emotions, Gus didn't try to force her to do anything but what was comfortable for her in that moment.

"You're a priceless gift to me, Cam," he said in a low tone. Smiling against her hair, his cheek against her head, Gus felt her sink more surely into his arms. He held her gently, lovingly. And as he felt Cam begin to relax and fit the contours of her body against his, he felt a sob wrack her. Automatically, his arms tightened for a moment around her shoulders. "That's it, let it out. Let it all out, Cam. You're safe with me. I promise.... Just get it all out and I'll hold you...."

Chapter 12

"Don't worry, they'll do fine," Gus reassured Cam as they stood just outside the barracks, the harsh floodlights breaking up the darkness around them.

Cam absorbed Gus's nearness like a sponge. It was dark, and in the distance, she watched Luis and Antonio climbing into the Apache helicopter, the ground crew ready nearby.

"I just worry," she said, frowning as she crossed her arms against her chest.

Chuckling, Gus stood inches behind her. "Hey, you've flown with these guys every day for the last month. If they don't have their night ops down pat by now, and interdiction rules memorized, they're never gonna have them." He glanced at her shadowed profile. Seeing the concern etched in her face, Gus fought the need to put his hands on her shoulders and tell her not to worry. But he couldn't. They were in full view of the crew and it wouldn't be proper military etiquette.

"This will be the first night they're going up alone."

"You'll be here. You've got the iridium phone. You'll be in contact with them," he coaxed. "Besides, aren't you tired of flying with each of these guys? Aren't you looking forward to a night off?" Gus was worried about Cam. Since her two friends had left, he'd seen Cam turn back into a twenty-four-seven workaholic. He'd done what he could to take work from her and give her a breather, but she still had to do the biggest share.

"I know...." Cam whispered. She twisted her head to look up at his dark, serious face. How handsome Gus was to her. And how lonely she'd been without their daily meetings out at the grove. Everything had changed since Wild Woman and Snake had left. She had to fly each night with either Luis, Antonio or Gus, five to seven hours, teaching them interdiction in real time. The entire duty rotation had changed. She was flying every night, without a break. They had only two Apaches available, and while one flew, the other was being serviced. Gus wasn't up to speed yet on the finer points of interdiction himself. Cam had spent most of her time getting the two Mexican pilots qualified so they could work with one another. Tonight was their first trial by fire, without her guiding them.

"Hey," Gus whispered, briefly touching her shoulder, "come on, Mama Hen in the Sky. Let's go to the grove—something we haven't been able to do for a long time." He looked forward to the rare personal time with Cam. Ever since she'd walked willingly into his arms, laid her head on his shoulder and cried her heart out, things had changed between them. Gus was earning Cam's trust one small step at a time. She was worth it to him. Even though he had his own devils to contend with—his fears that she was in a dangerous profession and could get killed just as the other woman he'd loved—Gus couldn't fight his powerful attraction for Cam.

Cam hungered for his touch. As Gus's hand grazed her shoulder, her flesh tingled with wanting of him, and she turned, searching his face. "You know what? That sounds wonderful. Since we only fly at night, our whole world has been turned upside down. We're awake all night and sleep all day."

"Not exactly great," Gus agreed as Cam fell into step with him. They walked along the concrete path around the barracks, then moved away from the lights on the building. In the distance, Gus could hear the Apache revving up for takeoff. Cam had the iridium phone in her left hand. He hoped the two pilots, who had made an amazing about-face, would do everything by the book tonight so Cam wouldn't have to worry about them so much. If they screwed up, it was on her record, her watch. He didn't want to see her career torpedoed like that. She didn't deserve it.

"Where's your guitar?" Cam asked. How she missed hearing Gus play it. This last month, their former routine had been shattered, and she had discovered just how much she needed this hour alone with Gus. The grove had become a place of healing for her on so many levels, a place where she could, for a little while, leave her responsibilities behind.

He gave her a slight smile as he walked at her side. "It's already on the picnic table, waiting for you."

Giving him a narrowed look, Cam murmured, "Why do I think you've had this all planned out, Mr. Morales?"

With a boyish grin, Gus said, "Oh, I dunno, Ms. Anderson. Do I look like the type who has a plan up his sleeve?"

Chuckling, Cam said, "That's one of the many good things about you, Gus—there're no games. No manipulation." He wasn't anything like the men in her past. The afternoon Gus had held her in his arms, so many of the old walls and fears had dissolved within Cam. The last month had been tentative, hopeful, scary, and yet happier than she could ever recall. Gus made her want to trust him. His honesty at every juncture was evident.

Swinging his arms as they stepped off the asphalt and onto the sandy earth leading to the grove, he said with humor, "I can't say this isn't something I didn't cook up. It is." He held her hopeful gaze. "It's something you need," he said enigmatically.

"Uh-oh, I'm in trouble now," Cam laughed. His returning laughter lifted her spirits and made her heart pound with joy.

"Nah," Gus teased. Once inside the grove, he slid his hand into hers. In quiet moments, especially in her office with the door closed, Cam allowed him the privilege of touching her hand, her shoulder. And as her trust in him grew during the last month, she'd come into his arms on her own, just to be held for a quiet moment. Gus knew the gift she was sharing with him and never made a move to go beyond what Cam silently asked for. Oh, how he wanted to kiss her! But he didn't. He waited. If he pushed his will on her, the fragile trust between them would shatter. And there was no way Gus was going to let that happen. His desire for Cam was held firmly in check. He was going to behave.

Cam squeezed his large, warm hand as he led her into the grove. "What have you done, Gus? I can see that wicked glint in your eyes." Breathless because she needed this playfulness, Cam grinned up at him. His hand tightened around hers as if to quietly reassure her that it was going to be a good surprise.

"Oh," he hedged, "just some small stuff." And he led her to the table. Cam stood at his side, lifting her arm and placing it around his waist. Shocked by her bold move, and yet glorying in it, Gus lost his smile. Gently, he wrapped his arm around her shoulders. Cam leaned against him, her head resting against his chest. Joy sang through him. Clearing his throat and trying to think coherently, because he hadn't expected Cam's response, he gestured to the long redwood bench.

"I got your favorite dessert," he told her in a conspiratorial tone. "A cream puff." He'd found out that Cam loved them. One night she'd enthused about her mother's ability to make the world's best cream puffs.

Touched, Cam moved out of his embrace to the small baker's box sitting on the bench. "Ohh, Gus, you shouldn't have!" she cried, quickly opening it.

Just watching the childlike expression on Cam's face as she leaned over and opened the box did Gus a lot of good. Picking up his guitar, which had been lying on the table, he straddled the bench behind Cam and settled the instrument against him.

"Sit down and enjoy your just dessert," he teased, as he began to strum the instrument.

Laughing, Cam turned around and straddled the same bench, facing Gus, the box between them. He'd thoughtfully included several large paper napkins, and she placed one on her left thigh and one on his right. The music he played was beautiful to her. Picking up the first huge cream puff, which was oozing with whipped cream, Cam placed it on the napkin on his knee.

"This is yours," she told him, grinning. Picking up the second one, she eyed it wolfishly. "And this is mine!"

Gus watched as Cam eagerly bit into the pastry. She knew how to attack it without squishing all the whipped cream from the center.

"You're pretty good at that," Gus said, impressed. "When I eat one, it squirts all over the place."

Chuckling and closing her eyes, Cam enjoyed the pastry. "Mmm, this is wonderful, Gus! Thank you so much. It's so thoughtful of you!" Opening her eyes again, she gave him a huge smile.

Gus grinned. Cam had whipped cream on both sides of her luscious-looking mouth. She quickly slurped it away with the tip of her tongue and attacked the pastry again with great relish.

"Good thing cream puffs don't fly. They wouldn't stand a chance with you," he stated humorously.

Laughing, Cam melted beneath his dark, smoldering gaze. Still in his flight uniform, with a few rebellious strands of hair dipping down across his brow, he looked dangerously handsome to her. "Why don't you eat yours?" she challenged.

Shrugging, Gus said, "I'll get it all over me."

"Chicken."

Rising to her bait, he placed the guitar on the table beside him and reached for his pastry. "Okay, here goes...."

Cam gave a cry as Gus bit into it, and whipped cream spurted everywhere, including a blotch on her cheek. When he pulled the pastry away from his mouth, he had cream on his face, hands and uniform.

"What a mess you are!" she said, easing to her feet and scooting closer till their knees met. She picked up her napkin and began wiping cream off his smiling mouth. Drowning in his darkened, narrowed gaze, Cam found her hand slowing as she dabbed at the remainder.

"I warned you," he growled huskily, setting down the cream puff and wiping his hands on his own napkin. "You've got a big splotch of whipping cream near the side of your mouth. Want me to kiss it away?"

Heat shot through Cam as he gently cupped her face and tilted her chin slightly upward. Gus wanted to kiss her. And she wanted to kiss him. Her hand came to rest on his chest and Cam gazed wonderingly up into those warm, cinnamon-colored eyes that held such love for her. It *was* love, Cam realized despite her stunned, spinning senses. She saw his strong mouth curve into a gentle smile as he cocked his head and studied her.

"Y-yes, kiss the whipped cream away," Cam whispered unsteadily, her voice hoarse.

"Sure?"

"Very sure, Gus."

"This has to be mutual, Cam...." And it had to be. He saw the desire in her huge and luminous eyes. Gus saw fear in them, too, but he hoped that the trust he'd earned would allow Cam to surrender to him. His fingers tightened briefly beneath her clean jawline. Her skin was warm and firm. How badly he wanted to touch it, touch her and kiss her.

Closing her eyes, Cam stretched upward. "Kiss me?"

Never had two words meant so much to Gus. Leaning down, he met her halfway, his mouth moving slowly, provocatively across her parting lips. She tasted of sweet cream. Grazing her lips, Gus smiled and licked off the spot of cream from Cam's cheek. Hearing her moan softly, feeling her fingers tighten reflexively on his flight uniform, Gus placed a soft kiss on each of her closed eyes.

"You are," he breathed, "the most beautiful flower in my garden of life, Camelia Anderson." He allowed his lips to trail down to the tip of her nose, and then lower, to her parted lips. "You are so beautiful to me. Like the delicate flower you are, everything has to be right for you to bloom, to flourish. I want to help you do that, *querida*. Darling..."

Lost in the heat of his strong mouth closing over hers, of his breath, warm and moist, flowing across her cheek, Cam surrendered to Gus. She felt his hands move in a caressing motion across her hair, cherishing her as if she were some fragile, breakable treasure. Never in her life had she felt so loved, so cared for. His mouth was strong and giving, searching and coax-

ing. She tasted the whipped cream, the sweetness of
him, and felt the power of him as a man, held in
check.

Moaning, Cam felt his arms move around her
shoulders as he drew her more closely against him.
Sitting on the bench with their knees pressed together
didn't allow for complete contact, but she didn't care.
Holding him close like this was enough. Her
breathing became shallow. Hungry for his continued
touch, Cam felt her lower body begin to throb with
an ache that moved upward toward her heart.

"I need you...." Gus rasped against her wet, slick
mouth. "In every way, *querida,* whenever you say
the word..." And he crushed his mouth against hers
as she met and returned the fire that had exploded
between them. Pain knotted deep in his lower body.
Oh, how he wanted to make slow, delicious, mind-
blowing love to Cam! Gus knew in his heart that he
could please her and show her that not all men were
selfish takers, interested only in their own needs. Her
mouth was strong, searching, eager, as he met and
matched her sweet assault. Beneath that cool exterior
lurked a woman of immense passion, he realized with
happiness as he threaded his fingers through the
strong, silken strands of her hair.

Moving her hands across his chest and up his
thickly corded neck, Cam eagerly traced every inch
of Gus. The male odor of him was like a perfume to
her flaring nostrils. Heart thundering in her breast, she
eagerly slid her lips against his. As his tongue moved
in a slow, sensual dance against hers, she shuddered.
She wanted to mate with him, to become one with

him, and that desire shook her as she'd never been shaken before.

Tearing her mouth from his, Cam drowned in his smoldering, hooded eyes, which were focused on her like those of a predator. "I need you, Gus. I'm afraid, but I can't stop...." And Cam leaned upward and pressed her lips against his. Feeling a groan ripple through his chest against her flattened breasts, she shared that wonderful animal sound with him. As his fingers slid across her scalp caressingly, Cam lost herself in his arms. Somehow she knew she was safe with Gus, that he wouldn't take advantage of her. Everything was so right. So beautifully right...

Lost in the explosions arcing through him as her mouth caressed his over and over again, Gus felt his control disintegrating. Alarmed, because he didn't take Cam's words to mean that she wanted to go "all the way" physically, he prayed that he was reading her right. Otherwise, he could botch this and send her running.

Cradling her in his arms, Gus moved his mouth more slowly, sipping from her wet, warm lips. Laving her lower lip with his tongue, he covered her mouth with his, smiling against her. Cam was trembling. So was he. Savoring the weight of her arms around his neck, the pressure of her fingers opening and closing against his back, he absorbed her thirst for him. Feeling euphoric, he finally reached up and smoothed her hair away from her cheek.

"You are so beautiful," he whispered to Cam, their noses almost touching. Watching her eyes open, those long chestnut lashes flutter up to reveal her drowsy, desire-filled gaze, Gus gave a very male smile of appreciation.

"You make me feel that way," Cam whispered unsteadily. Just being in Gus's arms was wonderful. "I've never felt how I do now, Gus. You make everything seem so right. So good."

His mouth curved ruefully as he traced her arched brow with his index finger. "That's because we trust one another, *querida*. We've laid a good foundation, don't you think? We've had time to get to know one another. We've talked a lot out here." Gus lifted his head and glanced appreciatively around the quiet, darkened grove. Looking back down at Cam, he saw her mouth part and a soft smile touch the corners.

"Yes…we have."

"I'm going to turn you around so you're more comfortable," he told her.

Nodding, Cam eased away. Gus positioned her so that she was straddling the bench like him, her back against his chest, her head resting on his shoulder. When his arms went around her waist and captured her hands across her abdomen, Cam sighed.

"Better?"

"Much better."

"We're not pretzels anymore."

Laughing softly, Cam looked up and drowned in his dark, narrowed eyes. "No…"

"That's for teenagers," Gus chuckled. "At our age, comfort is better."

"Mmm, this is nice," Cam agreed, and she sighed, feeling languorous and sated on so many levels. Moving her fingers across his clasped hands, she added, "I don't know how you did it, Gus."

Holding her close, he pressed a kiss to her hair. "What, *querida?*"

"Got me to trust you." Cam frowned and traced his thick, hard knuckles with her finger. The back of his hand was darkly haired and silky.

"It was easy," Gus confided. "The first time I saw you, the doors of my heart just sprang open."

"Really?"

"Yeah. Kinda took me off guard."

"Because of the woman you loved and lost?"

Nodding, Gus rested his cheek against hers, content just to have Cam in his arms like this. It was an unbelievable gift. His heart was still pounding in his chest, and his lower body was in knots of need, but he refused to allow his raging desire to affect this moment. Everything was perfect. Perfect. Cam was in his arms, trusting him, and maybe…loving him? Gus wasn't sure about that. He did know that whatever they shared, it was mutual.

"Yes, losing her ripped my heart out of my chest," Gus said quietly. Feeling Cam's hands tighten comfortingly around his own, he closed his eyes. "I'm still not right with it all, Cam. I'm scared, too, in a different way than you. But scared just the same."

Cam nodded. "I'm always amazed at how our fears stop us." How wonderful it was just to be held by Gus, to be talking like this. She had been starved for such intimacy, she realized, for a long time. In part, Cam knew, the closeness of her women friends at BJS had filled that need in her. When she left for this assignment, however, she'd been cut off from that lifeline.

Gus compressed his lips and he tasted Cam on

them. Aching to love her, but knowing that wasn't possible now, he said, "You fear trusting another man. I fear having a relationship with a woman in a dangerous profession again."

"You're helping me get over my fear," Cam told him softly as she grazed his hand with her fingers. Gus tightened his arms briefly around her in response.

"And I'm getting to be friends with mine, too."

"Where does this leave us, Gus?"

"Afraid but moving forward, I think," he said, giving a short laugh.

Nodding, Cam closed her eyes. "Yes, I feel the same."

Sighing, Gus murmured, "We just need to keep pacing ourselves with one another. And we need to keep talking. I'm not a mind reader and neither are you. The last thing I want to do, Cam, is misread you or assume. That can get us into hot water real fast. The *last* thing I want to do is shatter your growing trust in me."

"Just keep doing what you do so well, Gus." She looked up and smiled at his very serious face. "You seem to have this sixth sense about me, what I need and when I need it. I'm in awe of it, to tell you the truth. I don't trust myself in thinking I know you, or where you're at, because I never could with the other men I was involved with, so I'm relying more on you than me. Does that make sense?"

He gave her a one-cornered smile. "Yeah, it does, *querida.* It just puts more pressure on me to read you right the first time, though. I'm afraid I'm going to screw up with you...and that if I do, it will wreck what we have."

Cam shook her head. "No, Gus, it won't. I've known you for a long time now, in a lot of very different and difficult situations, and you've been steady as a rock for me. Your morals and values, the way you treat me daily, have never changed, no matter what was happening around us." Searching his eyes earnestly, Cam reached up with her hand and slid it along the curve of his jaw. "I trust you—with my life. Just know that, okay? I trust you, Gus."

Those were words he'd prayed to hear. At the same time, as he caught her hand and pressed it against his cheek, they scared him even more. Unwilling to call what they shared love, because it was just too much for him to grasp at this time, Gus whispered, "I've always trusted you, Cam. You hold my life, my heart in your hands, whether you know it or not."

"I didn't know that, Gus." She sighed deeply. "I'm so inept at reading men."

"You're innocent," Gus said in a hushed tone, pulling her hand from his cheek and placing a slow, warm kiss on her palm. "Don't be hard on yourself. Innocence is forgivable in my book."

Her palm tingled deliciously as he rested his lips against it. Every fiber within her screamed to make love with Gus, but Cam knew it wasn't time. At least, not yet.

"I've never thought of myself as an innocent," she said, humor tingeing her tone.

"Well, you are in my eyes," Gus said, pressing a second kiss to her palm.

"You're wonderful, Gus," and Cam smiled up at him, into his deeply shadowed face, carved with the harsh lines of life. "Thank you for everything to-night...."

"Even the cream puffs?" He chuckled. Gus knew their time was drawing to a close. He knew Cam had to get back to her office and stay alert in case the Apache crew needed her help.

"Especially the cream puffs," she said, laughing softly. As Gus lifted her hand and kissed the back of it, she felt giddy. Effervescent and free.

"Hmm, I wonder if they're really aphrodisiacs in disguise. I should bring them to our next secret meeting in the grove."

Cam sat up and turned toward him, laughing fully. "Gus Morales, you are an incredible man." She placed her hand against his heart. Growing serious, she met his hooded gaze. "I don't know what life will throw at us, but I want you to know this—I'm in it for the long haul with you. I don't want a one-night stand. I'm not built that way and I think you know it. I want the time to get to know you. I want to laugh with you. Cry with you. I want to talk, and share life with you."

Pressing his hand to hers, Gus said in a rasping, emotional voice, "Cam, we want the same thing. Only our lives aren't our own here. Not really. We're going to have to make precious hours like this one happen when we can."

Nodding, Cam whispered, "Let's make them happen, Gus. For both of us."

Chapter 13

"Nasty night out," Gus grumbled as he leaned down, frowning at the green HUD screens in front of him. Cam was flying the Apache over the harsh, high desert in northern Mexico, roughly a hundred miles south of the Texas border.

Cam gripped the controls, trying to keep the Apache on course despite the rain and wind whipping them around. "Yeah, our first time together on a night flight in over a month and we get this."

The darkness was complete except for lightning bolts that sizzled cloud-to-cloud around them, or danced toward the earth. A U.S. Army radar balloon tethered at the border and floating three hundred feet off the earth, had detected two aircraft, one fixed wing and the other a helicopter, coming in over a well-known drug route. BJS2 had been called to intercept them.

At five thousand feet, the Apache strained and bobbled as Cam hit one jolting air pocket after another.
Sweat stood out on her brow. She had her nightscope,
which was hinged on the right side of her helmet,
positioned beneath her right eye, allowing her to see
objects out there in the darkness. It was a necessary
piece of high-tech equipment. With her other eye she
continued to monitor the instrument panel in front of
her. The soothing green color served to calm her
heightened sense of anxiety somewhat. Cam didn't
have a good feeling about this mission, but she said
nothing to Gus. After all, it was only an intuition she
had, and so far, nothing had confirmed it.

"I hate thunderstorms. They destroy our night vision capability," she groused. Sitting in the upper
cockpit, with Gus below her, separated from her by
an armor-plated wall, Cam pushed the nightscope
away with her gloved hand. It was useless with lightning dancing around them. They had to fly through
the edge of the huge storm in order to reach the val-
idation point where they'd intersect their targets.

"I can see why," Gus agreed. Peering at the
HUDs, he saw the two aircraft approaching from the
right. "I've got 'em painted on the screen." He
placed his gloved index finger on the television-
screen image in front of him. "One's a Cessna 150
and the other is a Bell helicopter, according to the
identification."

"Helluva night for either of those Tinkertoys to be
out here," Cam said. "They must have a lot of coke
on board to risk flying in a storm like this."

"Yeah," Gus said grimly, "a 150 is too light to
withstand violent up-and-down drafts. If that pilot is

in the wrong place at the wrong time, he'll get smashed into the desert below, like a fly hit by a flyswatter.''

Chuckling, Cam said, ''The flyswatter being a nasty downdraft that pushes him to the ground before he knows what hit him.''

''Well, as we know, druggies will do anything, fly in any kind of weather or circumstances, to get drugs across the border.''

Grimly, Cam turned the Apache to the south on an intercept course as Gus called out the coordinates. ''It's bad out here tonight. Those pilots have got to be sweating it out, too,'' she muttered.

''They're at fifteen hundred feet and going lower. They sure don't want to remain on radar very long.''

Cam knew that drug-running pilots were well aware of the radar balloons placed at certain points along the U.S.-Mexico border. The balloons were a first-warning line of defense to pick up their approach. Drug pilots tried to fly beneath the reach of radar, sometimes as low as fifty feet above the ground, or what was referred to as ''nap of the earth flying.'' It was dangerous at any time. Especially dangerous tonight, given the turbulence caused by the storm.

''Uh-oh, they're turning west. I think they're trying to avoid this storm altogether.''

''Right,'' Cam agreed grimly, easing the Apache downward to intercept them. ''They'd have to. This storm would kill 'em and they know it.''

''Okay, they're both hugging the earth. One thousand feet. Twenty miles ahead. We're going out of our box.''

''That's okay.'' The ''box'' was an area they normally flew in on a known drug route. They would often fly Bravo or Alpha box, specific latitude and longitudes, in a rectangular flight pattern at five thousand feet, hoping to intercept a drug flight coming north. Gus would have to notify the base back at Tijuana that they were moving out of the box now. That way, military personnel would know where they were located in case they had engine trouble and had to go down. Rescue teams would know what their last location coordinates had been.

Looking around, Cam saw the roiling, cauliflower-shaped clouds light up for a second above them. Right now, even with the jostling they were experiencing in the storm's turbulence, they were still safer in the Apache than those two pilots were in their lightweight aircraft. Her heart was pounding a little, and anxiety enveloped her. Cam didn't like storms, didn't like flying anywhere near them. Akiva and Joe's Apache had been struck by lightning and suffered severe software damage on their last mission, and she had no wish to be placed in the same position.

"They're outta the storm's reach," Gus said, following the radar images on the HUD, "and going down to five hundred feet."

"What's the terrain under us like?" Cam asked. This was territory they'd never flown over before. But fortunately, the Apache's state-of-the-art equipment gave them a good look at the terrain.

Gus chuckled darkly. "Brutal. My people's land. My mother was born about fifty miles east of here. It's high desert, very dry with lots of canyons and caves. It's not hospitable. No water."

"Nice place to visit but not live in," Cam said,

smiling tightly. Her eyes narrowed as she continued to sweep her gaze over the instrument panel. In the dark, a pilot could get vertigo. Especially with lightning causing havoc with her eyes and brain. It was more important than ever for her to watch her instruments and trust them. Guiding the Apache swiftly downward, she saw that they would intercept the other aircraft in a matter of minutes.

"Right on," Gus said. Reaching for his night-vision binoculars, he waited as Cam placed the Apache in position to get a positive identification of the two aircraft. The first thing they had to do was get close enough, without giving away their position, to retrieve the numbers on each aircraft's fuselage. Then Gus would type them into his computer and send a request to the Federal Aviation Agency's computers in Washington, D.C., to find out if either of the other pilots had filed a flight plan. Every plane was required to have one, especially if crossing from one country's airspace to another's. Aircraft without flight plans were very likely drug runs.

The registry of the plane, and the owner's name, would pop up on Gus's HUD as well. Those names would be cross-referenced with the FBI database in D.C., which held a list of pilots known to fly drugs. A match there—a frequent occurrence—confirmed it was a drug run. If there was no match, but the plane had been involved in other suspected drug flights— even searched and found clean—that info, too, would pop up on his screen.

All they needed, however, was a thumbs up from D.C. to confirm there was no flight plan. That meant they could go to work and force the pilot to land at the nearest airport, where Mexican soldiers could apprehend and search the plane.

"This is strange," Cam muttered. "Two aircraft flying together? You'd think they'd realize that two make a bigger dot to be picked up on the radar screen."

"Yeah," Gus said. With the turbulence so bad, he held the binoculars in his lap, gripped in both hands to prevent them from flying around the cockpit and injuring him. "Makes me wonder if they're really drug flights...."

Shrugging, Cam said, "I don't know. If they are, this is a new tactic, and we need to be super alert."

"It's odd that one's fixed wing and the other's a helo. Usually it's one or the other."

"A lot of things aren't adding up on this miserable night," Cam muttered. They were less than a mile from the fleeing plane and helicopter now. She would bring the Apache closer, without lights on so that they wouldn't be detected, and Gus would get the numbers on the fuselage by looking through the night-vision binoculars. At least that was the plan.

"Druggies are always tryin' new things," Gus stated. They were within a half mile of the fixed-wing craft. Turning in his seat, the harness biting into his shoulders, he lifted the binoculars to his eyes. Even in the rain, he'd be able to read the numbers. "Stay the course, I've got 'em sighted, Cam...."

Using all her flight skills, she held the Apache as steady as possible. For the most part, they were out from under the storm cloud, and the wind was lessening. That made it easier to fly the gunship and she was grateful. Rain was still falling, but conditions weren't as bad as before.

"Steady..." Gus murmured. "Steady...I got 'em!"

Cam grinned, hearing the crow of triumph in his voice. Within seconds, Gus had typed in the numbers and sent them on for verification.

"Bingo!" he said shortly. "It's a Javier Rios flight, a drug lord from southern Mexico."

"Excellent," Cam said with a short, tense laugh. "Akiva and Joe must be doing a good job down there. He's been sending more and more flights north to avoid interdiction by them over the Gulf of Mexico, where Akiva and Joe's black ops base is located."

Before Gus could answer, he saw something on his HUD that made his eyes go wide.

"Rocket! Rocket being fired at us!" he yelled. Disbelievingly, he saw the helicopter, which was half a mile behind them now, firing—at them!

Cursing softly, Cam saw the warning on her HUD screen as a shrill warning went through her headset, indicating that they were being painted by an enemy's firing array. Where the hell had that rocket come from? Mind whirling, she instantly took evasive maneuvers.

"Get online. We're returning fire!" Cam barked at Gus.

Too late!

She had wrenched the Apache out of the path of the rocket. The only problem was that the rocket was a heat seeker, and it followed the heat of the Apache's engine.

"Look out!" Gus screamed, and he threw his hands outward to brace himself.

Spinning the helicopter around, Cam tried to avoid the hit. Out of the corner of her eye, she saw a yellow flame. It was the rocket—coming directly at their tail rotor assembly. Fear filled her. She groaned as she worked the controls, trying to avoid being hit.

Seconds flew by, though to Cam they seemed to drag. Tensely, she gripped the controls. Her breath jammed in her chest. *No! Oh, no!*

The rocket exploded upon impact as it grazed the tail rotor assembly. Fire arced all around them. Cam felt the Apache shudder. The blades whapped loudly as the helicopter began to slowly turn in a circle, out of control.

"Hang on!" she yelled at Gus, her nostrils flaring. Cam knew what would happen. The tail rotor was gone. Without it, the Apache would turn in endless circles until it smashed into the ground.

Darkness cloaked them suddenly as their instrument panels went offline. Panic surged into her throat and sweat popped out on her brow. They were going down! In a hurry!

Mind whirling, Cam calculated their chances. They had been five hundred feet above the ground when they were hit. She had no idea what kind of terrain lay below them. Feverishly, she worked the pedals with her booted feet and twisted the cyclic and collective to try and stop the Apache from spinning. Vertigo chased her. She shook her head savagely, trying to clear it.

In the distance, a bolt of lightning flashed. It gave just enough light for Cam to see the vague outline of a canyon coming up. They were falling into it! The walls were steep and narrow. Breathing hard, she gasped. The blades would strike the rock! Hands gripping the controls, she wrestled with the sinking helicopter. She heard Gus gasp as well.

In the middle of their uncontrolled free fall, Cam dimly registered the fact that the helicopter shadowing the plane had been the craft that had fired at them. It had been a setup! They'd fallen for it. She hadn't taken adequate precautions. Her mouth flexed grimly. The earth was coming up fast!

"Prepare for crash!" she cried out.

Seconds later, the blades of the Apache struck the wall of the canyon, sending a sickening shudder through the bird. Jerked savagely one way and then another, Cam felt their slowing descent. Chunks of rock struck the canopy. The Plexiglas groaned but didn't shatter.

The helicopter suddenly groaned and turned on its side, causing Cam's harness to bite painfully into her shoulders. She let go of the controls and, trying to brace, threw her arms up to protect her face. Simultaneously, she lifted her feet away from the pedals. If she didn't, the impact would break her legs and possibly crush her feet.

The Apache's descent was slowed even more as the flailing rotor blades hit the wall of the canyon again. The blades snapped and sliced like scimitars hurling through the blackness, shrieking as they spun. The bird tipped backward, the tail hitting the ground first.

The impact was horrific. Cam cried out as she was flung toward the front of her cockpit. Her harness held, but the jolt was savage, straining every muscle in her body. Pain shot through her neck and shoulders. Slammed to one side and then the other, she heard the scream of metal being ripped apart. Helplessly she flung out her arms as the bird keeled over, nose first now, tossing Cam in her harness like a rag doll.

Every second felt like a separate nightmare. The Apache slammed down on its port side. Cam's helmet struck the cockpit Plexiglas, shattering it all around her. She felt the final death throes of her bird before it finally lay without moving.

"Gus! Gus! Can you hear me?" Cam cried, fumbling for her harness release.

"I hear you!" he gasped. "Get outta here! That helo could have followed us in. They could finish us off! Get out! Hurry!"

Cam knew the score. Whipping her gaze across the cockpit controls, she saw they had no electricity. No way to call for help. But the bird had a transponder. It would start emitting a signal immediately.

"Get out!" Gus shouted.

Another bolt of lightning illuminated the canyon briefly. Cam managed to unharness herself. She reached to the right and twisted the release mechanism on the canopy, which popped open. Relief swam through her. She wasn't seriously hurt, just bruised. Wind rushed into the cockpit, and so did the rain. Grunting and groaning, Cam threw herself out of the cockpit headfirst. She struck the fuselage and then bounced off, hitting the ground hard.

Above, she heard a helicopter approaching. On

hands and knees, spitting sand out of her mouth, she yelled, "Gus! Where are you?"

The night was so black she couldn't see anything.

"Here!" he groaned.

Scrambling to her feet, Cam took off her helmet and dropped it as she headed drunkenly along the bird's fuselage, leaning against it to steady herself. Rain whipped into her face and she raised her gloved hand to protect her eyes.

"Where?" she cried. "Where are you?"

The helicopter that had shot them down was fast approaching. Breathing hard, Cam held out her right hand as she stumbled over rocks.

"I'm here!" Gus yelled.

Cam nearly tripped over him. Quickly, she fell to her knees, her hands reaching, searching. "Gus?" Her voice was strident, off-key. "You hurt?"

"Yeah...dammit. That chopper's coming, Cam. Help me up! We gotta get away from this bird. They're gonna take it out!" And he reached out and connected solidly with her hand. Cam was strong, he discovered. Holding his broken left arm close to his body, he gritted his teeth and stood.

"This way!" Cam yelled. The whapping of the chopper's blades was puncturing her eardrums. Any second now, Cam knew the helicopter would fire another rocket at them. Gripping Gus and wrapping her arm around his waist, she gasped, "Come on!" as he leaned heavily on her. Slipping on unseen rocks and gravel, she lunged away from the Apache and headed down the canyon.

Another bolt of lightning flashed. Panting and dizzy, Cam staggered unevenly beneath Gus's weight.

He was groaning, obviously trying not to cry out. In the second's light, she saw a bend in the canyon. Only fifty feet away! If she could get them around that corner of rock wall, they might be safe from a rocket fired at the Apache.

"Run!" she begged breathlessly. Gripping Gus hard against her, Cam surged ahead, digging the toes of her boots into the hard, sandy soil.

Gus gasped. Pain made him dizzy. He tried to run and felt Cam steady him as she aimed for the bend in the canyon. It was their only chance! Breath tearing out of his contorted mouth, he tried to concentrate. *Run!* He had to force his wobbly, weakened legs to run! Somehow, he had to force his attention to the present.

Faintness rimmed his vision, and Gus felt himself physically failing. Felt himself leaning more heavily on Cam, until she groaned. *No! No!* He loved her! This couldn't be happening! They couldn't die now!

Those thoughts cleared his pain-filled senses briefly. Gathering his strength, Gus swung his feet forward, one in front of the other. The rocks and gravel made the surface slippery and dangerous. They ran brokenly, stumbling, almost falling. They had to make it to that bend or they were dead!

Breath ripping from her burning lungs, Cam swung Gus ahead of her with one, last superhuman effort. She heard the rocket being fired. They had only seconds. As Gus flew off his feet ahead of her, Cam dived headfirst after him.

Slamming into the earth, the breath knocked out of her, Cam heard a tremendous explosion behind them. The entire canyon lit up like Fourth of July fireworks.

With a cry, she rolled to the right. Safe! She was safe! Fire vomited past them with a roar. The wall protected them! As Cam scrambled to her knees, covered with sand and grit, her eyes widened enormously. The fuel from the leaking tanks on the Apache had exploded. The fireball raced past them and shot high into the night sky. The odor of burning aviation gas permeated her senses. Nostrils flaring, Cam threw herself farther behind the wall and landed squarely on top of Gus.

He cried out.

Cam rolled off him, gasping for breath.

As the fireball began to dissipate, the drug helicopter flew past them and on up the canyon.

"Gus!" Cam staggered to her knees and twisted toward him. In the light of the fire still crackling and popping from the destroyed Apache, Cam saw his shadowy figure lying on the ground. His teeth were gritted and he was holding his left arm. His face was stretched with pain. Looking down, Cam saw that her hands shook as she reached out to touch his left shoulder. The dark color of blood stained the entire upper arm of his uniform.

"No!" Cam cried softly. She gently held Gus down when he started to get up. "Don't move, Gus, don't move!" she chanted as she reached into her flight suit. She always kept a Swiss Army knife with her; now she needed it. Pulling it out and opening the blade with shaking fingers, she quickly cut away the fabric. It gave with a sickening, ripping sound.

Cam winced. "Oh, God..."

Gus lay there gasping for air. Sweat rolled into his tightly shut eyes and he clenched his teeth. Hearing

Cam's soft cry sent fear through him. He felt her hands on his arm as she carefully pulled the sleeve away. "I—broke it on impact," he rasped.

Swallowing hard, Cam could see blood spurting from beneath his arm. Worse, she could see the whiteness of bone sticking out of his torn flesh. It was a compound fracture, the worst kind.

"Just hold still," Cam said in a shaky voice. Digging into the left pocket on her thigh, where she kept all her emergency medical items, she found several dressings. Tearing them open, the paper fluttering away, Cam placed them where she saw blood spurting out. Gus was losing a lot of blood. Fast.

"This is going to hurt," she sobbed near his ear, "but I gotta do it. You're bleeding, Gus…. Just hold still…." And Cam pressed the dressing up beneath his arm and then applied downward pressure on top of his biceps, hoping to stop the bleeding. If she couldn't, Cam knew, he'd lie here dying before her eyes. Swallowing hard, she shut her eyes and concentrated. Gus couldn't die! She loved him. It had taken this crash for her to admit that to herself. What a fool she'd been to dodge the truth of how she felt toward him.

Gus groaned, his body arching upward. Closing his right fist, his hissed out a string of oaths in Spanish.

"I'm sorry…I'm sorry…" Cam sobbed. "I've got to stop the bleeding. This is the only way…." And she bent protectively over him, tears stinging her eyes.

Heart pounding with dread, Cam tried to get ahold

of her emotions. The crash had ripped away any pretenses. As she knelt over Gus, in an unknown canyon, without any prayer of rescue, Cam knew she loved this man, heart and soul. But was it too late?

Chapter 14

Cam shuddered inwardly as the dawn appeared, turning the sky over the canyon a dirty red color. She sat huddled against Gus, who was sleeping intermittantly, his head resting against her shoulder, his left arm in a makeshift sling. The coolness in the canyon depths made her shiver.

It had rained off and on for the rest of the night. Soaked, they had clung to one another, striving for warmth. Shaken and bruised, Cam studied the yellow and ochre walls of the canyon, sandstone cliffs that rose nearly a thousand feet straight up. They were lucky to have survived at all.

Gus stirred. Cam gently eased him into a sitting position. She saw him grimace, his right hand moving immediately to his left one in its sling.

Anxiety threaded through Cam. She saw how leached out he appeared, and she didn't miss the pain in his expression as he slowly opened his eyes. He studied her in silence.

"Are you okay?" he asked finally, his voice thick and rough.

Nodding, Cam whispered, "Yeah. Cold. Bruised. But okay. How's the arm?" She gestured toward it.

The bleeding had finally stopped with direct pressure, and Cam had never been so grateful. Looking at Gus in the grayish morning light, she could see the dark stain of blood all the way down his flight uniform to his waist. It was a grim reminder that he could have died last night.

"It hurts like hell," he muttered.

"What I'd give for some pain meds for you," Cam exclaimed, sympathy in her voice.

"I'd settle for a glass of water." He rubbed his face, trying to get alert.

"Oh, yeah," Cam said, as she slowly got to her knees. Her entire body ached. She felt as if she'd been in a multicar crash at high speed. There was a tightness along her shoulders and into her neck. *Whiplash.*

"Stay here," she said as she got to her feet. Dusting off her uniform, she ran her fingers distractedly through her hair. When she flew, she kept her hair tied up in a rubber band at the base of her neck. During the crash, the band had broken. Now her loose hair was littered with ash and sand.

"I'm going to check out what's left of the Apache," she told Gus, and rounded the corner of rock wall that had protected them from the explosion. The gravel crunched beneath her booted feet. Down in the narrow canyon lay the blackened, charred remains of the once proud Apache. Wisps of grayish smoke still rose from it as Cam approached it. The air reeked of spilled fuel and melted metal.

They had carried ammunition, but no missiles, and Cam was glad. The missiles could have detonated upon impact and she and Gus would have died in the cockpits. Running her hand through her hair again, Cam stood looking at the wreckage. There was nothing left to retrieve, she realized, now that the rain had doused the fire. No iridium phone call for help. No state-of-the-art computer equipment linking them with the outside world. Nothing.

Turning on her heel, she looked at the wall behind her. It was scorched and blackened from the original blast. Compressing her lips, she realized once more how narrowly they had escaped from death. By getting around that wall they had saved their lives.

Sighing, Cam frowned and walked around the crash site, looking for anything they could use. Right now, they were in high desert—outside the box where the search planes would start looking for them—and without water. The prospects were daunting. She knew that Gus hadn't had time to radio back their position; everything had happened too quickly.

Still, they were alive, and as Cam retraced her steps to see how Gus was doing, hope clung stubbornly within her heart. Unshaven, his hair tousled, he was sitting there, back against the wall, cradling his broken arm, his right hand resting beneath his left elbow. Pain was etched in his face, darkening his eyes. Cam's heart lurched as she knelt down on one knee near his left side. Reaching out, she gently grazed his bearded cheek. "At least," she said, "we're alive."

"That's a big one," Gus agreed, lifting his head

and holding her narrowed gaze. "Anything left of our bird?"

Shaking her head, Cam said, "No...nothing."

"I didn't get a radio message off to base."

"It's okay. We didn't have time."

Gus hung his head and scowled. "I should have seen that coming. I should have been monitoring that damned helo. I'm sorry I let you down."

"No," Cam sighed, "that was my call. I *knew* better, Gus. This is an old trick that the drug dealers used to play on us down in Peru. They would have two helos about two miles apart trying to sucker us in and shoot us down. We almost lost a couple of our Apaches to them before we caught on to their change of game tactics." Grimacing, she looked up. "I did lose one. I was commander on this flight. It's my fault. I knew better. I had that feeling, and I was ignoring it. Dammit..." She rubbed her dirty face with her hands.

"Hey," Gus rasped, reaching out with his right hand to touch her leg as she stood near him, "don't do the blame game. Neither of us knew that helo was armed with rockets."

"I'd just gotten a report yesterday," Cam said, regret in her voice as she held Gus's gaze, "from BJS. It came from Akiva and Joe. They said that Luis Rios, Javier's son, who runs four or five helicopters to shadow their coke shipments in fixed-wing aircraft, had been using that tactic with them as of late, and to be on top of it."

"That was a day ago," Gus said.

"Doesn't matter, Gus. As commander, it's my job to take these reports seriously and to change our interdiction approach as a result. I didn't.'' Her mouth flattened. Cam knew it would be a horrible black mark in her personnel jacket. More than likely she'd get yanked from her position as C.O., and someone a lot wiser and sharper would replace her. Cam shut her mind to that possibility. Right now, they had to survive this ordeal and get Gus medical help.

"They'll understand, *querida*."

The endearment brought tears to Cam's eyes. Kneeling down, she touched his thigh, then reached out and slid her fingers across his hair before she allowed them to come to rest on his cheeks again. "You know what? When all this was happening, the only thing I was praying for was for us to survive." She felt the warmth of tears running down her cheeks.

Gus lifted his uninjured hand to take hers and kiss it gently. "We're going to be okay, *querida*. And we're going to make it out of here." Her hand was dirty, smudged from greasy black smoke. Her face was streaked with a fine layer of gray dust that her tears had made tracks through. Whispering her name, Gus cupped Cam's cheek, wiping away the tears with his thumb.

"We're going to get out of this."

Sniffing, Cam sat back on her heels and self-consciously wiped her face with trembling fingers. "D-do you remember anything about the map of this area, Gus?"

He nodded. "Yeah, I do. That's what I was searching for in my brain while you were gone." He pointed down the canyon toward the opening, which wasn't far away. "I remember last night seeing a Yaqui village about twenty miles to the south of us, from our last location before the rocket was fired. Now—'' he gave her a lopsided smile filled with pain ''—it might be closer or farther away, because we were dancing around in the sky so much, trying to shake that rocket. But I know it's south of this canyon. I saw the canyon marked on my HUDs, and for whatever reason, I remember thinking that it was a Yaqui village probably a lot like the one my mom was born in. So I *know* it's there and I know the approximate location.''

Getting hold of her escaping emotions, Cam whispered, ''good,'' and ran her tear-damp fingers along the dusty fabric of her flight suit. ''I'm so glad you remember that. I didn't.''

Giving her a grin that felt more of a grimace because of the way his arms was throbbing like fire itself, Gus said, ''Funny how we all remember certain things at certain times. You know, I had the weirdest thing happen to me in the middle of that firefight.''

''What?'' Cam saw his dark brows draw down, a quizzical look on his face.

''I would swear that seconds before we got hit, I saw this jaguar covering our Apache. I know it sounds stupid, but I saw this apparition...or ghost, or whatever you want to call it. I saw the cat leap at us and the helicopter became a part of the cat.''

''Didn't your mother say she had jaguar medicine?'' Cam asked, fascinated by what Gus had seen.

''Yeah...that's right.'' Gus gave a short laugh. Grimacing because even laughter caused him pain, he looked up at her. ''Yeah, jaguar medicine. She said it protects her.''

''Well,'' Cam said wryly, ''I'm not Indian, but it

sure sounds like you either have a jaguar guardian angel or your mother's spirit is helping us survive.''

Shaking his head, Gus said, "You know, looking back on the whole thing, I remember how after that cat surrounded us, the rocket hit us. I remember thinking we were dead. I heard this growling sound in my helmet and felt a weird vibration going through me, and it wasn't the Apache coming apart around us. I heard you curse and I knew you were doing everything in your power to get us down and out of there alive. And it was weird, Cam. I felt like I was above the Apache, like a detached observer, just looking on. I saw you. I saw myself sitting there. And I saw the bird on fire.''

Cam smiled slightly. "This isn't as weird as you think. Maya, our C.O., is from the Jaguar Clan. We don't know a lot about it, or her, but talk goes around BJS about it. She has special powers because she's a member of that clan. Maya has this extraordinary sense about things. More than intuition. Snake, Wild Woman and I have all flown with her, and we've seen the power of the Jaguar Clan in action through Maya.''

"Maybe we were saved by my mother's Jaguar blood?" Gus wondered aloud. "This is the first time it's ever happened.''

"When we get back home," Cam said, "I'll be sure to share this with Maya. I'll bet she'll know what happened to you. She can clear the mystery of what happened, and maybe help you understand it better.''

"Yeah, because I never felt my arm break. I never felt the pain, Cam, until you helped drag me away from that bird.'' Gus shook his head, wonder in his voice. ''I never felt the crash.''

Rubbing her aching shoulder, Cam muttered, ''I sure as hell did. I feel like I've got whiplash.''

Gazing at her, Gus felt his heart open. ''You had to be in your body to get us down safely,'' he said. ''You'd have felt everything. For whatever reason, and I don't know how it happened, I wasn't in my body during the crash.''

''Be nice if your were that way now. I can see the pain in your face.''

Nodding, Gus said, ''No kidding.''

Looking around, Cam took a deep breath. ''Well, come on. We've got a long walk ahead of us. I want to take advantage of the cloud cover and time of day. We'll lose less water this way.''

Frowning, Gus said, ''Go alone, Cam. I'd just slow you down.''

Her heart pounded once, strongly. She stared at Gus, her lips parting. ''No way!'' Her voice echoed down the canyon. ''I'm not leaving you here!''

''Hey, calm down,'' Gus said gently. He raised his hand toward her. Cam's face was a mass of raw feelings, and he saw the anger and anguish in her eyes. ''I'm really weak, Cam. I lost a lot of blood. I don't even know if I *can* walk. You can't carry me, not with this arm the way it is. I weigh more than you do.'' Gus forced a smile he didn't feel.

Cam's face grew dark and her mouth twisted. ''Gus, I'm *not* leaving you!'' She heard the desperation in her voice. Inwardly, she was shaking like a leaf caught in a massive storm. Her stomach knotted. ''How do I know if I leave you that the druggies won't come back here looking for us? Hunting us down?''

Gus touched the holster positioned against his right thigh. "I'd hold them off."

Snorting, Cam rasped, "Not for long! We each have one clip in our pistol and another on reserve and that's it! There's no way I'm leaving you here, Gus. I just won't!"

The anguish in her voice tore at him. Tears were splattering down Cam's cheeks. He saw the turmoil in her eyes, the way her mouth contorted and her lower lip trembled. Feeling bad, he said, "Listen to me, will you? I'm in no shape to go anywhere. You can walk a lot faster without me. Twenty-minute miles, Cam. You can make it there in ten hours."

"Tough. You're coming with me, Gus. I don't care if it takes twice that long, I'm not leaving you behind." Her voice had risen to an almost hysterical level. Shaking, Cam scrambled to her feet. "I left Maya. I swore after that that I'd *never* leave another person in the field. I just won't do it!"

Closing his eyes, Gus remembered how Cam had told him of the awful decision she had had to make on a previous mission. She had to leave Maya, who was unconscious, behind to be captured by the druggies, or stay with her and be captured along with her. Opening his eyes, Gus held Cam's teary gaze.

"This isn't the same, *querida*," he said in a quiet tone meant to soothe her. "I'm not Maya. There are no druggies. This is different."

"It's no different to me!" Cam cried. She leaned down and slid her arm beneath his right armpit and around his back. "Now get up, Gus! We're doin' this together or not at all!'' And she reared upward, taking his full weight with her.

Weakness seeped through Gus. Cam's quick, strong movement caused him to grow temporarily light-headed. Wrapping his good arm around her shoulders, he steadied himself against her as his feet found purchase beneath him. Knees feeling mushy, he gasped as the effort created waves of unrelenting pain up his left arm.

''Hold still....'' he rasped.

Cam was breathing hard, but holding Gus firmly. Unmoving, she saw his face blanche almost white. Her heart sank. Maybe he was right. Maybe he couldn't be moved. Cam felt him struggling to get his feet beneath him and become stable. A gasp tore from his taut lips as he managed to stand on his own. She loosened her hold slightly, but not much, unsure if Gus really could balance himself.

Though he understood why Cam wouldn't leave him, Gus knew they'd be in trouble if they tried to make the trek together. But he also knew that because of her past, Cam would rather sit here in this canyon waiting for search parties to find them, than leave him alone. Oh, he knew that Luis and Antonio had probably put in a call for help when they saw he and Cam hadn't returned to base on time. That was a given. But the search would be concentrated within the box designated by their FAA flight plan. Rescue aircraft wouldn't be searching outside of it for days, not until they'd combed that area first. Without water, Gus knew, they could die before they were found. The rain that had fallen wasn't enough to create puddles. The desert had been dry and instantly sucked all the moisture up.

Grimly, he forced himself to stand on his feet, planting them apart. Feeling Cam's strength, her steadying arm about his waist, he kept his right arm around her shoulders just in case. Biting down hard on his lower lip, he allowed the waves of heat and throbbing pain to pass through him. Slowly, the pain began to ease as he remained still and standing.

"You know what?" he said, his voice scratchy and low.

"What?" Cam breathed, watching him closely.

"I think we can do this...."

Her heart soared with gratefulness. "Okay," Cam muttered, "then let's try, Gus. One small step at a time. I know every time you put your foot down, it's going to jolt that broken arm of yours...."

"Yeah, and I don't want to rip open that artery that's just clotted shut, either," he reminded her dryly. "I don't want to bleed to death."

"No," Cam whispered, her voice off-key, "I don't want you to, either."

Raising one eyebrow, Gus asked, "You ready, partner?"

Cam fought back the tears. She was highly emotional at the moment. Part of it was the letdown after surviving a fiery crash, the aftermath of the huge surge of adrenaline. The other was fear of abandoning Gus. He didn't fight her on that, and she was relieved. "I'm ready, partner. Let's go. One small step at a time."

Girding himself, Gus nodded. "Yeah, very careful, mincing steps."

"I'll hold on to you," Cam swore. "I won't let you go. I promise."

Those words packed a lot of power and emotion behind them, Gus realized, as he began to take tentative, careful steps forward. Cam matched her stride to his. Every step jolted his arm. It was agony. But it kept his head clear. The sand beneath them was littered with gravel and small rocks. Gus concentrated on not slipping.

"At this pace," he groaned as they moved slowly down the canyon toward the exit point, "it will take us two days to reach the village."

"That's okay," Cam said. As they left the canyon behind and climbed slowly upward, the desert around them gradually revealed itself. Above, the low-hanging clouds, like strips of bumpy cotton kept the rising sun at bay. There was cactus here and there on the flat yellow reaches. In the distance, very far off—maybe fifty miles, in Cam's estimation—rose dark blue mountains, their peaks sharply pointed. Gus headed in that direction.

The desert floor was a dark yellow color due to the recent rains. The only vegetation was cactus.

"We're in luck," Gus told her. "See that cactus just ahead?"

"Yeah."

"It's a prickly pear. You got your Swiss Army knife on you?"

Cam nodded. "Yeah. What do you want me to do?"

"Let's stop here, let me rest for a few minutes." His knees were feeling like jelly. "First knock off some of those oval, flat pieces. With your knife, cut out the thorns. And then we can skin them. The pulp inside will give us the water we need."

Heartened, Cam gently helped Gus into a sitting position, his legs crossed. "Sounds good. My mouth feels like dried plaster." It was tough to form words properly, and she had been slurring them as a result of her mouth being so dry. The idea of a water source bucked up Cam's spirits.

Gus watched as Cam did exactly as he instructed. The prickly pear was a series of leathery, leaflike appendages, oval shaped, growing out of one another. They didn't have a lot of thorns, and contained enough water to survive on.

As Cam nudged the thorny pieces toward him with her boot, he drew his knife out of the lower pocket of his flight suit. Unable to open it, he handed it to Cam, who straightened the blade and gave it back to him.

"Thanks," he said. "Now watch me. As a kid, my mom taught me how to skin a cactus without ending up like a pincushion in the process." And he flashed Cam a grin.

Kneeling in front of Gus, she watched him expertly dethorn the prickly pear. Placing the tip of his boot on one end of it, he made several criss-crossing cuts through the tough, leathery surface. Once the skin had been scored, he used the tip of his knife to pull it off, leaving only the pulp. He was good at dethorning the fruit and she marveled at his skill and speed, even using only one hand. "Who would ever think that something like that, taught to you as a kid, would come in handy now?" she laughed. Hope pounded through Cam. Gus looked a tiny bit better. He was still wan, but there was some pink to his cheeks beneath his dark growth of beard.

"Yeah, you never know," Gus said, returning her smile. With her help, he skinned the cactus. "Now, cut up the pieces into bite-size chunks."

Cam followed his instructions, then held up the first morsel. "Here…"

Taking it, Gus popped it into his mouth. The water in the cactus tasted delicious.

"Try it," he urged.

Cam took a piece herself. The cactus was firm and fibrous, and she tasted a slight astringent bitterness, but water was released as she chewed.

"You can chew on it, get the water out and either swallow it as a food source or spit it out." Gus grinned and took another piece she handed him. "The only bad news about this is your stomach might feel a bit nauseous because you aren't used to the taste or texture. But you should be able to keep it down."

Nodding, Cam knelt there sharing the cactus with him. Her stomach did roll, but she wanted to absorb the life-giving water too much to allow the sensation to stop her from eating.

Within twenty minutes, they'd sated their thirst. Gus looked better, and Cam felt stronger. Without water, it would have been a terrible journey, she knew.

"I'm glad," she told him, wiping her fingers on the thighs of her flight suit, "that you have desert survival training."

Grinning, Gus said, "You'd better hope we find that village sooner rather than later."

"Why?" Cam ask, melting beneath his warm

smile. She saw life coming back to his eyes, and her heart soared. As she stood, Cam stopped fooling herself. She loved Gus. Unequivocally. Without reservation. The crash had brought it all home to her. As she put their knives away, she wondered if he loved her.

"Because we need protein," Gus said as she helped him stand. The pain was intense as he leaned against her for support. Her arm, wrapped firmly around his waist, steadied him. "Protein in a desert comes in the form of critters. Insects." He saw her wrinkle her dirty nose.

"Ugh, I remember the survival training the army gave us back in school." Shivering, Cam muttered, "I sure hope we find that village soon. I *hate* eating bugs!"

Chuckling, Gus looked around the flat, quiet desert. He heard the lone cry of a coyote somewhere off in the distance. The day was getting brighter, and he saw rifts and openings in the clouds above, where slashes of blue sky appeared.

"I dunno," he said congenially, teasing her, "I've eaten my share of them. My mother's people know which ones are tasty and fortifying if they can't find a rabbit or peccary to eat instead."

Snorting, Cam felt his teasing banter bolster her hopes. The love she felt for Gus ballooned. Having him beside her—his strength, his warmth and closeness—was really all she ever needed.

"We've got pistols. I'm all for finding some poor rabbit to be our meal tonight," she muttered. "Let the bugs live."

Chuckling even though it hurt, Gus gave her a warm look. "You know what, *querida?*"

At the endearment, Cam felt heat spread from her neck to her cheeks as he held her gaze. They walked slowly, but together. "What?"

"I'm glad you're here. And I'm glad you decided to haul my sorry ass along for this walk."

Grinning, she said, "Thanks, Gus. That means a lot to me." And it did.

Sighing, he looked across the desert. "This is a beautiful place. Full of life. Most people don't ever think of the desert as being alive, but it is." He tightened his arm briefly around her shoulders. "And I'm glad I'm sharing it with you...."

Chapter 15

"**I**'m inspired," Gus told Cam as they camped within a small cave they'd found near sunset. She hunkered over a small fire just outside the cave, turning a freshly killed rabbit, which she'd skinned, over the fire. The meat was browning and sizzling.

Cam gave him a dirty look as she held the rabbit over the flames. "Yeah, so was I. There's no way I was gonna eat bugs tonight, Morales."

Grinning tiredly, he sat on the yellow sand and leaned against the wall. "See? I'm good for you in exciting and unexpected ways," he teased. Seeing Cam return his smile lifted his tiredness momentarily. Supporting his aching, swollen left arm with his right hand, he absorbed Cam's features as the shadows of the night stalked them.

Giving Gus a warm look, Cam tried to keep her worry to herself. Twice today, as they'd rested, she'd pulled off the bandage to check his arm. There was little bleeding, thank God. Still, his entire upper arm was swelling up like a balloon because the bone needed to be reset. Anxiety ate at her. She saw how wan Gus looked. Throughout the day, he'd been courageous in not complaining of the pain she knew came with every step.

The rabbit was a fat one. Cam had been looking for any kind of animal on their walk toward the village. Luckily, a male jackrabbit with long, black-tipped ears had bounded out in front of them. She'd used her pistol and shot the animal. Though she'd felt badly about it because she didn't like killing anything, she knew that in order for them to keep going and hopefully reach help by tomorrow, they needed food as fuel. Slowly turning the rabbit over the flames, she shifted the stick it was skewered on between her hands.

"That sure smells good," Gus murmured. The desert was quiet tonight after the storm the night before. The thirsty earth had soaked up all the rain that had fallen and was now a pale ochre color once more. He watched Cam from beneath half-closed eyes. They'd found a small pool of water in a rock crevice which had sated their thirst earlier.

"I'm starving, too," Cam said.

"You should be. You practically carried me all day long." Gus was surprised at her strength, both physical and internal. He knew Cam wasn't going to leave him behind. The stubborn set of her mouth and the burning look in her eyes told him that.

"How many miles do you think we made today?"

she asked, pushing her hair off her forehead. How she wished for a brush and comb.

Mouth quirking, Gus said, "Maybe ten… It's hard to judge out here."

Nodding, Cam said, "Yeah. That's what I thought. Around ten."

"If all things are equal," he said, "and we didn't fly too far from the last position on my HUD, that village should show up sometime tomorrow evening if we can keep the same pace as today."

Cam shoved the end of the long, sturdy stick into the ground and surrounded it with large rocks, leaving the rabbit at just the right height to sizzle over the flames. Getting up, she scoured the area illuminated by firelight to find more pieces of dry wood for their campfire. With mesquite shrubs growing nearby, sticks were easy to locate. Gathering them in her arms as she walked, her boots crunching on the yellow sand, Cam looked up.

The sky was darkening swiftly now; only a hint of the peach-colored sunset remained, a thin rim on the western horizon. Just above the eastern horizon was a glowing white star. Turning back toward Gus, Cam said, "That's got to be Venus in the east. Isn't she beautiful?"

The cave opening faced east, so it was easy for Gus to see where she was pointing. His gaze moved back to Cam as she placed the fuel near the fire. "What I'm looking at is beautiful. In fact, she makes the planet Venus pale in comparison." All day Gus had wanted to establish intimacy with Cam. But their dangerous situation hadn't warranted it. Now, he hoped, it would. When Cam lifted her face, shadowed by the flickering light, he saw the surprise in her features.

"You're prettier than any star or planet," he said, giving her a slight, one-cornered smile. No matter how he sat or what position he tried, Gus couldn't relieve the pain in his arm. It was growing worse, but he wasn't going to tell Cam that. She was worried enough, and knowing her, was probably feeling as if the responsibility for the loss of their Apache rested solely on her shoulders. All day he'd seen her waging an internal war between sadness and guilt over the incident.

"Thanks..." Cam said, giving him a shy look. "I've never had a guy see me like that before." And she hadn't. Gus had a very poetic and romantic side to him, a side she loved....

There was that word again. Frowning, Cam picked up the stick with the meat on it and began to rotate it slowly over the flames once more. The crash had shaken loose all her suppressed feelings toward Gus. Did he love her? Could he love another woman who took risks? She had no answers. And she didn't have strength to devote to anything but their survival right now.

Somehow, Gus wanted to take Cam's guilt and worries away. He understood where she was coming from, and he knew there would be a military inquiry into the Apache being shot down. But that didn't mean Cam would lose her C.O. position and be drummed out of the army, as she feared.

"Tell me something," he said. "What would you do in your life that you haven't done already if you could?"

"Uh-oh," Cam said with a quiet laugh, "the philosopher is coming out. Are you bored, Gus? Sitting over there, helpless? Feeling like you should be helping me or doing this?" Cam pointed at the rabbit on the skewer.

Forcing a smile, Gus felt buoyed by Cam's laughter in spite of the relentless pain that moved like grinding waves up and down his arm and shoulder. "Yeah, you're right on all counts. Are you a mind reader, *querida?*" He purposely used that endearment. Instantly, he saw Cam's narrowed eyes soften. Her mouth relaxed, too. How he wanted to take her into his arms and hold her, and whisper to her that all would be well. But he couldn't....

Shaking her head, Cam tested the meat. "If I was a mind reader, I'd have known that that helo was armed with rockets." The meat was dark brown and oozing with juices now. Cam peeled back a piece to see if it was done inside. It was. *Good.* Getting to her feet, she took the rabbit over to Gus. Sitting down on his right side, facing him, she held the rabbit between them.

As she pushed the end of the stick into the ground so that the meat hung between them and they could peel off chunks to eat, he gave her a thoughtful look.

"Thanks. You're saving my neck, yet again."

"You owe me, Morales. Big time."

Enjoying her teasing, he popped the first bit of meat into his mouth. It was hot and delicious, just what he needed. "I like owing you," he teased back. He saw her grin. "This is good. You're a great chef, Ms. Anderson. Five star, if I don't miss my guess."

"Let's stick to the owing one another, shall we?"

Cam forced herself to eat slowly and savor every bite of meat. Her stomach had been in knots all day with worry and anxiety. She hadn't realized how hungry she was until just now. But maybe it was the company she was keeping, too. Eyeing him tenderly, Cam saw that several strands of his hair dipped onto his brow. With her left hand, she pushed them back into place. She liked touching him.

"I'll write you an IOU," Gus said with a grin. "And you can collect it from me once we get back to base."

"You're on," Cam chortled. And then she became serious. "You know, the only good thing about this," she confided, "is that I can touch you whenever I want. I don't have to worry about prying eyes or military regs getting in the way."

His flesh tingled briefly where Cam had slid her fingertips against his brow. "I agree. We should use this time productively." Catching her hand as she lifted it away, Gus pressed a long, slow kiss to the back of it and then released it. The surprise in her eyes made him feel good. Without a doubt, Gus knew he loved her. Fiercely. Without compromise. Wanting to broach the topic with her, but not knowing when would be best, he watched a look of languor come to her eyes for a moment after he'd kissed her hand.

"You are so gallant," Cam whispered. Her skin tingled where his strong mouth had caressed her flesh. No other man had kissed her hand with such a flourish. No other man had kissed her hand at all. Gus was a throwback to an age where gentlemen were truly that, and treated women with remarkable respect.

"Me? What about you, *querida?* I don't think *gal-*

lant is a word reserved exclusively for men, do you?''
He ate another chunk of the meat and held her gaze.
''Gallantry is like chivalry.''

''Is that how you see me?'' Cam wondered out
loud.

''As a heroine? Yes. Courageous. Fearless.''

''Forget the fearlessness,'' Cam growled. ''I was
scared as hell up there last night. When that rocket
was fired, I about died. I just wasn't expecting it. I
should have foreseen the possibility, but I didn't. I
was too focused on getting the numbers off that first
plane.''

Shaking his head, Gus wiped his greasy fingers on
the thigh of his uniform and then reached out. ''Stop
it, will you? I've never seen anyone savage themselves like you do, *querida*.'' He stroked her cheek
in a loving gesture. Maybe he couldn't come clean
with his feelings toward Cam yet, but Gus wanted her
to know that he cared deeply for her, anyway. Judging
from the softness in her eyes after he caressed her
cheek, he knew he could lift her spirits and stop her
from worrying so much. It was a wonderful discovery. A powerful one. Maybe he couldn't help her
gather firewood, make a fire or find meat, but he could
tend the garden of her heart and emotions. In that
way, he could help her.

''I just can't shake it, Gus. I screwed up with Maya.
I've screwed up here. All I do is screw up.''

''No, you don't,'' Gus growled. ''I don't think any
board of inquiry is going to hold you accountable for
what happened last night. We lost a rotorcraft, but we
survived. They can replace the Apache. We're a lot
harder to replace.''

Pursing her lips, she saw that the rabbit was pretty much eaten. Taking the carcass off the skewer, she picked delicately at it and found a few more morsels, handing them to Gus. He needed it most because pain was stealing his energy, sapping his strength.

"Maybe you're right," she muttered.

"I know I am." Thanking her for the last bits of meat, he made sure she got half of them, anyway. Cam had already dethorned more cactus, skinned it and cut it into bite-size chunks. He handed her some. It served as a vegetable with their meal.

"I can't say I'm thrilled with prickly pear," she told him, chewing on a small piece to get the fluid out of it. The water from the small pool they'd found earlier was gone and Cam knew they had to get as much fluid in them as possible.

"No, it's not exactly a Starbucks mocha latte, is it?" He smiled.

"What a die-hard sense of humor you have." Cam looked out of the cave mouth. The darkness was complete. Above them, a canopy of stars twinkled overhead. From somewhere out on the desert came the lonely, serrating cry of a coyote.

"I don't like the other choice," Gus told her.

Cam turned around, her back to the wall, only inches away from him. She needed his closeness. His optimism. Tipping her head back against the rock, she sighed and closed her eyes.

"You're my counterpart," she told him in a low tone. After wiping her fingers on her flight suit, she opened her eyes and found his hand. Slipping her fingers into his, she closed her eyes again and sighed.

"You make me happy, Gus. You have a way of pulling me out of a tailspin of darkness."

"Isn't that what people who care for each other do?" he asked, squeezing her hand.

Right now, in that instant, Cam wanted to turn to Gus, seek refuge in his arms. It was impossible under the circumstances, so she focused on feeling the warm strength of his hand around hers. "Yes...it is...."

Frowning, Gus took a deep breath. Just getting to talk to Cam helped ease some of the pain he was in. "Listen, I need to talk with you, *querida.* I don't know if this is the right time or not, but here goes...."

Cam opened her eyes slightly and slanted him a look. The firelight outside the cave highlighted Gus's sharp, strong profile. She saw that his brows were knitted. "Okay..."

"The crash," Gus began in a low tone, "changed a lot of things for me, Cam. Before it...well, I thought I had my life pretty well figured out. But now I find I don't. Maybe I never did, and I was just fooling myself."

Her heart beat a little harder. Feeling his hand tighten around hers a little more firmly, she whispered, "Go on...."

"When we were falling out of the sky," Gus said, "I thought we were going to die. And I had only one regret."

Heart hammering as she felt his tension, she asked, "What was that?"

Lifting her hand, he kissed the back of it tenderly and held her probing gaze. "That I hadn't told you I love you, Camelia Anderson. That I was too scared because of my past to say anything. I didn't think I could ever put my heart on the line again with a woman who had a dangerous profession. I found out that wasn't true, *querida*. As we fell out of the sky, I was crying inside because I'd never said those words to you. I didn't want to die, or have you die without knowing that I love you...."

Gulping, Cam sat up and turned toward him. Gripping his hand, she stared into his smoldering cinnamon gaze. "You love me?"

"Yeah. Why are you asking it that way?" His mouth hitched up slightly. "You're looking at me like I'm an alien from outer space who just landed in front of you."

"Well..." Cam hesitated, looking to the right, then the left, and finally back at Gus. He had such a tender and patient expression on his face, filled with love for her. That was how he felt. An incredible warmth spread through Cam's chest and moved downward.

"I never thought," she began lamely, "that you could...well, like me, much less love me. I just never expected that, Gus. I knew your past. I tried to tell myself that because of it, there was no place for me in your life."

"And where did you want to be in my life?" he whispered, holding her sparkling green gaze, which glimmered with tears.

It was put up or shut up time, Cam realized. Gus was being brutally honest with her. He deserved no less for his bravery. She held his hand between her own and stared down at it.

"I didn't dare dream that you could love me, Gus, the way I was falling in love with you." Her voice broke. "From the moment I saw you, my heart was doin' crazy things. You seemed unreal to me."

"Why unreal?"

"Because—" Cam cleared her throat nervously "—you seemed too perfect, like the guy I always dreamed about meeting and falling in love with. But I always thought that guy was a dream. That a man like you could not exist in reality." Cam managed a self-deprecating smile as she looked up and connected with his heated eyes. Her body responded hotly to that look.

"Dreams can come true," Gus told her. "I ought to know. The woman I never thought would exist is here right now with me, and holding my hand."

"Oh, Gus…"

"We're both knee-jerking from our past," he said. "We're both fearful, for different reasons."

"Yeah…" Cam muttered. "There's that word again—*fear.*"

"Amazing how much fear runs our life, eh?" Gus grinned a little through the haze of pain. Despite that, he felt his heart opening and the resulting warmth turn down the pain a few notches. It was a miraculous thing. Moving his fingers along her slender wrist and long fingers, he whispered, "I think we've faced the worst fear of all—death. And we've survived, Cam. Maybe we oughta reorder our attitudes and tell fear to get the hell out of our lives so it doesn't muck up anything else for us."

"How long have you felt like this toward me?" she wondered, her flesh tingling wildly as he traced each of her fingers and then the palm of her hand.

"Since the minute I saw you."

"Then…we both—"

"Yeah, got knocked over the head and heart by one another."

"Only," Cam said wonderingly, "neither of us had the guts to admit it to ourself, much less to one another."

"Yep," Gus said. "But air crashes have a way of leveling the playing field, you know?"

Nodding, words choking in her throat, Cam slowly got to her knees. She faced Gus, her thigh against his as she gently placed her arms around his neck. Taking care not to put any weight on his left shoulder, she smiled at him. Their noses were inches apart. She could feel the warmth and moisture of his breath against her skin.

"Your courage deserves to be rewarded, darling…." And she leaned down and found his mouth with her own.

Gus raised his right hand and slid it across her strong back as he cherished the feel of her tentative, searching lips against his. Groaning softly, he whispered, "I wish I could love you right now, *querida.* We'd lie down here, together, in one another's arms. We'd make this night sing with our happiness…."

Moaning his name, Cam drowned beneath his poetic words. Truly, Gus was a romantic of the most wonderful kind. She felt his hand graze her shoulder and then move in a slow, exploring caress down her spine. Oh, to be loved by him! Her body ached to be touched, tamed and molded by his hands. That was impossible, so Cam simply absorbed the feel of his mouth claiming hers strongly and hotly. As she ran her fingers through his hair, massaging his scalp and

memorizing everything about him, Cam's joy soared.
Gus loved her. She found that amazing. Wonderful.
Humbling.

Gus didn't want their kiss to end. Cam was being
so careful not to bump him or touch his left shoulder
as she kissed and caressed him. When she eased
away, he saw the rose color in her cheeks, the bright-
ness in her eyes and the love that shone in them—for
him.

"What we have," he told her huskily, "is so
rare...." Taking her hand, he kissed it tenderly. "Life
is so tenuous, *querida*. I want to take every minute I
have and live it with you."

"I feel the same, Gus," she whispered, her voice
off-key. Cam's mind went to all the sordid possibilities that could destroy what they'd just admitted to
one another. Gus was right: life was so tenuous. Last
night they'd nearly died. Today they had professed
their love to one another. Feeling beat up inwardly,
yet glowingly alive, Cam knelt at his side, unable to
speak.

"Come on," Gus urged her gently, "let's get ready
to go to bed. We've got a long day ahead of us tomorrow, and a good night's sleep will help a lot."

Biting back her worry, Cam nodded. "I wish I
could sleep in your arms."

"So do I, *querida*. Someday. Soon," he promised.

Worry edged out her joy as she released his hand
and slowly got to her feet. Things had to be taken
care of around their camp before she could join him.
He slowly moved from his sitting position and laid
down on his right side, placing his right arm beneath
his head as a pillow.

Cam smiled down at him. "I'll be there in a little bit. I want to get rid of this rabbit carcass first. We don't need a pack of coyotes coming to visit us tonight."

Gus nodded and smiled. "You're a great outdoorswoman, *querida*."

Cam had other worries other than coyotes, but she didn't mention them to Gus as she moved out of the cave. How did she know for sure that the druggies who'd shot them down wouldn't try to find them? She'd underestimated them once. She wasn't about to do it again. By tamping out the fire and sleeping in a cave, they were less likely to be found.

No, life was tenuous, as Gus had said. And they weren't out of danger yet—not by a long shot.

Chapter 16

Gus staggered drunkenly against Cam as she supported his full weight. Her cry of relief at the sight of the Yaqui village, not two miles in the distance, made him continue putting one foot in front of the other. The sun was low on the western horizon, sending long shadows through the brush and cactus that littered the hard sand surface around them.

Cam could barely contain her joy, though she forced herself to continue the same, slow pace. Gus was sagging more and more against her as the day wore on. He had a fever and that worried her greatly. That meant infection from the compound fracture. Now, more than ever, the urgency to get him to a hospital for treatment and surgery thrummed through her.

"We're going to make it!" Cam said, her voice breaking with joy. The Yaqui village was small and laid out in a circle around a main flat, dusty plaza. Squinting, she saw a number of women in long, colorful cotton skirts moving about the adobe buildings.

Grimacing, Gus whispered, "Yes...." His head swam with fever. He wasn't always sure where his feet were going to land. Yet Cam was so strong and steady for him. A fierce love of her swept through him. Today had been a special hell on him. When he'd awakened early in the grayness of the dawn, he had broken out in a heavy sweat with a raging fever. All day he'd fought the vertigo, the throbbing, pounding pain in his left arm, and kept trying to think clearly. Without Cam, her soft coaxing voice, her strong arm around him, Gus knew he'd never have made it this far. It seemed with every step her determination to get them to help grew. Amazed by the strength he felt radiating from her, Gus truly began to appreciate her inner toughness and resiliency in an emergency.

"Listen," he gasped, carefully stepping forward, "the Yaqui..." He grimaced, tightening his lips and closing his eyes as Cam steadied him.

Breathing savagely against the pain, Gus opened his eyes. Cam kept up their slow, mincing pace. "The Yaqui," he rasped. "They have a woman leader and a man leader, though they're matriarchal. They'll speak some Spanish intermixed with their own language. In case I go unconscious, tell them that I'm the son of a Yaqui woman. They'll give you extra special care. They take care of their own, Cam. Okay?"

"Yeah," she said, "I hear you." She saw several people walking toward them now that they had been spotted. "I just pray they have a phone—anything—so we can get you help pronto."

"Don't be disappointed if they don't," Gus warned her. Sweat dribbled into his eyes and he blinked it away. The fever was making him feel light-headed. He knew his temperature was high, maybe 103 degrees. If it went any higher, Gus would become delirious. Already he was seeing things that weren't really there. Every once in a while, he'd see a gold-coated jaguar with black crescent-moon spots walking near him. He'd blink and the apparition would disappear. And then, as he gave in to the fever again, the jaguar would reappear. Not wanting to mention it to Cam for fear of scaring her even more than she already was about his deteriorating condition, Gus forced himself to concentrate on one thing only: putting one foot ahead of the other.

Heart speeding up, Cam raised her hand as three people, all middle-aged, began to trot toward them. Hope flared in her. "They see us, Gus. They see us!"

Hearing the joy in her voice, he groaned. The ground was flat, but small pebbles made the sole of his boot roll, causing him to momentarily lose his balance. Cam's arm would automatically tighten around him to keep him upright. Hanging his head, he clenched his teeth. His left arm felt like a huge, swollen sausage. And it looked like it, too. Gus worried about losing his arm. If they couldn't get him medical help soon, he worried that partial loss of his arm's function would be the very least he would suffer. If that happened, he could no longer fly. Traumatized by the possibility, he pushed that aggravating fear away.

Within twenty minutes, Cam met with the village elders. Two were women in their fifties, with steel-gray hair and black, flashing eyes. The man—she assumed he was the other leader—was also gray-haired, with dark brown, weathered skin. As they drew to a halt, Cam saw their eyes widening. First she saw fear there as they stared at them. And then, when Gus raised his head and began to speak in Yaqui, Cam saw the fear go away and relief replace their original looks.

She knew only Spanish, and not the mother tongue of these short, thin people. They were dressed in colorful cotton garments, with leather sandals on their feet. The man carried a rake over his shoulder, as if just coming from a garden somewhere near the village.

Gus smiled tightly. "Okay, Cam, here's the deal. They have no phones. Senora Marquez, the woman to your left, who's wearing the red skirt, is the leader of this village. Her husband, Juan Marquez, is also a leader. He's the guy with the rake." Gus halted, pain ripping through him. Biting back a groan, he said, "I told them who I was. They want us to come back to the village with them."

"Good," she said, smiling and nodding to them in thanks. They smiled and nodded back.

"There's more," Gus groaned. "There's a drug dealer that comes once a week to their village. If these people don't find peyote buttons on the cactus, and give them to him to sell, he pistol whips someone in the village. They're basically unprotected out here. They have no way to defend themselves against this guy."

Frowning, Cam looked around at the flat stretches of the desert, at the mountains, jagged and black, rising loftily behind the small town. "Well…does this guy come by car?"

"That's the bad part," Gus whispered. Sweat ran into his eyes. He could feel himself beginning to weaken. His knees felt like jelly. "He flies in by helo once a week. And he's armed. His name is Robert Clark. He's a *norteamericano* drug dealer. Apparently, he works for a local drug lord out of Tijuana. That's all they know."

"I see," she said grimly, looking around. "Okay, let's get you to the village, Gus. We'll worry about these other things later. Right now, all I want to do is contact someone for help."

With all the water she wanted to drink and hot food to eat, Cam felt like her old self within the next two hours. The Yaqui village was small; perhaps thirty people lived here, all related to one another. Gus lay in the headwoman's adobe home on a pallet of soft grass with a blanket thrown across it. The medicine woman, Senora Ramos, had cleaned Gus's wound, placed damp, warm herbs around the ugly red, swollen flesh and rewrapped it with a clean bandage. He was sleeping, the fever having taken a terrible toll on his strength.

Worried, Cam walked around the village. Night was coming, the eastern sky darkening while the red-and-peach-colored sunset spread in a breathtaking wash on the western horizon. She was followed everywhere by curious children of all ages. Their Spanish was broken, but she managed to converse with them. Earlier, Senor Marquez had taken her outside the village that wrapped around the plaza, to where the helicopter would land.

Cam had seen how the dust had been disturbed by a powerful blast of rotors. When she tried to find out what kind of helicopter the drug runner flew, the kindly gentleman had shrugged and opened his hands. He'd smiled, revealing a gap where his two front teeth were missing. More than anything, Cam wanted to know if the chopper was armed.

Her thoughts swung back to Gus as she reconnoitered the area around the village. It was flat desert with a lot of brush, and a few stubborn trees that defied the heat and still survived through the summer. The Yaqui had a well, a shallow one, but it supplied water to their massive gardens, which were sprinkled about the area.

"Señor?" Cam asked as they walked back toward the center of the village. "When does this helicopter come to your town?"

Shrugging, Juan said, "No one knows when he will fly in on his devil bird, Senorita Camelia." He waved his hands in a frustrated gesture. "You will hear him coming. The devil bird is loud. Everyone—" he waved his hands, sadness in his tone "—runs and hides in their adobe homes. They fear him. He lands over there and comes with his gun drawn. If I do not bring him a bag of peyote buttons right away, he will go through each home, tearing it up, breaking our pottery, ripping things apart, to find them."

"The bastard," Cam whispered tautly. She flexed her fists in rage. "How long has he been doing this?" She looked down at the lean farmer, who wore a long-sleeved, white peasant shirt and a pair of faded jeans that were frayed on the bottom.

"Just the last year, *señorita*. He came out of no-where—" Juan pointed to the west "—out of the place of death."

Cam nodded. That was where Tijuana lay, to the west of them. "How far from this city are we, *señor?*"

Laughing, Juan shrugged. "Oh, many, many hours, *señorita*. The nearest phone that you speak of is fifty miles farther to the south. There is a Catholic mission, a small one—there at San Anselmo." He pointed in that direction.

Grimly, Cam's mind spun. Fifty more miles. "And you have no way to get there? No car? A truck?" She'd not seen a single vehicle.

"No, *señorita. Nada.* None. You must walk. Oh, you could take one of the donkeys that we use to plow with, to plant our corn every year, but you are much larger than the poor beast. You would do best to walk there."

"I see...." Cam said. They entered the village, where long shadows were falling across the main plaza. A number of black pots hung from tripods there, the small fires beneath them tended by women. The odor of rice and beans wafted temptingly through the dusk. Dogs and children were standing around each cooking pot, which was being stirred by a woman.

"Tomorrow," Juan said, patting her arm, "I will have Jose, my son, who is our strongest young man, take you to San Anselmo. Your man, Senor Morales, is very sick. He needs help we cannot give him."

Nodding, Cam halted at the door of the man's dark brown adobe home. There was a bright red wool blanket in place of a door. The house had three rooms. Thanks to their generosity, Juan and his wife had given up their bedroom to her and Gus. "Thanks, Juan. And yes, if Jose could be ready to leave early tomorrow? Say at dawn? We might be able to make San Anselmo in a day's time."

"Sí, sí," Juan agreed eagerly, gesturing for her to enter. "Come, come, my wife makes tortillas for dinner. Please, come in...."

Gus groaned as he felt a damp, cool cloth being pressed against his hot forehead. Lying on his right side, a lumpy pillow beneath his head, he barely opened his eyes. Because his fever was high, everything was blurred in the semidarkness. Seeing Cam leaning over him, cloth in hand, her eyes filled with worry, he managed a twisted smile.

"You're the most beautiful apparition I've seen so far," he muttered. Feeling thirsty, his mouth gummy, he tried to sit up.

"Take it easy," Cam whispered, and supported him as he eased into sitting position so that his back was against the earthen wall. Searching his washed-out face, and seeing the fever in his darkened eyes, Cam reached out and wiped his sweaty face with the cool compress. "Are you thirsty? Hungry? It's nearly 2100."

The flickering of an old oil lamp in the corner of the room made shadows dance before Gus's eyes. Blinking, he saw a jaguar, he'd seen the same one earlier, sitting in the doorway where a dark blue cotton blanket separated this room from the next one. He was having another feverish hallucination.

Lifting his chin, he looked up at Cam. "Yeah…I'm thirsty…."

Nodding, Cam reached for a bottle of water. "Let me help," she murmured, crouching at his right side. Gus looked terrible. When he tried to lift his hand to help guide the bottle to his lips, his fingers shook badly.

"Easy," Cam crooned softly as she placed her arm around his shoulders. Gus was weak—alarmingly so. His hand fell limply at his side. He couldn't hold it up at all. When she held the lip of the flask to his mouth, he drank deeply.

Dribbles of water trickled from the corners of his mouth when Cam took away the bottle. Sated, he tried to lift his right hand again. He couldn't. "I feel like a baby," he confided, his voice husky. "Useless…"

"You've got a high fever," Cam whispered as she sat back on her heels next to him. "Are you hungry, Gus? You need to eat. You have to keep your strength up. Senora Marquez slaughtered a chicken. She made you some delicious chicken soup. Want some?" Cam hoped he did.

"These people shouldn't be cooking their precious chickens for me," Gus said, frowning. He saw a pottery bowl filled with hot, steaming soup nearby. But he wasn't hungry. The fever had him in its clutches.

"Hey, you're like a son to them," Cam chided with a smile. "They wanted to do something to help you, Gus. You're one of their own. Everyone is worried for you."

"I'm worried for myself," he joked weakly. He

watched as Cam reached for the bowl and brought it over to him. She sat down facing him, the wooden spoon in hand.

"Tomorrow morning, early," Cam told him, as she placed a spoonful of clear broth into his mouth, "I'm leaving for a Catholic mission, San Anselmo. It's a day's walk from here. They've got a phone, Gus. Once I can get to a phone, we're home free. I can call in the help we need." She gave him a tender look as he patiently slurped the soup she fed him.

"You're going with a guide, aren't you?"

"Yes. Juan's son, Jose."

"Good," Gus muttered. He forced himself to eat half the contents of the soup bowl, a mixture of shredded chicken, potatoes and onions. The soup was salty and tasted good, but his stomach was roiling threateningly because of the constant pain he was in.

"You did good," Cam said, giving him a soft smile as she wiped his mouth afterward. "Keeping water and food in you right now is the best thing possible. It will keep you going."

Snorting softly, Gus looked around the shadowed room. It was small and warm. There was a square window, but no glass in it, only a blanket pinned into place. "I feel like a weak baby—completely helpless, *querida.*"

Arching at the endearment, Cam put the bowl aside, along with the damp cloth. Gus's uniform was dirty and damp with sweat. She wanted to get him out of it, but feared that moving his left arm might start the bleeding again. No, he might be in dirty clothes, but he was stable, so she let that idea pass.

"I had a dream about us," Gus told her in a quiet

tone as she came and sat cross-legged facing him. "A
little while ago…"

"Yeah?" Cam smiled, reaching out and grazing his
darkly bearded jaw. The stubble only accentuated
Gus's high cheekbones, showed how sunken his
cheeks had become in the last two days. Trying to
put her worry aside, Cam allowed herself the privilege
of wrapping her fingers around his good hand, which
lay at his side. His fingers were hot and damp. She
could see the wildness, the fever, gripping him.

"Nice dream…" Gus tipped his head back and
closed his eyes. "We were at this incredibly beautiful
place, like a Garden of Eden. There was jungle
around, and in the distance, big, beautiful mountains
with snow on the peaks."

"Sounds nice," Cam murmured, "but it sure isn't
around here."

His mouth twitched in a slight smile. Squeezing her
hand, he said, "No…I don't know where it was. You
were with me. We were sitting on this sloping, grassy
hill that had an oval pond at the bottom of it. The
water…" Gus forced his eyes open and drowned in
Cam's tender look "…was incredible, Cam. It was
like living, vibrating turquoise. It was clear, and as I
sat there with you, the desire to walk down there and
step into it was almost overwhelming." He closed his
eyes and quirked his mouth. "I knew if I walked into
that water, if I submerged myself in it, I'd be healed."

"Wow," Cam murmured, "that's pretty far out.
Wish I knew where this place was. You need it."

Hearing the humor in her voice, he nodded slowly.
"Yeah, this place…I'm telling you, I felt like I was
there. It was so *real*, Cam. So real…"

"Well," she whispered gently, "maybe when you go to sleep in a few minutes, you'll go back there. Next time, get in the water, okay? We need all the miracles we can lay our hands on now."

The humor revived him slightly. Gus opened his eyes. "Help me lie down? I'm so dizzy I feel like I'm going to pitch over...."

Getting to her feet, Cam eased Gus onto his right side. Once he was as comfortable as he could be, she tucked several blankets around his shoulders to keep him warm.

"Thanks..." he whispered wearily. "I love you, Camelia Anderson. All the way. With all my heart."

His gritty words flowed through the quiet room and touched her heart. As sick as Gus was, and in such unrelenting pain, he could still share that with her. Getting down on her knees, Cam leaned over him. Gus had already shut his eyes. His brow was beading with sweat again. She could see the pain and how it pulled his face into lines of unrelenting tension.

"And I love you, Gus Morales. Sleep, just sleep..." She stroked his damp hair with her hand. "Go back to that beautiful garden with the pond."

Her words lulled him into a deep, spiraling sleep. The fever had him once again. Even with his eyes shut, Gus could see the female jaguar sitting near the curtained doorway. She was looking at him with sparkling sun-gold eyes. A sense of care and protection emanated from her. As he felt Cam's hand stroking his head, Gus sensed, for the first time, that things were going to work out. Cam's words—that she loved him—embraced him and flowed through him. How nurturing she was. Like a sponge, he absorbed each of her tender touches. Tomorrow was a new day, he told himself. Tomorrow, Cam would go for help. Maybe by tomorrow night he'd be in a hospital getting the medical attention he needed.

As Gus drifted off, he heard the low, rumbling growl of the jaguar, who seemed to be very close to him now. He couldn't see her, could only feel her strength and presence. In his fevered brain as he spiraled into sleep, Gus thought it must be his mother's guardian, or perhaps his own, come to protect him. He had grown up listening to stories of the mountain and desert jaguars that had once roamed this part of Mexico. Oddly, Gus felt comforted by the apparition. That, and Cam's closeness. Hope flowed through him as he drifted off into the dark, feverish realm of sleep.

Chapter 17

Cam didn't want to leave Gus, but she knew she had to. He lay huddled beneath the warm blankets they'd shared last night. She'd lain against his back, her body curved against his. Half the night he'd been delirious with fever. Only when she slid her arm around the dampened waist of his flight suit, pressing her palm against his chest, did Gus cease his restless thrashing. He stopped muttering in Yaqui and Spanish, two of the three languages he'd grown up with.

Picking up the holster now, Cam strapped it around her waist and buckled it. Dawn was just touching the horizon, so the room was shadowed. Though she was barely able to see him, Cam made sure that a bottle of water was within Gus's reach for when he woke up. And she picked up his pistol, which had eight bullets left in it, and put it near the water. Her mouth tingled in memory of the kiss she'd pressed to his damp brow. Worried, Cam knew she had to meet Jose, who waited in the next room, and make that long, fifty-mile trek to San Anselmo. Giving Gus one last look as he lay sleeping deeply, she whispered, "I love you, Gus Morales. I'll be back, I promise...." And she quietly exited the room.

Jose, tall, lean and in his mid-twenties, nodded deferentially to her as she slipped into the main room. He wore a backpack on top of the lightweight dark green jacket over his upper body. Handing Cam a threadbare blue knapsack that sat on the wooden table, he said, "There is food and water in there for you, *señorita*. Are you ready?" And he smiled.

Liking the young man's quiet manner, Cam nodded. She quickly slid her arms into the knapsack straps and adjusted it against her back.

"I'm ready, Jose. Let's roll. I want to get to San Anselmo before dark." She saw his dark eyes sparkle as he opened the curtain at the front for her.

"I hope you are in good shape for a lot of trotting and little walking then," he teased in a low tone.

Outdoors, the morning was crisp, clean and cold. Cam could still see the stars above them. Everything was quiet. It was a peaceful quiet that fed one's spirit. Turning to Jose, who stepped out from the blanketed doorway behind her, she grinned at him.

"Let's start our trotting then, shall we?" Cam wanted to get to San Anselmo as fast as they could, even if it meant pushing herself to her maximum. She hoped that her daily three-mile runs and regular workouts at the gym at the base would hold her in good stead.

"*Sí, señorita,*" Jose said. He put an old, floppy

cotton hat with a wide brim on his head. Handing her another one, he said, "The sun is going to be merciless today. Wear this to protect your head and eyes."

Cam nodded and put the cap on. "Thanks, Jose. Now I look like one of your people."

Laughing softly, Jose said, "*Sí*, you do. Shall we?" And he took off at a trot across the hard-packed earth of the plaza, heading due south.

A growl of warning vibrated the air around Gus. He jerked physically, sending pain radiating from his left arm into his shoulder and neck. The sensation pulled him out of a deep, deep sleep. Where the hell was a *growl* coming from? His eyelids felt like weights, Gus discovered. He felt so weak he couldn't seem to force them open. He was warm and it felt good to just lie still.

Another growl. This time it felt like the animal, a big cat of some kind, was sitting right next to him and making the sound, which vibrated through his entire body. That forced Gus to drag open his eyes. Feeling fear, he slowly rolled onto his back, his right hand stabilizing his left elbow to minimize the pain. The room was a murky gray. Was he dreaming again? When the fever went high, he'd have hallucinatory dreams—nice ones, the only good thing about it. His fever was down now, he realized. It always seemed to be lower in the morning, and then, toward noon, would start to climb and he'd become delusional for the rest of the day and late into the night.

Right now, as he lay there, the blankets twisted about him, Gus tried to shove the sleep from his

barely functioning mind. The first thing he realized
was there was no big cat next to him. The room was
empty. Cam was gone, too. Vaguely, he recalled that
she was going to get up at dawn, meet Jose and hike
to San Anselmo today.

A wave of relief moved through him. She was going to get them help. That was good. Gus was quite
worried about his broken arm, and the fact that he
couldn't feel any sensations in his left hand at all now.
Was there nerve damage? If so, that meant he might
never be able to fly again, and that scared him.

Cam... He lay there, eyes closed, feeling such a
fierce love for her. She had kissed him so tenderly
last night that it had brought tears to his eyes. With
the unrelenting fever, Gus found himself highly vulnerable to the emotions he normally kept closeted
within. Not now. Cam's gentleness with him brought
out every emotion he'd ever known. And when she'd
come to lie at his back, curving her long, firm body
against his, he remembered feeling loved and protected by her. It was then that he'd drifted into a healing sleep, with her palm pressed against his chest,
over his beating heart. Yes, Cam owned his heart.
And his spirit. She was such an incredible woman.

Another sound, far off, caught his scattered attention—helicopter blades turning. Frowning, Gus felt
sweat beading his forehead once more. Blades. Helo
blades. What time was it? Lifting his right wrist, he
held his watch close to his face so he could read the
glowing dials. The fever made his vision blurred and
slightly out of focus.

It was 0800. Gus dropped his arm across his belly
and lay still. Was he hearing a helicopter because he

was hallucinating once again? Did he want to be rescued so badly that his fevered mind was making up the sound, as it did that big cat's growl? Or that female jaguar he'd seen off and on at the entrance to the room? Blowing a frustrated sigh from between his lips, Gus decided it was probably that. But his fever was lower, and although his mind was sluggish, he didn't seem to be hallucinating. Maybe the cat's growl in his ear had just been a bad dream.

Hearing excited Yaqui voices outside in the plaza, Gus frowned. The helicopter sounds were growing stronger. It was flying closer and closer to the village. *Was* he hallucinating? Gus opened his eyes. With a huge effort, he slowly and carefully moved to a sitting position, his right hand cupping his left elbow. Giving his head a slight shake, he keyed his hearing.

No, those were helicopter blades! Suddenly, Gus gasped. Could it be a rescue helo? One from Tijuana? Maybe Luis or Antonio had found them? His heart beat hard in anticipation. Lifting his chin, Gus looked toward the blanketed entrance. Outside, he heard more and more excited voices. Yes! That had to be a rescue team!

Hoping that Senora Marquez was in the house, Gus called for her, though his voice was rough and weak. Again, he called for her in Yaqui.

No one came.

The helicopter was almost upon them. Gus could hear the strong whapping of the blades, and it made his heart quicken with joy. The aircraft was landing just outside the village, so close that the vibration was palpable. They were going to be rescued!

As he heard the helicopter power down, the shrieking of the engine die away, Gus took a deep breath. How badly he wanted to get up, but he was still so weak. Cam had set a bottle of water and his pistol nearby, he noted. Anxious to meet whoever had come for them, Gus focused on trying to get up.

It was then he heard a scream—the scream of a little girl. And then he heard the shouts of panicked adults. Frowning, Gus tried to hear what they were saying. It was impossible.

He heard a warning growl—again. This time it seemed to be over his head and shoulders, the sound vibrating down through him.

What the hell was going on? His mind churned, confused, as he sat there.

More shouts. Screams. Someone was begging for something.

Something was wrong. Desperately wrong. Gus cursed.

It couldn't be a rescue team, then. So what was going down? Feeling shaky and unsteady Gus forced himself to his knees. Throwing out his right hand, knees spread, he assumed a tripod position to halt the dizziness that threatened to pitch him headfirst onto the earthen floor.

Another scream. Very close this time.

Suddenly, the curtain was ripped aside.

Gus jerked his head up.

"*Señor!* The *bandito* is here! Quickly! You must hide!" Senora Marquez whispered.

Gus saw the fear in the older woman's eyes. He saw blood dribbling from the corner of her mouth. Someone had struck her.

"What the hell is happening?" he demanded in Yaqui.

Senora Marquez quickly stepped into the room, wringing her hands. "*Señor,* the drug man is here— Robert Clark! He holds little Maria hostage, a gun at her head. He demands peyote buttons, but we have none! It is the wrong time of year. They do not grow now. But he wants some!" She gave a sob. "He is threatening to kill Maria if we don't bring him any."

Gus grabbed the pistol, which was inches from his hand. He forced himself to his feet. Staggering badly, he leaned against the earthen wall. Breathing hard, the pain clearing his mind, he looked at Senora Marquez.

"Where is he?"

Pointing, Senora Marquez said, "Near his bird. He is holding Maria there and demanding we bring the sack of peyote buttons to him."

Rubbing his sweaty face with his right arm, Gus rasped, "Tell him to come in here, *señora.* Lie to him and tell him the sack is in here. Tell him he has to come and get it."

Her eyes grew huge. Eyeing the pistol in his hand, and then his face, she whispered, "You mean...?"

Grimly, Gus rested his back against the wall. He could barely stand. His knees felt shaky and unsure. "Get him in here," he told her harshly. "I'll do the rest. Just make sure the little girl isn't with him, all right?"

Eyes widening, Senora Marquez made a fervent sign of the cross. "Aiiee, yes, yes, I hear you, Senor Morales."

"Just get the girl out of the way. And keep everyone else away from here. I don't want one of our bullets to hit anyone. Understand?'' His heart was beating hard. Gus knew this plan could backfire. He could die.

"Yes, yes, I understand."

"Vamoose!" he ordered her.

Turning, Senora Marquez turned and fled from the room. He heard her crying for Senor Clark, her voice strident and high.

Cursing softly, Gus saw his Kevlar vest lying in the corner of the room. Well, the bulletproof garment wouldn't do him any good now. He didn't have time to try and don it, and couldn't do so with his broken arm, anyway. Cam had removed it so she could tend to his broken arm.

Situating himself in the corner opposite the blanketed door, Gus waited. He felt incredibly weak, and fought to save his waning strength so he could lift the pistol at the right time and drill Clark before he shot him first.

Would the plan work? Gus's mind spun with questions. There were few options. He didn't have the strength to walk out of the room and confront Clark. Besides, if Clark was holding the girl hostage, Gus didn't have the accuracy to hit him and not the child. No, this was his only choice.

Dammit. Nervously, Gus wiped his beaded brow once more with the back of his good arm. Pain was stalking him in earnest now, throbbing unrelentingly through his arm, shoulder and neck. It shredded his concentration.

He heard voices—raised, angry voices. A child was crying pitifully. More screams. More begging.

Breathing hard, Gus wondered if his plan would backfire. Maybe Clark would shoot Maria anyway. Maybe he would refuse to come into the room. Chest rising and falling with each breath, Gus waited, half standing, half leaning against the wall. His legs were trembling badly and his knees felt like jelly. Closing his eyes, he sent a prayer to his mother and asked for help. He recalled her telling him a long time ago, as a child on her knee, that his jaguar spirit guide was there to give him help. All he had to do was ask for it.

Well, he was asking now, because if he didn't get physical strength from somewhere, he was about to slide down the wall into a heap. Breathing chaotically, Gus struggled to stay standing. Opening his eyes, he felt an incredible surge of heat spiraling up from his feet, running up both his legs toward his head. A moment later he felt an incredible surge of strength. What the hell was going on?

Gus wasn't sure. What he did know was that he felt incredibly stable and suddenly very strong—much stronger than he thought possible, given his broken arm and feverish state. Unable to sort it all out, Gus heard the raised, angry voice of Clark outside the adobe structure.

"You'd better not be lying to me, Marquez. If you are, I'm shootin' your husband in the head. You hear me, bitch?"

Holding his breath, Gus waited.

He heard Clark come through the first blanketed door, cursing darkly as he did so.

"Which room?" he snarled.

"Th-there…in there, Senor Clark…"

Gus heard Senora Marquez's trembling voice. Lifting the pistol, he prayed he could hold it in position. Any second, Clark would come through that blanketed entrance.

As Gus stood there, back to the wall, time seemed to stretch out endlessly so that every second passed in slow motion. His heart was beating hard in his chest. Perspiration was streaking down the sides of his face. And then Cam's face appeared before him.

How much he loved her! Wanted to spend his life with her! But he could die, right now.... *No! No, I want to live. Let me survive this. Please...I want to love her...to share my life with....*

Nostrils flaring, the point of his pistol wavering slightly as he aimed it at the blanket, he waited. There was no sound. Everything quieted. Gus suddenly felt as if he were out of time and space. It was such a surreal feeling, that he wondered for a moment if all of this was simply a nightmare he was experiencing during his delusional fevered state.

The blanket was ripped aside.

Robert Clark was a tall, lean man with frosty blue eyes, black hair and a black mustache. He was wearing civilian clothes, a suede tan jacket over a white shirt and black chinos. The gun he held was raised in caution.

When he saw Gus, he halted for a second. His eyes widened tremendously as he stared at the U.S. Army pilot in the shadowed corner. Was he seeing things?

"Drop the gun, Clark," Morales ordered, his voice deep and threatening. When the drug runner ignored the order and raised his weapon, Gus fired. The crack of the gunshot caroomed around him, hurting his ears.

The pistol bucked in his hand. Gus saw Clark knocked off his feet, landing hard on his back in the room beyond. The pistol flew from his nerveless fingers.

There were shrieks and screams, panicked sounds surrounding Gus as he forced himself out of the corner. Drunkenly, his legs rubbery once more, he moved as fast as he could toward Clark, who lay unmoving on the floor of the next room. Breathing hard, Gus kept the pistol aimed at the druggie. Seeing a red stain in the center of the man's chest, rapidly eating into the white of his shirt, he staggered to a stop. Breath tearing in gasps from his mouth, he saw Senora Marquez at the door, her hands pressed to her mouth, her gaze on Clark.

"Get someone to check his pulse," Gus rasped. Leaning against the doorjamb, he felt the strength begin to drain out of him, like an ocean tide leaving the beach and retreating back out to sea. Sweat stung his eyes. He blinked several times.

The whole village seemed to be crowding around the doorway. Senor Marquez came forward, moving cautiously around Clark.

"Get the gun," Gus ordered weakly. "Get it away from him."

Leaning down, Senor Marquez picked it up as if it were a snake that might bite him. He started to hand it to Gus.

"Lay it at my feet," he said. "Then check his pulse. On the side of his neck. See if you feel anything?" Gus thought the man was dead. He hoped so. Every second, he felt weakness stalking him once more.

Gus saw the eyes of the villagers crowded in the doorway, looking at him and then at Clark. There was such terror on their faces. A sense of satisfaction moved through Gus. He didn't like killing anyone, but he had no problem doing so to defend these people.

"There is nothing!" Senor Marquez said, holding his brown, work-worn fingers against the man's throat.

"Good," Gus rasped. He closed his eyes. "Get him out of here. Go bury him…" And that was the last thing he remembered.

"Gus? Darling? Wake up. It's Cam. Gus?"

Cam's low, urgent tone filled his darkness. Gus felt heavy. He also felt the constant, gnawing pain in his arm and shoulder. But something else—a warm hand caressing his bearded cheek—caught and held his attention. Then he felt her lips upon his mouth. Soft. Tender. The kiss drew him out of his sleeping state.

Forcing his eyes open, Gus felt Cam's lips ease from his. Focusing on her face, he saw that her green eyes were glittering with tears. But she was smiling.

"Uhh…what happened? Are you okay?" The gunfight started resurrecting from his clouded memory.

Laughing softly, Cam whispered, "Yes, darling. I'm fine. Everyone is okay."

Forcing himself awake, Gus saw that the room was filled with daylight. Cam was kneeling over him, smiling. Her hair was tousled and in need of combing, but even in its wild state it was like a chestnut halo around her head.

"W-what time…?" he asked, his voice thick and rasping.

"Eight hundred hours."

"You're back?"

Cam sat down next to him, her hand on his right shoulder. Gus was feverish. She understood his mind was shorting out. "Yes. We saw the helicopter coming in. Jose recognized it as the drug dealer, Clark. We were roughly six miles away when we saw it heading for the village." Cam quirked her mouth. "When Jose told me that, we headed back here at a dead run. Of course, six miles is a long way, Gus. I couldn't run that far. By the time we got here, you'd taken Clark out." Her voice quavered and her smile disappeared. "You could have been killed, darling."

Giving her a ragged smile through his pain, he rasped, "I didn't have many options left open to me. The bastard had a little girl hostage…."

"I know," Cam murmured soothingly, running her hand across his damp hair. "You were wonderful. It was a smart call, Gus. The Marquezes told us everything."

He saw her eyes lighten and become mischievous. Joy radiated around her and her cheeks flushed a rosy hue. Just feeling the caress of her hand on his head made him feel peaceful. Hopeful.

"What's up?"

"A lot. Clark's helicopter is available to us to use. Do you realize that?"

Blinking, Gus muttered, "No…I didn't think…"

"You're injured and feverish, that's why," Cam soothed. "I just put in a call to our base in TJ. I got ahold of Luis. I told him everything. Then—" Cam smiled broadly ''—I contacted the Naval Medical Center in San Diego. I told them we were coming in shortly, and that you were wounded. I gave them all the information on your broken arm, Gus. They're waiting for us, darling. Are you ready to leave here and head out?''

Tears jammed into Gus's eyes as he stared up at her. He saw tears rolling down her face, too. He heard the quaver, the relief and joy, in her hushed tone.

Gripping her hand in his, he whispered brokenly, ''Yeah...I'm ready to go home, *querida.*''

Chapter 18

"Hard to believe we were out in the desert wondering if we were going survive only seventy hours ago," Gus said dryly. He lay in a private room of the Naval Medical Center in San Diego. Cam sat on the edge of his bed with her hip against his blanketed thigh, facing him.

Cam slid her fingers into his. "It was like a bad dream," she agreed quietly. Morning sunlight was streaming through the eastern window. Outside, Cam could see the sprawling city, the streets filled with rush hour traffic. Since she had nothing to wear except her dirty green flight suit, she'd gone out and bought some civilian clothes.

Gus gave his left arm a worried glance. It was encased in a movable cast and suspended at an angle that promoted the best healing. At least he'd be out of the contraption by tomorrow morning and into a regular sling. That was progress. Looking up at Cam, he saw that she'd recently washed her chestnut hair, which curled around her shoulders. Dressed in a long-sleeved pink blouse and dark blue slacks, she looked like a young college woman and not the combat pilot she was.

"You're worried about Maya's reaction to the loss of the Apache, aren't you?" He squeezed her hand gently as he saw her green eyes become shadowed.

"Yeah, I am…and what's worse, Gus, I haven't heard a *thing* from her. Normally if you call Maya, you get a fast response." Biting down on her lower lip, she gazed at him, absorbing his caring concern.

How much better Gus looked now. He was clean and freshly shaved, his dark hair combed and tidy. Cam knew he had his own worries, but he wasn't going there. The break in his arm had been severe. Because he hadn't gotten prompt medical attention, there had been some nerve damage that affected his left hand and fingers. The doctors weren't sure at this point whether he would ever regain full use of his hand or not. Gus faced being drummed out of the army as a helo pilot if that happened.

Cam didn't know how she'd handle it if it were her, but Gus seemed easygoing about it. When he'd awakened shortly after the operation and the navy surgeon, Dr. Hannah Orbson, had told him of the possibility, Gus had given her a lopsided grin. He'd lain there and announced that no one was going to take him out of the seat of the Apache for any reason. He'd do the physical therapy it took to get full use of his hand back—or else. Cam loved him fiercely for that kind of spirit. She wasn't sure she'd have taken the news as well.

"I missed you last night," Gus told her now in a low tone, holding her worried gaze. Cam had been given a voucher for a room at a nearby hotel. The navy was taking care of her basic needs because Morgan Trayhern had made a call to the right people to see that she was not only okay, but given full and complete access to Gus.

"I didn't sleep well, either," Cam confessed, giving him a gentle smile. Lifting his hand, she brushed a kiss on the back of it. "I like sleeping with you."

"A bad habit," he teased.

Cam laughed shortly. Tension thrummed through her. Why hadn't she heard from Maya? She was afraid her C.O. would pull her from the BJS2 team and relegate her back to pilot status in Peru because of the screwups. It was only a matter of time, Cam was sure, before she'd hear her sentence from her larger-than-life leader. The iridium phone had been burned in the crash, so the only way Cam could reach Maya was through the Perseus office. Morgan had made sure the information was passed on to Maya, though Cam hadn't been able to talk to her directly. And she wanted to. She wanted to apologize for the loss of the twenty-million-dollar Apache.

Just then the door opened. Cam thought it was Gus's breakfast being wheeled in, since it was 0800. Her eyes widened. Major Maya Stevenson, in full U.S. Army uniform, stood there. Her black hair was knotted at the nape of her neck, just above the collar of her jacket. Cam's lips parted. It was the first time she'd seen Maya in her Class A olive green uniform,

with the many ribbons above her left breast pocket,
and the gold wings above them. Generally, she saw
Maya in her plain black flight uniform, which had no
markings whatsoever because they were a black ops,
except for the squadron patch.

"Maya!" Cam gasped. She released Gus's hand
and stepped forward quickly as her C.O. closed the
door quietly behind her.

"You two are a sight for sore eyes," Maya said,
grinning. She took off the hat she wore and hung it
on a peg near the door. As Cam came to attention,
she muttered, "Relax, will you?" Then she opened
her arms. "Come here!"

With a sob, Cam relaxed. When Maya smiled and
opened her arms, Cam felt such relief. This was her
C.O.; to hell with army regulations when prying eyes
weren't around. The fierce hug she gave her told Cam
better than anything could that Maya wasn't angry
with her.

"It's so good to see you, Maya," she whispered,
quickly wiping away her tears.

Maya grinned and patted her shoulder. "Makes two
of us. Gus? How are you?" She moved to his bedside
and looked down at him. Extending her hand, she
gripped his right one, squeezing it gently.

"I'm fine, ma'am." It was the first time he'd seen
the legendary leader of the Black Jaguar Squadron.
Gus stared up at her. She was powerful, warm and
charismatic. Bowled over by the energy swirling
around her, Gus absorbed her smiling features and her
large, emerald green eyes, which danced with life.
When her hand met his, he felt a distinct electrical
spark, and even now, as she stood holding his hand,

he felt those tingles moving up his right arm and into his left one. There was immediate warmth, almost an unpleasant burning sensation at the break site. Blinking, Gus knew something was happening, but he didn't understand it.

"Just receive the healing," Maya murmured. She looked over as Cam came to stand on the other side of the bed.

Gus nodded. Who could tell this woman no? Beginning to understand why Cam idolized her C.O., Gus found himself drawn to Maya himself. She was such a strong, nurturing woman—bold, yet with a fierce tenderness. She had the look of a warrior, but she wasn't aggressive. No, more like a powerful cat who knew her abilities and didn't need to show them off to anyone.

"Well," Maya said, humor in her tone, "I hear we lost an Apache. The good news is that you two survived. I'd rather lose a bird than two of my best pilots." She gave them each a measured look of pride. "I'm proud of what you did to survive."

Relief started to trickle through Cam. She stared at Maya. "Then...you aren't angry? It was my fault, Maya."

Shrugging eloquently, Maya said, "I read your report, which Morgan passed on to me. How could you or Gus even begin to think, in the middle of a thunderstorm, at night without a visual, that a lousy little civilian helicopter would be armed with rockets? It's one of those things, Cam. Accidents do happen. All you can do is learn from them and not make the same mistake twice."

Gus began to feel the heat flowing into his left arm

become more intense, almost painful. Remembering that Cam had said Maya came from the mystical Jaguar Clan, he realized she must be a medicine woman, like his mother. His mom used to lay her hand on his forehead when he had a fever or flu, and make the illness go away. Only now, whatever energy Maya was pumping into him was powerful. When she moved her intelligent green gaze to him, Gus had the distinct feeling she was reading his mind.

"Just a little longer, Chief Morales. I want you back flying a lot sooner than that year the docs are giving you." Her lips twisted enigmatically.

"A year?" Gus muttered. "No way." He focused on the energy she was giving him.

Cam sighed. "Thanks for your help, Maya. I never expected it."

"Why wouldn't I be here?" She grinned dryly. "Of course, having to fly commercial and in this get-up—" she gestured to the army uniform "—isn't something I looked forward to, but regs are regs. I miss my black flight suit. Infinitely a lot more comfortable," she chuckled.

Cam brought a chair to Gus's bedside and sat down. She saw the look of awe on his face as he kept his gaze riveted upon her C.O. "Are you healing him?" Cam asked.

"Well," Maya murmured, "let's put it this way. My jaguar spirit guide is sending Gus energy to help heal up that nerve and bone damage. You feelin' pretty uncomfortable about now, Gus?"

Giving her a twisted grin, he said, "Ma'am, my mother, who is Yaqui Indian, is a medicine woman for her people. When you sent that heat through me,

I knew what you were doing. It's okay, and I know it will help. I'm grateful. I want to fly again, more than anything.''

Maya's black brows rose. "Really? You'll do *anything* to get back into the seat of an Apache, Chief?"

"Yes, ma'am, I will. If I have to move heaven and earth to do it, that's what I'll do." Gus looked over at Cam. "I want to fly with her again. We're good together. Even though we got shot down, I blame myself for what happened. It was a bad night, ma'am. The winds were throwing us around. We had lightning dancing all around us, destroying our night vision. There was no way we could get a visual on that helo that shot us down."

"At ease, Chief. You don't need to convince me of what happened. Akiva and Joe down on the Gulf, at their black ops base, face the same weather conditions almost nightly when they interdict drug flights there. I'm aware of the circumstances. No one is finding either of you culpable. Nothing is going into your fitness reports that will indicate any unprofessional conduct. So take a deep breath and let's get past this, shall we? I have other fish to fry with you two."

Gus gave Cam a warm look. He was so relieved that she wasn't going to be singled out as at fault for the incident. "That's good to hear, Major. Thank you...from both of us."

Releasing his hand, Maya patted him in a motherly fashion and then smiled slightly. "You're welcome. Well, Gus, you said you'd do anything to get healed up so you could fly again?"

He felt the heat begin to saturate his broken arm.

The discomfort was slowly leaving after Maya had released his hand. "Yes, ma'am, I did."

"You meant it?" Maya shifted her gaze to Cam, who was frowning, obvious questions in her eyes.

"Yes, I did. Why?" Gus saw a feral smile cross the major's mouth, as if she were a cat and he, an unfortunate mouse that had just been trapped. Gus could feel so much around the woman, and yet he wasn't able to translate all of it to understand it—or her. Cam had said she was powerful, and now he clearly knew it was true.

"Okay, you two," Maya murmured as she took out some folded papers from inside her blouse and handed a set to each of them, "here are your TDY orders for the next two weeks." She opened Gus's and gave it to him to read. Cam took hers and carefully unfolded the typewritten orders. "TDY" meant temporary duty, so the two pilots knew they were being sent someplace, but not where. Maya waited in silence as they read the new orders.

Cam frowned. "Village of the Clouds? I've heard of that place. From…Inca, your twin sister."

Gus frowned, too. "Is this a military base? A hospital?"

Grinning, Maya said, "Yes to all the above. Gus, when you were delirious, you remember seeing a female jaguar? A big one with black half-moon spots over her golden coat?"

Jarred, Gus blinked. Maya stood before him, serious now, her hands folded in front of her body. Stunned, he took several seconds to respond. His mind whirled with questions. How could she know that? The mystery surrounding this woman shocked him. "Er...well, yes... But it was a hallucination brought on by my high fever," he managed to reply. Shooting a glance at Cam, who was smiling at him, he wondered where this conversation was leading. Seeing merriment dancing in Maya's eyes and a smile on her lips, he wondered what the hell was up.

"Yes, well, you see, Gus, you weren't actually imagining that jaguar. She's real. As real as you or I, right now. She's your spirit guardian.... Your mother is a member of the Jaguar Clan. Did she ever tell you that?"

"Er...yes..." Gus's head was spinning with a hundred questions. The jaguar was *real?* How?

Maya's smile widened. "Yes, she is. That means you, as her direct descendant can go to the Village of the Clouds for training, if you want it. It's also a place where people go to heal. There's a small pond known as the Pool of Life. If you go sit in that healing water, it will heal any disease or wound." She pointed toward his left arm. "If you want full use of that arm again, you have to go there and bathe in the waters every day for two weeks. It's not going to be dog duty, Gus. The place is like a Garden of Eden. You saw it already. You visited it in your dreams. Do you remember? The green slope leading down to that beautiful water?"

Dumbfounded, Gus nodded. "Yes, ma'am, I do recall that now...but I thought it was all—"

"I know, hallucinations brought on by high fever." Maya chuckled darkly. "Sometimes, when we're sick, we go to another place to heal, to help ourselves, Gus, and that's what you did. Would you like to know more about this place and what it offers you, since by heritage you can become a member of the Jaguar Clan if you want?''

Gus looked up at Cam. ''Has she got the same set of TDY orders?''

Maya laughed softly. ''Yes, she does. I think Cam deserves a little R and R with you, Gus. She's been busting her hump for months squaring this little TJ operation and getting it in order.''

''But,'' Cam said worriedly, ''what about the BJS2 mission? If I'm not there to run it?''

''Snake and Wild Woman are coming up to stand in for you two for the length of the TDY,'' Maya told them. ''And my X.O., Dallas Klein, will run the place for you. When you return from the Village of the Clouds, they'll come back to BJS and me.'' Maya held Cam's worried gaze. ''And upon your return, Cam, you're still the C.O. Gus is still your X.O. Things will move on just like they did before this happened.''

Frowning, Gus muttered, ''But...I won't be able to fly at that time. I'll just be a deskbound X.O., and Cam's going to need another pilot.''

Maya's grin turned sardonic. ''Really, Chief? Well, I guess you're gonna have to trust me on this one, aren't you? By the time you return to TJ, you'll be ready to fly.''

Cam laid her hand gently on Gus's left arm. ''Darling...believe her. I know it sounds impossible, but when Maya was wounded in action when Dane was flying with her down in Peru, and they mixed it up with a Black Shark, Inca flew in from Brazil. She laid her hand on Maya's wound and healed it instantly. We all got to see it.

"A number of us dragged Maya down from that Apache cockpit, and she was hemorrhaging. Our doctor got the bleeding stopped, but Maya was dying because she needed a blood transfusion. Luckily, Dane had the same blood type. A day later, Inca flew in—she's a well-known healer from the Jaguar Clan. All she did was lay her hand on Maya's arm where it got sliced open, and in ten minutes the wound was *gone.*"

Hearing the hope in Cam's voice, Gus gave Maya a strange, assessing look. The major stared back at him, her gaze bold and confident. "Two weeks?" he challenged huskily.

"Two weeks, Chief. I know you don't believe me, and that's fine. But you'll see." Maya moved to the door, picked up her cap and settled it on her head. She gave them a broad smile. "Morgan is sending you an overnight, top-secret packet. In it are your commercial airline tickets to Tarapoto, Peru. And Mike Houston, his right-hand man, who is also a member of the clan, has put in written directions on how you are to get to the village from there. Have a good trip...." She lifted her hand and waved to them.

"I don't believe this," Gus whispered. The place in his dream *was* real. He sat on the same grassy knoll that led down to the oval-shaped Pool of Life and it looked just as he had imagined. Except in reality Cam was at his side, dressed in a loose-fitting white cotton top and slacks. Her feet were bare, snuggled in the green grass. The sun was warm, but not hot, the sky a light blue, with rolling clouds. In the distance the peaks of the Andes, clothed with snow, were barely visible.

Cam sighed and put her hand on his right shoulder. Gus wore a pale blue, short-sleeved top and loose, cotton pants. He, too, was barefoot. Around them, the jungle closed in, embracing the beautiful spot as a lover would. The profusion of orchids in the trees overhanging the aquamarine pool below did indeed make this look like Eden in Cam's mind.

"This place is mystical," she said. "And so wonderful. Walking over that bridge earlier today and meeting Alaria and Adaire, the keepers of the village, was like meeting old friends. I swear, they're like grandparents to us."

Nodding, Gus stared at the vibrant water of the pool. The color was unearthly. It reminded him of that translucent hue he'd seen on icebergs in the Atlantic as they drifted southward. "I felt such love for them instantly."

"Me, too…" Cam sighed. "Why don't you go into the water, Gus? Alaria said you need to do it once a day for about ten minutes."

Nodding, he slowly stood up and walked down to the edge of the pool. Cam went with him. She helped him out of his shirt by unbuttoning it and gently removing it from around his arm, which was in a removable plastic cast. Kneeling down, she tugged off his pants, leaving him in a pair of boxer shorts. She then divested him of the sling and eased open the cast and removed it. The ugly red scar where the doctors had operated to put his bones back in alignment was a glaring reminder of their traumatic crash. It hurt Cam just to look at it.

Getting down on her knees, she dipped her fingers into the placid water. "Ohh, it's so warm! Like a hot tub." She twisted her head to look up at him, smiling. Cam knew that Gus really wanted to believe Maya— that by doing this, he could be healed. His two left fingers, the last two on his hand, didn't work at all. He couldn't move them.

Understanding his anxiety, Cam said, "Come on, I'll help you in, Gus. Nothing ventured, nothing gained."

Taking a deep breath, Gus set aside his questions and stepped into the pool. The gently sloping bottom was sandy and the water was deliciously warm and soothing. Instantly, he felt a delightful bubbling sensation against his flesh wherever the water embraced him. Moving out to the center, which was neck deep, Gus turned and looked up at Cam, who stood on the bank. He loved her fiercely. He wished he could make love to her, but it was impossible right now with his arm the way it was. Seeing the hope burning in her eyes, he said, "It tickles."

"What does?" she asked, laughing and sitting down at the edge, placing her feet in the water.

"That's the feeling," he told her, looking around the glade. "The water is like champagne bubbles all around me. I can feel their warmth and it's like…well, going *into* me. It's a strange sensation, but it feels good."

"Yes," Cam said, startled, "I feel it, too!" She pointed to her feet and ankles, which were immersed in the pool. "Wow, this is something else, Gus! Oh, won't it be wonderful if it helps your arm and hand?"

Hearing the hope in her voice, Gus nodded. Indeed,

he felt the water working energetically around his wounded arm, felt heat penetrating the wound and moving down his limb to his hand. To his surprise, he tried to flex his fingers. They all moved. Gulping in surprise, he tried it again. Before, his last two fingers would not flex because of the nerve damage. Now they did.

"I moved them," he exclaimed in a strangled whisper, giving Cam a wide-eyed look of surprise.

She grinned. "Yeah? Your fingers? They moved? Really?"

"Yeah...they did!" Gus flexed them again as if to persuade himself it had really happened.

Tears flooded Cam's eyes as she sat there, watching Gus in the center of the pool. His face looked at peace for the first time. The strain of the accident was gone, all the tension washed away from his strong male mouth. A soft breeze riffled his hair, lifting a few short strands and settling them against the smooth line of his brow. There was such hope burning in his cinnamon-colored eyes as he looked down at his left arm through the jewel-toned water.

Her heart pounded with hope. Hope for him. And hope that he'd fly at her side once again. Never had Cam wanted anything more. She trusted Maya. And she believed her statement that Gus could be whole once more, even if he himself was uncertain. He hadn't spent three years with this mysterious and powerful woman as Cam had.

"Just stand there and let yourself heal," she called to him softly, tears trailing down her cheeks. "I love you, Gus Morales, and I *know* you're going to be a hundred percent in two weeks."

Chapter 19

Gus ambled into their thatched hut, which sat beside a creek of cool, burbling water. It was dark. The weather was warm, in the mid-seventies. The village was quieting down for the night, for there was no electricity here. He'd grown used to the low light, the candles set in glass globes in every hut. To the left was their sleeping room. Seeing Cam sitting on their large pallet, with a globe flickering in the corner, giving her just enough light to write in her diary, he halted in the doorway and smiled softly.

She didn't hear him come in. He'd been quiet on purpose. Tonight was the last night they'd be here at this incredibly wonderful, healing village. He'd already said his farewell to the grandparents, Alaria and Adaire, who together ran this mystical community. Tomorrow morning, Gus and Cam would cross that wooden bridge over the stream and move out into another world, another life.

His heart expanded with joy. Cam would be at his side. He couldn't get any luckier than that. His lips curved in a wider smile as he observed her writing, her chestnut hair alive with red-gold highlights, her brow scrunched in concentration.

Gus hadn't understood the importance of being given a journal upon their arrival here, but now he did. Every day one of the teachers at the village would lead a number of them in some kind of visualization. They would then write down their experience afterward, their emotional response to it. The next day, the same group would gather with that teacher and share the experiences they'd had. The amazing thing to Gus was that all of them had the same experience. That told him that whatever was going on was real, and not a figment of his imagination. No, the last two weeks had been empowering to him and had given him a clearer understanding of his own Yaqui grandmother, and the valuable heritage she'd passed on to him.

"I want to take a photograph of you through my heart's eyes in this moment," he whispered to Cam.

Instantly, she lifted her head as she heard Gus's low, deep voice. His words cascaded over her like a warm blanket. In the thirteen days they'd been in the village, they hadn't made love because of his broken arm. But how she looked forward to sleeping near him, even if she couldn't snuggle in his arms.

"That's a beautiful thing to say," she murmured.

"I'm looking at a beautiful woman. Why wouldn't I say that?" His mouth drew into an enigmatic smile.

Eyes widening, Cam realized he was leaning ca-

sually on the doorjamb—against his left shoulder. The
one that had been so badly injured.

"Gus, aren't you in pain?" she asked, pointing to
his arm. This was the first time she'd seen him do
that. He had already regained the full use of his fingers and hand, just as Maya had promised. It was a
miracle, but then, Cam had realized very quickly, miracles were an ordinary part of life here at the village.

"Hmm?" He glanced down at his left side. "No,
I'm fine. There's no pain. Nothing."

Relieved, Cam rested her hands on the diary and
smiled up at him. "That's so wonderful, darling. I
can't believe it, but it's real. You'll be able to fly
again when we get back to TJ." She saw his hooded
eyes narrow on her. Heart pounding in anticipation,
Cam wondered what that look meant. Gus held something in his hands, but she couldn't see what it was.

"In a way, I'm glad to be going back," Gus told
her, glancing down at what he was holding. It was a
small ring he'd fashioned for Cam in the last several
days. He'd asked Adaire if he had any silver wire
around, and the old man had beamed. Taking Gus to
their craft shop, a large thatched hut at the outer pe-
rimeter of the village, he'd shown him much more.
And for days, after lessons, Gus would go there and
work. He'd made the ring for Cam—to symbolize a
hope in the future for both of them.

Cam looked around and sighed. She gently closed
her book and set it near the wall. "I know how you
feel. But there's a part of me that doesn't want to
leave this peace and quiet."

"But the other part, the warrior, wants to get back
into action, right?" he chuckled. Pushing away from

the door frame, Gus quietly shut the woven-palm door
so that no one would accidentally enter the room.
Then he turned back to Cam, who sat cross-legged
on the soft, springy pallet stuffed with freshly dried
grass. She was wearing a simple white cotton nightgown.

"You're right. I'm itching to get back to flying. I
miss that most." She watched Gus walk across the
room and close the purple curtains at the two windows, left by day to allow fresh air to flow in. Cam
had grown used to his nightly routine. It was time for
bed. He had just come from bathing, because he was
wearing only his dark blue cotton pants, and the black
hair spread across his broad bare chest still looked
damp.

Coming to the pallet, Gus knelt down in front of
her, less than a foot away. Cam's face was free of
tension. He'd never truly realized the pressure on her
until he saw how peaceful she seemed during these
two stress-free weeks. As she lifted her chin and
smiled up at him, her lips parting, he groaned inwardly.

"I made you something," he said in a low tone.
"Hold out your hand. I want to give it to you."

Thrilled and surprised, Cam did as he asked. When
he placed the piece of jewelry in her palm, the slight
touch of his fingers on her skin sent wild tingles of
longing up her arm, to her heart.

"Oh, Gus. It's a ring!" Cam picked up the delicately made piece and looked at it closely.

Nervously, Gus said, "I want this ring to symbolize
us, *querida*. Our future...our possibilities with one
another." He waved his hand. "I used gold and silver

wire, weaving them together to make a stronger band.''

Amazed by his painstaking work, Cam noted that seven tiny polished stones were woven into the ring, each a different color. ''It's like a rainbow ring,'' she whispered in awe. In the candlelight, the precious stones glinted and gleamed. It's beautiful, Gus...so beautiful!'' Cam choked up with emotion as she held his hooded gaze.

''It's for a beautiful woman who stole my heart the first day she walked into my life. I loved you then, Camelia Anderson, but I was a scared guy. There you were—a confident woman warrior, smart and foxy, who had three years of combat under her belt—my teacher and commander.'' He managed a sour smile. ''I didn't know I'd become your executive officer. That blew me away, but in a good way, because I wanted to spend as much time with you as I could. Through it all, I hungered for you, *querida,* even though I never let on to it.''

Smiling softly, Cam said, ''No...you never did. You're very good at hiding your motives, Gus Morales.'' She smiled into his eyes.

''And I had my own monsters to wrestle with,'' he told her huskily. ''I had my past to settle—the loss of another warrior woman I'd loved.''

''I understand,'' Cam said. ''I was afraid to love you, too, Gus, for different reasons.'' She gazed back at the ring, still in awe. The fire within each colored stone was breathtaking. Her fingers tingled as she touched the object. This was no ordinary ring, she realized.

Gus took it from her and held her left hand, her

long, graceful fingers extended toward him. "We've
both faced our fears and worked through them," he
said in an emotional whisper. Seeing her eyes tear up
and fill with love for him gave Gus the courage to go
on. He slid the ring onto her finger. It fit perfectly.
"This ring symbolizes our love for one another, *querida*. What I hope for us in the future. I know we're
in a dangerous business. I also know, now, that I'm
going to savor every second I spend with you from
here on out, because we may die suddenly."

Gulping, Cam drowned in his eyes, which burned
with desire. "Oh, Gus...this is so beautiful! Your
words, the ring..."

"Do you want to wear this ring for those reasons,
querida?" He prayed she did, but he had to ask. He
couldn't assume.

Tears drifted down her cheeks. "Oh, yes, Gus.
Yes! I feel the same about you...about us. That crash
where we almost died ripped away any misgivings or
worries I had about us. Seeing you hurt like that, and
knowing that you could die if we didn't get rescued,
helped me get real clear real fast about my true feelings for you." Sniffing, she whispered, "I love you.
I think I loved you from the moment I set eyes on
you. I just didn't want to admit it. I was too scared."

Caressing her hand and gazing down at the delicately wrought ring, he murmured, "Two emotional
cowards who finally got courageous enough to fight
our own dragons to win the prize—one another?"

With a laugh, Cam nodded. She wiped her tears
away with her other hand. "Yes...yes, exactly."

"That's what I wanted to hear," he murmured.
Getting up, he went over to the corner and blew out

the candle. The shadows in the room deepened, but bright moonlight pierced the semi-opaque curtains, filling the hut with a muted radiance.

Cam moved the blankets aside as Gus slid into bed beside her. This time, he maneuvered her onto her back and lay on his right side. With his left hand, he caressed her warm cheek.

"I want to love you tonight, *querida.*"

His low, vibrating tone feathered through her. Cam sighed and smiled softly as his fingers grazed her temple, cheek and chin. "I've wanted to do this for so long, but your arm..."

"My arm is fine now," he assured her. Drowning in her dark green eyes, which were filled with yearning, he ran his fingers down her shoulder to caress her breast beneath the fabric. Her eyes fluttered closed. A soft moan of need rose in her throat as she pressed against his exploring hand. How guileless and trusting Cam was! That humbled Gus as nothing else could. Despite her troubled past with men, she was trusting him so sweetly. That was the power of love, he realized, as he leaned down to seek her lips.

Kissing Cam was like kissing a flower opening to the sun for the first time. Her lips were like soft, warm petals yielding to him adoringly. Gus realized that Cam was innocent and not very experienced in love-making. That cautioned him to go slow, to remember that she was new to real intimacy between two people.

"I want this night to be one you'll always remember, *querida,*" he rasped against her wet lips. "Fly with me? Let me give you wings, Camelia. Come fly with me...."

His urgent words aroused her, and Cam moaned, "Yes... Gus, I love you...." And she arched against him, her own urgency real, her hunger making her body glow as if lava pooled in its core, ready to explode.

Lost in the haze and heat of his lips crushing hers, she scarcely registered the fact that he was tugging at her nightgown, slipping it up her body and running his warm hand over her bare skin. Cam reluctantly broke away from his searching mouth. Sitting up, she divested herself of the shift and set it aside.

Gus's eyes gleamed as he looked at her. "You're so beautiful." He reached out and caressed her small, firm breasts with his hand. Seeing the languorous look in her eyes, he smiled boldly and urged her to lie at his side once more. "I want to explore you," he whispered, kissing her nose, her chin, the length of her slender neck. "I want to learn every contour with my lips, my hands, and put it into my heart," he added, placing one wet, provocative kiss at the top of her breast, the side of it, and finally, closing his lips over the tight nipple.

Hands clenching, Cam closed her eyes as he suckled her and brought her fully into his arms. Swept up in a heated tide, she felt his strength as a man and reveled in it. Urgency filled her as his mouth left her nipple and found her mouth once more. Hungrily, Cam returned his passionate kisses. His breath was warm and rasping against her nose and cheek; his hand ranged artfully downward, exploring her rib cage, her waist and the curve of her hip. Even his wiry chest hair pressing against her sensitized breasts was a wonderful sensation.

When his fingers moved gently across her scalp, making it tingle, Cam rested her head on his right arm and looked drowsily up into his dark, burning gaze. "I ache, Gus...I ache for you...." she told him in a husky tone.

Cam saw the pleased smile come to his strong male mouth. Just having him trail his fingers through her hair was a wonderful and unexpected sensation to Cam. She felt like the most cherished woman in the world as he caressed her lovingly.

"That's good, *querida*. I ache, too. It's the ache of love...." Easing her upward, he lay on his back, grasped her wide hips and drew her above him. There was a look of surprise in her face as he did so, but under the circumstances, he had no wish to stress his newly healed left arm. Besides, his instincts told him that although Cam was not a virgin, it had probably been a long time since she'd made love, and this way he wouldn't accidentally hurt her.

He understood on some instinctual level that Cam needed to be given the freedom to flow with the needs of her body without him orchestrating their lovemaking. Gus knew that others had used her, forced her on her back and then, after their own gratification, got up and left her, not caring about her fulfillment. He was damned if that was going to happen tonight. Or any night they spent together. In the silent language of love, he was going to teach her about her womanly body, her own power and sexuality, and how she could reach the ultimate gift of it—with him.

As her legs straddled his narrow hips, she felt his erection graze her wet, throbbing core. A sigh tore from her moist, parted lips. When she rested her hands on his well-sprung chest, Gus moved teasingly against her, and when he settled her fully against him, the pooled wetness of her body met the hardened power of his. Fingers digging into the tight flesh of his chest, she moved downward of her own accord. A sense of newfound power, of being a woman, ripped through her like a bolt of lightning as Cam opened her body to him.

"Easy…" Gus whispered, gripping her hips to guide her. "Take your time, *querida*. This should feel good, not painful…."

His words drummed through her wildly pounding heart. Oh, how good Gus felt to her! Her body sang, the blood throbbing through her as she felt his masculine power at the doorway to her feminine darkness. Gulping, Cam could only feel right now. As he slowly eased his hips upward, and she felt him sheath a little more into her tight confines, the fiery sensations tripled. Breathing raggedly, Cam closed her eyes, lost in the hazy, exploding sensations. Never had she felt such joy, such honesty and beauty with a man as Gus was sharing with her right now. Oh, this was what love, real love, was about! In the spinning golden halls of her mind that were shorting out with the pleasure of their mutual coupling, Cam realized that Gus was controlling himself for her sake, to introduce her to a realm she'd never, ever explored before. Her breath was growing ragged. She wanted more.

"Take me," Gus rasped darkly. "Take me when you want, *querida*. I'm yours…all yours…."

With one powerful movement she did so, and the resulting pleasure moved through her like a tidal wave. Surrendering to her body's hunger, to her heart's desire to love Gus in every way possible, Cam sank downward. And then his hands were on her hips, moving her, grinding her body against his as he arched upward to create even greater pleasure for her.

Feeling as if she were in a storm, tossed by violent updrafts and air currents, Cam let the animal nature of herself take over. With each wet, gliding movement, the hunger grew, until finally an explosion unlike anything she'd ever experienced before took place within her. As Gus's large hands closed around her lower back, pulling her closer still, the violence of her climax took her by utter surprise.

Gus felt Cam stiffen. He understood what was happening. With a grimace of arousal, he finally released his tight control. As she arched her back with a sharp cry of pleasure, he quickened the rhythm between them, deepening his penetration and prolonging the pleasure for her. And just as her climax reached its peak, he allowed himself his final release into the hot, fluid depths of her loving body.

Cam groaned and slumped forward. Lost in a glowing haze, breathing hard, she lay across Gus, her head buried beneath his jaw. Weakly stroking his hair with her fingers, she felt their hearts beating in unison together like drums. Her mind was mush. She couldn't think, and speech was impossible. Wonderful radiating waves of warmth and light pulsing through her body held her total attention. Now she understood how sex, good sex, could be incredible, and she smiled against the curve of his sweaty neck. All the while, Gus was stroking her spent body, his strong hands moving gently down her spine and across her hips.

"You are my heart," he whispered into her ear, her silken hair tickling his face. "And this is what love…real love…is all about, *querida*. I wanted to show you that a man can love his woman as an equal partner. We don't always take and run, like you've experienced in the past." He smiled when she lifted her head to look into his eyes. "Loving is giving and taking. It's about sharing. It's about wanting to make the person you love happy." Reaching up, he grazed her flushed, damp cheek.

Drowning in his glittering gaze, which was filled with tenderness, Cam whispered brokenly, "I never knew, Gus…not until now…."

Satisfaction made him growl. "Well, now you know the difference, *querida*. This—" he stroked her shoulder and back caressingly "—is what we have to look forward to from now on. Pretty great, isn't it?"

Cam purred beneath his ministrations. "Yes…oh, yes!"

Sliding his hand to her cheek, he guided her mouth to his, cherishing her soft lips for a long, long time. When they finally eased apart, Gus whispered, "I'm going to love you forever, Camelia Anderson. Forever…"

Chapter 20

"Hey, welcome home!" Sergeant Angel Paredes called when Cam stepped into the barracks of the Mexican Air Force base in Tijuana.

Cam grinned and threw her arms around the Peruvian paramedic, who had worked at BJS since its beginning. They called her the Angel of Death because countless times Angel had managed to save the life of someone in the worst of circumstances—patients not expected to make it. She'd cheated death of many good people.

"Hey, great to see you here!" Cam replied. Glancing over her shoulder at Gus, she quickly introduced him to the Quero Indian. Angel was small and stocky, having descended directly from the Incas, proud rulers of an empire that had covered much of South America at one time.

Cam saw Angel's large brown eyes light up with

pleasure as she pumped Gus's hand. Then Lieutenant Dallas Klein, Maya's X.O. back at the base in Peru, appeared at the door. Giving the tall, slim, Israeli-born pilot a huge grin, she called, "Hey, I'm relieving you now. You can go home!"

Dallas laughed and rushed to embrace Cam. "Good to see you! You look great, Cam. That two week R and R did you a lot of good."

"Yeah, life is kinda wonderful now." Cam looked around. "Where's the rest of my tiny squadron? Luis and Antonio?"

"Oh," Dallas said with a mischievous grin, "I've got them doing some serious work over the mountains. They're learning some finer details of nap-of-the-earth flying, with Wild Woman and Snake in the other Apache."

Chuckling, Cam moved into her office. It felt good to be home. Her heart was light, her feeling about the future of this mission positive.

"Take your chair," Dallas said, walking in behind her. "Maya sent Paredes up here to give you your official FAA medical exam. It's protocol, but it's gotta be done before you and your X.O. can strap an Apache on your butt again."

"Fine," Cam murmured. "Not a problem." She ran her fingers over her battered old green metal desk. Dallas was a neatnik compared to herself. Everything was in little organized piles, unlike Cam's style, which was messy at best.

As she sat down in her squeaky chair, Gus and Angel entered the room, and Dallas went to the coffee dispenser and started pouring cups of the freshly made brew.

Gus closed the door and leaned against it, his gaze on Cam. She looked so happy, with her cheeks flushed, her eyes radiant. He knew why; their love was having the same effect on him.

Sergeant Paredes fetched her emergency medical pack and set it up on Cam's desk. "Let me check you two out, and then Dallas and I can take off, okay?" She gave them a swift smile as she pulled out a stethoscope and blood pressure cuff from her red canvas bag, which said Medic in Spanish and English.

"You first, Gus?" Cam asked as Dallas handed her a cup of steaming coffee. "Thanks, Dallas."

Gus nodded and eased away from the door. He knew the drill. Rolling up his right sleeve to above his elbow, he came over to where Angel had pulled out a chair for him.

"Right here, Chief Morales," Angel said, pointing to it.

Gus liked the energetic Quero woman. Her skin was a coppery color, and her black eyes reminded him of a night sky with stars dancing in its depths. "Gotcha," he murmured, and sat down. Angel was quick and professional, fitting the blood pressure cuff around his right arm.

After passing out the coffee, Dallas sauntered over to Cam's desk and rested her hip on one corner, her own mug in hand. "Maya said she sent you two to that village. I'm jealous. Angel has gotten to go, too."

"Well," Cam said, sipping her coffee, "I wondered why Angel looked so happy when she came back. Now I know why."

"Yes," Dallas chuckled, "I keep hoping my turn will come."

Cam gave her friend a narrowed look. "You've been with Maya since the beginning. You work with her day in and day out."

"Yes," Dallas murmured.

"And I think you know a lot about her…well, her other powers?" Cam wasn't sure how to approach Dallas on this topic. She didn't know how much Dallas knew about the mystery of Maya's past or how it figured into her present. Cam searched the woman's oval face, her shining sable hair and olive skin as the X.O.'s eyes grew thoughtful. Cam wondered if she'd made a mistake by asking at all. Still, she burned with questions.

Dallas took her time and sipped her coffee for more than a minute before answering her. "Maya has other powers. But from what she's shared with me, I wouldn't say they are superhuman ones. I've heard her say many times that anything she, or her twin sister, Inca, can do, anyone can, with proper training." Dallas looked over at Gus as Angel flashed a penlight into his eyes to make sure his pupils dilated properly. "Like Gus's broken arm…"

"Yes, that," Cam said. "We all know it's impossible for bones to knit and heal in less than six weeks, and yet in two weeks his serious break is *gone*. It's as if it never happened." She waved toward his arm. "Even the scar from the surgery is gone. I can barely see where it was."

Shrugging, Dallas murmured, "Maya has often said that truth is stranger than fiction, and that the world we live in is but a reflection of how we *want* to see it, not how it really is."

"I had a long talk with Grandmother Alaria. She's

the elder who runs the village along with her husband, Adair. I asked her about it, and she just laughed. She wasn't laughing at me, but rather, with me. Patting my hand, she told me that miracles are possible every breathing moment of everyone's life.'' Giving Dallas a questioning look, Cam muttered, ''I felt like such an ignoramus there.''

Nodding, Dallas said, ''Maya refers to it as the study of metaphysics, or the unseen realms that surround us. She says they're there all the time, even if we're not aware of it. When we meditate, we become more in touch with the other dimensions and energies surrounding us.''

''You seem to have a handle on this,'' Cam declared good-naturedly, ''and you've never been to the village.''

''I'm Jewish. We have the cabala. It's an ancient metaphysical and spiritual tradition that I think, at least from what Maya has shared with me over the years, parallels her beliefs very closely.''

''Oh...'' Cam said, frowning.

''Did you get asked to come back?'' Dallas inquired.

Nodding, she said, ''Yeah, they extended an invitation to Gus and me both to come back for training.''

''That's a compliment to you, then,'' Dallas said, smiling slightly. She watched as Angel finished her examination of Gus.

''That arm looks incredible,'' Angel murmured, shaking her head. ''Someday I'd like to go back to that place. Awesome!'' She grinned up at her firends. ''Okay, next poor slob?''

Loving her upbeat spirit and teasing nature, Cam raised her hand. "I'm the next victim."

Laughter filled the room. Gus vacated the chair and rolled down his sleeve. With a flourish of his hand, he invited Cam to sit down in his place.

"Thank you, kind sir," she murmured, giving him a warm look filled with love.

"A pleasure, *señorita*," he answered. His heart blossomed with so fierce a love that he knew he wasn't able to hide it from either of Cam's colleagues. Somehow he knew they approved, and it made him feel good.

Dallas slipped off the corner of the desk and ambled over. She picked up Cam's left hand. "My...what's this? Isn't it gorgeous. New, hmm?"

Cam responded to her playful inquiry. "Gus gave it to me. He made it. Isn't it beautiful?"

"I was eyeballin' that thing, too," Angel said in a conspiratorial tone as she pumped up the blood pressure cuff around Cam's right arm.

Feeling heat come to her neck and cheeks, Cam looked up into Dallas's smiling eyes. She knew. And Cam wouldn't hide it from her best friends.

Gus came over, crossing his arms against his chest. "I made it for Cam while we were at the Village of the Clouds."

"You were inspired," Dallas said, holding Cam's hand so that the fluorescent light showed off the highly detailed, intricate work.

"Very," Gus answered, giving Cam a wink. He saw her lips pull into a grin.

"*He's* inspiring," Cam announced.

"I feel love in the air," Angel sang in a high

falsetto tone. She threw her hands up in a dramatic flourish.

"Calm down, Angel," Dallas laughed. "Angels of Death are supposed to be serious, you know?"

Giggling, Angel shook her head. "Angels of Death have gotta have the blackest humor in the world to work with the likes of all of you. Hanging ten over the surfboard of life out there every day. Just darin' those druggies to come try to shoot you down. Hell," she muttered, her mouth twisting in a mirthful grin, "if it wasn't for my humor, some of you would already have died and gone to Inca heaven."

Chuckling, Cam sat still as Angel placed the stethoscope against her chest to listen to her heartbeat.

"Don't laugh now," Angel said, wriggling her black, arched brows, "or you'll blast my eardrums."

"I know...."

"Just don't talk for a moment, okay? It's tough enough trying to hear your red-blooded American heart pounding because the guy you love is nearby. You laughing and making croaking sounds with that voice of yours only makes it worse."

Gus couldn't help but laugh deeply. Angel was leaning near Cam, stethoscope in place, her face intent. "Is she always like this?" he asked with a grin.

"Oh," Dallas said, "count on it. If you work at BJS, you have to have a die-hard sense of humor to carry you and your buddies over the hurdle when all hell breaks loose."

"Which," Angel said proudly as she straightened and took the stethoscope away from Cam's heart, "is daily. We boogie down there, Chief Morales. I come from Inca heritage, and we call this thing we do the dance of death. Every day one of our women flies to intercept a druggie in the air, she's layin' her life on the line—for all of us.'' Patting Cam's shoulder, she said drolly, ''You'll live.''

''Whew. I was worried.'' Cam pretended to wipe sweat from her brow.

''Yeah, sure you were.'' Angel gave Gus a sly look as she tucked her medical tools back into her red canvas bag. ''I prescribe doing more of whatever it was you were doing back at the village. Normally, you have low blood pressure, Cam, but now it's normal.'' She flashed Cam an evil, knowing grin. ''So do it daily.''

Gus couldn't curb his grin when Cam's face turned a bright red. He heard Dallas choke, trying not to laugh, her hand against her throat. Unexpectedly, Angel turned to him after she'd zipped up the bag and put the strap across her sturdy shoulder.

''I assume you're the prescription she needs, Chief Morales?''

Now he was the target. ''Er…''

''Yes, well, I can see you are,'' Angel said primly, giving Cam an even broader smile. ''This is the best medical condition I've seen Cam in. So I'm gonna sign the FAA medical certificate allowing her back to flight status.''

''What about me?'' he asked, suddenly alarmed. He watched as Angel walked toward the door, the huge red bag against her left hip.

Turning, she gazed at him seriously. ''You've passed, sir. Just keep doin' what you're doin'.'' She motioned to his left arm. ''Obviously, you got well in a helluva hurry.''

Relief flowed through Gus. He wasn't used to the raucous, intimate teasing between enlisted people and officers he was experiencing right now. Cam had warned him that the lines between them were greatly blurred and usually nonexistent down at BJS. Seeing the deviltry dancing in the Quero's eyes again, he gave a sour grin. "Oh, I think I can manage to do that, Angel."

"Good." Angel gave them all a fond look. "I gotta hoof it to the commercial airport in San Diego. The major wants me back pronto. And I want to see my guy, Burke, again." She waved her left hand, the ring flashing on it.

"You're always missed," Cam told her, meaning it. They had one doctor and two paramedics to take care of the huge squadron of women and a few men under Maya's command. It was a daunting task on good days. Elizabeth, a U.S. Army doctor, considered Angel her right hand. Without her around, she was usually overwhelmed by the many small medical problems that routinely happened in the squadron. But now that Burke, a special forces paramedic, had signed on to be with Angel, the load had been considerably eased.

"I know I am. I'm absolutely indispensable." She giggled as she opened the door.

"Better get on over to San Diego," Dallas said. "I've got a car and driver waiting downstairs to take you to Lindbergh Airport. And," she warned, arching one dark brow, "don't forget to let Burke know how much you missed him."

Angel grinned. "Roger that. Loud and clear."

"No one accused you of being slow on the uptake,

Sergeant Paredes. Adios, amiga. Have a safe trip back to Peru.'' Dallas lifted her hand to the woman.

''Adios,'' Angel call softly. She became suddenly serious. ''Cam, Chief Morales? You stay *safe,* you hear? I don't wanna have to come back up here to requalify you for flight duty again....''

The room grew quiet when the Angel of Death had departed. Cam turned to Gus, who stood a few feet away from her, while Dallas finished her cup of coffee.

''I really miss the women of BJS,'' Cam said.

''Yeah, we're like a bunch of wildcats in the same bag, yowling, screaming and howling,'' Dallas chuckled. She put the cup near the coffee urn and looked over at Gus. ''You took us in stride, Chief.''

''Black humor is my specialty.''

''It is,'' Cam told her. ''You should hear him quipping in the cockpit when we fly.''

''Good,'' Dallas said. She went over and picked up her helmet and gloves. ''Well, we've officially changed commands, Cam. You're back in the hot seat again, and the chief is your X.O., again. I'm going to take some time to talk with the Air Force generals and give them a report on our actions here. I'll be leaving for Mexico City in an hour.''

''I'll miss you,'' Cam said, going over to hug Dallas goodbye. As she released the Israeli from her embrace, she saw Dallas smile and nod.

''We miss you, but we know you're doing good work up here. Like Maya said, we've spent three years honing our combat skills, and now the rest of the world has decided we got what it takes, and wants us to teach them what we know.''

"So the BJS pilots are like seeds in the wind, being blown here and there," Gus said.

"Bingo," Dallas murmured. She halted at the door, helmet dangling in her left hand, her green flight gloves jammed into it. "Morgan Trayhern and Mike Houston. Those two can't stop bragging about us, I guess, and the word is getting out at the top levels."

"Maybe BJS women are going to be sent around the world because we're the only ones who have the combat training needed to teach others," Cam said.

"Maybe," Dallas said, lifting her hand in farewell, "maybe our luck is changing. *Hasta la vista, amigos....*"

"Take care," Cam called after Dallas softly. The door stood partly open and Cam smiled, knowing Dallas had left it that way out of habit. Down at BJS, Maya always instructed her officers to keep their doors open, so they could be available to their people. Cam would try the same thing here, once they were assigned a permanent H.Q., which would probably happen after Dallas talked to the head honchos down in Mexico City.

"Welcome home," Gus murmured. He leaned over and pressed a kiss to Cam's smooth, unlined brow. How beautiful she looked, even in her genderless green flight suit. He knew what lay beneath that fabric—the heart of the woman he'd love until he died.

Sighing, Cam stretched up and kissed his mouth quickly. Hotly. But now was not the time for loving. "Sure is different from the Village of the Clouds, isn't it?" she murmured, releasing him and moving back to her desk.

"Yeah," Gus said as he ambled over and stood

near the desk as she looked at the flight schedule Dallas had drawn up for them. "But I have you. So I don't care where I am as long as you're at my side."

Touched, Cam turned the clipboard around for him to see. "Well, darling, it looks like we have the duty tonight. Together."

He took the clipboard and looked at it. "Yeah, Luis and Antonio are due back here in about an hour. They'll be exhausted."

"Dallas worked their butts off."

"That will make them appreciate your gentle but firm hand," Gus declared with a grin. Cam was a softy. Gus knew that as time went on, she'd grow into her role as C.O. of this mission. Much of her wavering was gone, replaced with a confident look— that of a leader who knew what she was doing and what she wanted to accomplish. As he set the board on her desk, Gus knew that his love for her gave her confidence, too. It was wonderful to see Cam growing daily before his eyes.

"Maybe it will," she said with a wicked smile. She saw the smoldering look in Gus's cinnamon-colored eyes and her body hotly responded. "Hey, you know this weekend?"

"Yeah?"

"Let's snoop around south TJ and see if we can find an apartment to live in. I don't want to keep living here, do you?"

Shaking his head, Gus said, "No. One apartment or two?"

"One."

"One bedroom?"

"One bed. The two of us in it."

"Roger. I hear you loud and clear."

Laughing, Cam sat down at her desk. There were a bunch of manuals to look through, read and then create written orders from. "Good."

Gus watched as she pulled the manuals in front of her. "Do you think Maya is going to mind about us?"

"It will be all right, Gus. She won't send you packing to another base, if that's what you're worried about. A number of her pilots have met guys—fallen in love and married them. They all work at BJS in one form or another." Cam knew he was worried about their intimacy. Normally, office romance was discouraged by the military. If they became engaged, as he and Cam had, then it was a dicey situation. Gus knew in a regular army mission he'd probably be sent away—permanently.

"Dallas liked the ring," he said, pride in his tone.

Lifting her hand, Cam looked at it, then sent a warm look in his direction. "Yes, she'll tell Maya. I'm sure that Sergeant Joanne Prater, Maya's desk clerk, will wag that tale all over BJS in short order— another woman pilot has crashed and burned and found a guy." She laughed and shook her head. "Prater knows what's gossip and what's top secret. When she hears Dallas describing your beautiful ring to Maya, she'll go racing out the door to tell everyone."

Gus smiled with her. "I hope someday to go down there, to BJS."

"I'm sure you will—with me."

He tapped the desk with his fingertips. "And we've been asked to go back to the village. Grandfather

Adaire said because of my Indian blood, and my mother's gifts, they want me to do more training."

"I know," Cam said, leaning back in the chair. "Is that high on your list of things to do?"

"No...not yet," Gus murmured, holding her luminous green gaze. A fierce love swept through him. "My heart, my soul, are centered on you, *querida.* On our life here." He looked around, his brows dipping. "We're in combat mode every time we fly. Our lives are on the line. I just found you and I don't want to let you or what we have go." And then his mouth crooked. "Maybe in a couple of years I'll think about it. But not now..."

Cam slid her hand into the one he held toward her. "I like the old-fashioned approach we're taking, Gus."

"What? A year-long engagement? That's what my father did with my mother—courted her nonstop. And that's what I'm going to do with you. I'm going to show you how many ways you make me happy, how you make my life feel like it's filled with sunlight every morning when I wake up. Then..." he lifted her hand, leaned down and placed a moist kiss on the back of it "...if all goes well, I'm going to be asking you, next year at this time, to marry me."

"I like your plan, Chief Morales."

He reluctantly released her hand. They were on active military duty now, and personal wants and desires had to be laid aside. Still, it was tough for Gus to do. He'd made love with Cam last night, and early this morning once again, just before they'd left the village. His body tingled hotly in memory of her warmth, her fierce response.

"What do you say we go down and check out our steed then?" he suggested. Gesturing to the manuals, he coaxed, "Leave them for later. Let's get into some sunshine, blue sky and fresh air. Together..."

On sale 16th July 2004

*Available at most branches of WHSmith,
Tesco, Martins, Borders, Eason, Sainsbury's
and all good paperback bookshops.*

0804/009/SH76 V2

NEW YORK TIMES BESTSELLING AUTHOR

DIANA PALMER

Some rules are meant to be broken…

LAWLESS

Published 16th July 2004

A
dangerous
marriage

The
Country
Club

Book 11 available from 16th July 2004

Escape into...
SPECIAL EDITION™

Life, love and family.

Special Edition are romances between attractive men and women. Family is central to the plot. The novels are warm upbeat dramas grounded in reality with a guaranteed happy ending.

Six new titles are available every month on subscription from the

READER SERVICE™

GEN/23/RS3 V2

Escape into...
SUPERROMANCE™

*Enjoy the drama, explore the emotions,
experience the relationship.*

Longer than other Silhouette® books,
Superromance offers you emotionally involving,
exciting stories, with a touch of the unexpected.

Four new titles are available every month on
subscription from the

READER SERVICE™

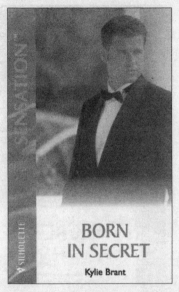

Escape into...
INTRIGUE™

Breathtaking romantic suspense.

Romantic suspense with a well-developed mystery.
The couple always get their happy ending, and the
mystery is resolved, thanks to the central couple.

Four new titles are available every month on
subscription from the

READER SERVICE™